T0278638

THE ONLY LIGHT LEFT BURNING

Also by Erik J. Brown

All That's Left in the World

Lose You to Find Me

THE ONLY LIGHT LEFT BURNING

ERIK J. BROWN

BALZER + BRAY
An Imprint of HarperCollinsPublishers

Balzer + Bray is an imprint of HarperCollins Publishers.

The Only Light Left Burning
Copyright © 2024 by Erik J. Brown
All rights reserved. Printed in the United States of America.
No part of this book may be used or reproduced in any manner
whatsoever without written permission except in the case of
brief quotations embodied in critical articles and reviews.
For information address HarperCollins Children's Books, a division
of HarperCollins Publishers, 195 Broadway, New York, NY 10007.
www.epicreads.com

Library of Congress Control Number: 2023944074
ISBN 978-0-06-333827-2

24 25 26 27 28 LBC 5 4 3 2 1
First Edition

For Michael Miska, and the family we choose.

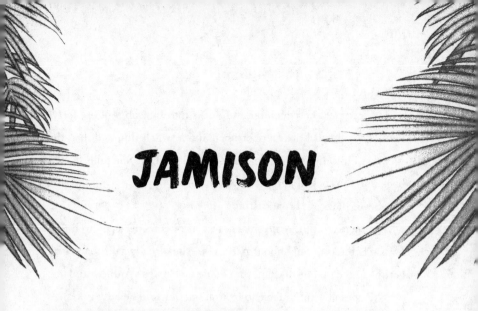

JAMISON

I USED TO LIKE SILENCE. THOUGH MAYBE *like* isn't the correct word for it. *Appreciate* would probably be more appropriate. I appreciated the silence of my house before my mom came home from work each night. *She* didn't appreciate it so much; she preferred to have music playing at all times. As soon as she got home, she'd connect her phone to the linked speakers in the house—the kitchen, living room, dining room, bathrooms, her bedroom, but not mine—and her favorite playlists would begin to pipe out. I could always tell how her day went from the music she played.

I wish I had streaming music now. Something to fill all the silence.

"Stop that."

I look up from the gears and metal fasteners on the boat deck to see that Cara is scolding me without even looking my way.

"Stop what?"

"Everything you're doing right now. Moping or whatever it is."

"It's not moping, it's thinking."

"About what?" She glances at me as she uncaps the OneDrop winch oil.

"Music."

Cara recaps the winch oil and ducks into the cabin of the forty-two-foot sailboat. I hear a door open and a switch flip, and then the speakers built into the cockpit seats crackle briefly. She pulls herself back into the cockpit and points at the helm.

"See if Blanca is broadcasting," she says.

I smile as gratitude fills my chest. Cara knows perfectly well that I wasn't thinking only about music, but she already said she wasn't getting in the middle of whatever's going on between Andrew and me.

She doesn't want to have to hear about our issues every time she's with one of us. It's bad enough that Andrew isn't on the boat crew anymore and so she only gets to see him for a couple hours on the weekends and at the monthly socials.

I stand and turn on the radio. Static. Blanca broadcasts on the same channel every time, but the hours are iffy. There's no set schedule, and even if she's said there is, we don't really understand it because Daria is the only one on the boat who speaks Spanish. She's translated a few broadcasts while we listened, but so far it's just been radio DJ stuff—making announcements for the Cuban settlement, music requests or dedications from people on the island, and once a guest who played guitar and sang live in the studio.

I flick through the AM stations that bookend the one she broadcasts from, hoping to hear her come through even just a little bit. But there's only static on every station. She must not be on the air right now.

Like us, she's probably working on something else at the moment. In the apocalypse, the job of radio DJ is appreciated, but not necessary.

She most likely only gets to broadcast when she has downtime.

I lower the volume but leave the radio on so the crackle of static drones in the background. It's better than the silence.

"It was worth a shot," Cara says, and goes back to rebuilding the winch that's been sticking.

We're supposed to leave on Sunday morning—the day after my birthday—and we'll be gone for seven whole weeks.

Seven weeks without seeing Andrew.

When he got kicked off the crew a couple of weeks ago it seemed like a nightmare. I told Admiral Hickey right away that I didn't want to be on the boat if Andrew wasn't there, too. That's when Andrew freaked out. He spoke for me and told Hickey I was staying on the crew, even though I didn't want to. That night we had a big blowup. He was pissed at me because I was so willing to give up on the boat mission; I was pissed at him for minimizing my fears of being separated from him. After that we got quiet, and the quiet—something I used to enjoy—has now grown into awkward stiltedness. So at first I was scared about being away from him, but the closer we get to the day, the more I think the separation might be a good thing for us.

I *hope* it might be a good thing for us. That the absence truly will make our hearts grow fonder—or at least make *his* grow fonder, because he's the one who snapped at me. The one who didn't talk to me for a whole day and has been staying late with the kids to avoid me.

"You're doing it again," Cara says, rubbing a gear with grease and placing it in its spot in the winch.

"I'm just tired," I tell her. "Didn't sleep well last night." It's not a lie. I haven't been sleeping well *any* night for the last week and a half. I

3

wake up in the middle of the night and can feel how far apart Andrew and I are.

He used to yell at me playfully—he made it clear that he thought it was adorable—because he says I sleep like a goldfish grows, expanding to take up whatever space is available to me. So each morning I would wake up half on my side of the bed, half on his, with him pressed up against me.

"I'm looking forward to the winter when your furnace body will be helpful instead of making me sweaty and gross," he said.

I told him to just push me back to my side, but he refused, giving me a devilish grin. "I like your furnace body making me sweaty."

But every time I've woken up these past few weeks, he's been hugging his edge of the bed as if he's trying not to touch me.

He says he isn't mad at me and he was just upset in the moment that he was kicked off the boat and that I would give up on the trip north to bring back Amy's mom. But the crew can do that without me. And I don't understand why staying here with him would be such an issue. So I didn't press any further, but it still doesn't feel like we've gone back to normal.

Across from me, Cara lets out an annoyed breath through her nose. She opens her mouth to say something, but the radio crackles and finally Blanca's voice comes through the speaker. My heart leaps and I stand, reaching over to turn up the volume.

I'm happy for the distraction, and Cara seems to welcome it, too, giving me a wan smile. But then the smile drops.

Blanca is speaking quickly, her voice fast and higher than it's ever been. It's not her usual, almost sensual radio DJ voice. It's panicked—at least it sounds that way in between waves of static.

Maybe it's excitement? For all we know she could be announcing a new guest who's in the studio with her. I turn to Cara, who crouches near the speaker, listening intently.

"Do you know what she's saying?"

Cara doesn't speak Spanish, but she can understand some. A word here or there that she can pick up and piece together into some semblance of context clues that she'll repeat to Daria. Then Daria will nod or clarify. But Daria isn't here. She, Admiral Hickey, and Trevor are all at a Committee meeting going over the plan to head north on Sunday. To scavenge the coast and return with Henri, the woman who is the reason Andrew and I found the Key Colony in the first place.

"She's talking too fast," Cara says.

More static. Then Blanca comes back and yells something we can't comprehend. In the background there's more shouting followed by a high-pitched whistle. The static returns, cutting through her voice like waves crashing against a shoreline.

Movement from the dock catches my eye. Hickey, Daria, and Trevor are on their way back. I cup my hands to my mouth and call out to Daria.

"Something's going on with Blanca! Quick!"

Daria, a Black woman in her late forties with her hair in locs, runs the rest of the length of the dock—Hickey and Trevor following behind her—then jumps onto the boat. I hold my hand out to help steady her and she grabs it, leaping into the cockpit. Her face clouds as she tries to listen. Hickey and Trevor come to a stop at the end of the dock, and we all listen to the static in silence.

5

Blanca's voice breaks in with another shout, but the whole sentence doesn't come through.

Daria shakes her head. Then another man speaks. He gets a few words out before the static returns.

"A hundred and ninety kilometers?" Daria says.

Cara and I share a look, trying to figure out what the 190 kilometers could mean. She seems just as puzzled as I am.

The man's voice returns, speaking faster, sounding more desperate.

Daria gasps and covers her mouth.

"What is it?" Hickey asks behind her. Hickey is an old navy admiral from before the world ended—and one of the reasons Andrew isn't on the boat anymore. Daria holds up her hand to quiet him. When there's a longer stretch of static she speaks.

"The Cuban colony got hit by a storm. Hundred and ninety kilometers is the wind speed."

Hickey does the calculations in his head. "That's almost a hundred and twenty miles per hour."

"Then it's not just a storm," Cara says. "It's a hurricane."

The static disappears and Blanca returns. Her voice comes through loud and clear for a few moments before static takes over again.

"The island is flooded," Daria translates. "Pray for us, pray for yourselves."

We listen to the static, but neither Blanca nor the other man comes back.

ANDREW

LISTEN. I UNDERSTAND THAT WHEN THE WORLD ends, society collapses, and we as a species want to make an attempt at civilization, round two, we're going to need people who do the jobs that no one wants to do.

But why do *I* have to be one of those people?

I know this makes me sound like a piece of shit, and I'm only saying it because I'm having a bad day—seriously, catch me on a good day and I'll talk your ear off about how amazing work is—but being a babysitter is not exactly my postapocalyptic dream job.

It's not that I have delusions of grandeur. I don't want to be a doctor or a scientist or the New American president. Honestly, I'd rather be a farmer. The agricultural people in the Keys are figuring out how to get a handle on sustainability and pest control. This time last year everyone was thinking about short-term survival. Now, though, we're feeling the full-on collapse of the bird link in the food chain. There are still birds—we all look up and point them out when we see them—but they're like us, few and far between. Maybe a couple million of them, at most, across the entire globe. And that means more insects and pests to destroy crops. And more rodents that might have otherwise been hunted by birds of prey. But the Key farmers are trying their best to deal and evolve with the times. It wouldn't hurt if I learned how to grow crops. Embraced my destiny as a Plant Gay.

I stop daydreaming to count the kids on the playground, and damn near have a heart attack. I regroup and count again. But I still come to the same number. Twelve. My lucky number thirteen no longer lucky. Which means one of the kids has gotten away from me. Again.

And I know exactly which one.

My heart races, somehow to the beat of Daphne telling me that kids can drown in seconds. But back on the beach side of the playground I still don't see him. Daphne's voice in my head goes from lecturing me about drowning to giving advice on looking after them.

Kids are creatures of habit. They're going to keep doing the same thing, even when you tell them not to.

Let's see, when was the last time I yelled at the Kid for disappearing?

"Dammit."

I sprint to the playground equipment, because Daphne has already been gone for fifteen minutes and could come back at any moment. I whistle hard.

"Taylor!" I shout at the top of the monkey bars. Thirteen-year-old, too-smart-for-her-own-good Taylor looks down on me—I mean, what else is new? "I need you to watch everyone for a second, okay?"

"Did you lose him *again*?"

"Okay, if we're going to place blame, you should have seen him

8

wander off from up there."

"*I'm* not an adult."

"No," I mutter under my breath. "Just reincarnated Damien from *The Omen*." I bet she has a 666 birthmark hidden under that braid.

"What?"

"Keep an eye, please? I'll owe you an extra cookie tomorrow." Shit, wait, did she just call *me* an adult? I'm only, like, three years older than her, what the hell?

Mustering the best impression of my own little sister I've ever seen, Taylor gives me a "sigh-fiiiiine," then, Satan love her, counts the kids playing around her. I sprint in the opposite direction toward the water park.

But it's not a water park anymore. The engineering folks still haven't figured out water treatment given the limited amount of power we have, so the fountains and the flower-shaped sprinklers are still turned off.

That also means the pool is empty. But there's no reason the Kid would need to go to the pool, so he isn't there. He can't be. Because I definitely won't be able to live with myself if I have to look over the edge and see him lying at the bottom of a concrete pool.

He's six. He knows better than that. I have to give him more credit.

But the closer to the pool I get, the more anxious I am.

Then relief—because there he is, on the sky-blue painted floor of the water park, under the nonfunctioning daisy sprinkler.

"Kid!" I call out with enough authority in my voice that I know my dad is looking down on me with a twinkle in his eye. Every time Andrew uses his big-boy voice, an angel gets their wings.

The Kid looks up from the stuffed hippo in his hands. I call him Kid because he's never told anyone his name. He has no parents or family to tell us who he is, and when we ask him his name he won't answer—even the name game doesn't work on him, and the other orphans eat that shit up. Daphne was vehemently against calling him "Kid," but even she's broken down and uses it when talking to me. Not to his face, though.

It seems to be okay when I do it because whenever I shout it, he answers.

When he sees me, the Kid immediately looks guilty, and it breaks my damn heart. I hate yelling at these kids. I understand why we need to, but it's not fair that *I'm* the one who has to do it. I mean, technically there's four of us swapping off the responsibility, but I do like to hand it off to Daphne as much as possible. Probably because *she* yells at me enough.

I come to a stop next to him and crouch down. "Dude. You can't run off without telling me."

His attention returns to his hippo. "Bobo needed fresh water." He makes a splashing sound.

Bobo's a stuffed animal, Kid; the less water he gets, the better. Instead of saying this aloud, however, I nod. "Well, now that he's had his fill, we need to get back to the others, okay? Ms. Daphne will yell at us if we're late for lineup."

That gets his attention, so he takes my hand and we head back to the playground. When we arrive, Daphne still isn't back—thank God—but Taylor is down from the monkey bars again, talking to another adult.

There's three full seconds of anxiety before I recognize the tattoos covering every inch of flesh visible around a cutoff denim vest littered with pins and buttons, and I relax a bit.

"Rocky Horror," I say when we reach the edge of the playground. "I've never been happier to see another human being in my life." That's extremely untrue, but I do love me some Rocky Horror.

He smiles wide and holds out a tattooed fist for me to bump. All the other kids have suddenly noticed Rocky Horror's arrival and the bravest of them are coming forward to ogle him.

Yes, his name is Rocky Horror. No, not first name Rocky, last name Horror. His first and only name is Rocky Horror. Like the Kid, he won't tell anyone what his legal name was before what he calls "Teotwawki"—the End of the World as We Know It—and honestly why should he? Rocky Horror's a great fucking name.

After our fist bump, he leans in and we make a loud show of kissing each other's cheeks. He puts on a Moira Rose lilt as he speaks. "Andrew, wonderful to see you as always."

"Isn't it?"

He goes back to his normal, gruff voice. "No. Where's Daph?"

"She ran to the loo." Bathrooms don't really exist when there's no running water, and calling them outhouses is boring, but it's not like I can say "brick shithouse" in front of the kids. Loo is whimsical.

One of the kids steps forward. Uh-oh, No-Filter Frank. Wanna guess why we call him that?

"What are those?" NFF points at the pink scars on Rocky Horror's bare, hairy, tattoo-covered chest. The scars being the only part of him—at least to my knowledge—not covered by tattoos.

He opens up the vest so the kids have a better view. "That? Just some scars from surgery. But they're old, so it doesn't hurt anymore."

"Especially since they put titanium over his ribs," I add with wide eyes.

He puffs up his chest and lowers his voice. "Now no one can hurt me!" He lets out the air in his lungs and adds, "Physically, I mean. Emotionally, on the other hand . . ."

Before NFF or one of the other kids can ask any more questions, Rocky Horror heads over to one of the benches. As soon as he's out of the vicinity of the playground, the kids disperse—probably realizing Rocky Horror is not going to go down the slides or play tag with them like I do. I bend down so I'm eye level with the Kid and Bobo the hippo.

"I'm going to go talk to Rocky Horror. But I want you to stay on the playground, okay?"

The Kid nods and walks off. I keep an eye on him until he sits on one of the swings.

"What's in the bag?" I ask Rocky Horror as I sit next to him, pointing to the backpack at his feet.

"Present for Daphne."

"Oh, so she gets a present but you still haven't handed over Jamie's birthday gift yet?"

He turns and stares at me in silence and, yeah, I may have walked into what I know he's about to say. "Oh? Are we still giving Jamie his gift?"

"Why wouldn't I?"

He shrugs and picks at dirt under one of his fingernails. "What use is a radio when you're not talking to your boyfriend?" Jamie's birthday is Saturday and my plan, once I was kicked off the boat, was to have Rocky Horror put together a long-range radio that we could communicate with. But he hasn't finished the radio yet, and we're getting dangerously close to the boat leaving. Two things giving me anxiety.

"We talk plenty." If the definition of *plenty* is "good morning," "good night," "hey," "fine," and "I'm not hungry, thanks."

"I'm not going to pretend I know what happened between the two of you—"

"It's simple, he—"

Rocky Horror waves his hands at me. "Pssh, uh-uh, no thanks. I said I wasn't going to pretend, but I also don't care. I know both of you well enough now to know that, whatever it was, the only reason this situation has gotten as far as it has is because—even if you are talking 'plenty'—you're not talking about what happened."

Yeah, he's got me there. So I shoot back with my own dig. "A single man of your age? Forgive me if I don't take relationship advice from you."

"Risky read considering I could have lost a loved one during the pandemmy, but . . . yeah, I was single, so maybe you're right. But if you want some non-relationship advice, stop letting it distract you and live your life. Figure out the Jamie shit on your own time."

"I'm not distracted."

"According to teacher's pet"—he nods in Taylor's direction—"you can barely be trusted to watch the kids."

"Gossipy little shit. The Kid's different. He's always sneaking off to find fresh water for Bobo."

Rocky Horror—a man *named* Rocky Horror—has the sheer

audacity to arch an eyebrow at the name Bobo. I double-check to make sure the Kid is still on the swing.

"These kids cramp my style," he says. "I don't know how you do it."

I pull at the denim vest. "This is style?" He swats my hand and I shrug. "It makes the days go by more quickly."

Though I'm not sure if that's a good thing or not yet. Being on the boat was boring and the days did tend to drag. But at least I got to hang out with Jamie and Cara all day. Sure, Trevor was a dick sometimes.

That's all. End of sentence.

And of course, the admiral hated me from the moment he joined the boat crew. His scowl grew scowlier with every joke. Honestly, I feel like he would have done better in Fort Caroline, the authoritarian settlement that hunted Jamie and me down the coast of Florida and almost succeeded in killing him. What's not for the admiral to love there? Structure, patriarchal rules, white supremacy. It's just like the navy!

"Obviously I know the answer, but speaking of things going fast . . ." He gives me a side-eye.

"No." I cut him off.

He groans and shakes his head. "I really wish I could be your age again."

"Right, because fifty years ago was so great to our kind."

"Excuse me, I am forty, you skinny bitch. And I mean right *now*. Because now we're all more or less on a level playing field." He elbows me. "And you're both wasting the precious time you have left."

"Here we go."

14

"No. For all we know, one of you could get appendicitis and die tomorrow. And you're not even talking to each other about what you want. Or why you're mad at each other—which clearly isn't because of the sex stuff."

This is all because I made the mistake of going to Rocky Horror for sex advice a little over a month ago when I found out he was a counselor in the before times. As one of the few queer men in our neck of the Keys, Rocky Horror was the clear answer.

Unfortunately, his advice was, and apparently still is, absolutely batshit: "Talk about it!"

Talk about it? How am I supposed to *talk* about sex with Jamie when we're only talking "plenty"? Maybe that's our issue. We couldn't have makeup sex after our fight, so we just fell into this awkward lull we're in now.

Still, even before the fight I didn't know how to talk about sex without making it weird. Who's doing what part, and do we still use condoms even though I'm a virgin and I think Jamie's a virgin, too? I mean, we've done other things and haven't used them, but are we supposed to use them for sex-sex even if we're monogamous and virgins and don't have the ability to become pregnant—and, side note, where does one find lube in the apocalypse?

At first we were waiting because Jamie was still healing from being shot by a bunch of authoritarian lunatics from Georgia. But then it became more about making sure the time was right and that we were both comfortable and safe—like, apocalyptically safe, because see above re: condoms. But then the longer it went on the more difficult it felt to bring it up. Then came the other worries.

What if he doesn't like it?

Or what if he doesn't even really like all the other stuff we've done but he's just horny and then doing *this* makes him realize he doesn't like any of it and by definition also doesn't like . . . me?

Before you get on me for the biphobia in that worry, I already know! Rocky Horror told me when I brought it up to him. But I can't help it. It's called being insecure, which I very much am but also very much want to work through.

"You look like you're going to throw up," Rocky Horror says, patting my shoulder.

"Must be the appendicitis."

He sighs. "There's no rush. Really, Andrew. You both love each other, and it will happen when it happens. But before it does you do need to talk to each other about it. So you should do it—talk, I mean. And *soon*. I'm not only talking about the sex stuff. You can lie to yourself, and me, all you want. But you and Jamie both know you're being dummies and you need to talk your shit out." It sounds like there's a warning in his voice, and his gaze moves over my shoulder. "And if you need help on that front . . ." He pats my knee and stands, grabbing the backpack between his feet.

I turn to see Daphne De Silva—bestselling romance novelist—returning to the playground.

Rocky Horror takes Daphne's hand and kisses it. Then he reaches into the pack and takes out a plastic device with a long cord hanging from it, handing it over to her. While she's distracted, I lock onto the Kid—no longer on the swing but sitting in the sand with Bobo—and count the twelve other kids.

A white woman in her midsixties, Daphne keeps her hip-length gray hair pulled up into a big messy bun and only wears sundresses, even if it's raining. Which, come to think of it, may happen soon. I rub at the scars on my leg, the bone aching slightly.

"What's that?" I ask, pointing at the rectangular plastic box in her hands. Daphne counts the kids and sits down next to me.

"A cassette player!" She holds it up and I see a speaker and little window to put the cassette in. "The library still has a bunch of old books on tape. I figured we could play some of them for the kids so you don't have to stay so late coming up with stories for bedtime."

"Oh, yeah, great idea."

With my excuse to "stay late at work" now in jeopardy, maybe Rocky Horror is right. Maybe it is time to talk to Jamie.

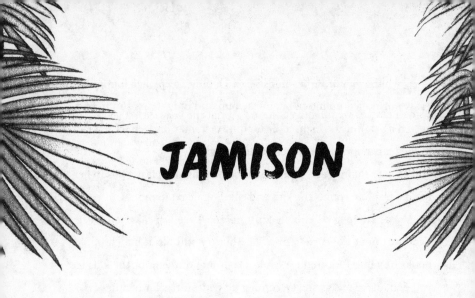

JAMISON

IT'S ONLY A LITTLE PAST FIVE, SO when the front door opens I expect it to be one of the other guys who live with us, but Andrew walks through the kitchen entryway. I stand a little straighter, awkwardness filling my gut.

"Hey," he says. There's a friendly tone to his voice but it sounds forced. Instead of coming around the counter to give me a hug or kiss, he sits on a stool at the other side.

At least he didn't go right upstairs.

"Hey." I'm about to offer him something to eat—expecting him to say he ate with the kids and the other caretakers—but then remember that he couldn't have. The social is tonight.

"How was your day?" he asks.

My chest tightens. Seeing him almost made me forget about Blanca's radio transmission. "Oh! Did you hear anything from Daphne yet?" I don't want to tell him the story again if he already knows and is just asking me sarcastically.

After the transmission, Hickey and Daria left again to tell the

Committee what they heard. If Cuba got hit by a hurricane, there's a small chance we might get hit, too—or at the very least a few days' worth of bad wind and rain, possibly enough to delay the boat voyage north another week. Especially if the storm is moving up the coast.

"Just the usual town gossip," Andrew says. "Nothing super salacious. Why?"

"We might be delaying the trip," I say.

Andrew's face clouds and the sad excuse for a smile drops. "Why?"

He's probably going to blame me again. To jump down my throat and call me selfish or say I don't care about Henri.

"The Cuban colony is getting hit by a hurricane. Radio Blanca broadcasted it late this afternoon. Hickey and Daria are talking to the Committee and figuring out the best course of action. They're worried that we could get some severe weather in the next couple days or that the storm might head up the coast. But it depends on what the Committee says."

He nods, his face softening a bit. "That's probably for the best, then."

"Yeah."

And that's it.

"You have to work at the social tonight?" I try. But I already know the answer. He does because he wants to. Though he'll make an excuse and say it's because Kelly was supervisor at the last social or he swapped with Daphne so she could have the holiday social.

But he shakes his head. "No, it's Kelly's turn."

I nod. "Cool."

"I should go wash up."

"Okay."

He stands and gets as far as the kitchen doorway, then stops and turns back. "You should, too. You smell like diesel."

I know he's only teasing me—though, yes, I do smell like diesel from the boat—but without the context of normal conversation it still feels like a dig. He must think the same thing because I see his mouth flatten.

"Do you want to come with?" he asks.

The idea of keeping this stilted conversation going all the way to the showers isn't at all appealing, but I also don't want to undo any of the progress we've made talking. And he *is* coming to the social tonight, so maybe having the buffer of other people will help us, too.

"I'll meet you there," I say. "I have to check with Cara to see if she heard anything else from Hickey or Daria."

He says okay and goes upstairs to get his shower caddy and towels. When he comes back down he has mine, too. He places it on the kitchen island.

"Don't take too long. There's bound to be a bunch of last-minute stinkers in line."

I frown. "Stinkers?"

He groans. "I've been hanging out with kids for too long."

I laugh as he leaves.

That was good—it almost felt normal. Or at least the most normal that things have felt since he got kicked off the boat.

It was Admiral Hickey's decision. He came to the Keys around the end of October, and the Committee figured who better to be on the boat than a formal navy admiral. The crew didn't realize that

20

meant one of us would be kicked off. There are only two bedrooms—berths—on the sailboat and the dining area converts into a bed as well. So with just Cara, Daria, Andrew, Trevor, and me, it all would have worked fine. Andrew and I could share a bed. Cara and Daria could figure out which other bed they wanted, and there would always be someone awake to sail the boat by night, which we'd make a schedule for. Sailing the forty-two-foot boat alone was difficult, but not impossible. And whoever was sleeping in the dining area would be on call in case of emergency.

With Hickey's arrival, things got more complicated. It also didn't help that Andrew jokes around all the time and Hickey is a no-nonsense naval officer. It would work perfectly in a Daphne De Silva novel, but in real life they butted heads nonstop. Andrew put a target on his own back.

I told him over and over to be careful, but he said he already knew he'd be booted off, it was just a matter of time.

Which is when I told him that if he didn't go, I wouldn't go either. Cara, Daria, Trevor, and Hickey could go on their own to bring Henri down here. Besides, Andrew and I had been talking about leaving and heading back to the cabin my mother had in Pennsylvania. Fort Caroline had sent people as far as northern Florida to hunt me down, all because one of their leader's sons tried to kill us. Of course, they didn't care about that part, just that I killed *him* to save ourselves. So for weeks we talked about running back to the cabin. Alone, in the woods—just the two of us—it'd be harder for them to find us again. And maybe we should just go already before winter really hit.

That's when we started fighting. He argued with me in front of everyone and stormed off. When I chased him we kept arguing. Back and forth for over three hours. At the time I thought he was just pissed at Hickey and taking it out on me, but the longer we argued the more I wondered if it was something else. Something that had been brewing between us but had never been said out loud.

The next day when he avoided me, it only cemented that feeling.

And now I'm too afraid to ask him what it is.

ANDREW

I'M TRYING TO FORCE MYSELF TO HAVE fun but I'd rather be spending my time with Jamie. Rocky Horror is right: I need to talk this all out with him. Not the sex stuff; that's obviously on an indefinite hold until we work out our issues. But talking to him before the social wasn't so bad.

"Why don't you stop being a little bitch and ask your man to dance?" Rocky Horror plops down on the picnic bench next to me with a glass of hooch. The smell turns my stomach. They don't call it hooch, but it's absolutely hooch. Basically the cheapest, easiest way to make alcohol: citrus, water, sugar, and yeast that they bury in the sand for five days to ferment.

I look over at Jamie, who's talking to Daphne. "He's doing his goodbyes, in case he doesn't see people before Sunday. Probably pawning me off on grub duty with Daph while he's away."

"Grub duty?" Rocky Horror waves away the flies that have already gathered around us because of the hooch.

Daphne is an Islamorada local. She spent her winters here even before the bug, and the greenhouse behind her little bungalow is one of the few places in the Keys—maybe even the world—still growing tomatoes. This past year has been a nightmare for her with the bugs. Apparently every time she picks off a cluster of grub eggs, there's at least one more she misses. Jamie helps her on Saturday and Sunday mornings—when he isn't doing boat stuff—in exchange for some tomatoes. I explain all this to Rocky Horror, who nods.

"Well," he says, "I have it on good authority that when this song ends, there's a slow one coming up."

The band is actually good tonight. No singer, which I some-times think makes it better. The only electricity is being used for the string lights hanging from the big tent's ceiling, so the band is just two acoustic guitars, a mandolin, an upright bass, and a viola. The five musicians have clearly been practicing together, because their acoustic-bluegrassy version of either Sia or Ed Sheeran almost sounds professional.

When I don't move, Rocky Horror adds, "I have it on good author-ity because I paid them to *make* the next song a slow one, so get up and ask Jamie to dance or you owe me fifty bucks."

I sigh and get up, making it halfway to Jamie before I turn around and walk back to Rocky Horror. "Fifty bucks? In what currency?"

He wipes the citrus hooch from his beard and flicks his hand at me. "It's a figure of speech. I just asked them to do it—what are they gonna do, say, 'No, we have too much artistic integrity to play slow music'?" He blows a raspberry and turns his attention to Amy and Cara.

I laugh and, sure enough, as the fast song ends and everyone claps, a slow one begins. I walk up to Daphne and Jamie, and Daph smiles wider when she sees me.

"Would you mind if I stole you for a dance?" I ask.

Jamie smiles and his cheeks flush. "Yeah, sure."

"I wasn't talking to you." I hold out my hand to Daphne, who lets out, legit, the best laugh I have ever heard from a human being in my life. Then she smacks it away and says, "You couldn't handle it."

"Wow! And I thought we were friends!" She holds her hands out to my face and I bend down to kiss her cheek as she kisses mine. Then she lets me take Jamie's hand and lead him to the dance floor.

But from there he leads me. He pulls me close and holds my hand out as we sway on the tiny dance floor surrounded by picnic tables.

"I don't want to ruin the moment," Jamie says, and I already know what he's going to ask. "But where is this coming from all of a sudden?"

"Here's the deal. I'm a proud person and I really hate apologizing, so save this in your mind grapes for a rainy day because it doesn't happen frequently: I'm sorry I've been avoiding you."

He feigns surprise. "He admits it." Then he dips me, and I grab on to him tighter.

"I'm always surprised when I remember you can dance," I tell him as he pulls me back up.

"Do I look like someone who can't dance?"

I look up at him. His broad shoulders, his stocky frame. "Yes, honey."

He laughs and leads me into a spin that gives me butterflies, then easily catches me and pulls me against him again. I love dancing with him. He feels confident, which makes *me* feel confident. We move in sync, and when he does things—like that twirl, for instance—I sense it coming and can lean into it.

The idea of him traveling without me returns and I feel awful again. Because on the one hand, I made such a big deal about him giving up and wanting to stay with me, and on the other, I do selfishly want that, but I'd never say it. Tears sting my eyes and I use it as an excuse to put my head against his shoulder.

"My mom taught me," he says, unprompted. "It was very embarrassing at the time, and I kept telling her no, but she said, 'Jamison, if you break your date's toes, she's never going to want to dance with you again.'"

I manage to blink away the tears and look up at him. "And who was this girl?"

"Lori Hauck."

"Gesundheit." He laughs and shakes his head. I open my mouth to ask more about Lori Hauck—totally ready with a "Lori Hauck-a-loogie" joke—when I see the admiral approach us.

"Jamison," he says. "Can I talk to you?"

Dammit. We were doing so well there for a second. I step away from Jamie as he gives me a look that asks if I'm okay with it.

"Go ahead. It's fine."

"I'll be right back."

I nod, but after I look around at the other dancing couples, I make a beeline back to the table, where Rocky Horror is frowning over his glass of hooch. Daphne is next to him with a disappointed look on her face. I drop onto the bench across from them.

"We were so close," Daphne says, shaking her head.

"Close how?" I ask.

"The two of you have barely talked the past two weeks, but you

26

seemed pretty cozy just now," Rocky Horror says.

Daphne turns to him. "I told you. Any time I have two characters in my books with a misunderstanding, I just force them to dance. Who slow dances in silence?"

"Sociopaths," Rocky Horror says.

"Excuse you both," I jump in. "We did *not* have a misunderstanding."

There wasn't anything to misunderstand. I said everything I needed to say to Jamie about how mad I was and why. I was annoyed that he decided to leave the boat after Hickey kicked me off. If it had just been left at that, it would have been fine. But then when I asked him to stay on the crew, he doubled down and kept telling me over and over that he didn't care about the boat trip, he just didn't want to be away from me.

I couldn't understand. Henri was the entire reason we were here, building this new family with everyone we've met. How could he just say "I don't care, I'll stay here" when the entire purpose of the trip was to go up and bring her back?

Back to her daughter, Amy. Not to mention her new granddaughter and namesake, Henri-Two. *Her* family. And ours.

It was a sweet gesture and I appreciated that, but I told him to stop being stupid and stick with the boat. For Henri, but also for Cara. Yes, Cara and Daria are friends now, but she's still dealing with her PTSD and gets panic attacks every once in a while. She needs more than just Daria on her side, especially with Hickey being as impatient as he is.

And, yes, this is absolutely what I lie awake at night thinking about. When Jamie and I were on the road with a shared goal, we seemed to work. But what if here, now that we've reached safety, we want different things? He started to talk about us staying up north after Henri gets on the boat, and going back to the cabin, just the two of us. And when we first got here, that plan made sense. We were scared that what happened in Fort Caroline—authoritarianism and bigotry—would happen here. But the Keys aren't like that. We have a community here. A family, even. And if Fort Caroline came a-knocking at our one-road-in, one-road-out island-chain community, that family would protect us.

I don't understand why he wants to leave that.

So, yeah, none of it was a misunderstanding. But it did get bigger than I thought it would. And Jamie being so willing to give up on our plans made it worse.

It felt like something had changed, specifically in him, and I don't know what it is.

"If it's not a misunderstanding," Daphne says, "then what is it?"

I shrug. "Maybe our relationship was just a codependent thing while we were on the road. We felt like we needed each other, and now that we're safe, things are just . . . different."

"Then why are you the one pushing him away?" Rocky Horror asks.

"I'm not pushing him away."

Rocky Horror and Daphne share a look that says they don't believe me.

"I'm not! He just . . . something is different. And I don't know what it is." We sit in silence for a moment, and I turn to see Cara at the next table with Amy, Henri-Two, and another woman with a baby around

Henri-Two's age. I know Cara's been listening, and judging by the look on her face, she understands what I'm talking about. She doesn't seem confused like Daphne—or bored-slash-annoyed like Rocky Horror. She seems sad. Pitying, maybe.

"Wait," Rocky Horror says. "I don't know why I'm still here dealing with this. Excuse me." He stands. "Daph, you need a refill?"

She says she's okay, and he gives me one last exasperated look before heading back to the punch bowl.

Daphne reaches across the table to take my hand.

"Whatever's going on between you two, I think you need to talk about it, for real, before you make any major decisions."

I nod, but that's easier said than done. How do I ask my boyfriend—are we even still boyfriends?—if he's changed now that we're living in what could be considered a functional society again? How do I not sound rude when I say I think it's selfish to change the plan so casually and forget about the mission to get Henri?

Jamie's voice pulls me from my thoughts, and I turn again to see him talking to Cara. She nods, her eyes wide with surprise. Amy and the other woman stop talking and turn to listen just as the band kicks into a high-tempo song and drowns out whatever he's saying.

Amy puts a hand to her mouth in shock.

"What's going on?" I ask Daphne as I stand.

Jamie turns to me. "We're not leaving Sunday," he says. "The broadcast earlier from Radio Blanca . . . the radio operator here lost touch with the outpost over there a few hours ago, and no one has answered yet."

Daphne is by my side now. "Is everything okay?"

29

"They don't know," Jamie says. "But they're making an announcement at the end of the social. We're going to prepare for the storm to hit us, too. Hopefully if it does, it won't be a full hurricane, but just to be safe, they're moving everyone into shelters. If it does hit, it will be tomorrow afternoon or evening."

"Where are we supposed to go?" I ask.

"There's a school in Marathon that used to be a hurricane shelter," Daphne says.

Jamie nods. "That's the one we're using. The southern Keys are going to the naval base in Key West, Key Largo is staying put and sheltering in a school up there, and from Tavernier down to us are heading to Marathon." He turns to me. "They want the boat crew to move supplies into the school overnight. You should probably start getting the kids' stuff together so you can all head over first thing in the morning. I'm going to grab stuff at the house first. Anything specific you want?"

So much for keeping the conversational momentum going. I shake my head, and he turns to Cara to ask if she's ready and she nods yes. The two of them leave, but he stops and jogs back to me.

He leans down and kisses me lightly on the cheek. "See you in the morning. But if the wind and rain start, don't wait, okay?"

"Okay."

When he leaves I can still feel the dampness from his lips on my cheek. And it makes my heart ache.

Maybe all we needed was a catastrophe to get back to normal.

That doesn't bode well.

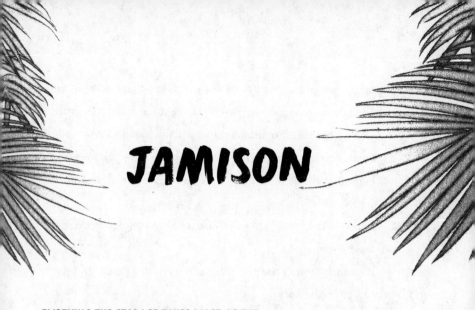

JAMISON

EMPTYING THE STORAGE TAKES MOST OF THE night into the early morning because we have to inventory everything first. I'm not sure when they came up with this emergency management system—judging by how logical it all is, I assume months ago—but the Committee wants to keep track of which supplies come from which Key so that afterward everything will go back where it was originally allotted.

The system by which everything was allotted to begin with is entirely above my paygrade.

It's tedious work, but it feels good to be doing something, even with the air of worry hovering over everyone. When the sun comes up, the sky is still clear and blue. But the afternoon quickly worsens as dark clouds creep in, and it starts drizzling as people arrive at Marathon High School. Cots have been placed in the gym, hallways, and several classrooms. The cafeteria is set up as it would have been in the before times, but with stacks of canned and dried goods surrounding the tables.

After we finish triple-counting the Islamorada stores in the caf, the people in charge tell me I'm free to go. I've only seen Andrew twice since we arrived, so I head toward the gym to find him. Outside, the rain is coming down steadily, and the wind howls in gusts.

I pick up bits of information and gossip from people in the halls.

"Sandy and her husband haven't slept in the same bed in—"

"Before, anything above a two was a mandatory evacuation for the Keys."

"I hope Fern is okay. Do you think we haven't heard because the radios were damaged?"

"It's a full moon, but we're heading toward low tide. If the storm surge hits at high, we—"

That last one almost makes me stop dead in my tracks. We have sandbags stacked on either side of every outside door, but I'm not even sure those would stop the floodwater if we're hit with a storm surge at high tide. We had a few hurricanes in Philly over the years, but most of them had weakened to a category one or tropical storm by the time they got that far inland. It was mainly the heavy rain we had to worry about. Once, after a pretty bad one when I was younger, the main highway through Center City was completely flooded all the way up to the overpass.

Marathon High School is a three-story building. If the water gets that high here, we might need to be on the roof—and the food that isn't canned will be ruined. I look back toward the cafeteria. The Committee people have already thought ahead, I'm sure.

It'll be fine. We'll all be fine. I just need Andrew to tell me he agrees, and I'll feel a whole lot better.

"Hell no, we're screwed," Andrew says. But as he holds a dodgeball just out of reach while one of the kids tries to jump up to take it from him, I still can't help but laugh.

"Can you stop torturing him?" I nod at the boy.

"This isn't torture, it's playing. You're having fun, right, Frank?"

Frank is smiling and it seems like he's about to say yes, but then he looks at me and grows solemn. All the kids in the Keys do that—well, the ones who have surviving family members don't. But the orphans all do. And it kinda freaks me out. It's like they can tell I'm an orphan, too. I wonder why they don't look at Andrew that way. Maybe they sense that I already have one foot out the door. That I want to take Andrew away from here and live the rest of our lives as hermits in a cabin in the Pennsylvania woods.

Finally, Frank speaks. "How come *you* don't have any scars?"

I have no clue why he's asking me that.

"Okay!" Andrew throws the dodgeball to an empty area of the gym. "Fetch, Frank." Frank runs off after it. "I always wanted a dog."

"What does he mean about scars?" I touch the side of my belly where I was shot. There's a dark pink indent that hasn't fully lightened to normal scar tissue. Not that Frank would know about it.

Andrew waves off my question. "The kid's obsessed with them. You should have seen him asking Rocky Horror about his top surgery scars."

"Oh! *That's* No-Filter Frank."

"Aptly named, yes." Andrew scans the gym, quickly counting the kids. He stops, recounts, then spins around, relaxing when he sees a kid sitting on a cot playing with a blue stuffed hippo. "But, yes, we're going to be okay. This place was a storm shelter for the area even before the bug, so it'll still work after."

I nod. Once we're past the worrying topic of a flash flood, he steps closer to me and lowers his voice.

"What about us?" he asks. "Are *we* going to be okay?"

My stomach clenches again and I shrug. "I don't know. I wasn't the one not talking to me."

He sighs as No-Filter Frank returns with the ball and tries to hide it behind his back. Andrew quickly snatches it, then throws it again, and Frank is gone.

"Everyone has been saying we need to talk about it, but I think I just wasn't ready at the time."

"And are you now?"

Again Frank returns, and again Andrew makes quick work of throwing the ball.

"Yes, this absolutely seems like the most opportune moment we've had for the past two weeks."

I laugh, but my stomach still tightens with nerves. If he's about to break up with me, this might be the worst possible time, surrounded by people and No-Filter Frank, who is probably going to ask why I'm crying, and I'll have no physical scars to show for it.

"I just need to know where you're at," Andrew says.

I don't understand. "In what way?"

"In our lives. You were so quick to pivot away from the plan to get Henri. You'd really leave Cara with the boat crew, alone, just because you'd miss me?"

He's trivializing it, making me feel childish. And that's not what I was doing at all.

Frank returns, and I have a moment to gather my thoughts as he gets better at keeping the ball away from Andrew. When he finally runs off to chase it again, I speak.

"Of course I'd miss you. But that's not it. Our plan was to go north, make sure Henri got on the boat, then go back to the cabin. I wasn't going to leave you here. And, yes, I would miss you, but 'where I'm at' in our lives is I don't want to be away from you. I left my home because I didn't want to be alone again. But now I don't care where I am. I just want to be with you."

"This is our home now, *your* home and mine." He motions to the gym around us. "These people are our family."

That gives me pause. I don't agree—the only person I would consider close enough to be family is Cara. Everyone else is just neighbors and friends. If Fort Caroline comes after me, these people aren't going to protect us. They want this place to stay safe, and that means giving us up if they have to.

"I understand what you mean," I say. "But I don't think you're right. You're my family. I trust you with my life, but—"

Frank returns and I cut myself off. He looks between us—as if he senses something isn't right—and Andrew takes the moment to steal the ball and throw it, this time aiming for the doors out to the hallway. It bounces out of sight and Frank runs after it.

"And you trust Cara, too," Andrew says.

"Of course." Without her, we wouldn't have escaped from Fort Caroline. Twice.

"So what makes these people different? What makes Rocky Horror or Daphne different?"

"They haven't lived through what we have."

"*Everyone* has lived through what we have!" Andrew says, his voice rising. I glance around to see if anyone is watching, but they all seem preoccupied, except for Cara, who looks up from the book she's reading across the room. "We all lost people we loved. There's a handful who still have the families they had before the bug, and then there's the rest of us, who are stuck trying to piece together new ones."

"Like you and me."

"And Henri and Amy. And RH and Daphne and Cara. There are plenty of people *here* who are becoming a family. At least to me."

I open my mouth to again say that, yes, they are our friends, but they aren't our family if we're planning to go back north anyway, when it hits me.

"You don't want to go back to the cabin."

He looks like he's surprised I'd say it out loud. But I'm a little pissed that I was the one who had to say it. If this was on his mind, why wouldn't he tell me? Why would we talk about our plans to leave for so long if he was having doubts? And these past two weeks of awkwardness, he was really going to let me go north without him.

"I . . ." He's looking at me, but Frank returns, ball in hand and a smile on his face.

A loud clap of thunder shakes the building and No-Filter Frank startles, dropping the dodgeball. Some of the adults go on with what they were doing, but all the kids have stopped, staring up at the gymnasium ceiling as though it's about to collapse. The wind whistles through the air vents, but the next roll of thunder sounds farther away.

I look to Andrew. He doesn't seem like he's planning to pick up our conversation where we left it.

I nod. "Guess it's going to be a long night."

ANDREW

THE THUNDER CRACK THAT WAKES ME FROM a twilight nap is sharp and quick. I sit up on the cot and rub at my aching leg. It doesn't ease the pain, since it most likely healed wrong after I broke it stepping in a bear trap near Jamie's cabin, but I can't help it. I glance around the gym, which is lit by small battery-powered lanterns. The kids are sleeping through it, but on the other side of the room, Daphne, Kelly, and Liz—the other members of Team Orphan—are all awake.

A few other people around the gym are as well. But not Jamie.

He sleeps through the storm, lying on his side facing me with his mouth hanging slightly open and his fists curled under his chin. The all-nighter he spent moving food into the cafeteria probably did a lot to help him pass out, because I haven't been able to sleep well since we talked.

I really didn't think we were on such different pages. Yes, I want to stay here, with this new family we're making, but I had no idea he wasn't torn the way I was. When we talked about the cabin, it felt like one of those fantasies we like to pretend are realistic. Like moving to

Spain randomly. How are you planning to do that? Do you have any idea how much it costs to immigrate to another country legally? What are you going to do for work? Where are you going to live? And do you even speak Spanish?

We knew where we'd be living, but getting there was a whole other nightmare we never discussed. Because the plan was the boat. We'd take the boat up to Bethesda and then keep on walking, knowing everyone else would return to Florida without us for their happily ever afters and we'd go back to the cabin for ours. We'd completely avoid Fort Caroline's authoritarian white supremacist colony in Georgia and we'd never run into the settlement near the cabin who stole most of our food and we'd be happy.

But that wasn't the fantasy for me anymore. And when they kicked me off the boat, I realized we could still make it here. Jamie could go up and we would miss each other. And when he got back, I'd be waiting by the dock in a flowy caftan and floppy sun hat I could borrow from Daphne, and slo-mo run to the end of the dock as he hopped down off the boat and scooped me into his arms as a classic 80s-sounding slow ballad blared in the afterlife movie theater where I'd rewatch this scene over and over. The other Best Original Song nominees at the Afterlife Oscars don't stand a chance, because there wouldn't be a dry eye in the house as Jamie returned home. To *our* home.

But to him, this isn't our home.

Thunder rumbles again as I stare at him. Seriously, he can sleep through anything. He even almost sleeps through his nightmares.

I'll hear him at night. Sometimes it's just a quiet "nuh!" But other times it's low, mumbled screams that progressively get louder and clearer until I have to shake him awake. I ask him what the nightmare was, and it's usually about his mom or the guy he shot to protect me—Harvey Rosewood. Sometimes it's Harvey's dad, Danny, or someone else from Fort Caroline. Other times he'll mumble that he doesn't remember, but I'll hear him tossing and turning the rest of the night. That's how I know he's lying.

But he seems to do fine with hurricanes.

Good for him.

Now that I think about it, though, it does seem awful quiet. No rain pelting the building. The wind and thunder quieter than they've been all day. I put my shoes on and walk out to the main hallway of the high school. LED lights are hanging on the walls, plugged into surge protectors and jury-rigged to car batteries. I wonder if we'll be in the dark for a few days or weeks until the solar panels we've been using are repaired. Or maybe we'll get lucky and they won't be damaged at all. They were probably created to withstand strong winds, right?

Sandbags have been placed at the entrance doors. Beyond them I can see the world outside, and the moon reflecting off the still surface of the water, which is almost up to the high school doors.

The moon?

Is the storm over? Maybe it was a tropical storm, not a full-on hurricane. Sure, the area seems to be flooded, but only a few feet.

Someone is whispering at the top of the stairs to my right. A door opens and then slams shut. I follow the sounds up to the second-floor hallway and onto an outdoor breezeway.

Outside on the hallway-slash-balcony, there's a line of about ten people staring up at the sky. I step to the end of the line and look up, then almost gasp.

The storm isn't over. And it's a hurricane, all right.

The black clouds swirl around us for miles, and right in the center is the open, starlit sky and a bright full moon. Clouds spin into tendrils along the eyewall. The sky lights up with a line of lightning, which follows the path of the churning clouds.

Everyone "oohs" as though we're watching fireworks.

It's beautiful. Scary, but beautiful.

I head back down to the gym. Things may be awkward between Jamie and me, but this is something he needs to see. I shake him lightly.

"Jamie, wake up."

He doesn't wake, so I shake him a little harder, hoping not to scare him. But there's no way I can describe to him later how cool this is.

"Hey! Jamie!"

He opens his eyes, then startles when he realizes we're not in our bedroom.

"It's okay! But I want to show you something."

Jamie sits up—the side of his hair that he was sleeping on is sticking straight up and I can't help but smile, feeling a warm pang of love in my chest. He looks around again and shakes his head. "No. Sleep now. Show later."

"There is no later for this. It's a once-in-a-lifetime thing, and you need to get your ass up right now before you miss it." I pull his legs off the cot and start putting on his shoes. He groans but works on tying them. "I'm getting Cara, Daphne, and the others, too."

I cross the room and tell them they have to see what's going on outside. "The kids will be okay for a few minutes."

Then we all head up the stairs. More people have woken their friends, and the number of people outside on the second floor has tripled. But we still have a great view.

"Holy shit," Jamie says as the sky lights up blue again. Thunder rumbles as if in answer.

"Told you you didn't want to miss this."

"As usual, you are correct."

"Usual?" Cara says under her breath.

I ignore her and pretend to hold a microphone up to Jamie. "Sorry, can you repeat that once more for the viewers at home?"

"Uh, sure." He bends down, pretending to speak into my fake microphone. "Andrew once had a wet dream about Gillian Anderson." Cara snorts.

"You said you'd never tell!" I throw the invisible microphone off the balcony.

After ten minutes or so, Jamie turns to me and says, "Thanks. For waking me up." He says it like he would have expected me to let him sleep through it, and it makes me feel awful.

"Of course." I hate this. How we talk in stilted, awkward sentences. Walking on eggshells. I never knew what that saying meant until we started arguing. Maybe that's not even the right saying for us. We're more like this storm, our past arguments and insecurities—hi, that's me—swirling around us. And then moments like this, where we're fine and there is no arguing. Just trying to keep up with the eye,

41

avoiding the destruction that the storm causes.

Or maybe only I'm doing that.

The thunder gets a little louder as the eyewall approaches the shore. The wind kicks up and we head back inside.

Once we're downstairs, I reach out and grab his wrist. "Hey, hold on a sec." He stops and turns to me as Cara and the rest of Team Orphan continue into the gym. I motion toward the hallway at the end of the front hall. "Can we try again? Talking, I mean?"

He nods and lets me lead him to a quiet, vacant area.

I sit down against the wall, and he settles next to me. Maybe it's easier to talk when we don't have to look at each other.

"You were right earlier," I say. "About me not wanting to go back to the cabin."

I see him nod out of the corner of my eye. "I figured." He still sounds disappointed, so I reach out and take his hand.

"I want to be clear. I don't want you to go back either." I turn to see that he's looking at me now. But he still seems sad. "I like the home we're making here."

He stares at the floor as though it hurts him to look me in the eye.

Finally, I ask him what's been on my mind since I first got kicked off the boat. "Why don't you?"

"I like it here, Andrew—"

"Then why do you want to leave so bad?"

"Why do you want to stay?"

"Because we *are* making a life here. We have friends. I'd call them a family." I turn my body toward him. It was easier to start this conversation not looking at each other, but I need to see him now, his face, his reactions. I need to know what he's thinking. Or at least try to. "We lost everyone in our old lives to the bug, and now we have a chance to start over and make our own family."

If he wants me to know what he's thinking, he's doing it all wrong because his face remains stoic and unreadable.

"We talked about this," he says. "Every night for weeks we talked about this. The last time we found a settlement this big, they hunted us down and shot us. Cara ran away from them."

"But she's still here."

"*Now.* She's still here *now.* You think if the Keys turn authoritarian, she wouldn't want to leave, too?"

"But this isn't like Fort Caroline."

"Right *now* it isn't, Andrew. That's what we talked about. What would happen if things went bad here or if Fort Caroline found this settlement? Yeah, Daphne, Amy, Rocky Horror, they would side with us. The people we like would obviously try to protect us, but aside from Cara, who would *fight* for us?"

I can't believe he's saying this. It's so not like him, and I don't know where it's coming from. Jamie saved my life when I was injured, and he didn't have to. He shared his medicine and took care of me. Then he followed me when I left. He leaves messages on trucks for passing strangers, letting them know there's still supplies in there. He killed someone to protect me. He sees the good in people more than the bad.

"All those people you mentioned would fight for us. If we make this place our home, they *will* fight for us."

"You're wrong." He reaches out and takes my face in his hands. "There are over two thousand people here—two thousand people who don't know us. And the world has changed. We've been lucky down here, but all it takes is a bad couple of days and they could turn on us. I don't want that to even be an option, so yes, I think we're safer on our own at the cabin. Where we can take care of each other and make our own decisions."

"What about the people who came to the cabin to rob us?"

His face darkens. "I told you I would fight for you."

My stomach turns and tears burn my eyes. I open my mouth to tell him I don't want that. To tell him his kindness is what I love. That here, we don't need to fight for our lives, we can just live. But something cold hits me, sending a chill up my back. I cry out, sitting up as water floods past us.

Jamie jumps up, too, and we follow the flow to one of the doors leading to the school parking lot. The sandbags go halfway up the doors, but the floodwater must have passed that point, because it's spilling through the cracks on all sides.

Behind us, toward the gym, someone shouts. Jamie spins and looks at me as though he's asking permission for us to go check it out. If the water is coming through everywhere, we might need to get everyone up to the second floor sooner rather than later.

I nod and we head down the hallway.

Water flows through the seams of the school's front doors. Outside, the rain and wind have picked up—if the eye hasn't already passed us, it's about to. I have just enough time to wonder how much pressure the glass doors can take when my thoughts are interrupted by someone shouting out orders near the cafeteria. More water flows from the caf, and the hallway is full up to our ankles. A guy I recognize runs past us.

"What's going on?" Jamie asks.

"The cafeteria's flooding," he says. "We're moving the non-canned supplies up to the second floor." He continues into the gym, probably to wake people and get more bodies moving the food.

Jamie curses under his breath. "I knew it."

We carefully splash through the floodwater to the cafeteria, where a group of people are already forming a plan. Cara joins us—silently listening. They tell us to go to the stairs and create a line to pass boxes up. Cara is heading for the stairs before we even move. Me, Jamie, and ten others form a line, each of us just an arm's length from the next, and start passing food up the stairs, where Cara hands it off to people who run it down the upstairs hallways. More people arrive, and along with them, I see the Kid emerge from the gym door, watching us.

"Go find Ms. Daphne," I tell him, taking a box from the guy next to me and handing it over the railing to Jamie.

But the Kid doesn't move; instead he watches the assembly line passing box after box, then looks down at the water around his legs—now halfway up his shin.

"Kid!" I yell.

"Hey!" The guy next to me is holding a box out, so I take it and pass it to Jamie. Taylor also emerges from the gym, and as I pass another box, I glance back at her.

"Taylor, you and the Kid get upstairs."

"What's going—"

"Now!" It's the most authoritative I've probably ever sounded. She rolls her eyes and, taking the Kid's hand, walks up the stairs behind Jamie and the others. I'm about to open my mouth and scold her, tell her to take *other* stairs that aren't being used, but the guy next to me seems to be getting impatient. So I pass the box he's holding to Jamie, keeping one eye on them until they reach the top and are out of my sight.

Behind me, Liz emerges from the gym, holding hands with a group of the kids, including No-Filter Frank.

"Where's Daphne and the others?" I ask.

"Hey!" the guy next to me says. "Focus!"

I hand the box to Jamie, ignoring him as Liz shifts her attention from the water spilling around the front door to me. "She's getting the other kids together."

"Upstairs" is all I have time to say. She takes a step forward but the guy beside me stops her.

"Use the other stairs!"

"Dude, chill," I say.

"It's okay," Liz says. "We'll use the ones on this side. Come on, kids." She steers them away from us, down the hallway that Jamie and I were just talking in.

The wind outside kicks up, and there's a loud bang and shouts from somewhere in the school.

"What the hell was that?" the guy next to me asks. I half want to yell at him to focus, just to be a dick, but I'm curious as well.

More screams, followed by another bang. The water around my shins begins to flow like a river. Behind us, Daphne emerges from the gym. She's soaked, and so are the kids holding each other's hands in a chain behind her.

She points into the gym. "The roof! The gymnasium—" If she

has anything else to add, I can't hear it because something snaps, and the wind outside is suddenly inside. The roaring storm has broken our shelter.

Daphne spins as wind and rain blast her from inside the gym. I jump out of line and grab her, pulling her away from the storm, trying to get the kids somewhere safe.

The rest of the line seems to have given up on the supplies and are running for the stairs. Jamie hops over the railing to me as I scoop up one of the smaller kids who fell into the floodwater.

The people in the line are trying to squeeze onto the stairs, pushing some over the railing into the water below.

"Andrew!" Cara yells down from the top of the stairs. I look up to see her pointing the way Liz and the other kids went. That's right, there are other stairs. I nod to her and turn back to Jamie to tell him to go the other way, where we came from. But another crash kills the words in my throat.

And a wave of water rounds the corner of the hallway we were just in—a brown, foaming wall coming right at us.

JAMISON

I GRAB ONE OF THE KIDS AND try to get between the flood and Andrew, but the water hits me hard, sweeping us off our feet and toward the cafeteria. Salt water fills my nose and mouth, burning my senses away. I try to stand, holding tight to the little kid in my arms, but I can't get my footing. We're moving too fast.

Then, all at once, we slam into a wall. All of us—Andrew, Daphne, the five kids with her—are a tangle of limbs grasping for purchase. The lights along the wall flicker as car batteries are ripped from their pedestals and the wires soaked.

The floodwater pulls us down the hallway again, and I roll to my knees, lifting the kid in my arms above the waterline. She gasps and cries out, wrapping her arms around my throat.

Next to me, Andrew manages to get to his feet, holding the hands of two of the older kids. But behind us, Daphne is still struggling both to stand in the rushing water and to keep her grip on the two kids in her arms.

I get to my feet, almost losing my balance as a folded cot bangs into my leg, and wade over to Daphne. Andrew helps me get her up, and the lights flicker again, then send us into pure darkness. The kids scream.

Outside the school, lightning flashes and a gust of wind howls over the thunder and rain.

"We have to get upstairs," I yell to Andrew.

The lights flicker on but at a low voltage, and I see him nod. I point behind him, down the hallway, where most of the debris is gathering against closed double doors.

"Go!" Daphne yells. The kids are the ones pulling *us* along. The hallways sound like an underground tunnel with a freight train barreling toward us. Back the way we came, something crashes, and the ground shakes beneath our feet. I stumble, losing my balance.

As I twist my body, holding the girl in my arms above the water, I feel Andrew's hands on me, trying to steady me. And when I stand, I see the other two kids, struggling against the current, also trying to help.

I doubt they can hear my thanks, but I catch my balance and move on with them.

Andrew reaches the door first and starts pulling away cots, boxes, insulation, and drywall. I readjust the girl in my arms so she's on my side, and then try to help. The kids and Daphne are all there, too, pulling things away from the door, but the water shoves it all right back. I stand on a cot, pushing it down, and reach for the door handle.

The door barely budges against the water and debris. Andrew pulls at the jamb, shoving his body into the widening crack to the other side. I imagine something big floating down the hallway toward us, smashing into the door and crushing him, and I pull at his arm, trying to get him away. But he's so determined he doesn't notice.

He pushes hard, using the other door as leverage and then pulling the kids to the other side one by one. Daphne ducks under his arms, then he looks at me and the girl I'm still holding.

"Come on, quick!" he says. His arms are shaking. I lean against him, pushing him through as I bring up one of my legs to prop the door open.

Before he can argue with me, I hand the girl over to him. Beyond him, Daphne is already ushering kids toward the stairs. There are more adults there, ready to help them up. Another, even louder crash sounds on the other side of the school, and again the ground shakes.

Andrew takes the girl, giving me an annoyed look. But then his eyes go wide as he looks behind me. "Jamie, watch out!"

I turn to see a wave of floodwater almost as high as the ceiling pushing wood and rubble toward me. With all the strength I can muster, I push the door out and slip through before it can crush me.

As soon as the wave hits the other side, the door splinters and a waterfall bursts from every seam.

"Go!" I push everyone toward the steps.

Behind us, the doors finally give, and the water and wreckage spill into the stairwell. I grasp the railing for dear life as the flood hits us. Andrew is a few steps above me, but he almost loses his grip.

The water passes the top of my head, and something slices into my arm. Burning-hot pain explodes from the cut. More debris brushes against my face and neck, scratching me and probably drawing blood.

I find my footing on the stairs and use the railing to hoist myself up. My lungs burn as I break free of the water, gasping for air. Andrew is there, waiting for me on the landing, holding out a hand.

There's blood spilling down the side of his face from a cut above his eyebrow, but other than that he seems to be okay.

I take his hand and he pulls me up, out of the water.

At the top of the stairs there are people handing out blankets and towels. Andrew wraps one around my shoulders. The cut on my arm goes from my elbow halfway to my wrist, but it isn't deep.

I wrap my arms around Andrew, pulling him to me. It's strange that we were just talking about our difference of opinion—the wedge driving us apart—and now I just want to hold him and keep him close.

He seems to feel the same way, because he wraps his arms around my middle and holds me tight.

Somewhere down the hallway, glass breaks. Wind whistles through the doors, making me shiver. Andrew squeezes tighter and I rub at his back.

Lightning flashes outside, and we go over to a taped-up window. The area behind the school where the baseball field used to be is flooded. The water churns as the rain continues to pour.

"Come on," Daphne says, breaking the hypnosis the storm seems to have over us. "Let's get away from the windows."

We crowd together with all the others in the upstairs hallways. People sit on the floors or squeeze onto cots, huddled together. Some people are crying; some let out startled shouts as the storm kicks up.

"Where's Liz and the other kids?" Daphne asks as she gets two of the kids to settle down.

"She took the other stairs on the gym side," Andrew says. He bolts back to his feet, the blanket falling from his shoulders. "Oh! Taylor and the Kid came up here, too."

"They're safe." I say.

If he goes looking for them in the dark, he's bound to trip or step on someone, and who knows where tempers are at right now. Our food is all on the flooded first floor of the school—where it shouldn't have been to begin with.

"Cara is with them, too. Just wait here till the storm dies down a bit," I say, taking his hand. I can barely see the outline of his face in the darkness, but I think he's trying to decide whether he wants to go or if he wants to stay with me. If he is, at least it means he's torn on the matter.

Not that I would ever expect him to choose between me and anyone else. But the way things have been going between us, it might not have been a hard decision. He sits down next to me on the floor, and I feel him shivering against me. I wrap the blanket back around him, pulling it tight.

"You okay?" I ask quietly.

"Yeah, I think. Yeah." He sounds wired—scared and anxious. I squeeze his hand tighter and he squeezes back, then puts his head on my shoulder. I lean over and kiss his forehead. For a little over an hour, every time thunder cracks or some part of the school clangs or smashes from the wind or debris, he startles against me. Each time I rub his back, and soon he doesn't startle anymore, and I can feel his breath grow steady and calm. He's asleep.

After what feels like a few hours, the thunder grows distant and the rain lightens. A little later, the wind dies down. And soon after that, just as the world outside is turning blue with the coming dawn, I fall asleep, too.

"Jamie." Andrew shakes me gently and the muscles in my neck, arms, shoulders, and back ache. I groan and try to stretch, opening my eyes slightly against the bright sun blasting through the classroom windows, as though Armageddon wasn't happening outside just a few hours ago.

"What time is it?"

"Still morning," he says. There's something in his voice that makes me focus on him, squinting against the brightness. His eyes are red and bloodshot as though he's been crying.

"What's wrong?" I look around the hallway. The kids are curled up around each other, fast asleep on the floor. Taylor is there, too, her legs pulled tight to her chest and her eyes puffy and red, tears streaming down her face. The little boy they call the Kid is asleep at her feet. She keeps a protective hand on his shoulder.

Andrew follows my gaze to her and nods in the direction of the stairwell we came up. I stand and follow him.

The flood on the first floor has only gone down about two feet, judging by the layer of mud up to the half landing. As soon as we round the corner, Andrew wraps his arm tightly around me. He buries his face against my damp, brackish-smelling chest and unleashes a howl of pain.

"What?" I ask, my heart racing. I don't think I've ever heard him make these sounds before. I hold him tight with one arm while rubbing his back with the other. Asking quietly what's wrong but knowing he can't verbalize it yet.

He cries like that for almost five full minutes before he says something quietly against my chest. I hold him close to me while lowering my ear to his mouth.

"What's wrong?" I ask, keeping my voice low, as if, if I get any louder, it will spook him and we'll have to start this process all over again.

It comes out in a croak. "They're dead."

My heart seizes. Cara. She wasn't there when I woke. My own legs feel wobbly and I try my hardest to stay upright. My mouth is dry but I manage to get out, "Who?"

"Liz. The kids."

Oh no. The kids who tried to go upstairs. They sent them the other way. The way the flood came. I wait for him to add Cara's name, but he doesn't. He sobs again and I wait, still expecting the news to get even worse. Then I remember Cara was already upstairs when the flood hit. I hold him tighter, hoping that he doesn't add another name.

When he's ready to go on he leans back, looking up at me. "The other side of the school collapsed."

My extremities go cold as my mouth drops open.

"Everyone who was in the gym, the people using the stairs on the parking lot side of the school, the people upstairs in that wing. They all got trapped. Crushed or drowned. Liz, Matthew, Lisa, Quinten, Jeremy, Lucy. Frank."

The last one he barely gets out before he breaks down again.

The little boy with the dodgeball. No-Filter Frank. That one breaks me, too, and silent tears stream down my cheeks as I try to comfort Andrew. My heart wrenches in my chest and I start to panic.

"What about Amy? Henri-Two and Cara? Are they . . . ?"

He lets out a long breath. "They're okay. Cara's a bit bruised, but Amy and Henri-Two were safe up here. Rocky Horror got up in time, too."

Good. At least that's something. Still, the number of people who must have died last night, trapped in the other side of the school—it's horrific. Even after all the death we've seen from the superflu, this somehow seems worse, though I'm not sure why.

We stay in the stairwell together, silently, for a while, eventually sitting down and watching the floodwater drop inch by inch.

After maybe an hour of silence, Andrew sits bolt upright and gasps.

I'm not sure if I can handle more bad news, but I ask anyway. "What is it?"

He looks into my eyes—his are still red and puffy. "It's Saturday." I don't understand what he means until he says the next part, and it feels like my chest is a pit.

"Happy birthday."

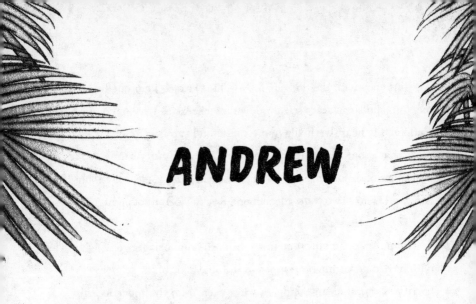

ANDREW

IT TAKES A DAY AND A HALF for the flooding to fully recede. By that time the high school and its inhabitants have grown ripe in the November heat. Thanks for being your hot, humid self, Florida.

Daphne says the Keys rarely get hit by storms like this, but when it does happen, it's particularly destructive. She's right. The devastation outside the school is unlike anything I've ever seen. The roads are cracked, large chunks sunken or pulled away entirely. Trees are bare or broken, and the bushes and shrubs are crushed beneath debris. Some buildings still stand, but many look like the half of the school that collapsed.

There's no real order to the day anymore because the portion of the Committee that's here is still trying to contact the other Keys. The last we heard, the folks on Key Largo are trying to regroup with their supplies, but there hasn't been any response from the group that sheltered at the naval base yet.

It's all overwhelming. There's so much to do but no one seems to know where to start. I know where *I* need to start, though. I just want to get clean. It's the only thing I feel like I can control right now.

I ask Daphne and Kelly if they'll be okay watching the seven remaining kids for a bit and they tell me to go ahead. I find Jamie and Cara talking near the flooded school buses in the school's parking lot.

"I'm going to wash up," I tell Jamie. "Do you want to come with me?"

He looks surprised that I'd even ask, which, yeah, fine. I get it. But of course I'd ask him. If nothing else, the hurricane and brush with death put a pin in our argument for a bit.

"Yeah." He turns to Cara as if he's about to ask if she wants to come, too, but I highly doubt the showers set up by the ocean are still standing, and I doubt even more that Cara wants to see either of us in the buff on the beach—title of my Jimmy Buffett cover album.

Thankfully before he says anything she tells us to go ahead.

"What were you two gossiping about?" I ask, trying to keep my tone playful. I need some kind of normalcy again even if that means ignoring whatever issues Jamie and I have.

"The boat."

Or, yeah, sure, let's talk about what drove a wedge between us in the first place.

"She talked with Hickey and Daria, and they're going to check the damage later today."

"You can go with them if you want." Not that I need to give him permission. I genuinely don't know why I said that. Probably because I didn't want to say, *Guess we didn't need to have that argument about you quitting the boat after all.* Especially because that would be reductive. It's very clear our issues are deeper than him thinking for a moment that he didn't want to be on the boat without me.

"I don't know." He nods at the row of houses to our left. They're all crushed against each other and half-buried in sand and silt. Also, I'm fairly certain they used to be on our right. "If the boat's still there, I doubt it's seaworthy."

I groan.

"What?" he asks.

I can't hold it in anymore. "I hate this entire conversation," I say, stopping in the middle of the road. "I hate every single thing about this boring fucking conversation because we almost died and all I want is some fraction of a millisecond of normalcy but I can't be normal around you because we just wasted the last two weeks and some odd days bickering—"

He smirks at me. "*We?*"

"Don't interrupt with your salient points, I'm on a roll here. We spent weeks bickering and arguing about what we want when all I want is you and me and being normal."

Jamie takes a step toward me, putting his hands on my arms. "That's all I want, too."

"Then I'm calling a truce. An armistice. I don't want to talk about Henri, or the boat, or this place, or anything else. Just for today. Okay? I want to pretend . . ."

My voice trails off because I legit almost said *pretend we're back in the cabin, just the two of us.* And that would violate the cease-fire I just declared. But my desire for the quietness of the cabin is only due to the chaos of our life right now. I forgot what that chaos felt like. It was like that on the road—every day a terrifying and unknown future. But we were together, and we could make the decisions for ourselves.

"Pretend things are normal?" Jamie helps.

I sigh. "Yes. I want that." Whatever "normal" is without worrying about Taylor crying over Frank. Or the Kid going completely silent. Or Daphne trying so hard to smile even as her eyes betray her heartbreak. I don't want to think about Liz and the kids who died, just for a few hours. Because I'm going to be thinking of them forever.

Jamie steps closer and pulls my chin so I'm looking up at him. He kisses me gently, slipping a hand around to my lower back and pulling me against him.

The world goes quiet and all I hear is my heartbeat in my ears. I imagine it keeping time with his.

When he pulls away, he keeps his forehead against mine, our noses touching.

"It isn't abnormal for us to disagree about something. Couples disagree all the time."

They disagree about what to eat and where to go, not how to rebuild a family.

"Then I just want to ignore one aspect of our normal relationship for the day," I say.

"C'mon." He takes my hand and continues walking. "When my mom came home after a particularly bad day at the hospital, she'd call me down to the kitchen. And we'd sit at the kitchen table and go back and forth naming one thing we were happy to have in our lives. It was never the days when the ER was just busy. It was the days when she lost more patients than she knew how to handle. This was all before the superflu, I mean. When that hit, the game stopped working."

"Repressing our emotions doesn't feel very healthy."

"It depends how long we repress them. If we do it for only one day, then it's just taking a break from the more intense emotions. Giving us time to rest."

I'm not sure if that's enough to make me feel better about all the people who died in the storm—so far they've counted 273 people missing on that side of the school. But it's enough to feel a little better about everything else. About Jamie not wanting to stay here and live a safe life—though maybe he was right, given the events of the last few days.

Shit. I do need this game. But I also need him to get me started.

"So what are you grateful for?"

He takes a second to think, then looks up at the afternoon sky. "The sunshine."

"Starting broad."

"I find it's best to think macro when things look like . . ." He gestures to the destroyed road before us, leading me around a fallen magnolia tree.

"Noted. My turn? I'm grateful for . . ." I take the time to look around, trying to find something. "I guess I'm grateful climate change will be slowed now that there are fewer people to destroy the earth."

"Flag on the play."

"I don't understand sports metaphors, sweetie."

"Use your context clues. You can't be grateful for something that requires cynicism. Find something else."

"Fine, I'm grateful for cynicism." He glares at me. "Okay! Okay. I'm grateful . . . Can it be something I'm *going* to be grateful for?"

"Sure."

"I'm grateful I won't smell bad soon." I pull my T-shirt up to my nose and pretend to retch.

"I'm actually grateful for that, too."

I nudge him. "You love my musk."

"That's not musk, it's *murk*."

I laugh and remind him it's his turn.

"I'm . . ." He pauses as we reach the beach. The sand is packed down and debris-ridden from the storm. We walk halfway to the shore, then sit down in the sand and take off our shoes and socks. "I'm grateful that we're here."

I look over at him, wondering if he means alive or in the Keys. Maybe he's had a change of heart. But I don't want to ask because it's breaking our rule. We're ignoring our real problems today and finding what we're grateful for.

He leans over and kisses me, putting his hand gently on my jaw.

"I'm grateful that I have my favorite person in the world," he says.

I'm not sure if it's the kiss or just the way he's looking at me—or maybe this really is working—but my heart feels lighter. Like there isn't a billion pounds of emotional weight shoved into every muscle in my body.

"I'm grateful that you know how to make me feel grateful again," I tell him.

He kisses me. "C'mon. Let's get cleaned up."

We leave our dirty, sweaty clothes on the shore and wade into the surf. As we use sand and salt water to scrub our bodies, we continue the game. And it does help. By the time we've washed and laid our clothes out to dry, I am very glad we're safe and still here.

It reminds me why I love Jamie.

And that makes me feel pretty damn grateful.

JAMISON

WE LEFT THE SCHOOL THE NEXT MORNING, but by then there were so many rumors swirling it was like its own secondary storm. I heard that there was a revolt against the Committee members at the naval base in Key West, which was why none of them had shown up. Another rumor was that their shelter was destroyed and everyone was dead. Either way, there hasn't been radio contact with them. We heard from Key Largo, but they had losses as well. Theirs plus ours came to 656 people dead in the storm.

The fact that we haven't heard from the southern Keys isn't a good sign.

People who lived in Marathon said their homes are gone, some flooded so badly they'll never be able to fix them.

The Key Committee members who survived told us the only plan they had: Go to Key Largo and regroup. Once there, we'd figure things out and wait until the folks down in Key West are able to contact us. I don't think they have any reason for this other than to get a total head count and reallocate the remaining supplies. Some people stayed at the school and started inventorying the supplies left over, getting them ready to be moved up to Key Largo. We set off with the rest of the crowd for Islamorada again. Me, Andrew, Cara, Amy, Henri-Two, Daphne, Kelly, and the seven remaining orphans. There we'll camp and rest until we set out to join the rest of the settlement in Key Largo.

Andrew held tight to the Kid's hand, but the Kid didn't seem like he wanted to let go either. It was a long walk, made even longer by the orphans' tiny steps. Thankfully a group of older folks didn't mind the slower pace, so we all stopped to rest overnight. It took a while to get a fire going, but when it did it was a big bonfire that kept everyone warm and comfortable. And with all the fallen trees, it wasn't hard to find fuel.

We got back to Islamorada today, in the late afternoon. But it looked a lot like the rest of the Keys we crossed along the way. The motel the kids lived in is still standing, but all the rooms on the first floor have been destroyed. We left Daphne and the kids and walked to our house, promising to come back.

Not that we have a choice.

The house we were living in is destroyed, the second floor crumpled atop the first.

Andrew looks at me. "I was thinking of renovating anyway."

I don't laugh. It's not our house anymore. And it never really felt like a home to me.

Andrew picks up a splintered palm trunk and throws it through the half-broken window of our bedroom. I follow with a smaller stick to break apart the remaining glass, then we both climb in. Everything is wet and already smells like mildew. Our bed, sheets, towels, the clothes we left.

Andrew pulls open the closet and the door falls right out of the soaking drywall around it, so he pushes it away. He squeezes salt water from some of the shirts hanging inside. "Maybe we can salvage some of this?"

He points to the collapsible hamper across the room, and I hand it to him so he can throw our clothes into it. I try to think if there's anything else we might need. And of course there is. I right the side table next to our bed and pull open the drawer. Water sloshes out.

Inside is the leather-bound notebook my mother left me when the superflu killed her. All the medical and general survival information she thought I could use for the apocalypse—and diary entries from before that I read sometimes, just to remember her voice.

"Ready?" Andrew asks, picking up the dripping-wet hamper.

"Are you okay?"

He gives me something halfway between a scoff and a laugh. "The best. I genuinely couldn't be any better. You?"

Point taken. But I knew that; I just wanted him to talk to me. Because maybe I want to say all the things I'm worried about, too. All the people who could be dead, how we might not be able to survive without the comforts we've had for the past few months. How it might not even be feasible to stay here anymore.

"You ready?" he asks again.

I am.

The following morning Cara and I sit quietly in the shade of the motel while Amy and Henri-Two nap upstairs, and Andrew and Daphne keep the kids occupied with playing a four-on-four game of steal the bacon—the Kid is sitting out by choice. We all stayed in two adjoining rooms last night. Daphne and Amy took the beds with a couple of the smaller kids—Henri-Two in a crib that had been on the second floor and so escaped the flooding—while the others just scattered around the floor alongside Andrew, Cara, and me. A couple of the kids had nightmares, and each time Andrew leaped up quickly to check on them, as though he had already been awake.

I can't stop watching Andrew. How he puts on this face for the kids, pretending he's okay when I know he isn't, because they need some sense of safety after everything that happened to them. I know how they feel.

Every day here, I worry about how safe we are. Even if Fort Caroline never finds us, there isn't anything to stop another settlement from coming and throwing the whole system into disarray. And who knows what that would look like for Andrew and me?

"Do you think I'm wrong?" I ask Cara.

She frowns and shrugs. "About?"

"Sorry. I forgot I haven't talked about this with you for a while."

She shakes her head. "I don't want to get between the two of you."

"I know that. I'm not asking you to. I just mean do you think I'm wrong about wanting to go to the cabin? I'm not asking you to side with me on anything, just trying to get your thoughts."

She chews at her lip, thinking. "I think . . . you are not *wrong*. But I also think you are not right."

"Thanks, Cara, super helpful. Great talk."

"Shut up and just listen. You got shot. By the same people I was trying to get away from, and for good reason—the getting away, not the getting shot."

"I was hoping."

"So, yes, I think you are not wrong to be worried about staying here. It makes sense to be distrustful. But you should also ask what it is about the Keys that makes you distrustful. I think your idea that Andrew would ever turn on you is obscenely misguided."

"I don't think that!"

"Then why is it your way or nothing? You think he won't pack up and leave with you the second he even hears the name Fort Caroline?"

It's not that at all. I turn back to Andrew, watching him call out the number two and Taylor and another girl run out to grab the bacon—a throw pillow from one of the hotel rooms—from the faded parking spot line.

I know he'd leave this place behind in a second if it became unsafe. But I can tell how much it's going to break his heart to do it. He would never admit it, but he was looking for family a long time before he met me.

He left his house in Connecticut after the death of his sister—his last family member taken by the superflu. And on the road in New Jersey he met a couple named the Fosters. He shared food and a fire with them, but that night they tried to rob him. He accidentally killed them while fighting back and from that moment decided he'd go south to Virginia and tell their remaining family what happened to them.

He found me first.

The Fosters in Virginia were long dead by the time we arrived, and I think he still feels the guilt from what happened to their parents— maybe not as often as he used to, but it's there. And every person we met—Henri; a kid our age at Reagan airport and his siblings; Cara; a girl in a shoe store outside Jacksonville; Daphne; all the kids—he treated them kindly. Not the people in Fort Caroline, though—but maybe he subconsciously knew they couldn't be trusted.

It wasn't until we got here, until he started talking to strangers, getting to know neighbors and making friends, that I realized he was trying to find the right people. The people he could make a family with again.

But I knew—*thought*—our time here was temporary, so I never did. I also didn't feel the need to. I like everyone fine enough, and Cara sometimes does feel like the older sister I never had, but in my mind we were always going to go back to the cabin someday. It would be me and Andrew—maybe Cara if she wanted to, but if not, I wouldn't mind as long as she was safe and happy.

Because I didn't want to be here if things did go bad. I didn't want Fort Caroline to find us, and I didn't want to watch this settlement go through the growing pains of rebuilding postapocalyptic society.

Before, if we had just told Amy where her mom was and then left, we would have been fine. We'd have no more ties to the Keys, and we could be happy that we'd completed our mission to reunite a family, then go live on our own at the cabin. Maybe even make a truce with the settlement nearby so they wouldn't bother us again.

But the longer we're here, the harder it's going to be for Andrew to leave. He'll never stop worrying about these people.

Especially because he already considers them family.

When Cara sees I'm not going to answer her question, she continues, "I get why you don't want to trust anyone. I feel the same way sometimes. But these people are different."

"And if they change?" I ask.

She doesn't have an answer for that. We sit in silence, and for a few moments I think that's the end of our conversation, but then she looks over at me.

"Since it doesn't look like we're going to get Henri anytime soon, what *is* your plan?"

I hadn't thought of it. But I didn't think I'd need to. Without Andrew on the boat, the plan was to come back, and maybe then the two of us could take the boat back up alone—or with Cara.

"I don't know yet," I say. "I guess we stay here and try to help wherever we can."

"And after that? After all this crap between the two of you over the last few weeks, you're just going to stay?"

No. Staying here was never my plan.

When it's clear I still don't have an answer, she speaks again. "If you do leave, I think I want to go with you. At least as far as Maryland."

"Why?" I know Cara is from Maryland—a town called Easton—but everyone she knew there is dead.

"I honestly don't know yet. But I've been thinking about it, too. My plan was to see how I felt when we went to get Henri and I was close to the Chesapeake. After my family was killed, I just walked. I wanted to get out of there, and any road that took me away was the right road. But now I wonder if I was running away. And maybe it's time to go back."

She's never put it that way before—saying her family was "killed," I mean. Andrew and I always assumed something happened in Maryland to make her leave, the same thing that was responsible for her

PTSD panic attacks. We also assumed it was something bad, but we'd never wanted to pry.

"You never mentioned wanting to go home before," I say.

"I'm mentioning it now."

"Is this new or have you been thinking about it for a while?"

"A while."

Before I can ask Cara for more information, I hear the low whir of electricity and turn to see Rocky Horror pulling up in a golf cart, wires running from the front up to solar panels mounted on the roof. One of the panels looks cracked, but the rest are fine.

Rocky Horror gives two quick, sad beeps of the horn. "Anyone want a ride?"

With the moment broken, Cara and I head down to the road while everyone else watches from the parking lot.

"Not sure you have room for all of us," I say. The golf cart is big enough to fit about six people; maybe an extra kid could squeeze in the middle, but not the front seat or the bench facing backward on the back.

Rocky Horror shrugs. "No. But the other three I rigged up should carry us all to Key Largo. Long as Ames is cool Britney Spears-ing it and holding Henri-Two in her lap." As if summoned by her name—or maybe it was the honks—Amy emerges from the room upstairs with Henri-Two and comes down.

Andrew joins us and climbs onto the side of the cart to see the solar panels on the roof. "You did all this in a day?"

"Yes, I'm a genius, I know. But I told you, them kids cramp my style. I am not a fan of camping, and if y'all are really planning on

69

heading up to Key Largo with the rest to regroup and figure shit out, I'm not walking with you like I did from Marathon." He puts one of his feet on the tiny dash. "And they don't make these shoes anymore, so I'm not planning on wearing them down more than I already have."

Amy joins us. "RH, if you weren't a gay man I'd marry you."

"If we're both single in our fifties, you can make a semi-honest man of me. We'll have a marriage of convenience."

She laughs. "Love that for us." Amy turns her attention back to Andrew and me. "Now get in the golf cart. I want to get the hell out of here. Cara, go with them."

I get in the back with Cara and pick up a chain saw from the floor. "What's with the chain saw?"

"Mosquitoes," Rocky Horror says, as if that answers the question.

Andrew gives me a shrug as he hops in the front, and Rocky Horror pulls a three-point turn—dodging a downed tree—to take us back to a storage facility. There are three other golf carts parked next to a pile of broken solar panels, and four rusted batteries.

Rocky Horror hops off and nudges the batteries with his foot. "Salt water fucked up most of the electronics, but I managed to get these three working."

"Where were they during the storm?"

Rocky Horror pulls open the storage garage behind the carts and points to a ramp going up to a wooden platform. There's one small two-seater cart remaining on the platform. Beneath it are four more carts pushed against one another, covered in dirt and sand. Their batteries have been removed.

"All the ones down here were a wash. Which sucks, 'cause those two in the back are eight-seaters. But we have four running; should be good enough."

After showing us how to drive the cart—I struggle a bit at first, since I never learned how to drive a car—we head back to the motel, where Amy, Daphne, and the kids are already packed up and ready. We tie bags to the roof supports and ask the older kids to hold some in their laps. Then we set off for Key Largo, where the rest of the Key Colony planned to regroup and repair.

ANDREW

LEAVE IT TO THE STATE OF FLORIDA to have a public library in a strip mall. It's the age-old question: What came first, the library or the Kmart it's attached to?

The Key Largo Public Library is the rendezvous area for everyone in the Keys after the storm. Its strip mall location has the added benefit of offering room and shelter for about twelve hundred people—the current tally, which, rumor has it, is not expected to grow much more.

We still don't know what happened on the lower Keys, but over the last three days there have only been a hundred or so stragglers. None of them were at the naval base.

There's talk about sending a few groups there to find out what happened, but mainly it's to get supplies. Because what survived the storm is dwindling fast. They're saying we might run out of food by Christmas, which is in five weeks. But that's another rumor. That's what happens when a committee of elected officials isn't able to give answers immediately and locks themselves away in a conference room in the library while they have everyone else doing supply runs and returning with waterlogged boxes of canned goods from around the

Keys. Rumors start. Rocky Horror has been off with a couple other tech people helping to get the radio tower going again so we can check in on the Cuban colony and a few settlements we've talked with up the coast.

Meanwhile the rest of us stay here, waiting for something to change. Half the people in the Key Colony are dead or missing, but I can't stop thinking about Liz and Frank and Matthew and Lisa and Quinten and Jeremy and Lucy. The seven people I saw every day since I got kicked off the boat but won't see ever again.

It's especially hard because I can't really take the time to grieve them without neglecting the kids who are still here. They're all orphans, and the ones who died were really the only family any of them had left. So I'm stuck trying to pretend to be strong while inside I have flu-year flashbacks of every person I knew dying. And I have to remind myself the kids all experienced that, too. And, yeah, sometimes Jeremy could be a real shit, and Frank had no filter, and Liz was a know-it-all who liked to scold me for every little thing as though I, personally, was going to destroy the kids' ability to function in post-apocalyptic society. But I still miss them all so much.

While I'm in the middle of thinking about them—distracted when I should be paying attention to the card game I'm playing with Taylor, though she doesn't seem to be into it either—a white guy with dark brown hair and a long beard goes over to Amy and asks to talk to her.

Amy gets up and walks about three feet away. I can hear almost every other word they say, something about the Committee and the Keys. He looks over at me and Amy follows his gaze. Then she thanks him, and he nods and leaves.

"What was that about?" I ask.

"Where are Jamie and Cara?" she asks.

I point over at the boat crew, who are doing a wonderful job making me feel excluded and keeping their meetings away from me. "Mourning the loss of their boat. Did you know that damn thing was struck by lightning *twice* and survived another hurricane when it was in New Jersey? Plus it's from the eighties. Maybe she needed to be put to rest. Right on top of a house."

"I need to talk to the three of you when they're done. Come find me?"

I don't like the tone of her voice. "What's up?"

Henri-Two fusses in the sling across her chest. "Just come find me. I'm going to go feed her."

"Yeah, all right." I watch her go, then turn to Taylor. "Can you help Daphne look after the kids while I'm gone?"

"You gonna tell me what she tells you?" She doesn't even look up from her cards. But next to her, the Kid looks away from Bobo long enough to glance between the two of us.

"Of course. But try and eavesdrop a little more on that lady who thinks her husband is sleeping with the rabbi." It's nice to know other people in the Keys still have their own relationship dramas despite the devastation from the hurricane. It adds an illusion of normalcy. I'm also thankful that all the uncertainty between Jamie and me has been on hold the last few days. That's a nice change.

I hand over my cards to Taylor, who begins putting them away. Admiral Hickey sees me coming, and Jamie follows his gaze over to me.

"Amy wants to talk to us about something," I tell him, then turn to Cara. "All three of us."

Cara and Jamie turn to Hickey, probably to ask for permission to leave. Without a word from either of them, he nods. "Go ahead; I'll send Trevor for you both when we're heading to the marinas."

Jamie and Cara follow me. "What was that about marinas?"

"He wants to find another boat," Cara says. "But not to get Henri. To do supply runs along the coast to see if there's anything we can bring back."

At least this means we can put a pin in Jamie's need to go back to the cabin. That fills my chest with a bit more hope. After everything, maybe staying here and helping out will make him realize we're a part of this community. It could make him change his mind about staying.

Especially since it seems we're going to be living with the remainder of Team Orphan now. And, honestly, I really want to. Losing the other kids and Liz made me realize exactly how much I care about them. Seeing people for ten-plus hours a day almost every day will do that.

I want to make sure all the others stay safe. That includes Amy and Henri-Two.

And double for Jamie and Cara.

We find Amy at the bank near the shopping center's entrance. She's under the awning of a drive-through teller window feeding Henri-Two.

"Sit," she says, motioning to the asphalt in front of her.

"What's going on?" I ask.

But Cara sits across from her. Jamie follows, so I finally sit, too.

"Rocky Horror sent someone to tell me so I could be the one to tell you all."

My stomach begins to tie itself in knots. What could they possibly be so worried about that they want to tell the three of us before everyone else?

"The radio's working again," Amy says. "They haven't been able to get in touch with Cuba yet, but there's a couple settlements up the East Coast who have confirmed that the worst of the hurricane missed them. It looks like the storm went from here up the western coast to the panhandle and then inland. A settlement in Alabama said they got some bad wind and rain, but nothing like what we had."

That doesn't explain why we needed to be the first to know.

"We asked a few of the East Coast settlements for help," Amy says.

That's when I start to connect the dots. Dots that look like the bullet hole in my boyfriend's side.

"You can't!" I say. It's the only thing I can even think to say. There's no way they can ask Fort Caroline for help.

Amy continues as if she didn't hear me. "The Committee has been in contact with them since before you both arrived. Initially the Committee agreed to never mention that you're here. But now they've asked those other settlements for help, and all but one said they couldn't."

"Why not?" I ask.

"There's plenty of reasons, Andrew. People are having trouble growing crops because of the pests. The supplies in stores have been spoiled by wild animals and rodents. Or maybe they just don't *want* to help us. Fort Caroline is the only one that's offered."

"They're lying," Cara says. "They would never help someone else."

She's right. Fort Caroline doesn't do aid. They once let a kid die because they didn't want to waste medical supplies on him.

"It's some kind of trap," I say. "They're coming here to take from you."

"There won't be anything for them to take," Amy says. "The Committee has been lying to everyone about how many supplies we have. Even with rationing, we'll be out of food just after the new year. Without fuel, we can't get out of the Keys to search for more supplies. We need help and they're the only ones offering."

"Find someone else!" I say.

"When will they be here?" Jamie asks.

Amy looks down at Henri-Two. "Probably a couple weeks. They're driving supplies down but will be stopping along the way to pick up more and find fuel as they go."

Cara gets up and leaves. I want to follow her, but I'm not sure if my legs will hold me up. My body is tense and my heart's racing.

"We'll be gone before they get here," Jamie says.

"No," I say.

He looks at me with pitying eyes. "We can't be here. If someone recognizes us—"

"They won't! We can just hide somewhere—the southern Keys, maybe. Wait for them to leave."

There are supplies down there. The bridges have been wiped out, so we haven't been able to go and get whatever hasn't been destroyed by the storm. And there could be more survivors there. Maybe they just don't have someone like Rocky Horror to fix their radio.

There's a solution here that doesn't involve us leaving.

There has to be.

"Andrew," Amy says. Her voice sounds broken. "They're coming here *for Jamie*. Fort Caroline has been sending out broadcasts warning the settlements about him for months now. The Committee gave in and told them he's here and that they'll turn him over in exchange for help and supplies."

My body reacts physically to the thought, like I'm a tire someone slashed a hole in and I'm slowly deflating. Jamie was right. He was scared they'd show up here and that the Keys would turn him over to them and he was right.

"We need to get your things together and you need to get out of here," she says. "Tonight."

"Okay." Jamie stands, but I still can't move. "Andrew. We have to—"

"What do you think is going to happen when they show up and Jamie isn't here?"

Amy nods as though she's thought of this already. She covers herself with her shirt and begins to burp Henri-Two. "I honestly don't know. But I don't think we should be here to find out."

We?

"If you don't mind the two of us coming along, that is," she continues. "We'll try not to slow you down."

"Of course," Jamie says. "And you won't slow us down."

"You said you couldn't travel all the way up to your mom with Henri-Two."

She sounds tired. Resigned. "I said I didn't want to. But I also never thought this would happen. As much as I want to stay here, I've also heard what you've been through with those people. I don't want to be indebted to them, and I don't want to raise my daughter in a place where a community turns on their own people."

That makes me think of the kids and what's going to happen to them.

Why did the Committee do this? Why did they agree to give Jamie up for food? There are any number of ways we all could have survived this, but they chose the only one we can't take back.

Everything is ruined now.

This place isn't our home anymore.

And we have to go back on the road.

I finally feel strong enough to stand and Amy does as well. I take Henri-Two from her so she can button up her shirt. Baby Henri is half-asleep, completely oblivious to the difficult decision her own mom has made. Amy holds out her arms and I pass her over. We walk back to our spot and I lock eyes with Taylor, who is talking to the Kid.

What's going to happen to them?

Jamie goes to Cara and tells her we're leaving with Amy and Henri-Two. But I can't stop watching the kids. Worrying about what will happen if we leave them here. Fort Caroline only wants the people who fit in with their rigid systems.

"Cara, what do *you* think is going to happen when Fort Caroline gets here and finds out Jamie isn't really here?" She lived with them longer than we did. She knows more about how they operate.

Her eyes cloud. "Nothing good."

"Will they kill them?"

"Probably not. They might convince the ones they want to come back with them. The rest they'll leave here to starve."

"The kids?"

Cara follows my gaze. "They'll probably say they can help take care of them. Then when they get to Fort Caroline, they'll put them in the school and train them for their army."

"Will they come down here with their army?"

"I don't know. Probably not."

"What are you thinking?" Jamie asks.

"We have to tell Daphne and Kelly."

He shakes his head. "We can't bring all these people with us. Someone will notice when we sneak out of here tonight with a group of kids."

"We can't leave them here. We don't know what's going to happen when Fort Caroline arrives and finds out they were tricked."

"We already have a baby, how are we going to take care of seven kids?"

"We'll figure it out." I turn away from him and he calls after me. I head over to Taylor first. I promised I'd tell her, and I keep my promises.

Also, she's old enough that she can make her own decision. But once I get through the backstory about Fort Caroline, it's a quick conversation. She probably knew she was going to leave with us before I even brought it up.

"We have to bring the others," she says.

"Good. I need your help convincing Daphne and Kelly, too."

She nods, looking older than just thirteen. As if she's grown three years since the storm. Together, we make our way over to Daphne.

We've talked about leaving—going back to the cabin—so often, and in our fantasy it was so simple. But now that it isn't a fantasy—now that we're facing the actual journey itself—it's clear it's a massive undertaking with a bunch of moving parts. And those moving parts are big and dangerous.

Daphne and Kelly are harder to convince than I thought they'd be. Especially Kelly. But Cara tells them what living in Fort Caroline was like, how the power structure was set up and who benefited from it—and how it would absolutely never be anyone from the Keys. The kids deserve better than becoming cannon fodder for Fort Caroline, too.

Finally, after several hours of discussion, Daphne agrees. But Kelly is still on the fence. Jamie made it clear he still thought it was a bad idea for them to come with us, but it's their decision now.

When Rocky Horror returns to camp, he comes right over to me, looking worried. "She told you, right?"

"Yes. We're leaving tonight."

He nods. "I'm coming with you."

"Seriously?"

"What, like I'm going to stay here and wait for the queer-hating authoritarian losers to realize the person they traveled four hundred miles for is gone? And how long till they find out I'm the one who tipped him off? Hard no."

I pull him into a tight hug. "Thank you. For telling us."

"Of course. Now let me go pack my shit."

I let him go, but ask if I can borrow the golf cart he pulled up in.

He looks up at the sky before handing me the key.

"Don't be long. Once the sun is down you've only got enough battery for maybe ten miles."

"Got it."

I tell Jamie and Cara to stay with the kids while Daphne keeps working on trying to convince Kelly to come along. She doesn't *have* to, but I wouldn't want to leave her here. Also, the more adults we have to help with the kids, the better.

I make it before sunset and park the golf cart in the last rays, hoping it will charge the battery a bit more to get me home. Especially since I'll need to have the headlights on.

Our bedroom smells even more like mildew and mold than it did five days ago. Maybe there really is no salvaging these buildings.

I reach up onto the top shelf of the closet. My hands find only dust at first—the water must not have reached this high, which is a good thing.

Then my fingers touch the cold metal of the handgun. Not in a safe, no lock on the trigger, just loaded and out in the open. Well, on the top shelf of the closet. I take it down and tuck it into the waistband of my jeans—first checking that the safety is still on, of course.

Then I reach up with two hands and take down the rifle. The one we still don't have bullets for, because we thought we wouldn't need them.

Unfortunately, the guns are important. Because there are people out there looking for us. For Jamie. And there are more dangers on the road than people.

If we're going to survive again, as much as I hate these things, we'll need them.

JAMISON

I WATCH AS DAPHNE, KELLY, AMY, AND Andrew help the kids pull on their backpacks in the darkness. Andrew is making sure the Kid is all set, pulling the straps tight and asking if it's too heavy. The Kid shakes his head.

"God, I hate this," Kelly mumbles to me. I can't help feeling guilty. They shouldn't have to leave this place, but Andrew and the others are right. They can't be around when Fort Caroline gets here.

Andrew, Daphne, and Amy have also carefully warned a few other trusted people. Telling them to leave if it looks like the Key Colony is having issues with supplies. But they've held back from telling them the whole story, hoping they'll be able to connect the dots tomorrow morning when rumors start flying about our disappearance.

As long as we make it out unnoticed, that is.

"Hey." Rocky Horror makes me jump as he appears from out of the shadows next to me. "Everyone ready?"

"Where have you been?" Andrew asks.

"Double-checking our escape route."

"Oh. Well, thank you."

Amy joins us. Henri-Two is awake and babbling in her arms, refusing to let her mom put her in the sling. "And how does it look?"

"Complicated. But not impossible."

I don't like the sound of that. "Complicated how?"

"Andrew," Daphne says, walking over to us, "do you have your water bottle?"

When he answers, he sounds annoyed. "Seriously? Yes." She puts her hands up and retreats to the kids, but it also reminds me to reach back and feel the side of my own bag to make sure mine is there.

"The gate across the bridge on Route 1 was destroyed in the storm, so the intersection where it meets up with 905 is heavily guarded. We need to be especially careful around there. It's a quiet night and there's no reason to think they're on high alert—"

"But they will be if they notice us missing," Amy says.

Rocky Horror nods. "Exactly."

"What's going to happen if they catch us?" I ask. If they're planning to turn me over, they won't shoot me. But I don't want the others getting hurt if they're only looking out for me.

And I don't want to say it out loud to anyone here, but if we have to run or figure out some other means of fast escape, the kids are going to slow us down.

"I say we worry about that bridge when it collapses, yes?" Rocky Horror says.

Andrew seems okay with that answer, but I'm not. When the others go back to Daphne, I pull him aside.

"They only want me," I say. "Maybe we should split up and meet back with the others when it's safe?"

"Okay, when will it be safe?" he asks.

I don't know what to say, and he pounces on it.

"Exactly. We're sticking together, Jamie." He goes over to the others without another word. I could sneak away right now. They're all distracted, getting the kids together. I could just run up the road. In the darkness, they wouldn't be able to find me.

But even now I can't leave Andrew. I clench my fists as the familiar wave of frustration comes back. Every time I think about Fort Caroline, and Danny Rosewood in particular, a pit of fire in my stomach tightens every muscle in my body. I picture Rosewood's son Harvey and his friend Walt holding us at gunpoint by a river. And I play through the whole scene again, only Harvey's friend Walt turns into Danny Rosewood halfway through. And this time I shoot *him*. Over and over. Then we'd never have to worry about Fort Caroline again.

"You ready?"

Andrew's voice snaps me out of the fantasy.

"Yeah." My voice sounds weak, and I feel a little clammy.

"You okay?" he asks, lowering his voice.

"Just anxious," I lie. Because I am not okay. I've had dreams like that fantasy—*nightmares*. In each one I kill Danny Rosewood instead, and every time all I feel is relief. Unlike the guilt, anger, and disgust I felt when I shot his son.

Every time I see Danny Rosewood die, I feel better. Like I can breathe.

And sometimes that scares me.

"Let's go," I say before Andrew can ask me anything else. And I take his hand and join the others.

We see the guards' flashlights before we even get to the intersection of Route 1 and 905. We extinguished our own lights a quarter mile back, and all of us are holding hands in the darkness. Every couple of minutes Daphne tells the kids to sound off and every time Andrew has to remind the Kid to say "here" since he won't say his name.

"Okay," Rocky Horror says quietly. "One last head count."

Once we confirm everyone is here, Andrew takes my hand as Rocky Horror leads us off the road. Amy is all the way at the end of the line, holding Kelly's hand and humming softly to Henri-Two, who is still fussing in her arms.

"We might have to wait for Henri-Two to fall asleep," I say.

"She's not that loud," Rocky Horror says, leading the way through washed-up sand and around a fallen tree. The moon above us is the only light we have.

"If she gets any louder it's going to be a problem," I warn.

"You're being louder than she is," Andrew says. I glance back at him but remain silent.

Once we're within earshot of the guards—their voices barely audible over the *shhhhh* of the ocean—we stop. Rocky Horror turns and puts a finger up to his lips. Daphne turns to the kids and reminds them of the fun game she taught them where they all try to be silent and whoever wins gets a piece of candy.

We don't have candy for them, but all the kids put their fingers to their mouths, some of them smiling and probably thinking it really is just a game. But one look at the Kid and I know *he* doesn't, and I feel like his anxiety is all my fault. And maybe it is.

I open my mouth to tell Andrew so he can reassure him, but he's distracted by one of the younger girls, who is whispering something to him. So I nudge the Kid with my right hand to get his attention. He looks up at me, then my hand. I turn it over, offering it to him, and after a moment's pause he takes it.

Rocky Horror continues, walking behind a Chevron station that has collapsed onto its empty gas pumps. He leads us to a quiet residential street a block off Route 1 and we walk quickly, quietly.

We're far enough away that we can't hear what the guards are talking about, but every so often we can hear their laughter drifting through the broken trees. Laughter is good; it means they aren't on high alert yet.

Once their lights are a good ways behind us—and the residential street curves back toward Route 1—Rocky Horror turns and nods.

"Okay," he whispers. "From here, it's a straight shot up the Overseas Highway. But we need to move quick, because if they catch us there, the only place we can go is over the side into the ocean."

"You're so motivating," Andrew deadpans. "I hope you coached Little League before the world ended."

Rocky Horror nods. "I was the captain of an all-transmasc softball team."

"Pun team name?" Andrew asks.

"No-Balls-All-Strikes."

"I knew I could count on you."

"Ready?"

We turn onto Route 1 and start across the bridge.

It takes three very long, terrifying hours to cross. Every few minutes I look back, expecting to see headlights. But once there's land on either side of us again, there still aren't any cars.

"Maybe they didn't notice we left yet," Andrew says.

Cara sounds less convinced. "They think we *wouldn't* leave. They're looking for us on the Keys."

She's right. They probably think we're hiding there or that we just went back to the motel or our houses. They won't suspect we're gone until they notice Amy and Rocky Horror are missing as well. Of course they'll check the Keys first, starting with the places we frequent. Then someone will mention that maybe we left.

I turn back, but there are still no headlights.

It's a few hours before we see another road. The kids are tired, complaining that they want to go home, and Daphne, Kelly, and Andrew try their best to calm them or to carry the ones who are especially tired.

"We need to find a way to transport them," I tell Rocky Horror. "They can't walk the whole way."

He nods. "We'll see what we can find."

A little before dawn, we stop and take shelter in an open storefront. Andrew helps Daphne and Kelly get the kids set up, and they're all passed out in seconds.

"Someone should keep watch," Cara says. "So we know which way they go when they come looking."

"I'll take first watch," I say.

"You sure?" Andrew asks quietly. "I can stay up."

"I'll be okay. Get some sleep. I'll wake you up in a couple hours, then you can take over." He gives me a light peck on the cheek, then slips into his sleeping bag.

No one from the Keys comes by, and when Andrew wakes up a few hours later I'm able to get a bit of sleep myself before the kids get up and we're back on the road again.

"Where are they?" Andrew asks Rocky Horror.

But it's Amy who answers. "They're probably getting things together. Making a plan and also turning it into a supply run."

That sounds like about what I'd expect from the Committee.

"Maybe they'll never come looking for you," Kelly adds. "They could have too much to deal with right now."

I nod, but I don't believe it. If they need supplies and Fort Caroline's help is contingent on turning me over, they'll be looking for me.

I turn to Amy, who seems exhausted with Henri-Two sleeping in a sling across her chest. "Do you want me to hold her?"

She lets out a low groan. "I do, but I'm worried she'll wake up if I jostle her. My back is killing me." She rubs at her lower back while keeping a hand under the one-year-old. "I need us to stop somewhere we can find a store that still has strollers."

I walk up to Andrew and nudge him playfully. "Gotta say, I preferred this part of Florida when I was dying of sepsis in a cart."

"Ah, the good ol' days." He turns his attention to the Kid, who he swings by his hands in front of him as a stuffed hippo balances precariously on Andrew's shoulder. "Hey, Kid, think Bobo wants a sidecar?"

"Uh-huh," the Kid says as he jumps up and lets Andrew swing him.

"And what is a sidecar?"

"I unno."

"Cool."

I laugh and hold out my hands. "Want me to take over?"

"Yes. Thank you. Kid, I need a break, Jamie's gonna throw your ass around a bit, 'kay?"

"Uh-huh."

Without skipping a beat, the Kid lets go of Andrew's hands and takes mine. I count him to three and he jumps as I swing him up and forward. Andrew takes the Kid's hippo and puts him on my shoulder.

He looks tired, too. We've been on the road for three days now. I forgot how hard it is to travel for so long every day. Even taking breaks every three hours, it's hard for the kids. They have to be carried if they get too tired. And if more than four can't walk at once, we have to stop for the night.

Andrew says Daphne is struggling, too, but every time I look over at her she seems in good spirits. And she never seems to tire of corralling the kids. I glance back at her as I swing the Kid in my arms. She smiles at me as she listens intently to the boy next to her tell a story about one of the kids he used to play with in the Keys.

"Did Cara tell you where we're hoping to stop tonight?" I ask Andrew.

"She said there's an airfield up ahead."

"I don't suppose Rocky Horror knows how to fly a plane?"

"You don't suppose correctly—I asked."

"Maybe Daphne does."

Andrew snorts. "Hey, Kid, you know how to fly a plane?"

"Uh-huh," the Kid says as he jumps into a swing.

"Knew it. We're saved." Andrew doesn't sound like himself. Maybe he's just tired, but it sounds like more than that.

"You okay?"

"As okay as I can be." I watch as he swallows hard and takes a deep breath. "I just never wanted to do this again. It wasn't fun the first two times and it's even less fun now. I miss the other kids, and Liz. The life we were building."

I want to wrap my arms around him and give him a hug, but the Kid is too busy using my arms as a swing set.

"I know you do," I say.

ANDREW

ROCKY HORROR LETS LOOSE ANOTHER STRING OF expletives from the truck cab behind us and I raise my voice, trying to drown him out with the best Stitch impression I can muster on a lack of sleep and sore legs from walking so much.

It's tragic that these kids will never get to see the real *Lilo & Stitch*, because it has to be the best animated movie ever made. But I am proud that it's my most requested movie retelling.

Though I'm certain that comes from the fact that we're all our own little fucked-up 'ohana.

Meanwhile, behind me, Cara and Rocky Horror's platonic lovers' spat has grown louder as he still struggles to hot-wire the five-seat pickup truck he said he could hot-wire almost an hour ago. The pickup would work well for us because it has a truck cap on the back bed that we could pile all the kids into. But I'm starting to worry we're wasting our time.

"And I think maybe we stop the movie here for now and go for a walk and potty break," I say, clapping my hands. The kids groan, but Daphne nods and she and Kelly jump in to coax them to stand.

Jamie even looks a little disappointed when the Kid stands up—the Kid who has become the bravest of the orphans and asked if he can sit on Jamie's lap during "movie" time.

"You were just about to get to the best part," one of the kids says.

I nod. "Yes, it's called antici . . . pation. Which reminds me to tell you the movie that Rocky Horror's namesake comes from."

Kelly snorts. "You packed gold bikini briefs?"

"No," I say. "But Jamie did." I wiggle my eyebrows suggestively at him as we herd the kids away from the corporate center parking lot toward the main road. And now I have a new item of clothing to look for when we stop.

"How come you never told me that one before?" Jamie asks as we head across the road where the trees and shrubs are overgrown, providing privacy.

"You never asked for it," I say.

"To be fair, I'm not sure I ever asked for any of them. But I do enjoy hearing the ones I've never seen."

I gape at him. "You've never seen it? Oh man, I need to tell you about the deleted scene." I always skip over the scene when Stitch takes the Ugly Duckling book into the woods because that scene makes me cry and I do not cry in front of the kids. But I bet if I can deliver it without sobbing, I can absolutely get Jamie to cry.

We walk into the woods and separate—Daphne and Kelly take the girls one way, and Jamie and I point the opposite way for the boys. The Kid doesn't move.

"Go ahead," Jamie says, shaking the hand that still holds his. "We'll be right here."

The Kid looks unsure but finally walks behind a tree.

"Okay," I say, keeping my voice low and steeling my nerves. "So while the kids are distracted, after Lilo and Stitch have their falling-out, Stitch goes into the woods—"

But a sound stops me. Jamie's eyes go wide.

It's a car. A vehicle of some kind. And it's coming up the road just outside the tree line, right toward us.

He pushes me down and we duck, peeking through the leaves of a bush. The sound grows louder, the tires humming against the broken asphalt.

There's a red-and-white pickup truck leading the way, followed by a black sedan. I hold my breath, hoping that they speed past and keep going.

Then I gasp. "Cara, Rocky Horror, and Amy!"

"They'll be okay," Jamie says. The cars are getting closer. I glance to the corporate park and, yes, there is a line of overgrown arborvitae blocking the lot.

I turn back, looking behind me to make sure none of the kids are coming. We've been trying not to scare them, so we haven't told them to avoid other people or cars. But hopefully they know. Or hopefully they're too busy going to the bathroom to run out and see who is coming up the road.

"Do you think it's someone from the Keys?" I ask Jamie.

He doesn't answer. The truck is closer now, about to pass us. I focus on the driver's-side window, trying to see who is driving it through the glaring sunshine.

My stomach drops.

The truck is moving fast, but I get enough of a glimpse of the

94

driver that I recognize him immediately. I turn to Jamie, and I can see he recognized him, too.

And why shouldn't he? He spent more time with Admiral Hickey on the boat than I ever did.

Which means the Keys *have* sent people after us.

We wait. When we hear leaves and twigs snap behind us, we quietly tell the kids to stay low. Daphne and Kelly join us, looking anxious.

After a few minutes I turn back to Jamie. "Think we're good?"

It's been quiet, no sound of engines or the whoosh of tires. They probably kept going. Or they stopped and are backtracking.

"Okay," Jamie says. "I think we can head back."

We move slowly, herding the kids across the road. Cara and Amy are waiting by the truck.

I nod at her and lower my voice. "It was Hickey."

"They're coming, then," Cara says.

"Can you map a route that will hopefully keep us away from them?" Jamie asks.

She nods and heads over to look at the road atlas. Meanwhile Rocky Horror still hasn't started the truck. I round the driver's side of the pickup, where he's lying under the steering column with wires dangling above his head.

"I stopped when Cara told me she heard cars coming," he says, not looking away from the wires.

"It's the Keys. They're looking for us."

"Then . . ." He touches two wires together and the truck engine cranks. He does it again and again, and on the fourth try, the truck roars to life. He smirks and scoots back out of the car, looking at the dashboard. "See? Told you I could."

"And just in time."

"Little over a quarter tank of gas," he says.

"It'll have to be enough."

After we get the kids loaded into the bed—it's a little snug with all of us, but the Kid doesn't seem too disappointed to have to sit on Jamie's lap again—Cara climbs into the passenger seat to be Rocky Horror's copilot and we're off.

And hopefully heading in a different direction from Hickey and the others.

JAMISON

THE TRUCK RUNS OUT OF GAS AROUND Sarasota. We find a large, empty house to camp in for the night, then set out first thing in the morning.

There's an extremely slim chance that Hickey and the others might run into us if we travel semi-parallel to them. Cara says if we can get to Tampa—about sixty more miles—without them finding us or another group catching up, there are plenty of other roads we can take.

Rocky Horror spends half a day trying to find another truck or van with enough gas, but to no avail, so we're stuck walking. Every empty stretch of road where we can't immediately run for cover is agony. Especially when they're straight and flat so the search party could see us from a mile away.

But after two days and no further sign of them, we start to relax a bit. Maybe they really did give up. When we stop for the night on day three—twenty miles till Tampa—Andrew holds up two of the large plastic jugs tied to his pack.

"We should probably get some water to boil for the kids," he says quietly. I nod, and once Cara points us in the direction of the closest body of water—a river about a half mile up the road into a residential area—we set off.

"Be honest," Andrew tells me as the road dead-ends and we walk alone toward a dock leading out onto the giant river. "How bad do I stink?"

Honestly, I can smell him from where he stands two feet away from me, but I make a big show and take a whiff. "Like a four on the postapocalyptic scale."

"Liar."

"You don't have to worry about your BO. I'm used to it by now."

He gasps. "*Used* to it? Jamie, that's the rudest thing you could ever say to me."

"I'm pretty sure I could say ruder. Like you're not very funny—"

"Well, that would be a lie, I'm delightfully irreverent."

"You have no style or sense of fashion." I'm setting him up for a joke I know he's going to hit without a pause, and it's nice to have this silly banter again. To be able to joke around and quote movies— movies I've never seen, of course, only heard him tell. But it feels normal, being on the road. And right now it's just the two of us.

Andrew takes the cue. "I think that depends on—"

"No, no. That wasn't a question."

Andrew laughs loudly and drops the plastic water jugs, then he pulls me close and kisses me. I can't remember the last time we kissed like this. Not just a peck on the cheek or a good-night kiss. An open-mouthed, I-missed-this-did-you-miss-this-too? kiss. My heart races, and though I can't feel his, I know it's matching pace with mine.

"You haven't even seen that movie." His voice is lower, as if he's also overwhelmed by the way we're holding each other.

"No, but I've heard you tell it so many times it's seared into my brain now."

"Yes, Meryl has that effect." He kisses me again, his face lingering near mine. "Still used to my BO?"

"Yes."

"But not into it?"

"That's not what I said." I drop my own water jugs on the dock and reach down to his legs, lifting him up against me. Our mouths open, our lips magnetic, breathing each other in. He wraps his legs around my waist, and I slide my hand up the back of his shirt.

How long has it been? Weeks. Weeks without a moment of privacy. Without worry and fear and death. But somehow all that's gone because right now it's just us, the soft lapping of water against the dock piling, and the cool breeze through trees thick with Spanish moss.

I lower us slowly onto the dock, but Andrew's legs stay tight around me. I peel off his shirt, his skin glowing in the setting sun, and put my face against his solar plexus, breathing him in. Not an odor, just the natural way he smells. I want to pull him into my skin and carry him with me and feel him on me all the time. Now *this* we haven't done in well over a month. Not since he was kicked off the boat and I was ready to leave the Keys then and there. With him.

This I absolutely missed.

He pulls me out of the thought, holding my face in his hands. He looks into my eyes, deadly serious.

"I want you to" is all he says. "I don't care what we don't have, I just . . . I want you." He kisses me. "Need."

My mouth goes dry and my heart races because . . . I want to, too. But I shake my head. "We can't."

"Yes." He kisses me, talking between kisses as his hands dip below the waist of my jeans. Holding me tight. "We can. We'll just. Go slow. It's not ideal. But I'm sure historically people have made it work."

"Andrew—"

"If it worked for Jake Gyllenhaal in *Brokeback Mountain*, I'm sure we'll be fine."

I laugh against his lips. "It's not that." I pull away and look into his eyes. I want him to see that I *want* to. I mean, obviously he at least feels that because of where his hand is.

But I want him to understand.

"I . . . I don't want it to be . . . quick." I laugh. "I mean, let's be real, it's probably going to be."

Andrew laughs, too. "Oh, totally. I'd say you've got about twenty seconds with me."

"No, I mean . . . I don't want it to be rushed. And this is rushed. We'll be rushed if we do it now."

"Who cares?" He laughs again.

"I do." I give him a look of sincerity, trying to really make him understand how special he is to me. And how I want *this* moment between us to be special, too. Quick, fine, but not rushed. Not forced because we're both horny and alone together for the first time in weeks and working through a rough patch. I need him to know I want to, but not now, like this.

He looks more hurt than understanding, and unlatches his legs

100

from my hips. "You're right. Sorry." He grabs his shirt and starts to pull it back on.

"Well, I didn't say you had to get dressed," I say, trying to sound playful and putting my hands back to his sides where I know he likes. He squirms and grabs my wrists. He gives me a light kiss, but this time there's no passion in it.

"They're going to worry where we are. And, honestly, if they're going to think we're having sex, I'd feel even worse that we didn't."

"I don't want you to feel bad." I hold his hands, squeezing them gently. "I want you. I *really* do. I—"

"No, I know, I get it. I'm sorry, I don't mean that I feel bad. I feel slightly wounded because it does feel like rejection even though you're right. Does that make sense?"

"Not really?"

"I know. But I can't help it."

"I'm not rejecting you." I hold his gaze. "You're beautiful. And you're my favorite person and I always want you. But I want our first time we have sex to be . . . you know."

He sighs. "It's not going to be. How can anything be perfect anymore? The world is dead and we're on the fucking road *again*! There will never be a perfect moment. The two of us together—that's what's supposed to make it perfect. Nothing else."

"I—I know that, and it will be, you're right, I know. But there can be a better place and time when we don't have to rush through it."

"Like when we were in the Keys?"

I flinch. "I never said I didn't want to."

"I know you didn't! I . . . ugh!" He puts his face in his hands and groans in frustration. "We can talk about this later, okay? Let's get the water for the kids and go back before people start to worry."

He grabs the water jugs and stands, walking to the edge of the dock and lying on his stomach to fill the jugs one by one. When I reach him with mine, he hands a full jug back to me and takes an empty one.

We fill them in silence, then walk back to the camp.

The next day Daphne is telling a couple of the kids the story of one of the romance novels she wrote called *Late Bottle Vintage*—a love story between a Portuguese port shipper and a sommelier in their fifties who try to create a successful port production company. It was her first book and, according to her, much tamer than the others. I'm walking next to Rocky Horror while the Kid uses my arm like a swing set.

Ahead of us, Andrew and Taylor are distracting a few of the orphans who are getting cranky about all the walking again. He and I haven't talked about the moment of horniness I ruined by the river last night. Of course.

"I can't believe I went from the pinnacle of postapocalyptic bachelorhood," Rocky Horror says, "to being fucking Mary Poppins." One of the younger orphans is asleep in his arms.

"Come on, RH. You love us." I laugh as the Kid swings on my arm one last time and then runs to Daphne.

Rocky Horror grunts, like he doesn't—but he does.

I lower my voice. "Can I ask you something?"

He takes the cue and slows his steps, letting the others get a few more feet ahead of us. I watch the Kid, waiting for him to notice I'm not next to him, but he keeps his eyes on the road, swinging his stuffed hippo by the arm.

"Sorry if you don't want to hear this, but I feel like the others are too young, and I know Cara doesn't want to talk about it. And Daphne's wonderful, but I think she's a little too optimistic and also I don't know her that well. Honestly, it's not like I know *you* all that well either, but you're the only other openly queer person here. And, I mean, usually I could look it up myself, but it's not like I can do that anymo—"

"Jamie, at the start of this, it felt like you had a question. I was getting big into the process of port making, so if you could focus back on that so I can finish listening to Daphne talk about this book of hers, I'd really appreciate it."

"Sorry, right." But just then the Kid sees that we've fallen behind and runs back to take my hand. Great, now I have to figure out how to say this so it's child friendly. "I . . . before . . ." I look up at Daphne talking about port. "Okay, I never had port before. And I'm assuming you have."

He scrunches up his face. "I mean, yeah. It's fine."

"No, RH, I mean, like, you've *had port*." I open my eyes wide and look down at the Kid.

Rocky Horror's confused face follows my gaze down to the Kid, and I'm about to give up when he scoffs and shakes his head. "Oh, Jesus Christ."

"Jesus Christ," the Kid repeats.

Rocky Horror snorts and glances down at the Kid. "Point

taken. Okay, yes, I've enjoyed *port* in my many years of queer . . . sommelier-ing."

"Well, Andrew and I were talking about trying it sometime, when we were back in the Keys."

"Yeah."

"But I just . . . I don't know, I kept getting nervous and I wanted it to be the perfect time for us to try port."

"Totally," Rocky Horror says. "You have to have the right atmosphere and food pairings. I mean, port and Mexican food do *not* go well together."

Now I'm confused, because I don't know what Mexican food is supposed to be a euphemism for. I'll try to figure it out through context clues. "Right, so I guess my main question is, is port . . . tasting, the first time you tried it, were you—"

He snorts again and it turns into a laugh. "You two fucking dummies are perfect for each other, you know that?"

"Fucking dummies," the Kid says.

"Hey," I say, giving his hand a gentle shake. "Don't repeat what Rocky Horror says."

"Was I nervous?" Rocky Horror continues. "Yes. I mean, a lot of that stemmed from some *major* fu—" His eyes drop down to the Kid again. "Effing gender dysphoria. But even after I started to get those things figured out, yeah, it's anxiety inducing and sometimes scary. And sometimes that makes port even better, but that's a lesson for another day. Look, you want to try port, right? Like you've thought it through on your own, you're into it, you want to try it?"

"Yes, of course."

"Specifically with Andrew."

I nod.

"Then the next time you two are alone, tell him. I mean, not right away—you can ask how his day went, and please get some privacy. And you can be nervous about it, but be nervous together. The point is, if you're with someone you love or connect with, port tasting is almost always great. Like pizza. God, I'm hungry. And I would love a drink. Even port, the real stuff, which, like, *port* is *not* like pizza. Let's kill the metaphors because I think I'm starting to confuse myself."

"Yes, please. Thanks, RH."

"You're welcome. Now, excuse me, I need to regroup with the *real* port shippers and reclaim the last remaining shreds of my dignity."

He walks a little closer to the group to continue to listen to Daphne while the Kid and I keep our own pace back here.

Rocky Horror is right, and so is Andrew. There is no real perfect time for us. I still don't want to rush it, but I also don't need to wait until we're off the road and safe. Neither of us knows when we'll ever be truly safe again.

"Hey," I say to Andrew when we stop for the night. "We should do a supply run in town." We're just outside a small town called Laureldale, and while we have enough food right now, things could get light if we don't look for more soon. Also, I want to talk to Andrew without anyone else nearby.

He nods and we let the others know.

"Look for some port while you're there," Rocky Horror says to me.

It isn't until he widens his eyes at me and grins that I get the joke and my cheeks flush.

No, we won't be doing that in a store. But we can at least talk about it.

Andrew leads me to a small mom-and-pop market next to a shopping center, but not before I notice the "Bob's Beds Mattress Emporium" next door.

Again I flush a bit, because that would be silly, even in the apocalypse. Maybe especially in the apocalypse.

Andrew heads for the canned food, but most of the chest-height shelf is empty. He takes what's left without really reading the labels, putting them in his bag. There are Florida-themed knickknacks scattered across the floor and on a couple of shelves at the front of the store. A wooden turtle painted neon green and pink with the word *Florida* on its shell catches my eye, and I snatch it while Andrew is distracted. I'll give it to him later. Just something for him to remember the good times we had in the Keys.

"I wanted to talk to you about last night," I say, taking the next aisle over to check the dry goods packaging for pantry moths or holes chewed by rodents.

Andrew shakes his head. "You mean my horniness-induced temporary insanity? Don't worry about it. I felt like a very unsexy dumbass last night, so I'm sorry."

"Okay, but I just wanted to make sure you know . . ." I have no idea why I'm having this conversation over the top of a shelf. I walk around to him and take his hands. "I want to make sure you know how much I love you and that I very, *very* much want to do that. Very much with you."

"Well, there's a mattress emporium next door, did you see?"

My cheeks burn again but I can't help but laugh. Andrew stands on his toes and kisses me.

"I love making you blush."

And he's very good at it.

We head back to the camp as fast as we can. As we turn the last corner a chill runs up my spine.

There are four vehicles by the camp.

From where we are, we can see everyone is okay. They're all sitting together on the ground with the kids. The people from the cars are standing by the road; there's about a dozen or more of them. And one of them is Admiral Hickey.

They found us.

Hickey turns and gives me a nod as the others point their guns at us.

ANDREW

ALL THE KIDS SEEM TO BE PHYSICALLY okay, but they look scared. Which, I mean, yeah, of course they would be. They've been on the road for several days, barely resting, and now people with guns show up.

"Both of you, on your knees," Hickey says.

Sure, Hickey, but let's see how many innuendos I can make. "Buy us dinner first." I expect Jamie to scold me, but when I glance over at him he's smirking as he drops to his knees. I follow his lead and we put our hands up while two men take off our backpacks and grab our guns.

"We're not going to tie you up," Hickey says as they check our pockets.

Two.

Jamie snorts beside me because he knows I'll keep going and, yeah, I can't wait to say it.

I pretend to be disappointed. "Aw, man, it's the one thing I was looking forward to during this whole thing."

Hickey's jaw tightens as behind him Daphne speaks.

"Andrew. There are children present." She scolds me like a mom.

"They don't get the innuendo, Daph."

"Some of us do," mutters Taylor, just loud enough for me to hear.

"You're not a child, Taylor." When I say that she actually smiles and seems a little proud.

Hickey focuses his gaze on me. "You realize if Fort Caroline showed up for Jamie and we didn't have him, they'd kill us, right?"

"They'd kill him, too, what's your point?" I ask.

"What was your plan? Just run?"

"Yes," says Jamie. "And then hopefully you'd lose us in the vast, empty openness of postapocalyptic America."

"If we didn't find you here, we'd find you in Bethesda." It's Trevor who says this, and it chills me to the bone. He turns and looks back at Amy. "That's where you're heading, after all."

Jamie shakes his head, playing it off better than I could. "*She* is going to Bethesda. The rest of us were just trying to find a new place."

"And if they find you there?" Hickey asks. "We're going to make an effort to protect you. Demand that you get a fair trial, that a jury made up of both their people and ours hears what really happened."

"You don't really believe they'll do that, right?" I ask. "You can't be that dumb."

Hickey just stares at me.

They pull us up, and one of them gives me a light shove toward the others. Daria avoids our gazes; she's the only one who doesn't have her rifle pointed at us. I stop as we get closer to the kids, locking eyes with the six people pointing their guns in our direction.

"Can you put the guns away around the kids, please?" I ask.

Hickey considers it for a moment. Then he opens his mouth, but something else catches everyone's attention. At first it just sounds like the wind blowing through the trees—just a low *whoosh*. But it's getting louder.

On the road to our right, several vehicles approach, led by an old-looking beige-and-maroon RV.

Their reinforcements have arrived.

"Christ," I say. "You really had to send this many people to find us?"

But Hickey looks anxious. He shakes his head. "They aren't ours."

Fort Caroline. No, no, no, they can't be here already. They said it would take weeks. But maybe Hickey radioed ahead and warned them to use a new route that wouldn't take as long.

Shit. I start to panic, trying to figure out how we can get out of this. How we can escape them again. But my mind is racing so much, thinking about how the last time this happened they shot my boyfriend.

My chest feels like it's going to cave in, and I can't breathe.

The RV slows as it reaches us. This can't be happening again. It isn't until I look away from the caravan that I notice the others in Hickey's group look confused. Like they weren't expecting anyone either.

Then the RV speeds up and the other vehicles follow suit. They pass us, and Hickey shouts for his people to stop them.

What is happening? All I know is the vehicles pass without stopping, and one of Hickey's men with a rifle runs into the road, pointing after them.

"Don't shoot!" Hickey yells. "Take one of the trucks. Follow them and see what their story is."

Three of his men get in the truck and speed after them. Which means there are three fewer people we have to escape from.

For now.

But I have no clue how to protect all the kids, Cara, Daphne, Amy, Rocky Horror, Kelly, *and* Jamie. We've been outnumbered before, but now we have others to worry about.

Sunset comes and goes, but the truck doesn't come back, so Hickey and his group set three large bonfires in the middle of the road. They have us set up the kids between two of them. The rest surround us on the sides of the road while two keep a lookout for the truck.

They leave us to ourselves, letting us feed the kids and put them to bed. Once they're all asleep—except for Taylor, who seems determined to be involved in the adult conversation now that I said she wasn't a child—we talk about our options.

To be honest, they aren't great.

Either we wait until they fall asleep and make a run for it (with seven kids) or convince them to turn on Hickey and let us go (unrealistic as well). We all agree to sleep for the night and think it over. While Amy, Kelly, Cara, and Rocky Horror get themselves ready for bed, Daphne and I check on the kids.

"How you doing, sweetie?" Daphne asks.

I look over at Daria, who watches us with a sad frown. She really does not seem to want to be here. Maybe that's something we can use. She might be able to convince the others to let us go.

"Fine," I say. "Just . . . tired, I think. Tired of all this shit."

Daphne reaches out and places a light hand on my cheek. When she speaks, her voice is low, barely audible over the crackling fires.

"If the two of you see a way to escape, take it."

"I can't leave the rest—"

"You can." Her eyes crinkle as she smiles. "You both deserve your happy ending. We'll all be fine, but the two of you are in danger. And the longer you stay, the more that danger grows."

"What about Amy and Henri-Two? Rocky Horror? They tipped us off. If the Keys find out and tell Fort Caroline . . ." I don't finish the sentence. Because I can't even imagine it.

But Daphne shakes her head. "Don't worry about them. They knew what they were doing when they took that risk. Besides, I'm the Gossip Queen of the Keys." She laughs that contagious laugh of hers that I can't help but smile at. "I'll take the heat. What are they gonna do? Kill me?"

My smile drops. "Yes, Daph, exactly that."

She waves a dismissive hand. "They won't. They could try, but I still have plenty of fans down there who will protect me."

That might be true, but what if Fort Caroline doesn't care about fans? Especially fans of a smutty romance writer.

"Get some sleep," she says, patting my hand. Then she leans in and kisses me on the cheek. "But remember, if you see the chance, you take it and get the hell out of here."

After I set my sleeping bag up next to Jamie's, he reaches for my hand. I take it and hold it until he falls asleep, then I tuck it into his sleeping bag so he's warm. But I can't sleep. With Daphne's words floating in my mind, I feel wired.

I'm looking for the chance she was talking about. Waiting to see if this could be it, and if Jamie and I could run.

But I don't know if I can do it. As much as I love Jamie, I don't know if I can leave all of them, knowing Fort Caroline is coming. I check that everyone around us is sleeping—six of Hickey's people are still wide awake and watching me like hawks—and then bundle myself back into my own sleeping bag. I stare up at the night sky, the fire popping as it devours the fresh wood.

It wasn't until the apocalypse that I realized exactly how many stars were out there. With zero light pollution left in the world, it's pretty awesome. Awesome meaning evoking awe, not plain old cool. That's a word that should be reclaimed in the apocalypse. Awesome. But only to be used in truly awesome situations.

I close my eyes, just for a second, but then someone screams. A woman.

It's a chilling, bloodcurdling shriek that raises my hackles instantly. I jolt upright, my sleeping bag unzipping itself. I must've dozed off because the sky has changed. Dawn is on the horizon. But somehow I woke from a dreamless sleep into a nightmare.

Someone else screams, this time a man. The kids are up, Daphne, too. I hear them murmuring, and there's more screaming. Even with dawn coming, I can't see them in the darkness.

"What's happening?" Jamie sits up, wide awake. I unzip my sleeping bag the rest of the way and crawl over to the orange embers of our fire. I throw more sticks on, trying to light the darkness that was so beautiful what felt like only moments ago. Cara is there in an instant, adding more to the fire. A gunshot cuts through the night and I hear Hickey's voice, and Daria's.

The kids are all awake, asking what's going on. The Kid is crying. Taylor asks what's wrong, her voice sounding so much younger than she's been allowing it to be.

I open my mouth to calm them, but the fire catches, lighting up the road as someone else screams farther away. So many screams. Including Cara, who points over my shoulder, wide-eyed with horror.

Because of the creature smiling at me from the grass on the side of the road. Pitch-black eyes, a long scaly snout, and a mouth full of teeth. A fucking alligator.

It leaps forward, snapping at me.

"Shit!" I fall back as the gator walks closer, snapping again. The guns! But Hickey took our guns. I reach into the firepit and grab the end of a burning branch. I put it in front of the thing's face, and thank God, it knows what fire is. The gator turns away, snapping at nothing.

Hickey's people are still screaming everywhere.

Rocky Horror helps me back on my feet, asking if I'm okay. I nod, and he turns to the kids.

"Taylor!" Jamie shouts. He moves quickly around the fire, grabbing a stick covered in leaves and Spanish moss and setting it ablaze. "Kids, all of you, over here."

"Where's Amy?" I say. My chest constricts as images of Amy and Henri-Two being mauled by an alligator flash in my mind. People are running, screaming. Dust flies up and gunshots ring out in the dark.

"Amy!" I shout. "Daphne! Kelly!"

"Here." Amy runs out of the darkness toward us, Henri-Two crying in the sling against her chest.

"Where's Daphne?" Jamie asks.

She shakes her head. I lunge at the alligator that came toward me, and it crawls off into the high grass at the edge of the clearing. I throw the stick back on the fire, along with every other piece of wood we have.

More gunshots, and someone else screams. A man stumbles forward, clutching his chest. Blood spilling through his fingers. He falls to his knees, then onto his face.

"Jamie, help!" I turn the man over. He's gasping, and blood bubbles from the bullet wound in his chest. Jamie throws his flaming stick onto the fire and joins me.

"Leave him," Jamie says, trying to pull me away from him.

I turn to him, my jaw falling open. "We can't just *leave* him." I don't have enough time to figure out how Jamie could even suggest such a thing—despite these people being here to drag us back to the Keys. Rocky Horror comes over and grabs under his arms.

"Help me get him to the fire." We drag him closer. The man tries to gasp three more times before he stops breathing. The chest wound releases a few more bubbles, then stops.

Another gun goes off. Then another, and another.

"Kids, get down!" I yell. But they aren't listening. How can they? It's chaos.

Beneath my hands the man jerks. He's alive? But when I glance down at his face, his eyes are wide open and he still isn't breathing. He jerks again and then I see the alligator at his leg, snapping and pulling.

"No!" I yell at the thing.

Jamie pulls me away. "It's okay." The alligator continues snapping down on the dead man's leg. Someone in the middle of the camp throws a flaming stick at one of the gators, but it goes over them, right into the tall grass at the edge of the road.

The grass catches fire almost immediately. Oh no.

"Where's the water?" I ask Jamie.

"Here!" Cara runs over to the jug but jumps back, screaming. Jamie spins with the fire, revealing three more alligators.

"Jesus! How many are there?" Amy asks.

And why are they here? Does this usually happen with alligators?

A few feet away the first alligator is still pulling at the dead man's leg. Jamie takes his flaming branch and runs toward him. The alligator rolls and the man's body rolls with it before his leg rips off and the alligator takes its prize into the grass.

I try to shield the kids from the view. Taylor is just out of my reach, staring at the man's body. Her face shines in the firelight.

I move over to hug her close and she lets me. Jamie pushes us all back toward the fires in the road, away from the alligators. The wildfire is spreading. Someone shouts to move the vehicles. With part of the field burning brightly now, I can see all the chaos around us.

Alligators—so many of them. There have to be at least ten.

They attack in bursts from the high grass surrounding us. People are trying to fend them off with fire and baseball bats or other blunt objects, but they keep coming. Those with guns shoot at the ground, but not even the gunfire scares them off.

How hungry are they that they seem to be hunting people in a pack like this?

When one of them tries to get close, Jamie chases it off with fire. Daphne comes out of the darkness covered in blood, and my heart stops in my chest. But then I see the huge knife in her bloody hand.

She holds it up to me. "Took this from someone, nearly got chomped in half." Then she lowers her voice. "This is the moment. I told you to *run*."

"You know I'd never leave you. But I am so damn happy to see you," I tell her.

She frowns but then shakes her head. "Well, given the circumstances, the feeling is mutual, hon." She looks down at all the kids. "All right, children? Where's the Kid?"

I spin to look at them. All six of them. No, there's supposed to be seven! Fuck! The Kid.

"Oh!" I jump up. "Kid!" I scan the chaos. People still shooting and screaming.

In the middle of it all, on the other side of our fire, the Kid is crying. Still in his sleeping bag.

Thank fucking God he's—

But then I see the light reflecting off something on the other side of the field. An eye in the moving grass. And teeth.

"No! Kid!"

But he's not moving. He's looking over at me with tears in his eyes. Crying loudly, Bobo held tightly against his chest.

I move, not thinking. Jamie screams after me.

The alligator lunges out of the grass, trying to beat me to him— and maybe if we were in water he'd be able to—but fuck you, asshole, this is land.

I leap over the fire and land on the other side. Right on the edge of a small pothole. My ankle twists as the edge of the asphalt breaks under my shoes. I eat it, face down on the road. The Kid is still crying. And he's still five feet away.

But the alligator is closer to him than I am.

No. No, no, no, no, no. He's not hurting the Kid.

I scramble across the road, pushing through the pain in my ankle and hands and knees.

The alligator lunges. I'm not going to make it.

But I have to.

So I do the stupidest thing I've ever done in my life. This coming from someone who stepped in a bear trap once.

I wrap my right arm around the Kid, pulling him to my side. But I put my left hand out, trying to push the alligator—the thing with a mouth full of razor-sharp teeth—away. Instead of pushing it, I get nothing but air.

And the alligator chomps down.

The pain is like . . . well, it's teeth. It's fucking teeth. I feel something in my hand snap and the alligator gives a quick head jerk. My shoulder pops, and every muscle burns with agony as I scream. The Kid is behind me now.

Safe.

But the alligator pulls again, dragging me across the asphalt, like it's trying to rip my arm out of its socket. And if it pulls one more time, it just might—the alligator rolled and ripped that guy's leg right off.

Oh, Christ, it's going to do that to me.

It opens its mouth and I try to pull away, but it snaps its jaws shut again and a fresh burst of horrific pain overwhelms every sense I have. Jamie is screaming something, but I don't know what it is. I see him run at the alligator with the rifle in his hand and even though I know it's not loaded—and Hickey had taken it—my brain doesn't even see the image as odd.

Jamie must remember the rifle's not loaded, too, because he's beating the ever-loving shit out of the alligator. The thing jerks again, pulling another burst of agony from my chest down to my arm, and I scream and scream and scream.

Only someone else is screaming now.

"Fuck you!" Movement catches my eye, but I barely have a second to register it before Taylor is jumping onto the alligator. Hitting it over and over and over.

No. Not hitting it. She has Daphne's knife. It's the size of Taylor's forearm, but she's holding it as though it's weightless. Driving it down into the alligator's skull over and over and over. The thing is probably dead—maybe it was after Taylor delivered the first blow—but she just keeps stabbing. It's like a horror movie. Blood flying, speckling her face, mixing with her tears.

Jamie uses the moment to pry open the thing's jaws and take my arm out. I cradle it in my other arm, crying out in more pain. It feels like it's been pulled from its socket, and I have no control over its movement.

Blood flows quickly from the ripped-up flesh of my hand and arm. My thumb is gone. My index and middle finger hang from broken, bloody sinew. I try to move them but my pinkie barely twitches. And all I feel is the pain.

Jamie wraps my arm in a shirt he grabbed from one of our packs, and I scream against his chest as the pain overwhelms me again.

"I know," he whispers. "I know, baby. But it has to be tight." I nod but still scream as he pulls the shirt as tight as he can, then ties it off. Within seconds it's darkened with blood. It throbs with pain, and I try to breathe, but each breath burns the muscles in my chest and back. Swollen and useless from my dislocated shoulder.

Taylor sounds like she's gasping, too. She's covered in blood, cursing under her breath with every stab into the dead alligator. Jamie cradles me in his lap, watching her. Probably wishing he could do the same.

I know Cara and the others are all watching, too. The fire takes up most of the other side of the road and the trucks and cars are right there, unguarded.

"This is our chance," I say. But it's so quiet no one hears me. My throat burns, raw from screaming.

And Taylor keeps stabbing. And stabbing.

Finally she drives the knife deep into what's left of the alligator's head. Then pushes herself off it, kicking away as though shocked by her own violence. She's starting to hyperventilate. I sit up with a groan of pain and hold out my good arm. She leaps into it and lets me give her a side hug as she sobs.

"Thank you," I say. "You saved my life."

She doesn't answer. Just continues to sob. I lie back, my shoulder still out of whack and my arm throbbing in pain.

"Are you okay?" Jamie asks.

I grab his shirt. "Now. We have to go now." Daphne is there and she locks eyes with me. My voice is hoarse. "You're right. This is our chance. For *all* of us."

She nods and runs to Amy, Kelly, and Cara. In the distance, Hickey and the others are still fighting off gators. Jamie asks me something, but I don't understand it. Maybe it's the blood loss, or the lack of adrenaline now that the attack is over. I close my eyes, barely paying attention to the sounds of everyone speaking around me.

They drift farther and farther away.

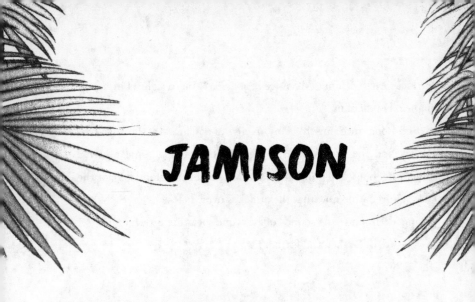

JAMISON

"ANDREW!" I YELL. "ANDREW, WAKE UP!" I shake him as guns continue to
fire in the darkness around us. To my right, the dry grass at the edge
of the road has created a burning force field to protect us. Daphne
calls my name again and I turn to her. She's pointing behind me.

I spin, expecting to find an alligator sneaking up on me. But she's
pointing at the cars parked beyond the fires.

Daphne yells to Amy, Kelly, and Cara, "Grab as many supplies as
you can and get the kids in the truck. Amy, drive them out of here,
we'll follow you. Cara, go grab a car."

Cara nods and follows as Amy and Kelly corral the kids into the
truck. Then Daphne turns back to us.

"Rocky Horror, help Jamie get Andrew to the car."

He nods and takes Andrew's feet, and I pull him up by his armpits,
then we start moving. Behind me, people continue to shout and shoot.
I turn to see Hickey's back is to us. But Daria is looking right at me.
She doesn't warn any of the others, and instead turns away, pointing
the rifle into the grass and pulling the trigger. Then she calls out to

the others and points into the darkness, drawing everyone's attention in that direction.

Daphne opens the back seat, and Rocky Horror and I slide Andrew in. The T-shirt wrapped around his arm is soaked through with blood. Amy starts her truck but keeps the headlights off. I turn to check that no one has noticed our escape yet, but everyone is still preoccupied. The gunshots have gotten farther apart, like a bag of microwave popcorn at the end of its cycle. The alligators must be retreating, scared off by the guns and fire.

"We have to get out of here," I say. "Before they notice."

"Wait." I turn to see Taylor beside me; I didn't even realize she was there. Without saying another word, she runs off toward the other cars.

"Taylor, we have to go!" I chase after her but stop when I see her slide the bloody knife into the tires of one of the cars. "Oh. Yes! Good job!"

She yanks out the knife, then slashes two more on the same car before moving on to another. While she does that, I run back to our little camp and snatch as many things left behind by the kids as I can. Backpacks, sleeping bags, a stuffed animal. My eyes drift past the dead man with his missing leg, but something catches my eye.

There's a gun holstered to his waist. I unclip it and take it with me. They took the handgun I left the cabin with, but this one will do fine.

I run back to the car just as Taylor has finished slashing her last tire. Cara pops the trunk for me, and I throw everything in the back. The truck Amy is driving is so far down the road all I see is the red taillights. Taylor, Rocky Horror, and I climb into the back seat, smushing together and trying not to hurt Andrew, who lies across our laps.

Cara does a three-point turn and the wheels screech. When I have a second to glance out the window, I see Hickey and the others have finally noticed our escape. They run after us.

"Hit it, Cara!" I yell.

"That's not helpful, Jamie!" she shouts back.

But she does punch it—narrowly missing a collision with one of the cars Taylor slashed—and speeds off into the darkness.

Cara follows Amy for about an hour, taking back roads until we finally get to a highway, where they pull over. The sky is turning light blue with the imminent sunrise. While Cara, Rocky Horror, and Daphne discuss which route to take and how long they should drive, I look after Andrew's wound.

As I pull the shirt away, I wince. It's still bleeding, but slowly. Andrew looks pale in the car's dome light, as though he's lost a lot of blood. I rinse his arm with my bottle of water, and the entire time I can't stop thinking about all the bacteria that's probably in these wounds.

He's going to need antibiotics, and fast. We don't have any at all, and when I needed them after I was shot, he stopped in every house he could, searching until he ran out of places to search. But we don't have time for that.

The Keys are chasing us. Fort Caroline is probably on the way, too. Unless the Keys have been trying to keep our escape quiet, which might make sense. Still, our world is getting smaller and smaller.

Andrew wakes up as I'm wrapping the strategically placed gauze pads around his arm. He winces and groans.

"I know," I say. "I'm sorry, baby."

He half opens one eye and mumbles, "Where are we?"

"On a highway. We got away from Hickey and the alligators."

"Yaaaay. Hickey and the Alligators? That's a terrible band name." He sounds so weak and tired. "Is the Kid okay?"

"Yeah, he's fine." Though I haven't seen him since Kelly was lifting him into the back of the truck. He could be traumatized for all I know. I wouldn't blame him. Taylor walks over to the other side of the car, looking through the open door.

"Is he awake?"

"Yeah." I cut off the last bit of bandage, tucking in the loose end, and Andrew exhales with relief.

"Someone was asking about you." She moves aside and lets the Kid step forward.

"Hey, Kid." Andrew tries to act more awake and even sits up, but he gasps. Now that he's not lying down, I can see how his left shoulder slumps; it's popped out of its socket. He leans against me and his eyes flutter as if he's getting light-headed. I reach around and brace him, holding his good hand with mine, which he squeezes gratefully. Then he tries his best to smile at the Kid. "How you doing?"

"I lost Bobo."

"Shit." Andrew actually sounds disappointed, not like he's faking it for the Kid's sake. "I'm sorry, Kid."

"Who's Bobo?" I ask.

"His hippo."

The stuffed animal. "Oh, wait!" I jump up and open the trunk. The handgun is right on top of the stuff I grabbed. I take it, making sure the safety is on, and tuck it into the back of my jeans. Then I move around the sleeping bags and find the blue stuffed hippo that had been lying on the road. But the arm I grabbed it by is stained with Andrew's blood.

Sorry, Kid, but at least Mr. Bobo is still alive and with us. I carry it around to him and his eyes light up.

"You rescued him from the alligators!" He reaches for the hippo and hugs it tight.

"Of course he did," says Taylor. "I mean, he's the guy who fought off a pack of lions."

"Wait, what?"

In the car, Andrew snorts and starts to laugh but immediately cries out, wincing. He puts a hand across his heart, his chest muscles probably sore as hell from his arm being pulled from its socket.

Taylor sees Andrew's pain and says to the Kid, "Why don't we let Andrew rest for a bit."

The Kid holds up Bobo's arm. "He's bleeding."

I open my mouth to tell him it's Andrew's blood and Mr. Bobo is okay, but realize it's Bobo's left arm. Just like Andrew. I reach into the car and grab the scrap of gauze.

"This should help," I say. "It helped Andrew, see?" I wrap the gauze around the hippo's arm, and there's just enough to cover the blood. "There. Brand-new, right, Mr. Bobo?"

"Bobo," the Kid says, like he's scolding me.

"Sorry. Right, Bobo?"

"You have to kiss it to make it all better," Taylor says, smirking. "Everyone knows that."

I look up at her and she hides her smile behind her hand. So I take

Mr.—sorry, *just* Bobo's—arm and give it a loud kiss.

"There. All better?" I ask. The Kid nods and Taylor laughs as she escorts him away. I put my head back into the car and Andrew is grinning despite his pain.

"What was all that about me fighting off a pack of lions?" I ask.

He snorts again but tries not to laugh. "Yeah, the kids were wired one night after too much sugar at a monthly social, so I told them about DC and the lions."

"And just made up the part where I fought off an entire pack of lions?"

He nods. "It was more interesting than 'big cats hate water and it started to rain.'"

So much suddenly makes sense. How all the kids looked at me like I was some awe-inspiring giant, how they were so scared of me at first. And No-Filter Frank asking why I didn't have scars.

"You're such a liar," I say. But I can't help but laugh now; of course these kids would be intimidated by a tall guy who could take on an entire pack of lions without a scratch. And now they have alligators to add to the myth.

"I prefer the term *storyteller*." I grunt and give him a side-eye. Then he slowly holds up his arm, wincing a bit. "You forgot to kiss mine and make it all better."

I lean across the back seat and gently kiss him. I don't let my hands touch him because I know he's in pain. One kiss. Two kisses. Three.

"How's that?" I ask.

"Good enough for a down payment. But I might need more later."

"As many as it takes."

ANDREW

THE SOUND OF SCREAMING SNAPS ME OUT of whatever sad excuse for sleep I was having. I sit up and the sore muscles from my formerly dislocated shoulder burn and spasm. I barely have time to groan in pain before my eyes are searching the darkness around the fire.

It's the second night since the alligator attack that the kids have woken up from nightmares. Different kids, same nightmares. Always with the monsters.

I scramble to my feet as fast as my injury will allow—clenching my teeth through the pain—and go to where Daphne and Kelly are crouching near the kids and trying to calm them down. Amy is trying to calm Henri-Two while Jamie points his rifle into the darkness.

Rocky Horror—after realizing we aren't being beset by alligators again—has turned over and tried to go back to sleep.

"Who is it this time?" I ask Daphne.

"The Kid. You want to take him while I calm the others?"

"Yeah." I walk over to the Kid, whose cheeks are wet with tears. He reaches up and wraps his arms around my neck, which hurts my arm so bad I have to bite back a groan and take a deep breath before I can speak. "Hey, hey, it's okay, you just had a nightmare."

"No! It was a monster. He was right over there." He spins and points into the darkness. But for some reason he points *up*, not at the ground, where alligators would be. And that kind of chills me to the bone.

"What did he look like?"

"He has a scary face and it was cut and it had this over his eye." He touches the gauze on my arm, and again the chills come back. This isn't just some reptilian creature with teeth. "And he had four arms."

Okay, so maybe that's more reptilian monster.

"Well, it looks like you scared him off." I point into the darkness. The Kid turns and looks over his shoulder, his eyes darting every which way. "So why don't you lie back down and Jamie and I will stay here and keep watch, okay?"

The Kid looks down at his sleeping bag and pulls it over him. Then he whispers, barely audible over the crackling fire, "I had an accident."

"Oh. That's okay! I'll get Ms. Daphne to help you get cleaned up—"

"No, you help." He looks up at Jamie. "And Jamie. Keep watch."

Jamie looks to me and then nods. "You got it, Kid."

I reach into his backpack and grab a shirt, underwear, and pair of pants. I have to do it one-handed while my arm throbs with more pain. When Daphne comes over to us, I whisper that we're going to change and ask her to unzip the Kid's sleeping bag and put it closer to the fire to dry.

Jamie walks with us as we head away from the fire so the Kid can have a bit more privacy. We stopped for the night in a library parking lot, and we walk around the side of the building where the fire is still visible, but it's a little darker.

I hand the Kid his clothes and tell him to change, and we turn our backs. Jamie still has the empty rifle.

"How many more nights of monsters do you think we have?" I whisper.

He shrugs. "Too many."

We're still in Florida, but in the panhandle. The truck and car we stole from Hickey ran out of gas yesterday—first the car, then the truck while we were all piled in the bed. Even if Hickey and the others changed out their flat tires and came after us again, we're on back roads so should be harder to find.

But in a couple of days we'll be in Georgia. Even though it's western Georgia and Fort Caroline is in northeast Georgia, I'm still anxious. It feels like we're going into their territory. Cara said she can remember most of the supply run routes she mapped out for them that headed west, but what if she forgot one or two? What if someone else from Fort Caroline shows up and they recognize Jamie?

There are a lot of what-ifs, but that's our life on the road. It's why I was trying so hard to make the Keys our home. But Jamie was right. They were never our home. These people we're with are, but the Keys *the place* was not.

So where is?

"Where are we going?" I ask Jamie while the Kid changes. We've been running for so long, it hasn't really come up *where* we're running to.

"Henri's."

"I mean after. You heard Trevor. If Fort Caroline shows up to the

Keys and we aren't there, they might tell them where we're going. We came down to get Amy to help reunite their family, not bring a militia to their doorstep. Also, Henri didn't exactly ask for seven orphans." Nine if we count Jamie and me, but let's not right now.

"Maybe we'll find somewhere on the way. People followed the rumors to Reagan Airport looking for help; they had to end up somewhere in the Maryland-Virginia area, right?"

The family of siblings we met at Reagan on our way south were going to Chicago in hopes of finding an aunt. Maybe that's what people would do: scatter and try to find whatever family might be left.

"For all we know," Jamie continues, "Henri has met others since we've been gone. There could be a whole settlement up there."

I glance over my shoulder and call out, "You doing okay, Kid?"

"Yeah."

Jamie snaps his fingers. "Cara said she was missing her hometown, that she might want to go back. Easton, Maryland, isn't far from Bethesda; maybe everyone could go there. Not permanently, but just to hide out until they know Fort Caroline isn't coming."

"That could work." In fact, it might be a great idea. But Jamie and I wouldn't be able to go. If Fort Caroline ended up traveling through Easton by chance and found us there—despite how low the odds might be—everyone would still be in danger. Without us, they could hide easily and pretend they never even met us.

As if he's reading my mind, Jamie reaches out and touches my good arm. "Then we go to the cabin like we always planned."

My chest tightens at the thought of leaving everyone.

"All done." I turn to see the Kid holding his wet clothes. I take them and we head back to the fire, where I lay out the clothes to dry off. We'll wash them next time we stop for water.

"You can use my sleeping bag tonight," I tell the Kid. "I'll share Jamie's." He gives me a quiet thank-you as I ask Jamie with a look if that's okay. He nods. We get the Kid settled—most of the other kids have already lain back down and are half-asleep or snoozing away.

Jamie fully unzips his sleeping bag, and we lie on top of the yoga mat he uses to pad the ground. "Should we get closer to the fire?" he asks me quietly.

"With your furnace body? I'd rather not die of heatstroke in the middle of the night, thank you." I lie on the side of my body that doesn't feel like it's been through a meat grinder and Jamie nuzzles up behind me, being very careful not to touch my arm or any part of my body that might hurt. But I reach over and take his arm, wrapping it around my middle to pull him closer.

Within seconds I start to laugh quietly.

"What?" he asks.

"You know *exactly* what."

"Shut up. I can't help it."

But I still shuffle back against him a bit more. This forced proximity is nice.

I've missed being this close. Even with imaginary monsters lurking in the dark, I can shut my eyes, feel my boyfriend's arm around me—and something else, of course—and I feel safe.

The next day we need to get on the highway again for a few miles, but before we do, Rocky Horror goes ahead to check for any signs of Hickey and the others.

We stay back about a mile from the on-ramp, and Jamie and I take the time to change my bandages. It isn't looking great, and I keep lying, saying it doesn't hurt. But of course it fucking hurts, I got attacked by an alligator.

The wounds aren't bleeding anymore, but there's a lot of gross pus that seeps through the gauze pads.

"We need to find antibiotics," Jamie says. "Maybe tonight we can stop early. I'll ask Cara to get us to a neighborhood and we can go door-to-door."

I nod. "Only if it's off the highway." I don't want to be the reason they catch up to us again. Jamie finishes wrapping my arm and by the time we rejoin the others, Rocky Horror is walking up. But he doesn't look relieved.

"Did you see something?" Cara asks.

He nods. "I think we should find another way. Remember the caravan that drove past after Hickey found us?"

The beige-and-maroon RV. I almost forgot in all the chaos. Hickey sent people after them, but they hadn't come back by the time we escaped. I remind the others about that and Rocky Horror nods.

"Which means they could be helping Hickey," he says.

"Did you see anyone?" Jamie asks.

"No one familiar, but they're also about half a mile up the road, so what do I know? I didn't see any of Hickey's cars."

"Maybe they left them," Amy says. "Just piled into that RV of theirs."

He nods and Cara says she's going to find us a new route. We go into the shade to rest—it's an oddly hot day for December. Though maybe not oddly hot for Florida.

About twenty minutes later, we hear the familiar sound of an engine and tires against the road.

Jamie and I jump up, looking at each other to verify we're both hearing the same thing. We should have gone back somewhere we could hide; instead we're in the open next to the road. I try to remember a building close by that we can run to, but then the RV rounds the curve ahead of us.

We're trapped. Again.

I curse under my breath and go back to my bag. As much as I don't want to, I take out the handgun Jamie stole from the dead man during the alligator attack. Jamie gives me the same look of resignation I must be wearing.

The RV comes to a stop—but there are no other cars behind it. For a while nothing happens, then the door swings open. The first thing I see is empty hands held up toward the sky.

A bald white man with a thick salt-and-pepper beard steps out. A few people follow behind him, but none of them are Hickey or the others from the Keys.

And none of them have weapons.

I lower the gun in my hand as they line up in front of the RV. One of the men catches my attention—a big burly white guy with a scar running down the left side of his face from forehead to jaw, and gauze over his eye.

"The monster!" the Kid yells. I turn and see him duck behind Daphne, who shushes him and tells him what he said is not nice. But the "monster" just laughs and looks at the others, who chuckle along with him.

The bald man shakes his head. "Kevin, I told you to stay hidden." He turns his attention back to us. "Sorry. Even before he was hurt, he looked like a monster."

"Fu—" Kevin cuts off the curse, glancing at the kids. "Screw you, Cal."

"Not much better," Cal says.

But I'm raising the gun again. "Wait. You've been following us? That was you last night?" And the night before. Lurking around us while we slept.

Cal raises his hands again as if to remind us he's not armed. And Hickey still hasn't come out of the RV. If they were following us—for at least two days—then maybe Hickey isn't with them. Why would he let us get farther away from the Keys if he was supposed to bring us back?

"Sorry," he says again. "We just wanted to be sure before we introduced ourselves."

"Sure about what?" Rocky Horror joins us. Cara and Amy as well. Amy holds Henri-Two in her arms.

"That the people holding you at gunpoint weren't still with you. We saw you all on the side of the road. Then two nights ago we saw you drive past us in some of the vehicles, and we thought it was them again. They sent some people after us when we drove past."

"Yeah," Jamie says. "We assumed they were sent to invite you to join up with them."

Cal shakes his head. "If that was the case, it was the worst invitation we've ever received. They pulled their guns on us immediately."

"Where are they?" I ask.

Kevin's good eye goes back to the kids and he shakes his head.

"Got a couple nice holes in the RV along the way," Cal says.

"Is that what happened to your eye?" Cara asks.

Cal speaks for Kevin. "No. That was . . . it happened a while ago."

"Why did you follow us if you thought we were Admiral Hickey and the others?" Rocky Horror asks.

Again Cal speaks, so I assume he's the leader. "We wanted to make sure we weren't running into them again. So when we saw your fire, we waited till you all fell asleep and then scoped you out. When we saw the kids, we assumed you were trying to get away from the others. That the way of it?"

"Yes," says Jamie. "We're all from the Keys. We got hit by a hurricane and the colony is struggling with what supplies remain. We decided to leave, and they didn't like that. The others you saw were sent to bring us back."

I notice how Jamie isn't telling them the whole story, and maybe that's for the best. If they don't know about Fort Caroline, they can't use us as leverage, too. For all we know, they could be *from* Fort Caroline. So before they can ask any further questions, I jump in with my own.

"Where are you all from?"

Cal looks to the others and shakes his head. "A little bit from all over. I'm from California, LA area. Kevin here is from Arizona." He points to a woman with light brown skin and black hair in a long braid. "Sandra is from New Mexico." The other three people are from Seattle, Nevada, and South Dakota. "We all met in a settlement in Louisiana."

A settlement they're no longer with. I want to ask why, but at the same time, do I need to? People don't leave settlements after the apocalypse unless they *have* to.

But Cara's curiosity is piqued. "What happened with your settlement?"

"Not a hurricane," says Cal. My eyes move over to Kevin again, and I start to put the pieces together on my own. "Listen, when we saw you, we weren't really in a place to help since we were a little outnumbered. But I think we are now. We'd like to invite you to travel with us for a while. We can't *guarantee* safety, but we can at least help you a bit. Get some more distance on the people chasing you—if they're still chasing you, that is."

Subtle way of asking if we slaughtered them, Cal. And his eyes flit down to my arm, so who can blame him? And maybe it's not that bad to have them think that. A little bit of fear might protect us.

"Thank you, but no," Jamie says.

Rocky Horror puts up his hands. "Hold on now."

"We'll let you discuss it," says Cal. "While we turn the RV around, you can all talk it out."

Then they get back into the RV and we go back to our group.

"We don't know these people," Jamie says.

Rocky Horror shrugs. "And? None of us here knew each other until we met at the settlement."

"That's different. We don't know if it's a trap. When they drive us back to their group, Hickey could be waiting for us."

I shake my head. "Hickey wouldn't have followed us for two days." Rocky Horror points at me, nodding aggressively. "And did you hear how cagey they were about their last settlement?"

It's Cara's turn. "No one in their right mind would leave a settlement unless they really needed to. Or unless they finally had a window to do so." She says the last bit very pointedly, hinting at her own exodus from Fort Caroline when she followed us. "If they're offering to get us a little farther, I think we should take them up on it."

"We're getting closer to Fort Caroline territory," I say. "If we can blend in with a larger group, it might be good for us."

Daphne and Kelly vote for riding in the RV, too, and after a few seconds, so does Taylor.

Jamie, clearly feeling like he's been beaten, finally nods. "Okay."

Just in time, because Cal hops back out of the RV and approaches us. We thank him for the invitation and he helps us corral the kids into the RV. I sit on the floor next to Jamie and put my hand on his knee, trying to communicate telepathically that we'll be okay.

And maybe it works, because he nods and puts his arm around me, resting his hand on my waist and pulling me tight against his body. Having him against me brings that familiar safe feeling. But the anxiety is still there, deep down.

Worried about who these people are, where they came from, where they're going.

And if we can trust them.

JAMISON

ONCE WE MEET UP WITH THE REST of Cal's group, we get back on the road. They tell us they aren't sure where they're heading yet, but that they've mainly been looking for supplies both to maintain their group of around forty—over fifty, including us—and, if they do meet a new settlement that's welcoming, to offer the supplies to convince the settlement to let them join up.

But they plan to be picky about where they're going to settle. They said one of the rumors they're chasing is Reagan Airport. We probably shouldn't say anything because that means they would take us all the way up to DC, when our goal is to get Amy and Henri-Two to Henri in Bethesda, but we don't want to deceive them. So Andrew and I break it to them that the European Union—if it still exists in any capacity—isn't coming. Cal and the others don't seem heartbroken and maybe not even surprised.

For now, like us, they're just nomads.

After a few hours, the radio on the RV's dashboard crackles to life and someone calls out to them. It's a scout they've sent ahead to look for a place to camp. The scout gives them directions, and within an hour and a half, we come upon a mall.

There are signs scattered on the ground of the mall parking lot—small, laminated with dark red letters that read "Distribution Center FL347." Some have instructions directing where vehicles should go; others say the distribution center is for authorized government personnel only and "ALL OTHERS WILL BE SHOT ON SITE." Though I think it was supposed to say "sight."

Some of the others have already started setting up their camp. Cal opens the door for us and looks down at Andrew's arm.

"If you need medical attention . . ." He points to a couple of pop-up tailgate tents. "Head over and see Dr. Jenn in the medical tent."

"Do you have antibiotics?" I ask.

He frowns and shakes his head. "We've been looking, too. So far, no luck."

Dammit.

Once Cal leaves us, Andrew turns to me. "I'm going to go see if there's anything they can do about my arm. Can you help Daphne and Kelly with the kids?"

"Of course."

He kisses me on the cheek and heads for the tent while I go to Daphne and ask what I can help with. We try to get the kids to set up their sleeping bags—it's late in the afternoon, and it's better that they have everything they need out and ready to go before the sun goes down. But they're all distracted.

The Nomads have kids with them as well, and the two groups of children are staring each other down across the parking lot, probably waiting for the okay to meet up and start playing.

Daphne finally gives our kids the okay to go say hi—walking along with a couple of the shyer ones—and Cara and I tell Rocky Horror, Kelly, and Amy we're going to check on Andrew.

"What kind of distribution center is this?" I ask Cara as we head over to the medical tents.

"They started setting these up during the flu-year fall. They did it in Maryland, too, but I don't think they ended up doing nearly as much. At least not like this."

There are a few trucks on the side of the parking lot closest to the mall. Two of the trucks are tipped over, their back doors broken open. Four are just blackened shells, the soot from the fire spreading all the way to the manufactured stone walls of the mall.

Cara continues but her voice sounds shaky. "The governor took over and gave an executive order that food and medical supplies would be stockpiled in distribution centers. Then the public would be told when they could come get aid packages—but they kept delaying it. I know in Maryland they were saying it was the politicians making sure they could keep their hands on supplies."

She stops me, taking my arm. I'm about to ask her what's wrong, but she takes a long, deep breath with her eyes closed, as though she's trying not to have a panic attack, before finally telling me.

"In Maryland, they took things from the supermarkets, too. No warning, just went in overnight and emptied everything out. When they did it in Easton, people panicked, and that's when everything started getting bad for us."

From the snippets of what I've learned about Cara before she ended up at Fort Caroline, I know that her family hadn't gotten the flu, but they must have died another way, because she said she was the only one left. I hold her hand because I know she doesn't want a hug unless she initiates it.

"Was that how your family died?" I ask.

She shakes her head. "That was later. More panicking, but because of confusion and rumors. It's not important right now. I just . . . I don't know, I wanted to talk about that part. The distribution centers. How they did it in Maryland, at least."

I nod. "FL347." So maybe there are three hundred and forty-six others out there, or more. That might explain why we had so much trouble finding supplies when we got to Florida. We thought it was the Key Colony, but maybe it's because all these distribution centers were stockpiling supplies.

"So there's supplies in there?" I ask, trying to bring the conversation around to something other than Cara's family.

Cara points to the smashed-in doors. "I think most of it's probably gone by now."

But there could still be something. Maybe canned food or some kind of antibiotics that someone overlooked.

After we check on Andrew and are back with our group, I tell them that I'm going to check the mall for supplies. Cara and Rocky Horror offer to come as well.

"Shouldn't we get a few people to help out?" Daphne says.

"I'll go," says Taylor.

"No," I say. "You stay here and keep an eye on things. It'll draw less attention if it's just the three of us. We can see what's in there first and then tell the Nomads. There are more of them than there are of us, so it's better if we can get supplies for us first."

"Jamie." Daphne gives me a look that feels judgmental. "These people are helping us—helping Andrew. We should be returning the favor, not taking supplies from them."

"We aren't taking supplies from them," I say. "We're taking supplies from the governor of Florida, who thought stockpiling them for herself was better than passing them out to people. We'll let the others know what's in there, and I'll even help them get whatever's left. But if there's only a few antibiotics, I'm making sure Andrew gets them. He got mauled by a wild animal, and if we don't find something to fight the infection, he's going to lose his arm."

Daphne frowns but doesn't argue anymore. We need to be careful now. There's no way these people would help Andrew before their own. The Keys decided to sell us out to Fort Caroline the second they needed help. We have to make sure we can get out of here, on our own, before the Nomads realize they have a bargaining chip in me.

We wait until the sun gets low in the sky before we walk around the back of the medical tent and over to the burnt trucks. We don't slink, we just walk—with our empty backpacks—looking like we're out for a normal stroll in the parking lot. If anyone notices us, they don't yell or point or run to see if they can come along.

I take one glance back but can't see anyone paying attention to us at all. There isn't even a lookout.

We enter through a store called Bealls, which I've never heard of, but it looks like a department store. Of course, there are no clothes or shoes—they've all been moved elsewhere. All that's left are mannequin limbs and empty perfume and jewelry counters.

There's also trash, leaves, and debris littering the floor. And quite a few bullet casings.

"Looks like they really did get raided," Rocky Horror says, nudging one of the tarnished brass casings aside.

On the floor ahead of us are two bodies lying face down. They're both wearing military fatigues. The gun holsters at their sides are empty, but I check their pockets for anything else. Not even a wallet.

The bodies are old, but they aren't just decayed; there's strands of muscle and tissue hanging from their faces and hands, left over from whatever bugs didn't want them. Holes have been torn in their fatigues by animals. Small, crusty animal droppings litter the floor around them.

"Be careful," Cara says. "There might still be animals in here wanting to protect their home. Or their food."

I flick the safety off the handgun. Rocky Horror has the rifle, but it still doesn't have any shells. There's a broken two-by-four ahead that I pick up and hand to Cara. She takes it carefully, making sure she doesn't get splinters.

The department store is mainly empty—as though they cleared it out to be a processing area for their stockpiled supplies.

But the stockpile isn't really a stockpile. At least not anymore.

Outside the department store, in a glass-ceilinged atrium, there are a few stacks of plastic tubs and cardboard boxes. Most have been ripped apart and are damp with mold and mildew. Dark red sunset filters through the cracked and dirty skylight above the atrium, and tendrils of ivy hang down through some of the larger broken panes.

Beneath the skylight is a decommissioned fountain that's full of stagnant green water.

It was probably drained before the government occupied the mall, but with the broken skylight has become a pond.

"Wait," I say, holding out my hand to Rocky Horror and Cara. I pick up a broken tile by my foot and toss it into the fountain. The sound of the splash echoes through the atrium and down the empty halls of the mall. Four birds—the most unexpected creatures we could see since so many of them have been wiped out—fly out of the cracked and open roof. Water spills out over the top of the fountain edge but nothing else moves.

"Just checking for alligators," I say.

"Good looking out," says Rocky Horror. Then we set about checking the boxes and tubs. I open one crushed cardboard box and fat cockroaches run from inside, scattering to the darker corners of the atrium. The cans inside the box have been crushed, and it looks like whichever ones didn't immediately open then exploded later, once the seal was broken and the inside started to spoil.

There's one can that seems like it might be okay. I grab it with two fingers, but its label is slick with fuzz and slime from the rest of the food that sat on top of it. I take it over to the fountain to wash off the sludge, checking again for any movements or eyes. A dead squirrel floating in the water puts me a little at ease. If there was something hiding in there, it would have eaten that thing by now.

"Jackpot." Rocky Horror is looking inside a large beige trash receptacle. He pulls out a black plastic tub and puts it on the ground. I throw the can into my backpack and join him.

He flips open the lid of the tub and right on top there's a package of gauze, sterile pads, and bandages.

Rocky Horror claps his hands. "I figured some government schmuck would try to hide his own stash to sell later."

Cara joins us and we stuff the medical supplies into our bags. There's also five bottles of rubbing alcohol, rubber gloves, over-the-counter pain meds, and burn gel.

"No antibiotics, though," I say.

"No, but let's keep looking. And let's keep an eye out for places where a grunt with a gun would try to hide things."

"The security office," Cara says. "The guards before the pandemic would have had lockers."

"You're a genius," I say.

She shrugs, smirking. "Why do you think I'm still here?" Then she heads over to a smashed plexiglass sign with the mall map on it.

There are four lockers in the security office and all four have combination locks on them. I pull on one of the locks, hoping it's old enough to just break, but it doesn't.

"Notice any hardware stores on that map, Cara?" I ask.

"No need," Rocky Horror says. He holds his flashlight out to me, and I take it. "Keep it on the dial for me." He pulls on the lock and starts spinning the dial until it stops. "Cara, remember eighteen." He spins the dial in the opposite direction, only this time it goes around a couple of times before finally stopping. "Jamie, you've got thirty-two."

"How do you know how to do this?" I ask. Cara has grown curious as well and is watching over his shoulder as he spins the two numbers

146

in order, then starts spinning in the opposite direction.

"I looked up a video online. Bike cops liked to lock up their bikes outside my apartment while they went into the coffee shop across the street." The dial finally stops and he spins it one last time to reset.

"All right, all together now."

"Eighteen," Cara says.

"Thirty-two."

"And five makes . . ." The lock snaps open. "Public domain version of Yahtzee."

He pulls the locker open, and I shine the flashlight in. Cara was right. Someone did use this place as a hiding spot for the supplies they wanted to trade once the superflu had burned itself out.

Only the locker is filled not with medicine or first aid but with candy and black binders stacked three in a row.

Rocky Horror laughs as he flips open one of the binders. "It's porn!"

"What?" I attempt to look but he pulls it away.

"No! You're underage. Cara, lookie." He giggles as he turns it around to her. She frowns.

"They're printed-out pictures of websites," she tells me from the other side of the binder. "Why bother stockpiling this?"

"Probably thought the web would go down eventually and he could use porn sheets as currency." Rocky Horror grabs another binder. "Aw, he didn't discriminate. This one's got bi porn!" He flips through it and flinches at whatever is on the next page. He snaps the binder closed and throws it back into the locker. "Oh, no. We don't need to look at that anymore. Grab the candy for the kids and I'll teach you how to pick those other locks."

147

We watch as he demonstrates on the second locker, then we try our own. Cara eventually gets it, but Rocky Horror finally has to take over and open mine. He takes the lock off, then snaps it closed again and hands it to me.

"You can practice later."

Rocky Horror's locker is filled with canned food and Little Debbie snacks that have probably gone very bad by now. Cara's locker is filled with clothes—but most are men's size XL so they would be pretty useless for her.

I open my locker and the first thing that catches my eye is the white pill bottle in the cubby up top. The label says clindamycin hydrochloride. I flip it sideways to read the directions, trying to figure out what kind of medicine it is.

"Jesus." Rocky Horror grabs something else from the locker.

"Is that weed?" Cara asks.

I look up from the bottle to see the large ziplock bag of marijuana.

"And that's not it." He picks up a package the size of a brick. "Gotta give the guy credit for diversifying his investments. Drugs, porn, and candy."

The bottle doesn't say what clindamycin is, and next to "dosage and uses" on the label, it just says "see accompanying prescribing information." But the name sounds familiar. Like I've heard it before.

Or maybe read it. I put it in my bag.

"What's that?" Cara asks.

"I'm not sure. But considering what it was stashed with, I'd say it's either prescription painkillers or antibiotics." I want to check my mother's journal before I tell anyone what it is. "Let's get back to the others. We can come back tomorrow when there's more light."

Rocky Horror puts the brick of drugs in his pack, and I raise an eyebrow at him. "Look, if it's heroin, it's a painkiller. I'm going to give the Nomad doc the option. Especially if they're going to have to cut anything off anyone out there."

I know he's talking about Andrew. If these aren't antibiotics, Rocky Horror is right. Andrew might need the heroin. I nod and we head back outside.

I was right. I had read the word *clindamycin* before. It's third down under the list of antibiotics in my mom's journal.

I open the bottle and pull the cotton ball plug from the top, then shake out one of the 150 milligram pills. They're green-and-blue capsules. My heart surges with hope because this is exactly what Andrew needs.

I take one of the pills and put the bottle back in my bag—replacing the cotton to keep it from rattling—then head over to where Andrew is lying atop his sleeping bag, awake but looking like he wishes he weren't. I hold out the capsule. "Antibiotics."

His eyes go wide as he holds out his good hand. "You found some?"

"Yes." I hand him my water bottle, and he downs the pill. "There should be enough for all of us in case something bad happens again. Even after your round."

He smiles, and it seems like the first genuine smile he's had in months. "Good. I think a couple others are going to need them, too."

I shake my head. "I mean *us*. Our group, not the Nomads."

Andrew stares at me as though he doesn't understand.

"There was only one bottle." I take it out of my bag and show it to him. "That's all we have, and my mom's notebook says you have to take a hundred and fifty milligrams every six hours."

"If I got bit by a crocodile every six hours—"

"Alligator."

"Whatever, I wouldn't take all those pills. We're giving them to the Nomad's doctor, Jenn, and she's distributing them."

"What about everyone else?"

"No, Jamie, what about *everyone* else."

"What if one of the kids gets sick?" I ask. "Are you going to be okay with them not getting antibiotics because we used them on strangers?"

He stares at me as though he doesn't understand how the kids might need them. They're kids. They could get sick; they could get hurt. One of *us* could get hurt. He rode up and down the eastern coast of Florida looking for antibiotics after I was shot and found none until we got to the Keys.

We lucked out with this porn-obsessed drug dealer. Maybe he's one of the bodies in the mall, maybe he's a body somewhere else nearby, but wherever he is, he helped us. We'd be stupid not to keep what we can when he was planning to do the same.

"What happened to you?" Andrew asks.

It takes me by such surprise I don't know what to say. So to buy time, I ask, "What?"

He's studying my face as if it's a mask he's never seen before. "You aren't like this. You don't *do* this. You're kind, Jamie. You care about other people—you kiss stuffed animals to make them feel better, for

Christ's sake—so how can you just say these people—who are helping us, by the way—aren't important?"

"*You're* important. Cara's important, and Amy, and Henri-Two. The others and the kids, they're all important."

He sighs and looks over to the group of Nomads at the fire closest to us. Our group is on the other side, separate from everyone else.

"I get what you mean. But you would never have said this last spring when we first met. I was a stranger, and you gave me the antibiotics and pain meds you had in the cabin."

"I wasn't going to use them all myself."

"Exactly. And we aren't going to use all this." He holds out his hand to me. I stare at it for a moment, understanding exactly what he's doing but still not sure I agree. Finally I hand the pill bottle over to him. "We're doing the right thing," he says.

"Okay," I say.

I know what he means. Morally, yes, we are absolutely doing the right thing. But morality is a construct of civilized society, which doesn't exist anymore. Now we shoot each other over supplies or out of revenge.

In the cabin, it was easy to pretend we were still playing under the original moral rules of society. Then the people came—Howard and Raven and the group of others who showed up and demanded our supplies.

About an hour after Andrew gives the antibiotics to Dr. Jenn, Cal approaches our group. He says hello to everyone who is still awake, then kneels down next to me.

"Can I talk with you?"

I get up and follow him off to a quieter area of the dark parking lot. I can see half his face in the dim light of our fires.

"I heard you and a few others went into the distribution center and found supplies."

"Yeah. We gave Dr. Jenn all the medical stuff, but we couldn't find much food."

He nods. "I just wanted to say thanks for helping us out. I know you didn't need to, since you snuck in—"

"It wasn't—"

He shakes his head, holding up a hand to stop the lie. "It's okay, I get it. Things are tough and you're looking out for your people. And most of your people can't look out for themselves anyway. I'm saying thank you for real. What you did shows great leadership."

"I want to take a few more people into the mall tomorrow and do a full sweep," Cal continues. "Every square inch, for as long as it takes. I'm sure it's been mostly picked over by now, but you guys got lucky, so maybe we'll get lucky again."

"Okay."

"Ask your people if any of them want to join. We'll split everything we find based on our people. Sound good?"

That means they get more than we do, but they also have more storage space in the trucks and RVs. Also, they have more people to help search.

"Sounds good."

He holds out his hand and we shake on it.

ANDREW

THE NEXT DAY AROUND LUNCHTIME, THE NOMADS and Jamie and the others came out and said they hadn't found anything except for some leftover food. Then they went right back in to keep searching.

Waiting in this parking lot is driving me crazy. Fort Caroline or the Keys—or both—could be getting closer every day, and we still aren't moving toward our own goal of getting Amy and Henri-Two to Bethesda.

Or toward figuring out what Jamie and I are going to do. We could go back to the cabin, yes, but what about everyone else? We'd be leaving behind people we've grown to care about.

I'm starting to worry about Jamie. He's gotten so guarded and anxious.

He was shot by the same people who are actively hunting us now, so I get where that fear and paranoia come from. But it isn't like him. At least not like the Jamie I fell in love with. These people are helping us, so why wouldn't he want to share antibiotics with them? We know they're trustworthy—they didn't turn us in to Hickey and the others.

And they sought *us* out and decided to help us.

"Would you mind helping me distract her?" Daphne has Henri-Two in her arms while Amy is trying to take a nap. Henri-Two has been teething and it's keeping her up most of the night—and therefore also keeping Amy up. I've been up, too, but that has more to do with the pain in my arm than Henri-Two.

Taylor, who has been sitting quietly next to me with the Kid, gets up and grabs a blanket, laying it out beside me. I motion for Daphne to put Henri-Two down. The muscles in my shoulder aren't as sore as they were a few days ago, but there's no way I can pick up Henri-Two and hold her for long. If she tries to crawl away from me, I can snatch her back or call Daphne over for help.

Daphne sets her down on the blanket and goes to get teething toys. I try my best to distract Henri-Two with my good arm, hiding a wince as the muscles in my bad one radiate pain. I lie on my back, and she begins playfully batting at my face.

"Yeah, girl," I say. "I know we need to get back on the road, but how can we when I'm like this and you're up all night yelling at your mom that your teeth hurt?"

She makes a series of squeals in return.

"Great point."

"She's good at those." Daphne sits down with some toys and a handheld fan and starts fanning herself.

"You okay?"

"Just sore from sleeping on asphalt," she says. "And tired from the same."

"Ditto."

"Excuse me?"

I look up to see a thin girl with dark brown skin who looks to be about Cara's age—a couple of years older than Jamie and me. Next to her is a younger Black boy who looks like he's around the same age as Taylor. And also like he does *not* want to be here.

"Hey," I say.

"I'm Niki," she says. "This is my brother, Jamar." Jamar scolds Niki under his breath and she turns to glare at him. I should have seen the resemblance immediately. Niki's hair is shorter than Jamar's— Niki's cut as short as possible with scissors, while Jamar's looks like a grown-out fade he's stopped upkeep on—but they have the same nose, and Jamar's ears stick out slightly more than Niki's, hinting that she grew into hers like he'll one day grow into his.

Niki continues. "There aren't many kids in our group around Jamar's age . . ." She turns her attention to Taylor. "I was hoping the two of you could maybe hang out? If you want?"

Taylor looks at us, almost as if she's about to ask permission, but then realizes she doesn't need to and nods. "Sure." The Kid looks up at her as she stands.

"Want to hang with us, Kid?" I ask.

Jamar's eyes cloud and he says, "Uh . . ."

"Oh, no, not you." I point at the Kid. "His name is the Kid. Kid, meet Jamar."

"Hi," says the Kid.

Taylor starts to walk away, then turns back to see if Jamar is coming. He gives his sister one final embarrassed look of contempt before he and Taylor walk off to stand by a tree and talk.

"How about you?" I ask. "Want to hang with a baby, the Kid, an alligator attack victim, and a romance novelist? We're thinking about walking into a bar later, seeing what happens."

She laughs and sits down with us. I notice her nails are painted but chipped. The color is a pale lavender.

"I like your nails," I say.

"Thanks. I know it seems ridiculous, painting my nails in the apocalypse, but it's therapeutic. Gives me a chance to relax. And thanks for helping me with Jamar. I know he's embarrassed, but he really doesn't get to talk to people his own age much."

"Taylor either," I say. We go around the circle and introduce ourselves. "You been with the Nomads long?"

She shakes her head. "We ran into them back in Arkansas. Jamar and I were pretty much the only two people left in our hometown when they came through."

"What was your hometown called?" I ask.

"Garland City. It's near Texarkana."

"Was that before or after . . . whatever happened to everyone?" I nod in the direction of the medical tent, and Niki's mood darkens.

"Before."

"We don't have to talk about it, hon," Daphne says, "if you don't want to."

She shakes her head again. "I heard a little bit about what happened to you all with your settlement in the Keys." But not about Fort Caroline. I glance at Daphne to see if she's going to say anything, but she just keeps her eyes on Niki. "It sounds like . . . I don't know. It sounds wrong to say your group wasn't as bad as ours."

"It's true," I say. Although I big-time disagree with how they handled things, the Keys *were* trying to find a way to help everyone. I just think we could have figured out another way.

"The settlement was in Louisiana," Niki says. "It was some church pastor whose whole family survived the flu. He said it was divine intervention and meant they were chosen to lead. When we first got there, things were fine; he wasn't a big fire-and-brimstone preacher like back home. He seemed like a good Christian who genuinely wanted to help."

But again my eyes drift over to the medical tent. While I was there having my injuries looked at, I saw all the other injured Nomads. Many of whom were burned, which seems pretty fire-and-brimstone.

"Then one night he died. Passed away peacefully in his sleep—or so his son, Phillip, said. But Cal says his son had a pretty cohesive plan to take over when his father died, so he and a few others think the son killed him. That's when things got bad. Supplies started to go missing, and his family seemed to be fine while the rest of us were struggling to find food. Some folks tried to raid the supplies instead of waiting for our weekly ration—they were trying to feed kids—but when they got caught, Phillip . . ." Her eyes drift down to the Kid, who isn't looking at her, but she's smart enough to know that doesn't mean he isn't listening. She mouths the words "cut off their hands" and mimes it with her own in case we missed it.

"Jesus," I say as Daphne puts her hand to her mouth.

"If he found out people were criticizing him, he would. . ." Again she stops, because the Kid *is* looking at her now. I think I know where she was going, anyway. "Let's just say it was all very Old Testament.

Some people believed in him, but most didn't. The people who knew his father and had listened to him preach in church every Sunday said Phillip was nothing like his dad."

There's a long silence. Fort Caroline hadn't gone full-tilt theocracy when we met them, but it seems like they were on their way. A chill run downs my spine at the idea of Phillip teaming up with Danny Rosewood to become the postapocalyptic supervillains of my nightmares.

"Sorry," Niki says with a shy laugh. "This is why we don't usually talk about this stuff."

"It's okay," I say. "We know how it is. I mean, not exactly, but we know how hard things can be post-poc. And it seems like you have a good group of people now." I have no idea how they all came together or what happened to the people in the medical tent, but I'm sure whatever it is, Niki doesn't want to get into it. The way she brightens when I mention her group proves my point.

"Yeah, and it's kind of nice, being able to travel around. I always thought I'd be stuck in Arkansas my whole life, and now I've seen Louisiana, Mississippi, Alabama, Florida. Which, yeah, maybe doesn't sound that great, especially considering the world ended and it's not like we've seen *fun* things . . ." Her eyes go wide and she seems to catch herself. "Not that I think it's fun the world ended. Oh, now I'm rambling."

We laugh and Henri-Two starts crying. Niki points to her. "Do you mind?"

"Go for it," Daphne says, nodding.

Niki reaches over to pick her up. She walks in a circle, trying to shush her and talking in a high-pitched voice. It works for a bit, but then the cries come right back.

"She's probably hungry," Daphne says, then she looks at me. "Have you eaten yet today, sweetie?"

I wave my good hand at her. "Yes, stop." She rolls her eyes, but then I see them scouring the ground, looking for proof—a can or wrapper, which she won't find because I haven't eaten. With the pain, honestly, I'm just not hungry.

Niki stops walking in circles and nods in the direction of the mall. "Looks like they found something."

I turn to see a few people walking with boxes and plastic totes. Including Jamie, Cara, and Rocky Horror.

"I hope it's food." Amy appears from nowhere, probably called to us by the sound of her daughter. "She's hungry, and breast milk and a handful of chickpeas aren't doing it."

Again, guilt racks me. She chose to leave with us, and now she's struggling to take care of her baby. I know it isn't our fault that the Keys tried to trade Jamie for food and supplies, but I still feel responsible.

We have to keep moving. Even if it hurts.

"If it is food," I say, "I think we might want to talk about leaving."

Niki turns to us. "Are you okay to go?"

"It's my arm, not my leg this time, so it will suck, but yeah, I should be fine."

Taylor and Jamar make their way over to us and Taylor asks, "Did they find food?"

"Hopefully," Daphne says, again looking at me and telling me with those motherly eyes of hers that she knows I lied to her. And, Christ, it works, because I do feel guilty.

"Good," says Jamar. "'Cause I'm about to add starving to death to the list."

Niki looks at her brother. "We forgot to add alligator attacks."

Without skipping a beat, Jamar says, "I'm surviving the apocalypse and I'm worried about the superflu, thieves, guns, pneumonia, a broken back, Canada having to dip into the strategic maple syrup reserve, cannibals, traumatic brain injuries, ingrown toenails, getting a bad haircut, hearing the phrase 'it could be worse'"—that one I legit guffaw at—"appendicitis, Christian fascism, waterborne parasites, burns, and alligators."

"You lose!" Niki teases. "You forgot beestings and cashews."

"I'm not the one allergic to those things."

"But you still have to say it. Point for me."

"You should add lions to your list, too," I say as Jamie joins us. He, Cara, and Rocky Horror have set the totes down near the medical tent, where the Nomads are sorting through them. And, yes, it does look like there's food.

"Oh yeah," Taylor chimes in. "You gotta tell them that story, Andrew." She turns back to Jamar like this is a magical moment she's been waiting to talk to him about. "It's wild. Jamison took out, like, three lions single-handedly."

Jamie puts his lips to my ear and murmurs, "They're going to be disappointed when a pack of lions shows up and kills us all." Then he kisses right behind my ear, giving me chills. I lean my head on his shoulder and he holds me close. Even though it hurts my arm.

By dinner the following day, they've searched the whole mall. They did find food but no more medicine. They divvy it up evenly among everyone, and Daphne, Kelly, and Amy get the kids fed while Jamie and I split a can of condensed soup. Cara is over talking to Niki.

"How's your arm?" Jamie asks. It's probably the fifth time I've heard that question today from him alone.

I mumble loud enough for him to hear, "I'm surviving the apocalypse and I'm worried about bear traps, lions, and finding sleeping pills because I'm exhausted and I'll take all of them immediately."

After dinner, Dr. Jenn comes by during her rounds to check on my arm and distribute my evening antibiotic. She points the light strapped to her forehead at my wounds. Jamie, standing off to the side and attempting to give me privacy, obviously can't help himself because he keeps glancing over.

"Wounds look okay," she says. "Any discharge?"

"Only when we have canned beans."

She snorts and shakes her head. "Pus, Andrew. Thick and yellow. Burning? Signs of infection?"

"Not as much."

Jamie—again, can't help himself—turns and says, "Tell her about the pain."

"That isn't infection," I say. "Just a side effect of being mauled by a goddamn alligator like I'm a born and raised Floridian."

"No," Dr. Jenn says. "We Floridians know how to avoid gators."

"You'll have to give me some pointers next time I return to this state, which will be fucking never."

She gives me an amused look but shakes her head. "What pain?"

"It's like an . . . intense, sharp pain. Just goes up my arm and into my shoulder."

"He said it feels like being shocked," Jamie adds, taking the moment to come closer, giving up the ghost of pretending he doesn't want to be a helicopter boyfriend.

Dr. Jenn looks at my hand. She touches the tip of her finger to the tips of my still index and middle fingers. "Feel anything here?"

"No." I haven't felt anything from those fingers except pain. Only it isn't pain in the fingers so much as my arm and brain telling me there's pain there.

"Sounds like nerve damage," she says. "Probably from the trauma. Do you feel any burning or tingling here?" She points to the stitched-up wound between my middle and ring fingers.

"Only when I move them." I show her what I mean, wincing as my index and middle fingers stay still and the pinkie and ring fingers barely flex. It's weird to see those fingers not moving. Like they should—my brain is telling them to—but they just hang there.

Dr. Jenn sighs. "There isn't a lot we can do. Nerve repair was tricky even before the bug, but it's impossible now. The pain could go away on its own, or you'll learn to live with it. When you *can* move without pain, you should try to move the fingers yourself. Sometimes injuries like this can cause post-traumatic arthritis."

"Arthritis?" I look over to Jamie. "We need to get a lawn so I can sit on the porch and yell at kids to stay off it."

Dr. Jenn opens her bag and takes out a metal tin. "Sap. We don't have antibiotic ointment, but pine sap has antiseptic qualities. It's a little old, so maybe put it by the fire to loosen it up before you apply it for the night. But make sure it's not too hot."

"I'll just stick my fingers in and see how it feels," I say.

She frowns, not enjoying my joke, and leaves to check on the others who are injured. Jamie takes the tin from me and puts it by our small fire, then gently takes my arm to look at it.

"How bad is the pain today?"

"Four?" I say, apparently forgetting how to pronounce the word *nine*. It's still throbbing, and the nerves feel like lightning bolts are running through them. "How was shopping at the mall?"

"Good. I mean, we found the stash of food in the Bath and Body Works storeroom and also got some wonderful-smelling soap for you."

"Saltwater Breeze?"

"Watermelon Mojito."

"Aw, nuts."

Jamie takes the tin from the side of the fire and twists the top off. He shakes his head and takes a wooden tongue depressor out of the small, mostly empty first aid kit we have. He stirs the sap in the tin and pulls out a long string of it, twirling the wood around in his fingers to separate it.

I hold in a sharp inhale as he places the sap against the stitched wounds, but he still sees the flinch of the fingers that remain mobile.

"Sorry," he says. "I'll be careful."

"It's fine." I put my good hand on his knee and squeeze. But this is definitely unsexy. I lower my voice in case anyone nearby might be eavesdropping. "Well, my hand jobs are about to become a lot more creative."

Even in the firelight I can see his cheeks flush. "You're a righty."

"Hey! You're all righty, too!"

"I'm not laughing at these awful jokes just because you're injured."

"Whatever. I think I'm funny."

He looks into my eyes. "Fine, I'll admit it. I think you're . . . delightfully irreverent, God help me, I don't know why—"

"Bitch."

"But you don't *have* to be funny. Not about this. You're allowed to be sad and hurt and in pain."

"Well, yeah, I'm all that *and* funny."

He scowls as he puts away the tin and begins wrapping my arm with a fresh bandage. "You don't have to perform, then. You don't have to tell shitty jokes to me as if you need to act like you aren't hurt. I still love you, and you don't need to pretend around me."

Be vulnerable? Ew. What is this, a Scientology intake quiz?

But what would that look like? Being vulnerable—not the Scientology, because that's silly alien junk. Would it just be me crying to Jamie that I miss my fucking thumb? There are people in Niki's camp who had their whole hands cut *off* for trying to feed kids. And Kevin-the-monster's eye injury gives a whole new eye-for-an-eye vibe I hadn't picked up on before.

And I feel even worse about the next bit, because it's so idiotically clichéd, but I don't know what this injury means for our future together. Hand job jokes aside, what if when he doesn't need to take care of me anymore, and my injuries are just scar tissue and unending pain and post-traumatic arthritis, he's repulsed by my missing thumb and dead fingers? Even if he was, he wouldn't tell me.

All that is giving me constant anxiety, but more than anything, I'm joking because I don't want to say that the pain is so awful and so relentless that sometimes—despite *everything* we've survived—I'm not scared of dying anymore. Dying would at least mean no more pain. Now, what scares me the most is the pain not going away. What if it stays hovering at a nine out of ten for my whole life and I become a nasty, miserable person because of it?

That's why I'm trying to joke. Trying to be funny and make sure the people I love don't get annoyed that I'm cranky because I'm in endless, agonizing pain.

Bright and early the next morning, Cal and Kevin come over to our group with news. They want to get back on the road, but they want to invite us to stay with them. Jamie and I share a glance that says we need to discuss it as a group, because we haven't yet. But for today, Cal says, they're going on a supply run farther up the road.

"How much farther out are you going?" Cara asks.

"Today? Pretty much as far north as we can while still getting back before nightfall, or until we find gas, whichever comes first."

"I'll go," Jamie says. I turn to question him with my eyes, but he isn't looking at me.

"Me too," says Rocky Horror. "If for no other reason than I'm curious to see how you get the gas."

"I'll come, too," says Cara. Cal tells them to meet by the trucks in ten minutes, and the three of them get packing.

"Why are you going?" I ask Jamie. "We have to talk about whether we're going with them or not."

"We can discuss it when we get back. We'll need food either way, and we can hit up more places on the way if we're riding in a truck."

"All the food is in these distribution centers."

"Not all the food. There are still empty houses and maybe a few stores that might have something. Or maybe we'll find another distribution center. One that wasn't attacked."

"Can you just stay with us?" I ask.

"And do what? They're finished checking the mall, so what am I doing here that's useful? Babysitting the kids?"

Wow, managing to dig right into my own insecurities of being dumped off the boat and assigned orphan duty. And also kind of belittling that job. We're like a heteronormative married couple arguing about whether taking care of the kids *is* a job. I'd make a joke if I wasn't so pissed off.

"Fine," I say. "Go watch football with your friends. I'll stay here with the kids." It's the best I can do.

He gives me a confused look but doesn't say anything. Instead he dumps out his backpack onto our sleeping bags, then dumps out mine, too. "I'll be back." And without saying *I love you* or kissing me goodbye, he, Cara, and Rocky Horror head off for the trucks.

I'm surviving the apocalypse and I'm worried about bear traps, lions, alligators, Christofascists—oh my!—and the arguments between me and my boyfriend getting worse.

JAMISON

CARA, ROCKY HORROR, AND I RIDE IN the bed of one of the pickups with three others, as well as tubes and fuel equipment that reek of gasoline. The Nomads had already hit the first two gas stations we passed and said there was nothing there. We stop at the third, but it's also empty.

One of the Nomads shrugs. "Maybe a lot of Florida folks were trying to get out and go somewhere they weren't stockpilin' the supplies."

We continue driving, passing dust-covered cars pulled to the side of the road. Some people were nice enough to write "NO FUEL" in the dust.

I remember the time Andrew and I found a blue Civic that ran for three whole hours before the fuel ran out. It was beautiful. The day was hot and humid, but feeling the wind blowing around us while driving down a silent, empty highway was incredible. Now, the wind blowing around us in the back of the truck is a little chilly. It's winter, which means the days in Florida are in the low-to-mid sixties. We'll need to stop to get jackets and winter clothes soon if we keep going north to Maryland.

After another hour, Cal pulls into a small three-pump gas station. They peel off the bottle-cap-looking metal plates in the station lot and send one of the tubes down until it meets resistance.

Rocky Horror—having learned how the pump worked at the last stop—hooks up the hand pump while another Nomad puts a second tube coming out of the hand pump into a five-gallon gas can.

We listen, at first hearing only the wind whistling through the tube in the can.

Then what sounds like bubbling.

"We mighta got some here, boss," one of the guys says. And soon the gurgles grow louder and the sound of fuel splashes into the metal canister. We cheer, and even Cara looks excited.

"Okay," Cal says, pointing to Cara, Rocky Horror, and one of the Nomad men. "You three, stay here, fill up as many tanks as you can. Make sure the truck gets some, too."

Then he points at me and two other Nomads. "You three are with me; let's head into that town about a mile down the road and see what we can find."

We nod and I go back to the truck to grab Andrew's and my packs, as well as Rocky Horror's and Cara's.

"Once it's empty or the cans are full, come find us," Cal says.

And we head down the road on foot.

The town is Grand Lemfort, Florida, and the rusted and dusty sign welcoming us on the side of the road says it's home to the oldest living person in the Florida panhandle. Which—judging by the age of the sign—may not have been true even when the superflu hit.

There are no houses or buildings, but dead palm fronds rustle across the road, fallen from the trees on either side. Farther down, something moves, crossing from one side to the other. It's a gray fox. A skinny one that gives us a quick glance, then runs off into the overgrown grass on the left side of the road.

After about a half mile, we come to what looks like quaint downtown Grand Lemfort. There's a public library, a "multiuse" center that looks like a sad little empty storefront, and something called G&F Supermarket, where the word *supermarket* is doing a lot of heavy lifting.

It's a one-story peeling white shiplap building a little larger than the library, which itself looks no bigger than four rooms. The front door to G&F is dusty and unbroken, but around it—at about knee height—are scratch marks in the peeling paint. Probably the fox. If it was pawing around the door, maybe there's food in there.

"How about over there?" I ask Cal. He nods and we walk over. The doors are locked. "Maybe a back entrance?" I try.

But Cal takes the rifle off his shoulder and uses the butt to smash open the glass. He reaches through and unlocks the door.

The grocery store is warm and musty, and smells a bit rotten. The shelves are pretty empty but some still have items on them.

"Check the dry goods," Cal tells the others, then he turns to me. "Let's check out the canned stuff and also see if there's any more med supplies."

I go up an aisle with canned food, but most of the cans on the shelves have exploded, their contents splattered across the ceiling or spilling down the shelf and dried out. The ones that haven't exploded are bulging.

Cal nods, picking up a seemingly fine can, but its bottom sticks to the shelf, and whatever was inside has turned to a putrid brown sludge. "This was the issue in some of the desert states, too. Without

AC, this place probably gets to around a hundred by noon. Canned stuff spoils and explodes."

"Have you thought about heading north?" I ask. I'm sure there are still plenty of places there that didn't get so hot inside. At least I hope there are.

"We were thinking of heading that way next. You're all from the Keys, so it's not like there'd be anything down there for us to find."

We move over to the medical section and grab boxes of gauze, antibiotic ointment, painkillers, and bandages. There are also several bottles of multivitamins and chewable kids' vitamins—all the gummy vitamins have melted into one large blob at the bottom of the plastic bottle.

"Yeah," I say, trying to avoid talking too much about the Keys. "And I heard a bit about your last settlement. I'm sorry." Andrew told me what happened with them, but he said he didn't think he had the whole story. He also reminded me to be careful with what I said about the Keys around the Nomads. We don't need any more people trying to turn us over to Fort Caroline.

Cal doesn't say anything as he stares at the almost-empty fridges lining the wall. The milk section is empty—thankfully. I'm not sure I'd want to smell rotten, exploded milk. But some of the soft drinks and cheeses are still there. The cheeses are a beautiful shade of fuzzy blue green.

"Let's check if there's a basement," he says, nodding to the back of the store. I follow him as he calls out to the others, "How's it going over there?"

"Got some pasta that's not ruined," says a woman whose name I haven't gotten yet. "And there's some nuts and cookies."

Cal pushes the back door open, and I take the flashlight from my bag. It's a battery-less flashlight that has a little hand pump on it, so I pump it to give it some juice. It's dim, but it does the job. There are various sizes of cardboard boxes stacked up against a wall.

"More back here!" Cal yells back.

"Heard!" comes a reply.

But some of the boxes have little holes eaten through them on the bottom. Which isn't surprising considering the small brown droppings and crumbs all over the back room. Mice or rats. Possibly squirrels. But the poor fox wasn't able to get in. Maybe it just waited for all the other rodents to fatten themselves up before eating them. At least now with the door smashed open, they can have all the pantry-moth-eaten food their little heart desires.

There's a rusty metal tread plate door in the middle of the back room next to a desk stacked with order forms and invoices. Cal leans down and pulls on the metal handle. The hinges squeal and rust flakes off.

A set of steep wooden stairs leads down to a damp-smelling basement. I look back at the boxes against the wall behind us. I don't see why someone would carry heavy boxes down these basement stairs if they were using the back room as storage. And it's not like this town has many options for "supermarkets," so I'd assume the owner knew exactly what kind of food to order and how much per week.

Still, I follow as Cal leads the way.

The basement is pitch-black and the rotten scent gets stronger. I shiver at the familiar sweet, putrid smell. There's something dead down here. My chest tightens, and I'd sprint back up the stairs if my legs could move, but they can't. The light in my hand dims and blood pumps through my ears in a cacophonous whoosh.

"More light, Jamie," Cal says. It shakes me from my paralysis, and I pump the light, trying to focus on that instead of on the dark around me. Or on the imaginary skeletons lurking in the dark, the people, the animals, or any other things that are waiting to scurry across my feet or graze the back of my neck.

I realize I'm still pumping the flashlight but it's not getting any brighter.

Cal is looking at me. "You okay?"

"Yeah. Claustrophobic," I say, which isn't entirely a lie. I'm scared of the dark *and* claustrophobic. The dark is less of an issue when I'm outside, but even if I have to pee at night, I won't go far from the fire. And if the fire is too low, I'll hold it till morning.

"Let me distract you, then," he says, turning back into the basement and waving away the spiderwebs refracting the LED light in the dark. "Do you think you'll all come along with us tomorrow?"

That is a good distraction, actually. Because I want to vote no, but I'm not sure how Andrew will feel about it. Yes, these people have been helpful, and they seem trustworthy. If they're not, I shouldn't be following Cal into a dark basement in middle-of-nowhere Florida. But my plan is still to get Amy and Henri-Two back to Henri in Bethesda and then go to the cabin with Andrew, though I'm not sure he'll leave everyone else. If we could convince them all to go with the Nomads, then maybe me, Cara, Andrew, Amy, and Henri-Two can continue on our own. It would be easier, just the four of us taking turns holding Henri-Two. We wouldn't have to find as much food, stop as much, rest for as long.

And if we find antibiotics and food, we can prioritize ourselves. But I'll be honest, I will miss a few of the others—specifically Daphne, Taylor, and the Kid.

I know it's the best solution for us. I just don't think Andrew will go for it.

"I'm not sure," I say. And the distraction kind of works because now I'm not freaking out about the dark, I'm freaking out about Andrew and me and trying to figure out what's next for us.

"Holy shit," Cal says. I focus the flashlight to his right. There's a ceiling-high shelf that goes all the way toward the front of the store, and on the left is another similar line of shelves, creating an aisle. They're all filled with non-exploded canned food. The basement is damp and a lot cooler than upstairs. It must not have gotten as hot through the warm summer months.

Though I still don't get why they'd stock shelves down here instead of keeping the cans in boxes in the back room.

Cal calls up the rickety stairs, "Hey! Get down here and turn on your flashlights!"

I'm checking out the cans on the shelves when the others come down, flicking on their lights. The extra light makes me feel a little more comforted. Everyone whoops in excitement and starts to load up their bags.

"Get a couple boxes we can fill and put in the truck," Cal tells one of them. "We'll take what we can today, then we'll come back with the whole crew tomorrow and empty the place."

If we split off from them, they'd come back without us. I put my bags down at the end of the row that's toward the front of the store and start loading up. But the flashlight reflects off something metallic on the other side of the shelf. I shine the light in and see another room. More food maybe. But then that sweet, rotten smell reminds me there's something else down here. A body or some animal that came down here and died.

My imagination runs wild with every possible thing that could be in that room. A rabid dog, foaming at the mouth and hiding in the shadows, waiting for the right moment to pounce. Thousands of rats cramped together and tangled into a giant, rotten rat king. A shallow eel pit that's filled with cannibalistic eels hoping for something else to eat.

Around the corner is a small plywood wall with a makeshift pressboard door on old hinges. Slowly I pull it open, pointing my flashlight at the ground in case anything crawls out. But nothing does. When I step inside, the smell of rot grows much stronger.

I point the flashlight to my left and let out a startled cry.

The others call out to me, asking if I'm okay.

"Yeah."

It's no eel pit. There's a metal cot in this room. The body on it has probably been dead for well over a year, and all that's left is bone, dried tissue, and clothes. Cal appears in the doorway, along with the woman. She points the flashlight at the body, and I can see it's curled up in the fetal position. There are dried, oily stains on the cot and basement floor next to some opened canned food.

A flu victim. They probably shut themselves down here as soon as they heard about the superflu, thinking they could ride it out as long as they didn't have contact with anyone. But that clearly wasn't the case. The way it infected people, it didn't matter how secluded you were. If you weren't immune, you got it.

"Jesus Christ." Cal points the flashlight at the far wall. There are about nine military-style automatic rifles hung on the walls. All of them framing a dusty, weatherworn Nazi flag.

"Finally, we have proof of the flu doing something right in the world," one of the Nomads says. "Adios, Nazi."

It feels weird seeing a Nazi flag in person. And it doesn't make my chest feel any less tight.

Though it does make me feel better about taking his food.

Under the flag is a wall-length built-in with drawers and cabinets. I go over to it, expecting to find Nazi memorabilia or the blueprints to the US Capitol, but instead it contains boxes and boxes of ammo for each of the guns on the wall. The cabinets in the center have more drawers, which house handguns in foam padding.

Cal joins me and takes a box of bullets for his handgun. There are a few boxes that have shells for the rifle I left back at the camp, so I take one of those, too.

Then Cal rips down the Nazi flag and tosses it into the corner.

"Come on," he says. His voice has an icy edge to it now. "Let's pack up some of the food. We can come back for more ammo and the guns."

I nod, but even taking the rifle shells from that room feels weird. I try to push the thought away and go back to stocking the bags with canned food and freeze-dried MREs from the shelves.

Rocky Horror and Cara show up about fifteen minutes later, and by the time their bags are full like mine, they're so heavy I have to

175

leave one down by the steps while I carry the other two out front. Cal comes back with me to get the last bag.

"The settlement you left," he says. "What made you leave them?"

I stop mid-reach for the bag at my feet. I don't know how much I should tell him. Their group seems to have chosen him to be their leader—although he does discuss major decisions with the others. While we were in the mall, he listened to other people and took their thoughts into consideration. And when someone had better ideas, he stepped back and let them take over. Still, if the Nomads have a leader, it's him.

And if we tell him the truth, that there's a settlement out there that's willing to pay for me, he might choose to turn me in. Or go back to his people and take a vote.

"The hurricane," I say. "We were at a loss for supplies and thought the road would be better for us."

"Why did the others follow you?" he asks. "Why hold you all at gunpoint and use up food and gas to come after you? And us when we drove past?"

It feels like he's been waiting to ask this question since we met. I hate lying. Every time I do it, I feel awkward and stumble over my words. But this time when I do it, everything comes out easily. Because it's not entirely a lie, it's omission and avoidance.

"We've dealt with dangerous people like you have. Ours weren't religious, but they wanted to control everyone anyway. They tried to kill me and my boyfriend, Andrew."

"With the arm injury?"

"Yes." I pull the bag up and shut the door.

"Why?"

I shrug. "Maybe they didn't like who we are." It feels like I should be telling Cal the truth, but that didn't help us in the Keys. Still, there's something trustworthy about him, like he wouldn't turn against us if given the chance. I never thought that about the Keys, but I almost do about him.

Almost.

I stop as I reach for the door back into the market. "Can I ask you something?"

"Go for it."

"What happened with your pastor? Is he still out there?"

His mood darkens more as he shakes his head. "No, he's dead. His followers, the ones who didn't fight us when we tried to take back the settlement, are probably out there somewhere. Or maybe not. Maybe they didn't figure out how to survive without their pastor telling them how to live. And we were all starving by that point, so who knows if they found food and safety. But the rest of us stuck together."

"How did he die?"

He looks at me like I should already know that, and I do, but I still want him to say it. "We killed him, Jamie. We knew how dangerous he was, so we took him out. Some people believe that makes him a martyr, but we knew we couldn't survive as long as he was still around."

"Did it make you feel bad? Killing him? Or do you feel better, I guess?"

And finally there's something that crosses his face that I can't read. Over the past few days of working with him and the other Nomads looking for supplies in the mall, I've learned how expressive Cal's face is. The way his forehead wrinkles when he's frustrated or thinking about something and the crow's-feet around his eyes grow deeper, but this is something that I've never seen.

"There's a lot in my life from the before times that sometimes keeps me up at night. Are you religious at all?"

"No." My mom raised me with the most basic religious beliefs— mainly what she was raised with. But she was brought up Catholic and said she didn't want to force me to think the same way. When I was seven, I asked why we didn't go to church and her answer was simple: "Because I got sick of tithing my own money to a church that makes women take vows of poverty while the priest is driving around town in a brand-new Cadillac." Through the years I've become more of a spiritual agnostic.

"How about some kind of higher power, everything happening for a reason?"

"What reason would justify killing off seven billion people in a matter of months? Not to mention those who've died in the fallout. The people who are sick or get injured in some kind of accident and don't have doctors anymore. The Americans who are outnumbered by guns by about ten thousand to one now. Why does everything have to have a purpose? Why can't the superflu just be a random oops, where that one patient-zero bird was supposed to fly into a window but didn't? The universe was created by accident, so why can't it end the same way?"

He laughs, and I realize how riled up that got me, though I'm not sure why. But he's nodding. "Yeah, I guess you have a point. But maybe some of those random moments have reason. Like a universal convergence, where all the right moments happen at all the right points in time. And just for a split second, things make sense. The bird realizing at the last moment it was about to fly into a window. It doesn't make sense to us because humans, and the bird, all died. But viruses are living things, too, so in that moment, everything converged to make it survive and spread."

All this has gotten a little too cerebral for me. I'm sure Andrew wouldn't mind having this conversation with Cal, but I don't know how we got here from talking about his Christofascist settlement. I shrug. "Okay."

"What I'm saying, Jamie, is not everything is going to make sense. And maybe not everything we do in life is something to feel good about, but sometimes—yes, even those maybe-random moments— things converge and it makes sense. But not for everyone."

Like his fascist pastor's death. It didn't make sense for Pastor Phillip, but it made sense for everyone else here, still alive.

That's how I was feeling after I shot Harvey Rosewood. There was guilt because I never wanted to hurt anyone. I never *want* to hurt anyone. But I would kill Harvey again if I needed to. To protect Andrew, I'd do it.

Over the past few months I've also thought about Danny Rosewood, and how his death would be the easiest thing for us. The more I thought about it, the easier that thought came. My stomach no longer turned; the guilt in my chest wasn't there. The thought was like a splinter embedded too deep in my finger; the skin healed over it and it became a part of me.

"Pastor Phillip liked to use that Bible passage about the meek inheriting the earth. Could be, the meek outnumber the others. And maybe now, without the structure of society, we're all learning how to fight back. If those random moments converge again—and honestly, it seems like with a smaller population left, it's happening a whole lot more—there's strength in numbers. Especially if the randomness of the world lets people like Pastor Phillip survive the flu. Or the people coming after you."

I absolutely clock that he's using the present tense. Maybe my gut is right, and he can be trusted. Still, he said there's plenty for him to feel guilty about from the before times. Maybe it's stupid stuff like shoplifting or lying to someone he loved. But it could be more.

"What do you still feel guilty about? From before, I mean."

"Next universal convergence," he says. "If you're still with us, remind me to tell you."

That doesn't make me feel great. Cal pushes open the door to the back room, and I follow him out to the truck, hopping in next to Cara and Rocky Horror.

As we drive out of town, I see the gray fox again, lying low in the high grass on the side of the road. I feel Cara's eyes on me and turn. She gives me an arched eyebrow, asking if I'm good, and I nod. But I can't help but think about her family. How they all survived the superflu only to die in some mysterious fire she escaped. Maybe that was another random convergence. One that involved others who sought to hurt. Once we're on the highway again, the wind is too loud to talk over, so I'm able to think about what Cal said.

We're all learning how to fight back. And maybe that's what we need to do. I'll always fight for Andrew; we just need to find other people who are willing to fight for us, too.

ANDREW

JAMIE, CARA, AND ROCKY HORROR COME BACK with plenty of food for all of us, and they said there's even more about an hour and a half drive up the road. Which is great news, because an hour and a half drive is probably about a day and a half walking. And there's apparently more food than even the Nomads can carry, so even if we don't leave with them, we can stop there and replenish some of the food we eat.

But we still need to figure that part out.

Shortly after dinner, while Jamie is off using nature's facilities, Rocky Horror sits down next to me.

"Cute nails," he says.

I hold up my right hand, where the nails have been painted a vibrant blue. "Thanks, Niki did them for me." She even painted the two fingers on my left hand that weren't wrapped. I turn to show them off in the sling my injured arm is resting in.

"How's the arm feeling?"

I know I can be honest with him. "Like shit."

"Yeah, I can tell 'cause of the cuntyness."

"I didn't say anything."

"You didn't have to. I heard you snap at Jamie earlier today—"

"I didn't snap at him."

"And most of it's readable on your face."

"It's not cuntyness you're reading, it's pain. Annoyance with pain. Like unending, throbbing pain that doesn't go away no matter how much I try to ignore it, or breathe through it, or I don't know what else."

I don't have to hide it all from Rocky Horror like I do with Jamie. It's kind of freeing. When Jamie asks how I am, I lie and say *fine* because he always wants to help. I love that about him, truly. But when nothing can be helped, he tries anyway, and that can make it worse. I'm in pain—so much goddamned pain—I'm tired, I'm hungry, and I'm just so sad. That's it. None of the big words are big enough to express how I feel. Sad is the only one that feels right. We lost our home for the second time since the apocalypse, and now our only option is to either go back to the original one and hope we can strike a deal with the people there, who expect us to pay them food taxes to stay, or join up with the Nomads and make the road our home until we end up wherever they decide to put down roots. Which just feels exhausting.

Rocky Horror nods. "I get it. This part sucks."

"It's my own fault for getting comfortable in the Keys. Should have known things would get dangerous again."

He scoffs. "Honey. Being queer is inherently dangerous. Even before the era of teotwawki. Just living our lives was dangerous. There's the obvious, like heading out into the dead of night to hook up with a headless torso you've only spoken to on apps who may or may not be a serial killer—or worse, a catfish!"

"The catfish is worse?"

"I always saw myself as the Sidney Prescott type. I can survive a serial killer."

"Of course."

"But then there was just walking down the street. Using a bathroom. Going to spaces specifically made for us only for an idiot with a gun to decide he's been tasked by God to cleanse the gays from the world. It only got worse for *everyone* when the world ended. And now we're all on a . . . I guess only slightly more even playing field."

I nod and look back at the Nomads, celebrating their scavenging finds for the day. That's what I've been trying to impart on Jamie lately. We're all on the same playing field, and maybe that means helping each other out and trying to win the game. Or whatever, I don't know—Jamie can figure out the sports metaphor.

"What's your vote?" I ask Rocky Horror. "Do we continue with the Nomads or go on our own?"

"Nomads. Safety in numbers. You?"

I nod. That's how I felt before on the Keys, only it didn't work out for us. But maybe the Nomads will be different. And if they have food and supplies, they could help keep us safe and get us to Maryland faster.

"I think you might be right."

He leaves and goes over to Cara, probably to gauge her thoughts before our impending vote. Daphne and Kelly are with the kids, trying to tire them out for bedtime. Amy is chasing a crawling Henri-Two around in circles on a blanket, making her laugh and squeal. I finally have a quiet moment to close my eyes.

I'm so tired. Trying to sleep while the nerves in my arm are firing lightning bolts of pain is damn near impossible, but I could probably fall asleep in seconds right now.

Even with my eyes closed I know when Jamie returns and sits next to me. His steps are quiet, but it feels like the air has been disturbed around us. I can also smell the gasoline on him still.

"You okay?" he asks.

"Yes," I lie. "Just tired." It's not as bad if I follow it up with the truth, right?

Once the kids are asleep—minus Taylor, who now gets to vote with us—we talk about our options.

"Do we know what their plan is?" Amy asks.

"Rocky Horror and I spoke to one of the guys this afternoon," says Cara. "They're heading north. They had similar issues with supplies in the red states."

"The hot states, too," Jamie adds. "Without AC, the canned food spoils at over ninety degrees."

"North means winter weather," Daphne says. But we're only in sweatshirts and jackets right now. The Florida days are in the sixties, but nighttime drops to the low fifties or the high forties.

Rocky Horror raises his hand. "I'm just leading with a yes. Let's go with them. There's strength in numbers, and so far we've been here for a few days and the Keys haven't caught up with us. These people have vehicles, fuel, and food, and if we need to, we can get away from the Keys and Fort Caroline faster with them than we can if we're on foot with seven kids." He looks at Taylor. "Sorry, six and a half kids."

Taylor rolls her eyes. But it's hard to argue with Rocky Horror's logic.

"Does anyone have any cons to counter Rocky Horror's pros?" Kelly asks.

I turn to Jamie, expecting him to remind us that these people are strangers. He didn't trust the people in the Keys and always had one foot out the door, so he has to be feeling similar about the Nomads.

But he just looks back at me, then around the circle.

Seriously? Nothing?

"They're nomads," Cara says. "They don't have any idea where they're going other than north. I know when we set out from the Keys we had a similar idea, but Amy, I don't think your mom is able to accept fifteen people into her home. So maybe we need to talk about what the plan is for all of us, too."

"Jamie and I were talking about that," I say, jumping in. "The way Trevor made it sound, they could tell Fort Caroline we're heading to Bethesda. Cara, you lived in Maryland. We were thinking maybe once we get to Henri, we get her to leave with us for a bit, maybe head somewhere else in Maryland farther from Bethesda. We camp out and wait there." I turn to Amy. "Then when it's safe, you can all go back home. Maybe we stay close by?"

But when I look to Jamie, he doesn't seem to agree with the last part. Cara doesn't answer me, either. She keeps her gaze on the ground in front of her, lost in her own thoughts. After about forty seconds of silence, Rocky Horror speaks again.

"That is something we can figure out in Bethesda. Right now, let's keep the question to 'Are we joining up with the Nomads?'"

"Well," says Daphne, rubbing at her shoulder, "I for one would love to be off the road. But we do need to discuss the rest soon. I'm okay traveling around with the Nomads for a bit, but it's not ideal for the kids. They've lost everyone they know. They need structure and stability."

That's true. We have to find a place for the kids first. Again, my mind goes to the poor kids who died in the hurricane. The guilt I still feel for not helping Liz get them to safety before the gym collapsed.

"Daphne's right," I say. "We have to make the kids a priority."

"What if we find another settlement?" Taylor asks. "If the Keys weren't safe, maybe another settlement nearby will be."

I glance at Jamie. We never told Taylor everything about Fort Caroline.

"We can also ask some of the Nomads if they want to *make* a settlement," Taylor adds. I know she's especially talking about Jamar, who she's grown close to over the last few days. She also very clearly doesn't know how much work would be involved in such a thing. Like us, by the time she showed up in the Keys, most of the hardest work had already been done.

Daphne reaches out and rubs Taylor's shoulder in a motherly way. "I love that idea, hon. But it's hard to start something from scratch. Maybe your idea of finding another settlement is better."

We discuss back and forth for almost two hours until we've started repeating ourselves and Rocky Horror finally calls for a vote.

"Let's make this a quick one," he says. "All in favor of taking on the nomadic lifestyle, raise your hands."

Kelly's, Taylor's, and Rocky Horror's hands go up instantly. Amy's follows shortly after. I look over at Jamie. He seems to be wavering back and forth like I am. Then he gives me a slight nod and raises his hand.

That's all it takes for me to make my decision, and my heart feels a little lighter. Jamie was trying so hard to distance himself from the people in the Keys—the people sitting by this fire, even—but he's willing to risk it now. Maybe he's turning a corner and allowing himself to have some hope.

Cara and Daphne are the only holdouts, but as soon as I raise my hand, Cara's goes up, too. Though she looks less sure than I feel.

Daphne rolls her shoulders and head, touching her sore arm before finally raising it as well.

"Okay," Rocky Horror says. "We'll head out with them tomorrow."

"We're going to have to find another vehicle," Cara says. "We can all fit in the RVs with the others at first, but it's going to be too cramped to stay like that for long."

"We'll find one on the road," Kelly says. "Maybe a school bus."

With our decision made, we turn in for the night. Jamie and I make the unspoken decision to sleep a little farther from the others than we usually do. Maybe there's more to discuss, but I'm worried he's trying to unpack whether we made the right decision. Something I don't want to talk about. He attaches his sleeping bag to mine and pulls me close against him. Not even the pain in my arm and hand is enough to distract me from how good it feels to be next to him.

To feel him next to me. Feel his hands on me.

"How is your arm?" he whispers as one of his legs wraps around mine and pulls me tighter against him. I've noticed his hands not touching it. His fingers graze up my thigh, hip, side, shoulder, then just float over my injured arm before finding somewhere else to land.

"Fine," I say. It still hurts, but I have no intention of whining about the pain. At least my leg aches from the rain have gotten noticeably less annoying. Jesus, I'm a mess. I have to stop injuring myself.

"Are you sure?"

I kiss him, biting at his lip. "Yes." I use my other hand to prove the point and he buries his face against my neck to smother his gasp. He rakes his teeth against my skin but then gently takes my injured arm, and the pain is sharp and instant. I suck air through my clenched teeth. He leans away from me as I clutch my arm to my chest.

"I'm sorry, are you okay?"

"Yes," I whisper, but the pain has taken me out of the moment. "It's fine, don't worry about it."

He scoffs and puts his hands to my cheeks. "I'm always going to worry about you."

"That's very sweet, but I'd rather you worry about this." I slip my good hand back into his underwear, but he grips my wrist.

"Hold on. You don't have to pretend you're okay if you aren't."

"Why not? I'm so good at it!" I try to kiss him, but he pulls away.

"No, you aren't. I can tell when you're lying, remember? And I spent several weeks with you after you stepped in a bear trap. I know what your face looks like when you're in pain."

"Talking about it doesn't help."

"It can."

"No! It can't. It's not psychological trauma, it's physical. Focusing on it makes it worse. You asking me over and over and over makes it fucking worse, because you can't do anything about it but you try, and it gets annoying very quickly."

Even in the dark I can see the surprise on his face.

Shit. I shouldn't have said the last part. Why did I say that?

"I don't mean it's annoying," I say, even though I do. It's annoying because *I'm* frustrated that he wants so badly to do something but can't. But I also don't want to talk about it *because* he can't. I know it's coming from a place of love when he asks me, and I absolutely love him for that when I think about it, but in the moment, yeah. It's annoying. Especially right now, when all I want to do is *not* focus on the pain and just enjoy being with him.

"It's okay," he says, but I can hear the hurt in his voice.

"I'm sorry," I say. "I'm a cynical bitch, but I don't mean that *you* annoy me. It's the pain and I'm taking it out on you." I kiss his lips. He kisses back, but it seems like an afterthought.

"You don't have to be a cynical bitch with me. You can be a regular bitch and I'll still love you."

"You say that now, but, girl, just so you know—"

"Andrew." His tone sounds like a warning. Like he wants me to stop joking around and be serious.

My cheeks burn and I feel guilty again. Silly, even. My boyfriend is scolding me like I'm a child. "It's a defense mechanism."

"I know it is." He runs his fingers up my back. "You don't need your defenses up around me."

"Everyone needs their defenses up these days." What the hell is wrong with me? "That was a joke, too. I'm sorry I can't stop."

"Try." He sounds serious now.

I don't know what to say. I know I don't need to be defensive around him, but every day there's more danger and despair and it feels like there's no end in sight. Rocky Horror even said it—being queer is inherently dangerous, but so is the world now. For everyone. Is this how our lives are going to be now? Tiny moments of joy and then awfulness the rest of the time?

Because if it is, yes, I do need my defense mechanism. I need to be a cynical bitch who can laugh because otherwise I'll go insane.

I put my forehead against Jamie's, and even though my injured arm still hurts, I hold it against him. He's going through the same things I am, but I don't want to be a helpless, miserable shell—which is what I'll become if I can't joke about what scares me.

"Just talk to me," Jamie says. He kisses me, and I realize silent tears are dripping from my nose. "And if I'm annoying you, then tell me, just don't make it a joke."

"You aren't annoying me." I sigh, but it turns into a sob. "And my arm hurts. So fucking bad. All the time it hurts, and it feels like it's never going to stop. I'm so tired."

He pulls me against his chest, squeezing me firmly but gently. It's not just my arm that hurts. It's everything. Every day. I'm so tired of being scared all the time. And I think he understands that—of course he does—because he whispers in my ear. "I know. I am, too. But we'll be okay." He repeats it over and over. And his whispers are the last things I hear before I finally fall asleep.

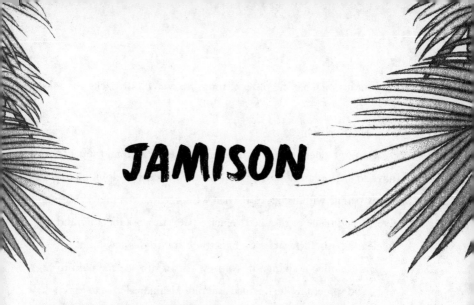

JAMISON

THE PAST THREE DAYS HAVE BEEN THE easiest we've had since . . . honestly, I can't remember when. Maybe since my first day out of the hospital in the Keys. Andrew and I spent that day walking around our neighborhood, meeting new people—it was the day we met Daphne because she had to be the first one to gossip about us to everyone. Cara kept to herself most of the day, but the three of us had dinner on the dock behind our house.

It was the first day since my mom had died that I felt hopeful.

Really hopeful. Not just wishing for something good to happen, but actually having good things happen to us—like it was a bridge being built before our eyes. On the other side of that bridge was supposed to be comfort and safety, but the longer we were there, the more I realized both sides were the same.

It's not that the Nomads are trustworthy—I think this is just how we live our lives now, with hesitation and caution. I trust them as much as I trusted the people back at the Keys. They're just trying to survive, like us, and they're going to do what they need to do. But it's nice having others around to watch our backs—at least for a while.

Also the driving.

Gasoline doesn't burn as efficiently when it's old and stale, so we have to stop a lot more often to find fuel. It's also helpful having so many people with us because when we come to a roadblock—like an overturned truck or disabled vehicle—we can work together and try to clear a path. Otherwise we backtrack and find a new road.

I also notice a change in Andrew. I can still see the pain in his eyes, and sometimes he'll wince and pull his injured arm to his chest, but he's calmer now. Once we've passed the sign welcoming us to South Carolina—"The Palmetto State"—he seems to relax a bit. And maybe I do, too.

We're taking the day off from travel so Rocky Horror and a few others can go out in search of fuel. We still haven't found another vehicle, so we've been pretty cramped in the two RVs. It also doesn't help that for the past two days it's been raining, and Rocky Horror, Andrew, a few others, and I have been traveling in the beds of the pickup trucks. There were ponchos and tarps for us to huddle under, but it's been getting chillier as we've headed north.

"The kids need some warm clothes, too," Daphne says. She's winded from chasing around Henri-Two and one of the other kids. The rest are playing with the Nomad kids—except for the Kid, who's by himself with his stuffed hippo.

"The next town over might have a department store," Cara says. She's by one of the tents set up under an overhang. We stopped for the night in an amusement park parking lot because there are large, flat metal awnings over some of the parking spots at the back of the lot. There's also a picnic area.

Cara gets out her road atlas to find our location and start mapping a route. Andrew is next to her, lying on the ground with his eyes closed.

"We can go check it out," I say. "There might be some stuff we can use. Maybe they'll let us take the other truck."

Behind me I hear a snort. "Definitely not."

Niki joins us. She and Jamar have been hanging with us a lot.

"They're a little worried about gas," she continues. "There's no way they're going to let you borrow a truck when they aren't sure if there's any gas around."

"Cara, how far is it?" I ask.

She stares at the road atlas a little longer, then glances up at me. "Maybe five miles?"

The sky is overcast, but it's still early afternoon. If we leave now, we can probably get into town, find a clothing store, and still get back a little after sunset. "Not too bad. Niki, you want to come along?"

She turns, looking at the groups of kids playing in the parking lot, probably trying to find her brother, who absolutely ran off with Taylor again. It was especially hard to tell the kids to stay away from the amusement park—Palmetto Park and Splash World Resort—so they made sure to station a few people in front of the park gates to keep them from trying to find a way in.

"I don't know," she says. "Do y'all know where Jamar and Taylor are?"

"They're out by the road," Andrew says without opening his eyes.

I thought he was sleeping. "I saw them walk that way about twenty minutes ago."

"Thanks. I'll walk that way with you all, but I think I'll pass on the trip to town."

I grab our bags and dump the contents into my sleeping bag. Andrew sits up. His arm is still wrapped in gauze, and he keeps it in the sling despite claiming his shoulder doesn't hurt anymore. He holds out his good arm for the backpack.

"Stay here and rest," I say.

"I'm rested," he says. "I'd rather get in some walking. This driving in the apocalypse shit is for the birds."

"The birds are dead, sweetie. Resting, like you ought to be."

"Then resting is for the birds, too. Tell him to let me come with you, Cara."

"Talking to either of you is for the birds," she says.

"Birds don't talk," Andrew says, snatching the backpack from me with a little too much gusto. He flinches and I can tell it hurt his arm.

"Parrots do," Niki says.

Cara puts away the atlas and joins us. "Parrots are smarter, too." She pushes past me and heads toward the parking lot entrance. Niki and I laugh as Andrew acts indignant.

"You know, I am injured. You should be nicer to me."

"I didn't tell you to stick your hand in an alligator's mouth," Cara calls back. "Even parrots know not to do that."

I wrap my arm around Andrew and kiss his temple as he humphs.

We find Taylor and Jamar sitting on a metal guardrail next to the road.

"Hey, guys," Niki calls out. "Can you come back up to camp where we can see you?"

Taylor stands, but Jamar turns to look at his sister. "Why?"

"Because I asked you to."

"That's not a good reason, Niki."

"It's fine," Taylor says.

But Jamar ignores her and addresses his sister. "We aren't doing anything."

"Then you can do nothing where I can see you better."

"Why? You think a stranger's going to roll up in his white van and offer us some candy?"

Andrew leans closer to me and lowers his voice. "I mean, it *is* the apocalypse. If that happened, I'd one thousand percent take the candy. Especially if it was Sour Patch Kids."

"We're not going to argue about this," Niki says, crossing her arms. "Now get to camp. Both of you."

Jamar finally stands, and Taylor moves to walk to the camp with him, but he puts his arm out in front of her. "No."

"Jamar."

"Nikita."

The siblings stare at each other, neither blinking nor backing down. I'm curious to know if this is what Andrew and his younger sister were like. From the few stories he's told me about his life before the end of the world, it seems very similar. Only maybe his younger sister was the one who was telling him what to do.

"I'm not going to talk about this anymore," Niki says. "Get over to the camp or else."

"Or else what? You gonna ground me? Take away my phone? Go figure out a better way to feel important and stop making me your project."

Even Taylor seems shocked by his words. I can't see Niki's face, but I do see her start in surprise. She takes two strides toward him but stops. Jamar holds his ground and so does she. Then finally she turns around and looks at us. Her face is unreadable.

"Fine. I'm coming to town with you all," she says.

"More the merrier," says Andrew.

"Do you want to grab your bag?" Cara asks.

She shakes her head. "Nope. Let's go."

"I'm coming, too," Taylor says. She gives Jamar a look, and I didn't have a younger sister like Andrew, but I recognize it immediately.

"Wait," Jamar says. "Why are you going?"

"Because you were rude to your sister," Taylor says. "She just wanted to make sure you were okay and that she knew where you were, and you were rude. And I'm not in the mood to hang out with you when you're being rude." She walks around Jamar—whose face has dropped in confusion and shock—and follows Cara.

"Fine," Jamar says. "I'll come with you all."

"No," Taylor says, looking back. "You can stay here. With the kids."

Niki smiles and turns back to her brother. She points at him. "Grounded."

Then she follows Cara and Taylor. Jamar gives Andrew and me one last look of desperation, his eyes begging us to do something. Andrew manages to shrug with just his right arm and shoulder, and we follow the others.

Once we're a good distance away, Taylor says to Niki, "I'm sorry about Jamar. I don't know what's gotten into him."

Niki laughs. "Girl, don't feel like you should apologize for him, because it's not your fault. I'm honestly kinda okay with it."

"Seriously?" Taylor asks.

"Yeah." Niki sounds different, like she's happy about it. "Ever since the world ended, he's been stuck to my side like glue. Always doing what I said without a word, looking for permission for every little thing. Once our mom was gone, I had to step up and take care of him and my grandma." I glance back at them, and Niki's smile drops before she continues. "But now he's a little more like he was before the flu. Defiant little asshole."

Taylor chuckles.

"I think it's a good thing," Niki continues. "Means he feels comfortable. Safe, maybe." Her voice turns serious again. "Now, that doesn't mean he can get away with talking to me like that. But it's still kinda nice."

"Hey, look." Niki points ahead, past a tractor trailer parked across a sidewalk. There's a big sign for a shopping center that lists all the stores in it. Big Lots, Kroger, and all the way near the top, Dick's Sporting Goods.

Across the street is another shopping center. This one has several fast-casual food joints, two chain restaurants, a Best Buy, and a Kohl's.

"Let's check the Dick's," Andrew says. "Because, one, I'm immature and just wanted to say that—"

"Naturally," Cara says with a frown.

"And two, they're bound to have some stuff we can use. Ammo, camping gear, maybe even some freeze-dried food."

"But the Kohl's is going to have more clothes," Niki says. "And we came for winter clothes."

"You three head to Kohl's," I say. "Andrew and I will take the Dick's."

Andrew snorts and Cara rolls her eyes as Taylor shakes her head. But no one argues, and Cara tells us to meet back by the overturned truck when we're done.

As we head for the Dick's, Andrew smiles up at me. "Did you make the inappropriate joke just to cheer me up?"

"Did it work?"

"Maybe."

"Then yes."

The store's automatic front doors have been smashed in by some kind of vehicle, but it looks like they must have been able to drive away afterward.

Inside, dead leaves gather in piles against endcaps and register aisles. Every once in a while, the breeze makes a leaf skitter across the floor. It's dark since the only light comes from the broken front doors and the sun is behind a thick layer of low-lying clouds. I take out my flashlight, and Andrew and I head for the clothing. There are overturned racks of yoga pants, shirts, and shorts. The sports jerseys on the far wall have been ripped down and only a few less-than-stellar teams remain.

I can't help myself and pick through a few on the floor, looking for a Phillies jersey or even an Eagles shirt. Of course they aren't there, which means either they were never here in the first place or the people of this town had good taste.

There are pillars of dark television screens that have been smashed to bits, and old signs ripped and thrown about. Andrew finds an empty circular rack and shines his flashlight on the ground beneath it.

"Here are some jackets."

I join him, picking up a bright green puffer jacket on top of the pile. Feathers tumble out and something moves.

No, *several* somethings move.

Andrew screams as a nest of rats the size of my forearm scatter, squealing and running in all directions. I shriek and jump as one tumbles over my foot. Throwing the jacket across the room, Andrew and I sprint in the opposite direction.

My flesh crawls and I jump up and down, groaning, as Andrew "yeesh"-es and clutches his arm to his chest.

"Shit!" I shout. "Ugh."

Andrew laughs. "I fucking hate the apocalypse."

"Hard same." I cringe again as the rats continue to scamper somewhere else in the store.

"Do we go back and see if any of the jackets are salvageable?"

I shine my flashlight over to the pile of jackets and down feathers. "If even some of them are okay, it might be worth it. And we can always wash them."

Andrew pushes me forward. "Cool, you go look. I'll check over here."

I shudder again and head back to the pile of clothes. I pick them up, one by one, examining each as I hold it between my thumb and forefinger. They're tattered and gutted. Down litters the floor, along with rat shit and shredded nylon. Still, I might be able to stitch some of these together.

"Jamie! Over here!"

I drop the coat in my hand and walk over to the children's section. Andrew has thrown several coats on top of a rack.

"Most of these aren't rat infested. Think they'll fit the kids?"

"If not, they'll grow into them." And maybe one or two that don't fit can be used to patch the larger ones. Then something clicks. "Oh. Wait here."

I run up to the front of the store—a rat skittering away from me makes me jump—but there's only leaves and more mess. This time it's shredded bags of impulse-buy candy and snacks from near the registers.

I point my flashlight down the aisles as I walk until I spot an empty dark green cart. I grab it and pull it farther down the aisle to the baseball equipment section. There are plenty of gloves left on the floor, ripped from their boxes. As my light flashes across it, more rodents scurry away. But there's a metal baseball bat on the floor. I take it and throw it in the cart.

On my way back to Andrew, I stop at the hunting section. There's a plastic deer on the ground that's been beaten to bits, its head halfway across the cordoned-off area and riddled with bullet holes and neon-feathered arrows.

"Jamie! What are you doing?"

"Just a sec!" I jump over the counter and almost land on a body. I try to right myself so I don't step on them, tumbling against the empty racks where the guns usually would be. The body is face down and wearing a backpack.

"You okay?" Andrew's voice calls out.

"Yeah. I just tripped."

"Please stop being so clumsy. We can't both be injured. The Nomads will put us out to pasture."

I have no idea why I lied to him. It's not like it's strange to find a dead body these days. But maybe it's because of how this person is dressed. As though he was on the road, long after the superflu burned out. And maybe because he still smells. Sweet and rotten like the basement neo-Nazi.

I slip his backpack off, but it's already light and unzipped. When I place it on the counter and look inside, there's no food or bullets, only clothes. And not even winter clothes.

I turn the body over and see the four bullet holes in his chest. His hands are empty, but I check his pockets. There's lint and a small pocketknife in one, and only a folded-up piece of paper in the other. I put the pocketknife on the counter. There's ink on both sides of the paper, but it bleeds out around the edges as if it's been stamped.

My blood runs cold.

On the back of the paper is a small square image that looks carved from a makeshift rubber stamp. It's a map that shows a convergence of highways and roads. In the center of the map is a black ink spot.

Above the spot are the words FORT CAROLINE.

Below the map is another stamp, but this one has ugly carved letters with instructions on how to reach Fort Caroline by any of the major highways. There's more ink on the back of the page.

I flip it over to find I'm wrong—this is the *front* page. This is what people would see first if these pieces of paper were plastered around a certain area.

The stamped letters at the top of the paper say *WANTED*.

Below that, someone has lined up several stamps carved with sentences that have no punctuation. Each stamp cants at different directions and the margins aren't lined up.

```
Fort  Caroline  is  on  the  hunt  for  an
escaped  fugitive  who  goes  by  the  name  of
Jamison
   He is 17 years old 6 foot 3 inches a large
build  light-brown  hair  blue  eyes
   Jamison  is  wanted  for  the  assassination
of  selectmans  assistant  Harvey  Rosewood
   He  is  armed  and  should  be  considered
extremely  dangerous
   Fort  Caroline  will  reward  anyone  with
information  that  leads  to  capture
   Or  if  Jamison  is  brought  to  us  we  will
pay  handsomely  with  food  shelter  and  more
```

Then, at the bottom, in the same size font as the *WANTED* above it is the word *ALIVE*.

Shit. They made *wanted* posters for me.

"Jamie!"

I flinch and almost rip the paper in half.

"Andrew, I'm looking for bullets. Stop yelling." But my voice sounds shaky. My hands, my whole body in fact, are buzzing with adrenaline and fear.

"We don't need them. The Nomads have plenty."

He's right. I quickly fold up the paper and put it in my backpack with the pocketknife. I look back down at the body one last time, wondering where he came from, and where he found this wanted poster. We drove all through Georgia and didn't see any. Part of me wants to show Andrew, but I don't want him to worry.

Then another thought comes to me.

What if Cal and the Nomads found one of these? We're already past Fort Caroline, but they could be talking to them on a radio and agreeing to another rendezvous point farther ahead.

For now I'll just keep this quiet. Maybe this guy was *from* Fort Caroline, and that's the only reason he had the paper in his pocket. I grab the cart—and another that's shoved against the counter—and head back to Andrew.

He smirks. "Why is there always a cart with one janky wheel?"

"It's store policy." I try to keep my voice steady.

We start loading up the kids' jackets.

"How are you feeling?" I ask. But before he can snap at me for asking about his arm, I clarify, "I mean about us being on the road. With the Nomads." Now, after finding the wanted poster, I want to be back in the cabin with him more than ever. Away from the roads and people and Fort Caroline.

He holds up one jacket, checking both sides for rat bites or some other kind of rodent holes. "Okay, I guess. I mean, it's hard to find things to complain about when we're being chauffeured around."

"Do you miss the Keys?"

He stops and looks up at me. "Do *you*?"

"No, but I know you were hoping things would be different."

He moves over to a display of hiking and camping clothes and starts picking up things from the floor.

"I was." He throws some gloves and hats in the cart, then stops and approaches me. In the dim light I can see the sadness on his face, and it answers all my questions about how he felt leaving the Keys. "I just—I know you were scared. And I know why. You got shot and you almost died. That's enough to royally screw up anyone's trust."

Hearing him say that out loud gives me a sudden sense of relief. It's such a comfort to know he understood where I was coming from. It means we haven't drifted apart like I was scared we had. I start to reach for the wanted sign in my pocket, but he speaks and it stops me in my tracks.

"But," he says, "I hope you know there's more people you can trust besides me. And Cara, too. Things have changed since the bug destroyed everything, but there are still good people who survived."

There's that worry again, though. That maybe the Nomads know Fort Caroline is looking for me. I can't get rid of it entirely.

"What if I fully trust only you and Cara, and hang on to the smallest bit of doubt about everyone else, to keep us safe?"

There's sadness in his eyes. He puts his good hand up to my chest. "It's not your responsibility to keep us safe. We have an equal share in that, and no one is ever one hundred percent safe. Even before the bug."

No, but post-superflu America is still more dangerous than it was before. Especially when we have two settlements out there looking for us now. And who knows how many people in between who have wanted posters with my name and description on them.

He gets up on the tips of his toes and kisses me gently.

"We'll be okay," he says.

I nod and he turns his attention back to the rats' nest of coats on the floor. He grabs a few of the least torn adult jackets.

"And you can sew these into a Postapocalyptic Coat of Many Colors."

"It's going to be hideous," I say, looking at the neon-green jacket with a shredded arm.

"Absolutely. I love it already."

We finish grabbing the best of the coats and take the cart out to the road. Cara, Niki, and Taylor are waiting for us with their own haul of clothes but not nearly as much winter stuff, so maybe it is good we split up.

Before either party can say anything, we hear a strange sound drifting through the quiet, supposedly empty town. It's music. And it's being played through speakers. It's a tinkly version of . . .

"Is that the Mexican hat dance?" Niki asks.

I turn my head toward it, listening to the music echoing through the dead town. Immediately I'm on edge, because that music is being played by a machine—it sounds as if it's being piped from an ice cream truck. Someone could be playing the music across town to distract us into thinking we're safe here while they're watching us from around the corner. My eyes dart everywhere, looking for more wanted signs, people crouched down, guns.

"I think we might have just ended up in a horror movie," Andrew says. The Mexican hat dance stops playing, but then seconds later, it starts over again.

"Then let's not stick around," I say. Taylor's eyes are wide and worried, and she's probably regretting making this trip with us. She and Cara are the first to turn and head back toward the highway.

I focus on every shadow, trying to discern movement. But the Mexican hat dance doesn't follow us, and by the time we're on the highway, we don't hear it anymore.

Back at the camp, Niki says she's going to tell Cal and the others to keep an eye out. Their ears, too—though I doubt whoever was playing the music would play it if they wanted to sneak up on us. Unless it really was a diversion. Or a way to draw people in.

"We should tell Daphne and Kelly, too," Andrew says. "Figure out the best way to tell the kids without scaring them."

"Then *you* shouldn't do it," I say, nudging him playfully. "I'll go find Daphne."

The sky above us finally gives up the ghost and a misty drizzle falls. We head toward the covered parking spots where we've set up our camp. Amy is following Henri-Two as she teeters around. Behind her the Kid sits quietly, still not playing with the others.

"Is the Kid okay?" I ask Andrew.

He looks sad when he answers. "He's always been kind of a loner. He got pretty close with Taylor after Frank died, but I think she's been a little distracted."

Taylor has, in fact, already run over to Jamar, no doubt to tell him all about our near miss with a slasher movie. I make a mental note to talk with Daphne and Kelly about how we can get the Kid to hang out with the others; I feel bad, seeing him sitting on his own.

When we reach Amy, Henri-Two looks up and does her clumsy half walk a few steps to us—Amy following and holding her hands at either side of her—then she stops just short and smiles up at us before turning back to her mom. Andrew follows, knowing the game well enough, and tickles Henri-Two's legs as Amy scoops her up so she can be at his height. Henri-Two squeals, babbles something, and buries her face in Amy's shoulder.

"Where's Daphne?" I ask as Andrew keeps making baby noises and tries in vain to get Henri-Two to look at him.

Amy smiles as Henri-Two giggles. "She's lying down." She nods to the grass, where I see Daphne lying beneath a blanket. "She didn't look too great, so I told her to take a nap. But we might want to wake her. It's starting to rain, and also we should get the kids fed and start the bedtime routines."

I nod. "I'll go."

Amy thanks me and I head over to Daphne and gently shake her shoulder. She opens her eyes slowly, looking up at me, not seeing me, then focusing.

"Oh, when did it start raining?" she asks.

"A couple minutes ago. We should try and get everyone covered up and ready for bed."

She sits up with a little help from me. "I miss the rainy days at my computer. A cup of tea and a steamy open-door scene at the ready. You know how many different ways I had to think of to say *erect penis*?"

"Please tell me all of them," I say as she stands. "I need a new way to make Andrew blush."

She laughs and winces, rubbing at her shoulder.

"You good?"

"Yeah. My muscles have been aching these last few days." She winces again, rubbing at her shoulder and neck. "Go ahead, make sure the kids get under cover while I pick up this stuff."

I nod and turn to go. Just as I do, I hear her cry out a soft "oh!" When I turn, she's bent over, her knees on the ground.

"You all right, Daph?"

She falls onto her side.

"Daphne!"

I crouch next to her. She's looking up at me, surprised, blinking against the light rain.

"What's wrong? What is it?"

But she isn't rubbing her shoulder anymore. She's clutching at her chest. Her breath is quick, and she's paler than I've ever seen her.

"Hey!" I shout at whoever will hear me. "Help! Someone help!" Rocky Horror sees what's happening and shouts that he's getting Dr. Jenn. Andrew is immediately at my side.

"What happened?"

"She fell," I say.

She manages to gasp, "Get the . . . kids away."

I turn to see a group of them watching us, their faces masks of fear and worry.

"Andrew, the kids."

He turns and sees exactly what she means. "Stay with her."

"I will."

And he's gone. I hear him, Amy, and Cara trying to calm the kids behind me, but I'm more focused on Daphne.

"It's okay," I say to her. "Dr. Jenn will be here soon, okay?" I hold her hand. It's wet, and her grasp seems so strong.

She looks at me, her eyes wide and her skin gray and wet from the rain. Her breathing comes in sharp inhalations. Then one long exhale.

She doesn't breathe in again. Her hand goes limp in mine.

"No, Daphne, wait!" I place the heel of my hand on her chest and start compressing. This was something my mom taught me well before the superflu, in case anyone ever collapsed near me when I was on the bus or subway on the way to school. She gave me a list of songs that were between 100 and 120 beats per minute and taught me how to do chest compressions until help got there, and to teach someone else when I got tired.

I thought it would be funny choosing "Crazy in Love" by Beyoncé, but it's not. I listen to the beat of the song in my head as I push down on Daphne's chest.

"I'm here!" Dr. Jenn slides to a stop, crouching down across from me in the rain, which is growing heavier. "Did you see what happened?"

"She was asleep, I helped her stand, and she seemed fine but then she fell."

"Was she complaining of any pain?" She reaches out and grabs my hand, stopping me as she puts two fingers against Daphne's throat.

"Her shoulder and neck. She said it was from sleeping on the ground."

She points a flashlight in Daphne's eyes and lets go of my hand.

I take that to mean I can continue compressions, but Dr. Jenn grabs my hands again.

"She's gone, Jamie." She reaches out to close Daphne's eyes, then sits back on her heels and lets out a long sigh. "She might have thought it was from sleeping on the ground, but it sounds like she had a heart attack."

A heart attack. That's so . . . mundane. We all survived a superflu— a superflu with a near-100-percent mortality rate, in which we were in direct contact with people who died from it. Most survivors believe we're immune. We're supposed to worry about escaped zoo animals and other survivors with guns and natural disasters and serial killers playing the Mexican hat dance. Not something as simple as a heart attack.

Dr. Jenn stands up and puts a hand on my shoulder. "I'm sorry."

I thank her and stand, then walk over to Andrew. He already knows what I'm going to say before I say it, and his face scrunches up into a look of grief. I pull him into a hug and let him cry into my chest as I whisper over and over that I'm sorry.

ANDREW

WE LEAVE DAPHNE WHERE SHE FELL, JUST for the night. We cover her with
a blanket and spend the evening trying to console the kids. Most of
them fall asleep pretty quickly once they get the tears out. But some—
Taylor and the Kid especially—can't sleep.

In the morning, Jamie wakes me up and right away I realize it's
not early. The kids are all awake and it looks like I'm the last one up.

"What time is it?" I ask, still feeling groggy. My eyes burn with
exhaustion, and it's started to rain harder.

"A little after ten."

"Why did you let me sleep so late?"

"Because you needed to. What time did you even fall asleep?"

I have no idea, but it was probably very late. I get up and go check
on Kelly. With Daphne gone, all these kids have lost another parental
figure. Now it's just the two of us on Team Orphan.

"We have to do something with her," Kelly says, looking over my
shoulder at the soaking-wet blanket lying over Daphne's body. "The
kids can't keep looking over and seeing her."

I nod. "I'll ask the Nomads if they have a shovel. Maybe we can find a nice place nearby to bury her. Do you think the kids will like that? I mean, not *like* it. But I mean, do you think it will help?"

"I do. A lot of them didn't get funerals when their parents died, and we never got to have one for Liz and the other kids, so it might be a way to get closure."

True.

I go over to Niki because she's the one we have the best relationship with. She shakes her head.

"I asked yesterday when I heard, but they only have garden spades for . . . you know."

I nod. We have some, too. And I'm not about to bury Daphne with the shit trowel.

"I'm really sorry," she says.

"Thanks."

I start toward the camp but the heaviness presses down on my chest. It's almost hard to breathe. Jamie must see it because he says something to Cara and jogs across the parking lot to me.

"You okay?"

I shake my head. Taylor is looking at me now. The Kid, too. And a few of the others. I fake a sad smile and try to hide behind Jamie's torso.

"I need to go have a mental breakdown away from the kids."

Jamie nods and looks out over the parking lot. Then he takes my good hand and squeezes it gently. "C'mon."

I let him lead me away as silent tears stream down my face. He takes me around the side of the amusement park to the staff entrance.

"We need to get in there," Jamie tells the three Nomads guarding it. "We're trying to keep up a front around the kids, but he needs somewhere away from them to grieve for a bit."

One of them, a woman with curly auburn hair and a freckled nose, nods and pushes open the door for us. "Go ahead. We're sorry for your loss." The lock has been broken and lies in pieces on the other side of the door.

As soon as it shuts behind us we take several long strides into the park. I turn abruptly and wrap my good arm around Jamie's neck. He hugs me gently against him, careful about my injured arm. It hurts. Everything does. I bury my face against his chest and sob again.

"I know," he says. It's raining and we're both soaked, but I don't care. I just needed to break down. To let this all out without the kids seeing.

I know the Keys Committee put me with Daphne because she requested it after I got kicked off the boat. I also know she requested it because she saw me as one of those orphans, too. She pretended that I was the "helper" and, yes, I did help. But all along, she was watching after me, too.

And now she's gone.

"Come on," Jamie says when my cries start to slow. "Let's get out of the rain."

I let him lead me past silent, broken-down rides. A carousel, a drop tower, bumper cars, a two-story slide. He's heading toward a covered concession area when I stop him.

To our right is a red, pink, and purple building. Above it, a dark sign lined with heart-shaped lights reads "Jingle Jaguar's Tunnel of Love." A cartoon jaguar wearing a raspberry beret winks suggestively at us from the corner of the sign.

Jamie smirks and shakes his head but lets me lead him to the ride entrance, a covered platform that shelters us from the rain. The ride track before us looks like it used to be filled with water. But there are only small puddles left beneath the red-and-pink heart-shaped boats. The track that steered the boats is rusted.

There's a red plexiglass-covered control booth to our left. I push gently on the door, expecting it to be locked, but it swings open. I step inside and Jamie follows me. There are four dark monitors, no doubt used to make sure nothing untoward was happening in the tunnel of love—or maybe to *watch* the untowardness. The controls are simple start and stop buttons, clearly labeled and colored green and red.

I press the green button, but of course nothing happens.

Under the control panel is a first aid kit. I open it. It's full and hasn't been used.

"See?" I say. "My emotional breakdowns can be extremely useful to us."

"Sure."

I look for anything else that might help us out, but all that's there is a giant Maglite flashlight. I pick it up and already know we aren't bringing it with us. For one, it needs batteries, and who has the time to stop for those when we have the hand-crank flashlights? Also, it weighs about twenty pounds.

Still, I click the button and it turns on.

Oh, I have a terrible idea. I hand the flashlight to Jamie and take his other hand, pulling him back out onto the platform.

"Come on, love," I say. "Jingle Jaguar built this tunnel just for us."

214

Jamie pulls back on my hand gently. "I don't like our history with tunnels." But he's talking about the Fort McHenry Tunnel outside Baltimore, which flooded and had cars full of dead bodies—very much *not* a tunnel of love.

"Then let's change it. Come on, there's no bodies in there. The amusement park was closed down just like all the movie theaters and sports arenas. And it's not flooded because look." I point to the evaporated troughs that acted as the river.

"What about animals that have made it a nest?"

"We'll run from them. Please?"

Jamie frowns, but he hops down into the empty river between two of the boats, then turns and holds out his hands to help me. I crouch at the edge of the platform as he grabs my hips and effortlessly lifts me down without jostling my bad arm.

Then he lets me guide him around the boats toward the plywood entrance, which is heart-shaped and painted pink. The words *Tunnel of Love* were supposed to light up, but they're dark now. Torn red metallic fringe hangs down from the top of the heart, but the elements have pulled most of the plastic strips down.

As we pass under, into the darkness, Jamie clicks on the flashlight.

The first room is a letdown. It's just a white tunnel. I put my hand out to touch it and the wall gives. It's fabric.

"There must have been a projection or something," I say. "On the other side of the fabric."

"If it's all like this, it's going to be a boring trip in the love tunnel."

"Title of your sex tape."

I turn to see if he's blushing. He is. I give him a playful peck on the

215

cheek and continue to the next room.

This one is much prettier. The sides of the tunnel are filled to the ceiling with brightly colored fake rosebushes. String lights loop across the curving roof above us. There's another curtain of pink fringe ahead that we push through.

"Wow," Jamie says, pointing his flashlight around the next set piece. It's a long, straight tunnel that's painted to look like the outside. In the ceiling and to our left are little lights in the shape of stars. To our right is a small-town street lined with a dock. Animatronic heterosexual couples sit on wooden benches—the man's arm around the woman's shoulder—or hold hands in the street or share a milkshake with two heart-shaped straws at the Fountain d'Amour ice cream shop. All the animatronics are dressed in ragtime-era clothes and the streetlights are shaped like hearts as well.

"And you were worried," I say.

"I still am. These animatronics are creepy." He shines the light on the guy in the background of the Fountain d'Amour shop. He's smiling wide and holds an ice-cream cone while watching the couple in his storefront window share their milkshake. Jamie has a point—some of them are very creepy.

The next winding tunnel is a repeat of the rose room—this time with an emergency exit hidden at the end with a dark exit sign above it—and then we reach the biggest set piece. If my sense of direction is still good in the dark, we should be in the center of the ride.

It's another place painted to look like the outside sky. The ceiling is pitch-black but I can see where they've attempted to put pin lights in the shape of some constellations. We're in a garden filled with topiary hearts, dogs, and a unicorn. More fake rosebushes line the wall, breaking the horizon's line of sight so it looks like the garden could go on forever.

In the center is a waterfall that's gone dry. Next to that is a fake moss-covered island with stone pavers placed in the shape of a heart. At the top center of the heart is a large, fake willow tree. And if you look close enough, the leaves are all shaped like hearts, too. Smaller rosebushes dot the island.

"Is it weird that I love how tacky this is?" I ask.

"No, I think that's about right for you."

I laugh. But whatever happiness I feel is gone just as quickly as it came because I'm thinking of Daphne again. How she used to tell me some of the more sordid storylines she'd written in her romance novels. Before we left the Keys, I had been planning to ask her for a copy of her most Hallmark Channel Original Movie-ish book to give to Jamie for Christmas.

I don't know why I thought going into a tunnel of love would give me time to *not* grieve her. In fact, she would have loved this place. The tackiness, yes, but also because of all the different ways she'd say she could use it in a book. Either in a near-drowning meet-cute or a big love confession climax. Then it clicks for me. How perfect this place is.

"Oh my God."

"What's wrong?" Jamie asks.

"I know what we can do. Come on."

I pull him back to the second rose room, heading for the emergency exit.

An hour later, we're back in the Tunnel of Love. Only now we have seventeen others with us. And Daphne.

Jamie, Rocky Horror, Cal, and another Nomad named Jim carry Daphne's body—wrapped in a white blanket—onto the island next to the dried-up waterfall. Because of my arm, I can't help, so I stay back with the Kid, who holds tightly to my good hand. They place her gently beneath the fake willow tree with heart-shaped leaves.

Taylor is crying and laying her head on Jamar's shoulder. Behind him, Niki holds a candle in her hand. The adults hold the younger kids so they can watch—their flashlights pointing up at the ceiling to diffuse the light a bit more.

We decided that Amy would lead the ceremony since she knew Daphne the longest. She hands Henri-Two over to me and I tuck her against my right side, away from my injured arm. Jamie looks down at the Kid, then crouches and asks him something I can't hear.

The Kid looks up at everyone else, then nods. Jamie turns around and the Kid wraps his arms—and Bobo, his arm still bandaged just like mine—around Jamie's neck. Jamie grabs his legs and stands so the Kid is piggyback and can see everything going on. My heart flutters just a bit.

"I met Daphne ten years ago," Amy says. "It was the week after I opened the shop, and she came in asking if I had any Daphne De Silva novels. Thankfully I already had several of her books on the shelves. She promptly took out a Sharpie and started signing them. I thought she was some disgruntled fan." Everyone gives a chuckle. "Her picture in the back of the book was from years ago, and she was all done up and . . . well, here was this woman just scribbling in my books. So I snatched one right out of her hand, yelling at her. Messed up the signature. She just laughed and said, 'You can have that one, sweetie.' Like they weren't all my books since I *bought* them!"

More quiet laughter; this time some of the kids understand the joke and they laugh, too.

"I think that's the thing I'm going to miss the most about her. Her laugh was so warm—you knew she was never laughing *at* you, but always with you. And she absolutely would have gotten a kick out of a Tunnel of Love being her mausoleum."

Everyone laughs again, but it's the kind of laughter that comes from nervousness. Like they aren't sure if putting Daphne's body here is rude or something she'd want. I'm glad Amy is on the same page. I can even hear Daphne's warm laughter.

I'm going to miss it, too.

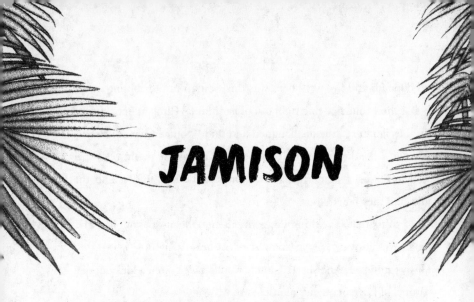

JAMISON

FOUR DAYS AFTER WE LEAVE THE AMUSEMENT park behind us, we're somewhere in North Carolina. I haven't seen any more wanted posters, and the Nomads haven't been acting jumpy or suspicious at all. Andrew has been trying to fill the gap left by Daphne, but I can tell he's missing her just as much as the kids do.

He, Kelly, Amy, and Taylor have taken them into the woods for a potty break while Rocky Horror, Niki and Jamar, Cara, and I watch the road with Cal and a couple other Nomads. We're always at the end of the seven-vehicle caravan. We have younger kids, so we have to stop more often than the others.

"Sorry," I say to Cal as he scans the open field next to the road. "About all the stopping." It's the Kid. Andrew says he's been having some stomach issues the past day or so. And unfortunately the RV bathroom isn't really an option.

Cal shakes his head. "You in a rush?"

A rush, no. But I do want to get off the road once and for all. I want to get Amy and Henri-Two home and figure out where the others are going—then go to *our* home.

Our home. The thought alone makes my chest ache. I can't wait to see the cabin again. It's also good to hear Cal say we're not in a rush, as it means he probably doesn't know about the wanted posters. I should show Andrew soon. Right after I found the poster, Daphne died, and I didn't want to cause any more worry or stress, so I kept it to myself. But it's still in my pack, tucked away in a pocket.

"I guess not," I say. "But it still feels like we're slowing everyone else down."

Cal doesn't answer and instead turns his attention to the left, where Kelly, Taylor, and a few of the kids emerge from the line of trees, followed by the others.

I walk over to Andrew, who's a little farther behind with the Kid. "How you feeling, Kid?"

He doesn't answer, and Andrew holds up his good hand and wavers it. I was feeling bad for slowing the Nomads down, but now I'm feeling worse for the Kid.

"Should we stop somewhere?" I ask Andrew. "See if we can find Pepto or something? Can kids have Pepto?"

"Great question. When we stop for the night, let's ask Dr. Jenn."

"Horses!" the Kid shouts next to us. I look down at him pointing out at the field to our left, and he's right, there are horses out there.

My stomach drops.

Two horses with riders on them—and me with a secret wanted posted with my name in it in my pack. Everything feels very Wild West all of a sudden.

"Shit," I say. I move behind Andrew and he puts a hand on the Kid's back to hurry him along to the road. Cal nods and unbuttons the holster clipped to his belt. The horses are trotting over to us. I reach back and grab the baseball bat I took from the Dick's in South Carolina out of a side pocket of my pack.

Cara, Andrew, and the adults stand in a short line in front of the kids, waiting to see what the people on horseback are going to do. I step forward with Cal and the Nomads, but none of them have guns at the ready.

"What do we do?" I ask Cal.

"Just wait. See what they want. There's more of us than there are of them, so I'm not worried, but we don't want anyone to get hurt if we can help it."

I nod. "I never did thank you for not pulling your guns on us."

He looks at me. "We did have guns on you, you just couldn't see them."

The idea chills me to the bone. They must have been focused on us in the RV. If we made one wrong move, they could have killed us. And the same might be true right now. Everyone on our side is standing here in the road. But whoever these people on horseback are, they could have more people watching us.

My eyes scan the trees around the field, looking for movement.

As the horses get closer, I notice that if the riders are armed, their guns aren't in their hands. The taller one raises one hand in a hello, while the other holds the reins.

As they reach the other side of the highway, I see it's a middle-aged East Asian woman wearing a blue baseball hat, her hair pulled back in a long ponytail. The boy next to her is Asian, too, and probably around Jamar and Taylor's age, maybe a little younger.

The woman turns the horse around in a wide circle and I see that she does have a gun—it's holstered on her right. But when she stops her horse next to the other, she seems to give us a friendly enough smile. I see Cal take his hand off his gun. He steps forward and the rest of us follow a few paces behind.

"Hi," she says. "I'm Hannah." She nods to the boy next to her. "This is my son, Alex." Alex gives us a friendly wave and Cal introduces himself.

"And everyone else." He waves behind him. "The rest of our group is up the road waiting." It sounds innocuous, but I know it's a warning—that we have people waiting for us, and if we don't show up they'll come looking—and I think Hannah takes it that way.

"Where you all from?" she asks.

Cal laughs and makes a big sweeping gesture. "All over."

Hannah smiles. "Yeah, us too. We're from Cleveland originally. Lots of folks in our settlement are from all over, too."

Lots of folks. I wonder how many.

I don't know what else to say—none of us seem to—so Hannah speaks again.

"Well, our settlement is up the road here. If you're all interested in spending the night, we'd like to extend the invitation."

Cal glances back to me, then his people. I look back to Andrew, Rocky Horror, Amy, Cara. It looks like none of us know exactly what to say. I don't want to speak for the group, but strangers offering hospitality these days is not always the best sign.

Hannah holds up her hands. "No pressure. You can talk it over. But if you do decide to join us for the night . . ." She points up the road. "Take the second exit, make a left. Head on down the road for a mile and a half and then make a right at the coffee shop shaped like a boot."

But something isn't sitting right with me. "Why are you inviting us?" I ask. Cal turns, surprised that I said something, and maybe I am, too. But I want to see what Hannah's answer is. We told her there were others waiting for us, and she has no idea how many. For all she knows, we could number several hundred, and her settlement might be only twenty.

Or her settlement could be several hundred, and ours is seventy-one.

Still, I'm not willing to trust her so easily. And judging by what I've learned about Cal and the Nomads, maybe they aren't either.

Hannah looks at me, then her eyes drift to the kids, who have gathered to look around the adults in front of them. She shrugs. "It's Christmas Eve. Think of it as goodwill toward . . . survivors."

Shit. I had totally forgotten. Holidays are hard to remember without the constant barrage of consumerism and nostalgia. Our minds have been more focused on finding food for survival than gifts. Andrew and Kelly look surprised, too. Amy and Cara either remembered and didn't tell us, or they have great poker faces. Well, Cara absolutely does.

"Think about it," Hannah says. "We do hope to see you, though."

She and her son bid us goodbye and head back the way they came. Hannah stays facing forward, but Alex turns back to look at us, like he's not sure we're trustworthy.

We wait until Hannah and Alex are far enough away before we gather in a big circle to talk about it, weighing the pros and cons. The pros are food, safety, shelter, companionship. The only con is, they could be trying to kill us. It's Rocky Horror who comes in with the logic.

"What's the point? I mean, we don't know how many there are, but they have to know we aren't carrying that much on us. And 'come join us for Christmas dinner, but also no pressure' isn't the most enticing way to lure in a buncha rubes."

"Excuse me, what is a *rube*?" Andrew asks.

Rocky Horror claps his hands together. "That settles it, *I'm* going. I need adults to hang out with."

I turn to Cal, who turns to Kevin, who's basically his second-in-command when we're separated like this. "Radio the others, get their thoughts." He nods and leaves.

"What if it is a trap?" I ask as the circle breaks up. Andrew joins me.

Cal shrugs. "That's why we ask the others."

"But if they say yes, we should have a plan, right?" I ask. "If it's a trap and they attack us, we should keep the kids back so we don't have to worry about them getting hurt."

"Good point," he says. I can feel Andrew's eyes on me, but Cal turns to him. "You and the kids will be in the RV. Tell Rocky Horror, Niki, and Cara to stay in the truck."

"Wait," Andrew says. "You can't really be planning to kill these people."

"It's the backup plan," he says. "Not the first plan."

"No, the backup plan should just be not going. If you think these people are that dangerous—which I doubt, by the way, because what would the point be? But if you really think that, why wouldn't we just keep going?"

"What if they have supplies we need?" I ask. "The Kid's been sick for almost two days."

Andrew turns his attention to me, his eyes wide. "Don't think it's worth killing a whole bunch of people for *Pepto Bismol*, Jamie."

"And if he needs something more?"

"Then we figure it out! What the hell is wrong with you?" He's addressing only me now.

Kevin comes back. "They said they'll leave it up to you."

Cal looks at me and says, "Universal convergence." Then he turns back to Kevin. "We'll go ahead and see. Tell the others to stay back at that boot café until we give the okay."

I guess that's a good enough compromise. He heads for the truck as Amy and Kelly start trying to corral the kids into the RV. I go to Cara to ask if she wants to get in the truck with us or the RV, but before she answers, the Kid is pulling at Andrew's jacket.

"I have to go to the bathroom."

Andrew looks down at him. "Emergency?"

He nods.

"Okay, come on." Andrew gives me one last desperate look, and I know he's asking me to get in the RV and wait with them. But I'm not going to do that.

"If something happens, get the kids out of here. Take the RV from them if you have to. The Nomads don't know about Bethesda, so just go and get Henri out of there." I kiss him. "I love you."

"Don't do this," Andrew says.

"We don't have a choice."

"Of course we do! The choice is to not go. Or stay with us—Cal and the others don't need you, there's plenty of them."

"It's not fair to send only the Nomads. Rocky Horror says he wants to risk it." I turn to Cara. She seems unsure and is also unarmed. Cara doesn't like guns and only uses them when she has to. For instance, to save our lives.

"I'm with Rocky Horror," Cara says. "I don't think it's a setup."

"Andrew," the Kid whines, pulling on Andrew's arm.

"It'll be okay." But I can't know for sure. Andrew follows the Kid toward the field but stops and turns back, running to me, wincing as he tries to keep his arm steady. He kisses me hard on the lips.

"Don't do anything. And don't die. Please."

"Promise," I say, trying to keep my voice light.

He turns to Cara. "Either of you. Something happens, get Rocky Horror and get the hell out of there."

Then he runs back for the Kid. Cara turns to look at me.

"You better not be getting me killed tonight," she says.

"I promise?" I sound even less sure this time. I make sure to tell Amy and the others to stay with the RV until they hear from us on the radio. But while they aren't looking, I grab the handgun out of Andrew's pack. I double-check that the safety is on, then tuck it in the back of my jeans.

About twenty minutes later, after making a left at the boot café, we find ourselves greeted by two men with rifles. My stomach tightens and I reach down to feel that the gun is still there.

They introduce themselves and instruct us to park on the side of the road. We pull over and they lead us the rest of the way up a gravel and dirt road, past a sign that reads "Faraway Lodge and Campground."

Rocky Horror sticks his head between me and Cara and whispers,

"Camping was *not* what I had in mind when she said shelter."

I shrug. "So it's the same as every other day."

"Merry Christmas to all," Rocky Horror mumbles.

But the end of the road opens up onto a clearing with a massive three-story lodge. The plexiglass-covered sign to our right has a map with labels written in what looks like faded dry-erase marker. Written over the section labeled "campground" is "farm." On the northern section is a large lake. A small square drawn on the plexiglass says "WT." To the west of the lodge are a group of scattered cabins labeled with numbers.

I expect to see more people with guns pointed right at us. But it's quiet.

Hannah trots down the short hill from the lodge to us. "You came!" She holds out her hand and we all shake. "Welcome to Far-away."

"The others are behind us," Cal says. "You're sure you don't mind? There are about seventy of us altogether. We do have our own food."

"When they get here, we can talk food. We're planning a feast for tonight, so some additional provisions will be greatly appreciated."

My eyes flash to the windows of the lodge. Then the roof and the trees around us. There really isn't anyone else. The men with the rifles have gone back to their positions at the entrance to the driveway.

I see Cal reclip the holster on his gun. My own gun is digging into my right butt cheek, but I don't care. Cal may feel safe, but I'm not ready to let my guard down.

Hannah offers us a tour and we oblige. But first Cal turns to Kevin and tells him to check on the status of the others in the caravan. Which

I assume is the all clear. Then we follow Hannah as she starts the tour.

Cara leans in close to me. "We should go on a supply run tonight."

"You think they left anything in the town?"

"Not food. It's Christmas Eve. I don't know how many of these kids still believe, but it'll be a pretty fucked-up Christmas if they wake up tomorrow and the other kids in this place all got gifts and Super-flu Santa didn't leave anything for them. Especially after just losing Daphne."

Shit. She's right. I nod and make a mental note to have the others watch the kids after bedtime. Maybe Rocky Horror, Niki, Cara, and I can go. Andrew, too, if he's up to it. But I don't think he'd be willing to leave the kids.

During our tour, I learn the "WT" by the lake stands for Water Treatment. There's a pump powered by a solar panel that pulls from the lake and sends it through several natural filtering systems. Hannah points out a smattering of cabins for us, saying that's where we'll stay for the night—Rocky Horror brightens at that.

Then she takes us past their fields, which all look to be cut away.

"How were your crops over the summer?" I ask.

Hannah sighs like it's a major annoyance. "Not great. We tried, but it's hard to keep up with the pests, and we had issues troubleshooting our irrigation system. We spent most of the year trying to get us to a point of sustainability, which we've almost reached. We hope to make the goal by next fall, then we can focus on keeping the crops pest-free."

They had the same problems with the rodents and insects that we saw down south.

"It's going to be a while before the food chain stabilizes," Hannah continues. "The birds that are left are going to have to try a little harder to repopulate. There were some flocks flying south over the past few months. But for now we're trying to figure out new ways to roll with it. Next year we might get rid of the cabins and use the foundations for greenhouses. Set up a little airlock-type system to keep out the bugs. But . . ." She shrugs. "We're okay for now."

She continues the tour by leading us into the lodge. "This is where most of us stay."

The lobby has a rustic cabin feeling. The walls are stone, and to our left is a massive stone fireplace, the roaring blaze inside keeping the lodge warm. Ahead of us, between two doors, is a large grandfather clock, its pendulum swinging back and forth. "There's thirty rooms, a common area, kitchen, dining hall."

On the walls, string lights have been hung from small nails. They're off, but there's enough light coming through the windows for now.

"Electricity comes from the solar panels on the back of the roof. It's only enough to keep the lights going for a few hours after sunset. But tonight it may not last as long because of this." She pushes open the double doors to the right of the grandfather clock and we follow her into what looks like the common room.

On the far wall, next to several sliding glass doors that lead out to a deck, is a Christmas tree, decorated with ornaments and unlit string lights, the star at the top just touching the fifteen-foot ceiling.

Cara gasps and covers her mouth.

"Shit," says Rocky Horror. "I'm not a Christmas gay, but that's a great Christmas tree."

Hannah nods, looking proud. "Alex saw you with the kids and thought they might like a little normalcy. Oh, and if any of you are Jewish, we also have a menorah. Tonight is the first night of Hannukah." She pauses. "We think. Without a calendar it's hard to be certain, but the Jewish folks who did the math say they're ninety-nine percent sure it's tonight."

I never thought to ask the kids their religions and I feel bad. It seems like something Daphne would have done. I'll have to ask Andrew if he knows.

"Hey, Hannah," a voice calls from the doorway. It gives me a chill, and I don't know why. "Do you have the key to the root cellar?"

I turn and my stomach drops, every hair on my body standing on end.

"Chef needs some potat—" The man's voice falls off as he locks eyes with me. At first, it looks like he doesn't recognize me—like he's wondering why I'm staring at him—then his face drops, and I know he knows who I am.

I saw him look at me the same way five months ago, right before he shot me. His name is Grover Denton.

The sheriff of Fort Caroline.

The Nomads knew about the wanted posters all along. They were *bringing* us here to hand me over.

ANDREW

WE'RE DIRECTED TO PULL OVER ON THE side of the road instead of going
up the driveway. The other truck is there already, with the rest of the
caravan somewhere farther up the road.

We get out, and the men at the entrance usher us up the drive.
It looks like the place used to be a campground resort and someone
decided to turn it into a settlement. At the end of the drive is an empty
parking lot area in front of a lodge. The kids are immediately buzzing
with excitement because to our right, past a map of the resort, is a
playground where there are plenty of other kids.

"Oh boy," Kelly whispers. "I better get them over there. You all
go ahead." She turns to the kids and asks if they want to go play. Most
don't answer and instead just run for the playground.

Taylor sighs and turns to Jamar. "Come on." She drags him away
and I hear Niki tell him, sarcastically, to have fun. Taylor calls for the
Kid, who gives me a wary glance before following her.

I should go with them, but I want to find Jamie first. I walk up to
a woman who's passing by with a box of canned food. She tells us she

saw a group go into the lodge about five minutes ago. Amy, Niki, and I head for the lodge, too.

I can hear Jamie yelling as soon as I open the door.

I bolt toward his voice, and the voices of several others. Including Cara.

"Jamie, stop!" she yells. I push past a doorway into a dining hall area. There's a man with his back to us and Jamie is pointing a gun at him. Behind him, Cal and the rest of the Nomads have their guns out, but they aren't pointing them at anyone yet. Cara is standing between Jamie and the man, her hands out toward Jamie, while Hannah has her gun trained on him.

"Hang on!" the man says. His voice is familiar.

"Jamie, what's going on?" I ask.

Hannah points her gun at me in an instant and the man turns to look in my direction. My blood runs cold but somehow my face burns. The sounds around me get very quiet and my head feels buzzy. This is a nightmare. I'm asleep and this is a nightmare and I'm going to wake up any second. But the steady throb of pain in my arm tells me that's not true.

Grover Denton holds out his hands and backs away as though he's trying to soothe a cornered animal.

"Hold up!" Denton shouts. "Everyone just calm down!"

"Jamie, put down the gun!" says Cara.

"What's happening here?" Amy asks. She's turned Henri-Two away from everything and wrapped her arms around her, trying to protect her.

"Han, holster the gun!" Denton tells Hannah.

Rocky Horror steps closer to Jamie. "Jamie, what's going on?"

"Hannah!" Denton is still focused on her instead of me.

"He's the one who shot me!" Jamie says. That's enough for Rocky Horror, and he turns, stepping in front of Jamie, but still keeps his weapon on his shoulder. His eyes drift over to me, and I nod.

Denton stands upright and frowns. "I did not shoot you."

Jamie pulls up his shirt, showing the pink scar on the right side of his stomach. "What's that, then?"

"No, no." He shakes his head. "*I* was not the one who did that."

"Technicalities aren't going to settle this, dude," Rocky Horror says.

"He's the sheriff of Fort Caroline," I say. "He and a whole militia came after the three of us. First they sent people out to find and kill us—that was Harvey Rosewood and his friend."

Jamie jumps in. "But before they could hurt Andrew, I shot them."

Rocky Horror speaks out of the corner of his mouth. "Okay, saying *you* shot first isn't helping here, Han Solo."

Jamie flicks his head toward the Nomads. "This is a trap. They brought us here."

Cal's eyes go wide, and Kevin looks over at him with his good eye, also seemingly confused.

"Jamie, what are you talking about?" I ask.

"Look in my pack," he says. I slowly step behind him. "There's a piece of paper in the front pouch. Look at it."

I unzip the pouch and find the paper he's talking about. There's black ink stamped on it, bleeding blue a little around the messy edges from getting wet. But when I unfold it, the words on the front catch my attention more than the little map stamped on the back.

WANTED. ALIVE. And Jamison's name. My heartbeat quickens.

"Where did you get this?" I ask.

"I found it on a body when we were getting warm clothes for the kids."

The Dick's Sporting Goods. He went off somewhere and was quiet for so long. He must have . . . He found this and didn't tell me.

Why the hell would he keep something like this from me?

I hold it out to Cara, who takes it, her eyes wide. Denton reads it over her shoulder, and he seems just as surprised.

"They brought us here," Jamie says. "The Nomads. They knew we'd sense something was up when they took us near Fort Caroline, so they set us up to meet somewhere else. Because look who's here to bring me back and pay their reward."

"That's not true," Cal says. But I'm not sure I believe him.

"There was no universal convergence," Jamie says. That phrase again. "You were out *looking* for us. That's why the Keys haven't caught up with us. This is your settlement, isn't it? You let Cara get us this far so you could have Fort Caroline waiting here for us."

"Jamison, stop!" Denton yells. Cara's eyes haven't left the wanted poster in her hands. "This isn't some big conspiracy."

"We're just as confused as you," Cal says, stepping around so he can see Jamie. He also gives me a look, and I'm starting to believe him. Maybe Jamie is, too, because he looks away from Denton for a second to lock eyes with Cal, who nods slowly. "Just tell us what's going on. How do you know these people?"

"Just him," Jamie says. "He's from a settlement that tried to kill

235

Andrew and me. They said they were going to kill Andrew and make me watch."

"That was not what we sent them to do," Denton says. "And, Hannah, I told you already to put the damn gun away." She looks over at him, then back at Jamie, before putting her gun back in the holster. But she leaves her hand on it.

"Jamie," Cara says, taking the same tone of voice as Denton. "Put the gun down. I know Grover, he's telling the truth." Jamie doesn't move. Using a voice I've never heard her use—and one she probably hasn't used herself very often based on how shaky it is—Cara addresses everyone else. "*Everyone. Guns. Down!*"

Cal glances at Jamie one last time, then holsters his gun.

"Jamie!" Cara says. "You're pointing it at *me*."

I step around her and go over to him, gently putting my hand on his wrist. His heart is racing so hard I can feel the blood pumping beneath his burning skin. "Come on," I say quietly. His hands are shaking. "Put the gun down."

I move my hand to the weapon, holding my breath and waiting for it to discharge accidentally. Jamie would never forgive himself if he shot Cara.

But then I see it. The safety is still on. Seeing Denton must have scared him so much that he just reacted, not thinking about the safety. Now that I know the gun's not going to go off on its own, I use a little more force with my good hand to pull it away from him. I hold it out to Niki, who takes it from me and tucks it into the back of her jeans.

Denton takes a careful step forward. "Rosewood said you stole food and snuck out. We sent a few groups to find you and get the food back. They weren't supposed to do anything else."

"Well, you sent the wrong people," Jamie says.

"And we didn't steal," I add. "It was *our* food we left with."

"And that doesn't matter anymore because you came after us. All the way to Florida. And you shot me."

"I—" He stops himself from saying again that *he* wasn't the one who shot Jamie, even though he was the sheriff and was the leader of the group sent after us. He takes a moment and then says, "A lot of us didn't like the way that went."

I bark out a laugh. "Yeah, we didn't exactly like the way it went either."

"I'm sorry," Denton says. "Our goal was to arrest you and bring you back for a trial."

"And I'm sure it would have been a fair one," I say. I see Cal's eyes darting back and forth between Denton and Jamie, trying to piece everything together.

Denton's lack of answer is answer enough. His jaw tightens. "It doesn't matter anymore. You're alive, I have no intention of arresting you, all that's behind us."

"Then why are you here?" I ask. "Why aren't you in Fort Caroline? Where is Rosewood?"

Jamie looks terrified all over again, as if he hadn't even thought about the possibility of Rosewood being here but now he has.

"He's still in Fort Caroline," Denton says, fast. "A lot of people are. But me, a few others, we gave up on it."

"Gave up?"

He gestures to a few tables. "Can we sit down?"

Jamie looks to me and I turn to Cara. She nods and is the first to move. As Denton waits for us, I whisper to Jamie that it's okay and motion for him to follow her. We all sit, and Denton takes a chair across from us, still giving us space. Rocky Horror and Niki stand beside us while some of the other Nomads decide to continue the tour on their own. Cal stays put, standing by Rocky Horror. Amy remains by the doorway, probably worried that Jamie will go wild again and she might need to make a quick exit with Henri-Two.

"So," Denton starts, "after we got back from looking for you, Rosewood was pissed. He blamed me for losing you, which I deserved. I didn't want to go after you anymore. But more than that, it was a waste. He was using a lot of resources on a revenge mission. While we were gone, a few selectmen managed to change some of the laws to benefit themselves. Taking supplies, using labor for their own shelters, stuff like that."

"Taking advantage of people," I say. Next to me, Jamie's left leg is bouncing uncontrollably. I place my hand on it, and he stops. Out of the corner of my eye, I see his shoulders relax a bit.

Denton gestures with his hand as if to say *yes, obviously*.

"Rosewood still decided to try and blame me, but people liked me. He knew he had to get people to *not* like me. So—I have no proof of this, obviously, but it reeked of Danny at the time and no other option made sense—there was a bizarre uptick in crime. Bullshit offenses, fights and thefts, vandalism."

"Psyops," Cal says. Denton nods, looking impressed. Then Cal turns to the rest of us. "Psychological operations. It's when a population is manipulated to turn on whoever's in power. When people start to feel unsafe, they turn on you."

"Right," says Denton. "So, with the uptick in crime, Rosewood installed a few more deputies in the sheriff's department, people Nadine and I didn't know."

Denton turns to the Nomads, who weren't part of our Fort Caroline saga. "Nadine was my second-in-command, and one of my only friends who survived the flu. Anyway, the new deputies didn't answer to us and decided to make like the selectmen and start taking advantage. They'd blame people they didn't like for crimes they committed themselves—things I had evidence for. But to answer your previous question, Andrew: No. Jamie's trial wouldn't have been fair. Just like the others since haven't been."

"It wasn't a question," I remind him.

He nods. "Anyway, things went bad quickly. People turning against each other, power struggles among the members of the select committee. Things weren't ideal."

"You mean like the white supremacy and their fucked-up registry?" Jamie asks. His leg is bouncing nervously again beneath the table. My hand is still there, but I don't think he even feels it.

"Registry?" Niki sounds disgusted.

Denton doesn't even look at me when he says yes. "We—Nadine and me—we thought it would be okay. That we'd be able to live with it and that maybe by being in charge of Fort Caroline's law enforcement, we could make a difference. We needed a place to feel safe after everything that went down with the flu. Some normalcy."

I have no sympathy for him. Jamie and I wanted that, too. We all do, even now. But we saw what was wrong with Fort Caroline and we left. Just because Denton eventually caught on doesn't make me respect him.

"So why did you run away?" Jamie asks. "If you knew all this was happening and other people there saw it, too, why didn't you do what you wanted and make a difference?"

"We did," he says. "Or we tried. But we trusted the wrong person and we had to run."

Cara, who has been quiet most of this time, finally speaks. "Who ran with you?"

"Nadine and six others."

"Why didn't you leave earlier?" she asks. "You told me things were getting bad way before I left. You told me to keep my head down, do my work, and just wait. But you could have left before I did."

I could be wrong, but Cara sounds hurt. Like maybe she had asked Denton to leave with her before and he refused. And maybe that's why she finally decided to come with us.

Denton reaches out and puts his hand on hers. It's not a romantic touch, more paternal. "I was worried when you left. But I'm glad you were safe. I had a feeling that was you shooting at us when we caught up to you all."

Rocky Horror groans. "Okay, show of hands, who here in this room hasn't shot at someone else?" His hand goes up, and so does Niki's—probably not realizing Rocky Horror is joking. Trying to cut the tension that has filled the room.

Taylor comes into the doorway holding hands with the Kid. I can tell from the look on her face that she knows something is going on. Or maybe they've both been listening. She waves me over. I give

Jamie a reassuring squeeze on the leg and go to her while Denton asks if we've run into anyone from Fort Caroline on the road.

"The Kid has to go to the bathroom, but he won't let anyone else take him," Taylor says.

I look down at him. "I appreciate you, too, Kid, but your timing sucks." I turn to get Hannah's attention and she comes over to us.

"The Kid's been having some stomach issues the last day or so. Do you have any over-the-counter meds that might help? Also, which way to the bathroom?"

She nods. "Head out the front door, right past the cabins; we put in some outhouses. Come find me after and we'll get him some medicine and Pedialyte."

I thank her, and the Kid takes my hand. Jamie knows what's going on, so I turn back to give him another look of reassurance, hoping my telepathic support will be enough while I'm gone. Instead, he stands and walks across the room.

"Let's go," he says.

Taylor follows us. "What's happening in there?"

"Nothing good," I say.

Jamar is waiting for Taylor outside, and she separates from us as we walk in the direction of the outhouses. The Kid is pulling my hand, trying to get me to go faster.

"Go ahead," I say once the outhouses are in sight. The Kid runs to the closest one and Jamie and I hang back to give him some privacy.

"Why did you lie to me?" I ask. "About the wanted poster?"

He looks at the ground. "Because Daphne had just died, and I didn't want to worry you."

241

"I'm always worried; that's a terrible excuse. And you found it *before* Daphne died, so try again, only this time don't lie to me."

"I'm not lying. I didn't want to show you at first because it scared me. I knew it would scare you, too, and I didn't want to do that. *Then* Daphne died, and I knew I couldn't show it to you yet. I'm sorry."

I sigh, still annoyed that he lied to me, but I can put a pin in that for now because he's still scared. "Are you okay?"

He shakes his head. "No."

I hug him and he squeezes me tight, crouching down to put his face against my neck.

"This is just going to keep happening, isn't it?" he asks.

I rub his back with my good hand while the left one pulses with pain from the pressure of his body against me. But I bite back the agony and hide it from my voice. "This isn't the same as the Keys. Denton is running from Fort Caroline now, too."

I still don't feel bad for them, but better late than never, I guess?

Jamie leans back again but keeps his arm around my waist. "There are probably less than forty million people left alive on this entire continent—and that's just from the flu, not starvation or accidents or regular illnesses—but we still run into the same ones we're trying to hide from."

"They won't tell anyone. Denton has to know the reward on that poster is bullshit. And I'd bet real postapocalyptic currency they don't want Fort Caroline to know where they are."

"And what happens if Fort Caroline finds them?"

My stomach lurches. They wouldn't do that. Denton and Nadine ran from Fort Caroline, too. They know just how bad they are.

But I can only wallow in delusion for so long before logic brings me back to the real world. If Fort Caroline did find Denton and Nadine here, the two of them could offer information about us in exchange for safety. Because if there was a way to protect everyone here without fighting, they'd do it. I try to hide the realization on my face, but Jamie must see it. Of course he does. He nods.

"So what do we do?" I ask.

"I don't know."

The outhouse door opens, and I point at a sink below a water container. "Use your foot on the pedal there," I tell the Kid.

I watch as he soaps up his hands. Oh God, we really have to leave them all, don't we? The family we made in the Keys and on the road. Jamie was always right. It's not safe for them as long as someone is looking for us.

I love Jamie. I love him with all my heart, but I also love everyone else. Cara, Rocky Horror, Amy, Henri-Two, Taylor, the orphans and Kelly, even Niki and Jamar, who feel like part of the family now.

And the Kid.

Shit.

"We go to the cabin," I say. "Like we always planned. We . . ." My voice breaks as I try to say the words I don't want to say. "We let Kelly decide what she wants to do with all the kids, maybe stick with the Nomads. Then you, me, and Cara leave and get Amy home, and we let everyone else figure out what they're going to do on their own. We don't tell them where we're going. We just *go*."

If we were in the woods again, alone, I'd never know. I could tell myself they all lived happily ever after, couldn't I? If I was living happily ever after, surely they'd be doing the same.

That's *if* it was happily ever after for us.

"What happens to everyone else?" Jamie asks.

"Done." The Kid stands at my side, looking up at us.

"Come on," I tell him. "Let's get something to settle your tummy."

The Kid takes my hand and Jamie wraps his arm around my shoulders. What happens to everyone else can just be a mystery. But all the tummy medicine in the world won't make me feel better about it.

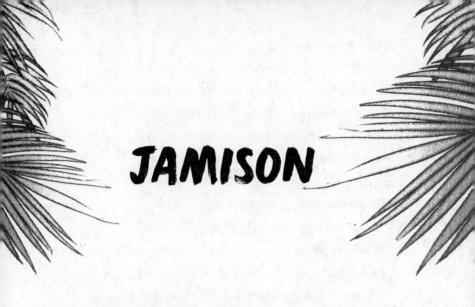

JAMISON

WHEN I WAKE UP ON CHRISTMAS MORNING, I feel strange. Not because we're in a new place, but because of everything that went down yesterday. The anxiety and fear of running into Denton again, then all that coming together with the optimism about Andrew, Cara, and I continuing on our own again after Bethesda.

This is a good thing, but there's still an uneasy feeling in my gut.

Maybe that's just because of the meal last night. I wouldn't call it a feast, exactly, but there was plenty for everyone, which is hard to come by these days.

I help Andrew and Kelly get the kids up and when we enter the common room, there's already food out, and something smells holiday-spicy, like cinnamon and nutmeg. Most are leftovers from the night before, but there's a tray of what looks like cookies and small quick breads.

The younger kids all run for the tree—several adults telling them to slow down and line up—but I'm drawn to the cookies and bread. I grab one of the loaves and examine it closely. It's dark brown and feels dense. It smells like cinnamon and citrus and looks like there's dried fruit in it. I show it to Andrew, who grabs a cookie.

"Orange cranberry." Hannah appears at my side. "The orange flavor is extract, but the dried cranberries are real. The cookies are just spice cookies. We ran out of real flour last year, so that's chef's special pine flour."

"Pine?" Andrew asks. "Like the tree?"

"The bark can be ground into flour."

He laughs. "Sawdust cookies, nice."

"I promise they aren't that bad." She takes one and heads over to the tree, where her son, Alex, is waiting patiently.

Andrew leans in and whispers, "Who knew pine trees had so many uses. Antibiotic ointment and now flour."

"Don't forget decor." I point to the Christmas tree across the room.

We join Cara and Rocky Horror—who tell me they're drinking "forager tea."

"Basically, it tastes like dirt," Rocky Horror says, but still takes a sip. We watch as the kids get handed gifts one by one. Even ours receive gifts. We asked Hannah if there was a place in town where we and a few of the Nomads could go to find gifts, but she assured us they had enough for everyone. And it looks like they do.

Across the room, I catch Nadine and Denton talking with Cal and a couple of other Nomads, including Kevin. Nadine locks eyes with me, gives me a curt nod, then returns her gaze to the other side of the room. The Lady Marine hasn't changed.

"Close your eyes and hold out your hands," Andrew says. When I turn to him, he has his good hand behind his back while his injured

246

hand is still held close to his chest despite not using the sling anymore. My smile grows and I do as he says. He places something light in the palm of my right hand. "Okay, open them."

It's a small, faded green ticket—like one from a raffle—with the words "KEEP THIS COUPON" flaking away.

"Are they doing a raffle?" I ask. The last time I saw a ticket like this, it was at my neighborhood's community development fundraiser.

"It's a movie ticket," he says. "Good for one movie that I will retell for you—to the best of my knowledge."

My smile manages to grow a bit more. "What if it's one you hate or don't know?"

He looks like he's already regretting this. "Any. Movie. Of your choice."

"An—"

"Within reason, Jamie, don't make me tell you *Citizen Kane* or some shit. It's so boring. Rosebud is the sled and capitalism is evil. There, that one was a freebie."

I laugh and close my hand around the ticket. "I'll make sure I choose a good one. Where did you get this?"

"Palmetto Park and Splash World Resort. There were a few littering the ground and I picked them up . . . you know." During Daphne's funeral procession. Yes, I guess that would make sense.

"Them? There's more?"

He shrugs. "Who knows!"

I put the ticket in my back pocket—already thinking about the movies I can ask Andrew to recite for me—and tell him to close *his* eyes. He does and holds out his good hand. I take the neon wood turtle I stole from the shop in Florida and put it in his hand.

He opens it and his smile drops. For a second I feel bad, like I made a mistake by choosing a gift from the place we had to flee.

"I thought it might be nice," I say, trying to salvage the moment. "I mean, for you to have something to remind you . . ." Remind him of the place we had to run away from. Because of me. "A souvenir. Sorry."

But he does smile, and when he looks at me, there are tears in his eyes. He laughs and tries to wipe them away. "No, don't be." He hugs me tight, then kisses my neck, then my cheek, then my lips. "It is perfect. Tacky and wonderful and perfect. Thank you."

After gifts, everyone pretty much splits off into groups to talk and have breakfast. I see the Kid sitting alone with Bobo and his new toy, a Pokémon plush he doesn't seem as interested in as his own hippo. I head over to him and sit down against the wall.

"You feeling better today, Kid?" He just nods, so I press him a little more. "Pretty cool that Santa still knows where you are, right?"

Again, just a nod. Maybe he knows Santa isn't real. Maybe when Santa didn't show up last year after society collapsed, all the orphaned kids in the world realized it was their parents who bought them gifts on Christmas. I feel Andrew's eyes on me from across the room, probably waiting for me to give him the look that we often share. The one that says *tag, you're in* so I can go to the sideline, and he can take over trying to make the Kid feel better. But now, knowing that we're going to have to eventually ghost everyone, I stay put.

I grab the Pokémon from the floor. It's not one I recognize, so it must be a newer one.

"What's this guy's name?" The Kid just shrugs. "Should we give him a name, then?" Another shrug. "I think he looks like an Edward."

That makes the Kid smile.

"No? How about Engelbert Humperdinck?"

The Kid finally laughs.

"Well then, what do you think?"

He finally takes the plush from me and looks at it, holding it up next to Bobo. I expect him to say something like Cece or Bobo-Two, but instead he says, "Albie."

I gasp. "I think that's an amazing name! Now, aren't you glad Santa brought him?"

The Kid's smile drops again. "Are you and Andrew leaving?"

I turn and give Andrew the look, and he joins us. "Are you talking about me?"

"Are you leaving?" the Kid asks. He must have heard us when he was washing his hands yesterday. Andrew gives me an almost imperceptible glance before shaking his head.

"We're all leaving. I'm not sure when, but don't worry, we're all going to stick together." He holds out his hand. "Let's go get something to eat."

The Kid takes his hand and Andrew gives me a guilty look. I return it with a nod. I know exactly what he's thinking because I feel the same. The Kid is going to be destroyed when we leave. Across the room, Taylor breaks away from Jamar to talk with the Kid for a second. She's going to be sad, too. But maybe she can go with the Nomads and Jamar.

Christ, then the Kid would be completely alone. This is why I wanted to keep our distance in the Keys. We weren't supposed to become friends with these people, and we weren't supposed to be a found family to a group of orphans.

I get up and head out to the front of the lodge where I can breathe a bit. My chest feels tight and my eyes burn, threatening tears.

"How you holding up?"

I turn to see Cal emerging from the lodge. He has a steaming mug of the forager tea in his hands.

"Good. Merry Christmas."

"Is it?" he asks, blowing on his tea. "After your . . . reunion yesterday. You and Andrew seem to be on edge."

I nod. "Hard not to be."

Cal takes a sip of his tea and winces. "This stuff tastes like shit." He throws it in the dirt, where according to Rocky Horror it should be right at home. "You never told me about this Danny Rosewood guy."

Of course I left out the part where I killed one of the leaders of Fort Caroline's only living son and had a bounty on my head. "I figured it would make me seem less trustworthy."

"Because finding out on Christmas Eve—and after weeks on the road together—that some authoritarian regime is hunting you up and down the Eastern Seaboard, yeah, that's a person we can trust." He says it with a smirk, though, so maybe he's not so pissed.

"We're going to leave," I say. "I'm sorry we didn't tell you, but Andrew and I are going to get Amy and her daughter home, then we're gone. On our own."

"And what about everyone else? What if these people catch up with us? Do you want us to lie for you?"

The answer is yes, but it's not right to ask that. Regardless of how long we've been traveling with them, they owe us no loyalty. So I shake my head. "You can do what you have to do. But I'm not telling you where we live."

"I know Amy's mom is in Bethesda. I can send them that far at least. Then what?"

My mouth goes dry. "Go ahead and tell them. Amy and her mom won't be there when Fort Caroline arrives, and they'll hit a dead end. But maybe chasing us all over the country looking for breadcrumbs is exactly how they fail. Using up all their supplies and fuel to find me, all for nothing."

Cal nods. "But what about the kids? And Amy, Kelly, Cara, Rocky Horror? You'd be putting them in danger even if they were hiding elsewhere."

I clench my jaw and try to look like I'm not lying. "And who would tell us if something did happen? Even if they lived here, happy and healthy for the rest of their lives, we'd never know."

"No, but it would be there. In the back of your mind." He watches my face, waiting for something, but I'm not sure what. I try to remain neutral, showing him that he's wrong. But he isn't. "I think this is one of those universal convergence moments we talked about, but from the moment we drove past you on the highway with people from the Keys. Or were they from this Fort Caroline place?"

"No, that part was true. After the hurricane, the Keys offered me up in exchange for the bounty Fort Caroline had out on me."

He nods. "They could have let us drive past without chasing us down. We agreed it was none of our business and wanted to stay out of it."

"So why did you get involved?"

"We saw you camped out. Andrew was injured, you had the kids. If you'd escaped them, we figured you could use some help, and you were resourceful enough to get away from your captors."

"And how is this supposed to be a random moment that makes sense again?"

"I was retired before the flu. But I worked for the CIA."

That's surprising. There's always been something cop-like about Cal, but spy wasn't even on my radar.

"Most of my time I was stationed in Afghanistan. We were required to withdraw in 2021, and the government promised us that our interpreters and assets who were still there would be evacuated and given US citizenship. Seven of my assets and their families were supposed to be rescued during the evacuation in Kabul. But they never made it, and I never found out what happened to them. So trust me when I say, you can run off into the empty roads of America, end up wherever you end up, and hope for the best for the others here. But you know how this world is. In the back of your mind, it's the uncertainty that'll drive you crazy."

He really just said all that to make me feel like shit, to make me feel guilty for not telling him. "Thanks, that makes me feel so much better."

"I'm not trying to make you feel better. I'm trying to make you realize something needs to be done."

I stare at him, trying to read his unreadable face. "Something like what?"

"You can't just keep running. And you can't stop them on your own."

The uneasiness I felt this morning. Hearing Cal say all this seems to help put those pieces together for me. I want Andrew, Cara, and me to continue on our own, but I'm worried about what might happen to the others.

"So what am I supposed to do?" We ran to begin with because we knew it wasn't safe. Then we kept running when they caught up to us, but this just keeps happening.

"If they did go down to the Keys to find you," he says, "that means they probably sent whoever they're using as a new military force to kill you or bring you back. Which means Fort Caroline itself is weak right now. There's probably only a skeleton crew or bunch of civilians with guns watching over them."

"So you're saying . . . we attack them?" That's the easiest way for Andrew and me to die. Yes, I'd shoot whoever I had to, to protect Andrew. It's very different from the deer I didn't want to shoot back at the cabin. Deer don't target humans; they don't try to kill us like people do. The memory of my own gunshot wound returns. I *want* anyone who would hurt Andrew, or the others in our group, to feel that pain.

But Cal shakes his head. "We don't attack. We destabilize. From what I learned yesterday, it sounds like this Fort Caroline place is already heading in that direction with the psyops they tried to pull with Denton. So what happens if we show up with you as our 'prisoner'"—he even uses air quotes—"say we're there to collect the bounty, and everyone else finds out the people in power have been wasting their supplies hunting you when we've had you all along."

"What's to stop you from just turning me in?"

"Because I don't trust them."

"But I'm supposed to trust you?"

"Yes. Because we've lived through all this before. We stayed up late last night talking with Denton and Nadine. Hearing them talk about their experiences there gave a few of us flashbacks of Pastor Phillip. Less religiously fueled, but the same tactics. Authoritarianism doesn't go away on its own. A few brave people need to push back, tell everyone who will listen what the future will look like if things continue. And I've told you what *your* future is going to look like. Worrying about my assets didn't end when the flu hit. I still think about them, and I know you'll think about everyone in that room there." He points at the lodge.

"And, honestly, I'd feel the same about all of you," he continues. "There's nothing I can do about the world ending. But I can at least wish for some peace of mind. And maybe that's making sure the people I've been traveling with—the people I've trusted with my life, despite them not trusting me—don't have to worry about being hunted down."

"What if it doesn't work?"

Cal nods. "It's possible it won't. But think of it this way. If it doesn't work, you don't have to worry about them anymore." He doesn't clarify who the "them" is. He could mean Fort Caroline, because I'd be dead. But I'm thinking of Andrew. And the Kid and Cara and Amy and Rocky Horror. If I went along with this plan and they weren't involved, it would mean they were safe.

"How do you imagine this destabilization would work?"

"We show up with you, we pretend a couple of us are the leaders of our group, while the rest of our people act as citizens. They plant the seeds of dissent, and we wait for them all to explode."

"So people still die."

"People always die," he says. "That's the price of freedom."

"There you are." I turn to see Andrew coming out alone.

"Think it over. The Faraway folks have invited us to stay another night. Let me know your decision tomorrow."

He nods to Andrew and then goes inside. "Think about what?" Andrew asks.

"He wants to know what our next step is," I lie. "I mentioned that we might be separating from them and heading to Henri's."

"It's going to hurt," he says. "But it's for the best. For all of us."

I nod. "Yeah. I think you're right."

"Come on," Andrew says. "They're doing some kind of Christmas toast or something." I follow him inside, and I can already hear Hannah speaking. Then cheers.

"Guess we missed it," I say.

We walk in and the kids are all celebrating, dancing, running around. The orphans, the Nomad kids, *and* Faraway's kids. Kelly wipes a tear from her eye, hugging a woman from Faraway. Cal locks eyes with me from across the room as we approach Cara.

"What did we miss?" Andrew asks.

She lowers her voice. "They just offered a place to stay for anyone who wants it. To live and work here with them."

Andrew's eyes are wide, and he looks at me as if shocked by this Christmas miracle. He slips his hand into mine and squeezes it gently, and I know exactly what he's going to do.

"We're not going to stay," he says. "We're going to take Amy and Henri-Two to her mom's and then go to Jamie's cabin. But we don't want to tell too many people."

"Because of Fort Caroline," she says. Andrew nods as Cara's eyes flit over to Grover Denton and Nadine Price. "So why are you telling me?"

"Because we're a family. You can choose to stay here if you want, or at Henri's in Bethesda. Or you can come with us. Right?" He looks to me for reassurance, to make sure I'm okay with him inviting Cara to live with us. Of course I am, but that means another person we have to protect.

"Yes," I say. "You're always welcome."

She nods slowly. "I'll think about it. I'm going to Henri's with you, so there's plenty of time."

Her eyes drift over my shoulder and I follow them to see Denton and Nadine walking over to us. I've avoided them as much as I could since yesterday. Every time I see him, rage flows through my body. It makes my throat tight and my jaw clench. I can only think about him tying our hands behind our backs, ruining the first kiss I ever had with Andrew—the one I thought would also be our last. I don't care if he says it wasn't him who shot me. It was *them*. And he was part of them.

"Can we talk to both of you?" Denton asks.

Andrew shakes his head. "Sorry we pulled a gun on you, but you did shoot my boyfriend, so I'm not that sorry. But whatever you have to say to us, it doesn't matter."

Nadine lowers her voice. "The invitation for the others to stay is contingent on both of you not staying."

Of course it is. It makes sense. Even if we hadn't already been planning to leave, I wouldn't be offended.

Denton closes his eyes. "Nadine."

"They need to know."

"Yes, and I was going to talk about it outside so as not to cause a scene."

Andrew scoffs. "Listen, I'm going to give you all a wonderful Christmas present. We aren't staying anyway. We'll leave tomorrow, so long as everyone else can stay." He grows serious. "Especially the kids and Kelly. They need a place they can call home, and if they stay, you need to make sure Fort Caroline doesn't go near them."

But I'm not sure that's possible. If they find out Denton is here and come after him, Faraway might trade information about us to save him. And Fort Caroline has shown they can't be trusted. They might say they'll leave Denton and the others here, but if they show up and are better armed than Faraway, they could kill the adults and take the kids.

"Understand?" Andrew asks.

Denton nods and turns to Cara. "You're allowed to stay, if you want."

Cara shakes her head. "I left Fort Caroline with them. I'll leave here with them as well."

Denton seems disappointed, but the look on his face says he understands.

"And look at that!" Andrew smiles wide and holds out his good hand like a magician doing a trick. "Without causing a scene. Be proud! Merry Christmas to all."

Cara glares at Andrew, but Nadine just takes his joke as her cue to leave. Denton stands there for a moment before looking at both Andrew and me.

"I also wanted to say that I'm sorry," he says. "I know now that I wasn't being brave. I was letting things happen instead of rocking the boat, and it still turned out bad. And I'm sorry you two got caught in the crosshairs."

Andrew sighs as though he's annoyed that Denton is apologizing. "Well, you weren't the only one there letting things go on, so try not to take all the blame." He stops short of saying anything about forgiveness, which I understand.

Denton nods, wishes us a merry Christmas, and goes back to the other side of the room. But his words still stick with me. How he regrets not doing more when he could have, and how others should have, as well. Maybe there are more people like that in Fort Caroline, just waiting for someone to say something.

Which means Cal might be right.

And it means we should try to do something about it.

I don't say anything at first. Instead, I let Andrew and Cara enjoy the morning feast. They talk to Amy and agree to leave the next day. It isn't until halfway through the afternoon that I finally have the nerve to talk to them. I tell them to come outside with me and we walk down to the lake.

"Should we invite Rocky Horror to come with us?" Andrew asks. "I'm not sure if he will, but he may not want to stay here without any other queer folks."

"Denton and Nadine are both gay," Cara says.

"No shit! Wow, they really were dummies for staying in Fort Caroline for so long. I'm not sure if that makes me madder or if I feel bad for them now. Dammit, Cara, why do you have to make me feel solidarity with them?"

I take a deep breath and say what I've been gearing up to all afternoon.

"I'm not going to Henri's with you."

ANDREW

I STARE AT JAMIE, TRYING TO FIGURE out when the bit is supposed to get funny. Like, oh, I'm not going to Henri's with you because I've decided we should all hop on a boat and go where the wind takes us. Which still isn't funny, so I'm hoping he's got something better.

"I was talking to Cal," he says. "He's worried that Danny Rosewood is just going to keep sending people after us. And I think he's right."

"How?" I ask. "They went down to the Keys and we weren't there."

"Trevor said he'd tell them where we were going. Once they regroup after the Keys, they might head there."

"Or they could give up," I say, looking to Cara for help. But she seems worried. "And we talked about this. We get Henri and Amy out, and they hide somewhere until Fort Caroline gives up looking for us."

"They've been broadcasting about me for months, Andrew. There are wanted posters—"

"One! One wanted poster; we haven't seen any others."

"Because we were on the western side of Georgia. They probably plastered them up and down the East Coast. Which is why we can't stay here, we can't go to Henri's, and we can't go to the cabin. Not until this ends."

Ends. I stare at him, trying to figure out what the hell he's talking about. Because he's not seriously considering sacrificing himself for our safety. That's insane, even for Jamie.

"Ends how?" Cara asks.

"Cal thinks they sent an army to get me in the Keys. I guess to intimidate them and because, as we already knew, there's no way Fort Caroline is helping anyone else. So they might be vulnerable now."

"You're going to attack them?" I ask. This plan sounds worse every minute.

But Jamie shakes his head. "Based on what Denton said about things falling apart, Cal thinks it'll be possible to start a revolution. Then, when their army gets back from the Keys, there's already new leadership in place and it becomes a democracy."

"That's stupid. No, you're not going based on months-old intel from Grover Denton and some random guy from California."

"Cal was in the CIA."

"I don't care if he kissed the president on the mouth at holiday parties. Jamie, you can't be serious about this."

"I'm tired of always looking over our shoulders!" he says. "I don't want to have to worry about everyone for the rest of my life."

I step closer to him and take his hands, even using my bad one, which hurts so awfully it brings tears to my eyes. Or maybe the tears are because of how scared I am of him doing this. "You don't have to worry about everyone. Just worry about us. They don't *want* everyone else. They just want the two of us."

He puts his forehead against mine. "Which is why I'm going. If they have me, they won't come looking for you or anyone else. And if we get there soon enough, everyone else in Fort Caroline will see what a waste this all was, and that whatever kind of villain Rosewood made me out to be, I'm just a kid that they spent months and who knows how many resources hunting down. All that time and energy spent on a revenge mission instead of making sure their settlement could be sustainable. And that's how Danny Rosewood is taken down."

"What if it isn't?" I ask. He seems confused by my question. "What happens if you show up and they kill you? Then they parade your corpse around town claiming the teenage boogeyman who stole seven cans of food and shot their leader's son is dead. What happens then?"

He shakes his head. "It won't happen like that."

"Why not?"

"Because if I have to, I'll kill Rosewood myself. And anyone who gets in my way." He sounds so sure. His voice doesn't waver and neither do his hands. Jamie's face is hardened in anger and frustration, and not even the boy I met nine months ago at gunpoint looked like this person who's in front of me now.

That boy would never say this. He'd never look at me like this. Before, when I broke into his cabin, he looked lost. As if it wasn't me breaking in, but him waking up not realizing where he was. I thought he'd kill me, but then almost immediately I could tell he wouldn't. I don't even remember if I thought that then or if I was just gambling.

When he gave me food, I thought he might be trying to poison me, but the longer he spoke, the safer I felt.

If I broke into that cabin today and saw this person . . .

I think he would have shot me.

"No." I shake my head. The old Jamie still has to be in there somewhere—this is because he's scared, that's all. We're all scared; I just have to remind him we can be scared together. I put my hands to his cheeks so his eyes are locked on mine. Blood is seeping through the bandage on my left hand and it's throbbing with pain. "You don't need to do this. I get why you think you do, but you can come with us and we're all going to be fine. No one is ever perfectly safe, not even before the apocalypse. But we can be happy, and we can try. All of us."

I turn to Cara for backup. *Please help me.* She nods and takes Jamie's hand.

"It's okay to be scared," she says. "We can all be scared, but staying together is what makes us strong."

He closes his eyes and for a second my heart leaps. We did it. He's going to stay with us.

But he gives a slow shake of his head.

My hands drop away from his face. There are no tears in his eyes, and he looks resolute.

"Denton is right. I killed Rosewood's son, and as long as he's alive, he'll never stop trying to find me."

I think the reason it's called "heartbreak" is because it really does feel as if your chest has split open and everything has fallen out. And then all that's left is numbness.

"Jamie, please," Cara tries.

He shakes his head. "And I don't want you to come with us either. I want you both, Amy, and Henri-Two to make sure you get to Henri."

My voice is icy when I speak. "I have no intention of going with you on a revenge mission, Jamie."

He seems surprised, as if he thought I would fight him on this or sneak onto a truck to come with him.

"It's not a revenge mission."

"Yes, it is. And I didn't see it before, but you've been like this for . . ." I shake my head. "Since you got shot. You pushed the people in the Keys away. You refused to let that be our home. You gave up on the boat mission after I got kicked off for someone who was a legit navy admiral. You gave up on getting Henri, which was the entire *point* of us going to the Keys. Then when we were on the road, you tried to hide medicine from the Nomads—the people who helped us and gave us food. You pulled a gun on Denton yesterday. This isn't about keeping us safe, no matter how much you're trying to tell yourself it is. It's a revenge mission. Because you don't like the person you've turned into and—"

I stop myself just in time, because I was about to say *I don't like him either*. But I don't want to say that out loud. Not that I need to. I can see in his face that he knows exactly what I was going to say.

"I love you," I say. "I do. Just please come with us."

And just like he knows what I was going to say, I know what he's going to say, too. He's made up his mind.

"I don't want to lose you," I try one last time.

"I'll come find you when it's done," he says.

I turn away from him. He calls after me, but I go up the deck stairs behind the lodge and straight into the dining hall area. Nadine is there, but Denton isn't. I walk up to her, interrupting a conversation she's having with another woman.

"Where's Denton?"

"Why?"

"Just tell me."

She looks down at my hands, probably checking that I'm unarmed. Smart move, Lady Marine.

"He went to the bathroom."

I leave without thanking her and head back toward the outhouses. Halfway there, Denton sees me coming and stops. Probably because he sees the anger on my face. I walk up to him and shove him with my good hand. Because it's only one arm, it's not enough to push him all the way onto his ass, so he just stumbles back a few steps.

"Hey!"

"Shut up!" I yell. "Whatever you said to Jamie worked, because now he's going to Fort Caroline on some revenge mission to kill Rosewood."

"What? Andrew, I didn't say anything."

"I don't care. You're sorry, right? You want to make amends? Then you fucking go with him. Make sure he doesn't get himself killed and . . ." My voice breaks and tears spill from my eyes. "You make damn sure he comes back. Stop him before he makes a mistake he'll never forgive himself for."

"Andrew—"

"I don't care! Whatever you have to say, I don't care. I told you what you need to do. Do it or don't." I continue past him to the cabins and start packing up my clothes. I don't want to say goodbye to Jamie. It's immature, but it's also my last-ditch effort to try to get him to change his mind. If I hide and he can't find me when he goes to leave, maybe he'll stay? I hope he will.

But he doesn't. He doesn't come looking for me in the cabin the other kids are sharing. And in the morning when I wake up with everyone else, I learn that Jamie and a group of the Nomads have left. Niki has left, too, which surprises me. I never thought she'd leave Jamar here alone.

Cara finds me by the lake, where I've taken some of Faraway's water to clean my arm. It's healing nicely, except for my hand, where I popped four stitches when I was trying to convince Jamie to stay.

"Are you okay?" she asks, keeping a few paces away from me.

"Not even a little bit." I'm exhausted because I couldn't sleep. My arm hurts because I strained it yesterday. I spent most of Christmas morning thinking about Daphne and Liz and the kids who didn't survive the hurricane. And then my boyfriend ended the afternoon by telling me he's on a revenge mission to kill another person. Something I know deep down he doesn't want to do. He's just scared. Like I am now.

"Let me help you," Cara says. She takes the cloth from me and dips it in the water. Then she gently cleans my arm, puts antibiotic ointment on it, and rewraps it. "We can stay here. I'm sure Amy will be okay with it. For a few days, we can rest and wait."

But that sounds awful. Waiting here for them to come back, only to find out what? That Jamie is dead? Or that he killed someone? I don't care how much Rosewood deserves to die; I don't want it to be Jamie who kills him. When he killed Rosewood's son it almost broke him.

I don't want to see that person again. He did it to protect me, but he's lying to himself now if he thinks that's what he's doing. Though I don't think he'll realize it until after it's done.

"No, let's get Amy home. Let's just get that done and then we can figure out what we're going to do."

She nods and helps me up. "I know there's nothing I can say to make you feel better."

For a minute she just stares at me. Then she shrugs. "That was it."

And I actually laugh.

"I talked to everyone last night," she says. "Amy's ready to leave with Henri-Two whenever you are."

"I think I want to go today. I'm tired, but if it's just the four of us, we can stop anywhere." I'm also worried that if we stay here too long, I'm just going to end up waiting for Jamie to change his mind and turn around. But if he does, he knows where we're going.

"Okay, let's go tell the others."

We go back and find Amy, Kelly, and Rocky Horror by the playground. Taylor and Jamar are there with the Kid as well.

Amy gives me a questioning look and I nod. She goes into the playground to get Henri-Two, who is playing with another toddler in a sandbox.

"You okay?" Rocky Horror asks.

I turn back to the others. "Amy, Cara, and I are going to continue on to Bethesda."

Kelly nods. "I figured as much. Amy mentioned you all might keep going."

Taylor walks right over to me. Jamar follows at her heel.

"'*You* all'?" she asks.

"I'm still leaving. I'm going with Amy and Henri-Two to Bethesda."

"I'm coming with you, then."

I shake my head. "You're safe here, you don't need to do that."

"What about Jamie?" she asks, looking past me for him.

"He went with some others to another settlement." She doesn't need to know where he really went.

"Wait," Rocky Horror says. "Where did he go?" I turn back to Cara, who looks guilty. She must have forgotten to tell him.

"There's another settlement that was like ours," Jamar says. "They're going to stop them. Niki went, too."

"Stop them how?" Rocky Horror asks. But I don't answer.

"Is he coming back?" Taylor asks.

"I hope so. But not here—probably to Amy and Henri or to the cabin his mom had in Pennsylvania."

She nods as if that makes sense. "Okay, I'm coming, too, then."

"Tay—"

"Screw you, I *want* to do it. Jamie is my family now. Just like Daphne and Liz were."

"What about the kids?" I ask. "They're your family, too, aren't they?"

"Yes, but the kids are fine here, and they have Kelly. I'm coming with you." She turns to Jamar. "I'm sorry. I can't stay."

"Then I'm coming with y'all," says Jamar.

"No, no, no," I say. "Niki would hunt us down and murder us."

"He's right," says Taylor. "You have to stay here. She's your sister. She can't come back to find you missing."

Jamar's eyes start to well up with tears, and Taylor hugs him tight. He sobs quietly as he grips the back of her jacket.

Rocky Horror puts out a hand. "Whoa! Hold on! I agreed to the Mary Poppins fuckery for the *trip*. I am not staying here so you can leave me with six kids!"

"You coming, too, RH?" I ask.

He scoffs. "I did not say that."

I smile. "Then chim chim cher-oo on outta this conversation and go help Hannah and Kelly babysit those kids."

Rocky Horror groans, looks at the kids on the playground, then back at me. He rolls his eyes and says, "Fine, stop begging, I'll come, too."

I open my mouth to tell him I was just kidding, but he holds up a hand. "I was only going to stay 'cause y'all were. I'm still not entirely ready to be done with you yet." He takes a few steps over to me and lowers his voice. "This place is great, but I'm going to be honest. There's just something more inviting about being on the road. I feel kind of . . . stagnant here, if that makes sense."

I *want* stagnancy, just not yet. Still, I nod.

I ask them all, individually, if they're sure. They tell me they are. And I do feel a bit better having them on my side. Jamar and Taylor still have tears in their eyes, though. They walk off to say their farewell as we say goodbye to the kids. They're sad to see us go, but I think they're happier to have a place to stay now. Especially since after we

269

hug, they run right off to their new Faraway friends.

Except for the Kid. He looks heartbroken.

"It'll be okay," I tell him. But he just nods. "You take care of Bobo and Albie, okay?" Again, just a nod. I ask him if I can have a hug, and he nods again but doesn't hug me back.

With tears in my eyes, I turn away from him. We have our things packed up and ready to go, and Kelly, Jamar, and a couple of the Nomads are there to send us off.

Just as we start to walk away, Jamar calls out to Taylor.

He runs down to her as she turns, and they stop three feet from each other. They just stare, both too afraid to speak or move.

Then Jamar takes a step forward and kisses Taylor on the lips. It's a long—adorably awkward—closed-mouthed kiss where they both keep their hands in fists at their sides.

They separate and look at each other. "Bye," he says. And promptly turns around and walks away as quickly as possible. Taylor turns back to us, her face pink.

"You good?" I ask her teasingly.

"Yes." She walks past me as her mouth slowly curls into a smile, and Amy and I have to bite our lips to keep from laughing. Then Rocky Horror, Cara, Amy and Henri-Two, and I follow her down the dirt-and-gravel driveway to the road. There, we say goodbye to the man and woman at the entrance, thanking them for their hospitality.

We're probably fifty feet away from the Faraway Campground when the woman at the entrance whistles behind us.

"Looks like you forgot one!" she calls out.

I turn to see the Kid running for us. Bobo and Albie flop in either hand, and he's hunched over with the weight of his backpack. I jog to meet him halfway and crouch down.

"Kid, you have to stay here."

But he shakes his head. "I want to come with you."

"It's safer here. For all three of you." I wiggle one of Bobo's legs, but the Kid shakes his head. "Please? I promise you're going to be okay here."

"I want Jamie, too."

Shit. I stand and turn to the others, using my eyes to ask for help. I could lie to him and say Jamie's coming back. But then the Kid grabs my hand and holds tight. I look down to see Albie and Bobo tucked under one arm. The Kid looks ahead at the others.

"We're not going to find Jamie," I say. "He had to go do something."

The Kid looks up at me. "But he's coming back here?"

I shake my head. "I don't know. He might meet up with us later."

"I want to come with you, then."

Cara shrugs and pats Rocky Horror on the shoulder. "Glad to have you back, Mary Poppins."

Rocky Horror groans, pretending to hate everything about this moment while the others give him a hard time. The Kid pulls me along, helping me give up a little easier. Because I definitely would have missed him, too.

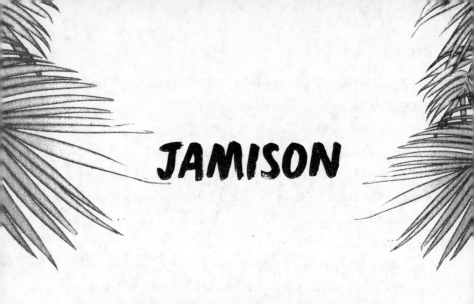

JAMISON

THERE'S TWENTY-FOUR OF US ALTOGETHER. INCLUDING GROVER Denton. I
have no idea why he's here, but his eyes keep darting over to me in the
back of the pickup truck. It's raining and we've covered ourselves with
tarps, but my pants are still soaked from the water pooling in the bed.

We've been driving since this morning—only stopping once to
get situated after the rain started. That's when I realized I still had
the road atlas we were using before we met up with the Nomads. Not
that Cal and the other guy in charge need it. They're taking the same
routes we took to Faraway, but will eventually cut across South Carolina to get to I-95. From there, Denton's given them directions to Fort
Caroline in Georgia.

After a couple of hours, the rain starts pouring down even harder.
The person driving the truck pulls over, and he and Cal get out and
come around to the truck bed. Cal motions for us to climb down.

"We'll swap you six with six in the RV so you have some time to
dry off."

The RV folks have already been chosen, probably because Cal

radioed back and asked for volunteers. We thank them and get into the RV.

They've removed the bed from the rear of the RV to make more room for supplies and for people to sit. One of the people at the dining room table looks up from the maps in front of her. She's an older white woman with messy brown-and-gray hair. She points behind her.

"There's a bathroom you can use to change," she says. "The plumbing isn't hooked up right, so don't use it. But you can throw your ponchos in the shower, and we'll hang them to dry when we camp for the night in Orangeburg."

The guy in front of me nods and goes into the bathroom. I have no idea how Cal managed to recruit so many people on such short notice. I scan their faces, looking for Niki, but she isn't here, so she must be in the back room of the RV. The people around me all look serious, like they're totally ready for this. They aren't doing it for me—I've said maybe fifteen words to anyone in this RV since we first met up with the Nomads—so they must have their own reasons. Denton isn't the only one from Faraway who joined either.

The bathroom door opens and I go in, throwing my poncho on top of the others in the shower. I change my pants, underwear, and socks—my shirt is a little damp but not bad—and look at myself in the mirror.

I used to be able to shave only every other week, but the hair on my face has been getting thicker. Andrew still gets away with twice a month, tops. He could do it even less, but it makes him itchy.

The moment I think of him—and how far away he is right now— my chest tightens, a wave of anxiety walloping me. My hands shake and I have to turn away from my own reflection.

I push the door open and head to the back room without saying anything to the next person. Some of the canned food, weapons, and ammo we found in the neo-Nazi hideout are stacked around us. The rest they left in Faraway.

Niki is sitting on the floor next to a stack of boxes. She gives me a wan smile as I sit down next to her and say hi.

"How is it out there?" she asks.

"Wet."

We're dancing around what I really want to know: why she left her brother back in Faraway and came with us. How did she go from worrying about him being out of her sight in an amusement park parking lot to leaving him in a new place while she goes to a white-supremacist settlement?

And she isn't the only Black woman in the RV. There's also a handful of other people of color who joined up with us for this mission. This whole thing is even more dangerous for them given Fort Caroline's racism. The silence seems to stretch longer between us, and she anxiously rubs her hands up and down her jeans.

"My grandma survived the flu," she says. "It was me, Jamar, and her who Cal and the others found in Arkansas. She was ninety-six. You wouldn't think it, though. When we got to Pastor Phillip's settlement, there was a law. We weren't allowed to share our own food with people over seventy. They got their rations, and anything else they had to find themselves."

"How?"

She shrugs. "It's not like we could walk several miles a day with her looking for food. Especially when they had taken everything already. They would have raids and double-check the rations they gave us to make sure we weren't hoarding food. If they found extra, they would take it. But the rations got smaller and smaller for the elderly, and my grandma . . ." She shakes her head. "They were just trying to starve the older people. They didn't see her value, and maybe they didn't want the old folks to talk about what things were like before the flu."

"That's awful. I'm so sorry."

"Jamar is a good kid. He's so sweet and sensitive. Grandma was getting so weak she couldn't even leave the apartment, so he gave her some of his food. And he hid a little bit. We had a surprise inspection and they found it. I knew it was him, but I told them it was me, so they arrested me, put me in their jail with a few others who had been trying to help the people they loved.

"Then they cut Jamar's rations, too. And Grandma wouldn't eat because she knew he needed it." Tears spill down her cheeks. "They let her starve; they let a *lot* of people starve while Pastor Phillip and his family ate well and lived in their mansion."

I hold out my hand and she grasps it, squeezing hard.

"This Fort Caroline. They'd do the same, wouldn't they?"

I say yes, but it's possible they'd do worse. It's also possible that Pastor Phillip's settlement did worse.

"I trust Cal," she says, turning to look at me. "And I trust you now, too. We're doing this for the people we love." Like she went to jail for her little brother. I nod and pull up my shirt.

"This is where they shot me. We left them, and even though we took only the food we'd brought in with us, they sent people after us.

One of those people was a leader's son, and he wanted to kill Andrew and me because we're queer. I'm doing this because I don't want them coming after us anymore."

Someone else walks into the back room and I look up. Of course it's Denton. His eyes drop to my scar then immediately away once I lower my shirt. He takes a seat on the opposite side of the room.

"What about you?" Niki asks, turning her attention to Denton. There's a little venom in her voice, and it makes me feel like she's absolutely on my side. I'm glad she's here. "I heard you the other day talking about how you and Nadine narrowly escaped. Why are you here?"

He stares at me, and after a few moments I start to think maybe he won't answer her—that he thinks it should be obvious. Or even worse, that he thinks it in some way exonerates him from getting me shot, which it doesn't.

Finally he says, "Because I don't want people like that growing into power unchecked. And I know a lot of people don't realize it, but our resources are dwindling. Everything that was made before the superflu is now in short supply, and it's going to be generations before we even get close to where we were before. The big settlements that don't collapse on their own are going to be the ones in power. And I'd like for them to be welcoming."

I don't know if I believe him. If he cared so much about a just and tolerant society, he would have left Fort Caroline before Andrew and I even got there.

A woman from the back of the truck—her name is Valerie—joins us, sitting between Denton and me. She adds her own context. "I think there's a couple people just in it for the chaos."

"Seriously?" I ask. I would absolutely not be here if I could help it. I'd rather be walking with Andrew and Amy and Henri-Two. Even in the rain if we had to.

"Oh yeah," Valerie says. "There's a girl up there who followed her boyfriend when Cal asked for volunteers. The two of them seem to be hoping it turns into a full-scale violent uprising."

I shake my head. "We're not doing that, though."

She shrugs. "Not to start. But convincing a bunch of people to turn against those in charge is rarely peaceful."

A younger white guy on Denton's side of the room shrugs, giving a wry smile. "I mean, I don't want there to be an all-out war, but I wouldn't mind some firefighting." His eyes dart to the guns next to the food. "But, you know, not front-of-the-line cannon fodder."

"So who do you think deserves to be cannon fodder, then?" Valerie asks.

The two of them start arguing back and forth. Denton just gives me a look that I can only interpret as him saying, *You did this.*

I give it right back to him until he turns and looks out the window.

ANDREW

THAT NIGHT, AFTER WE SET UP CAMP, I start worrying about Jamie. It's not the first time I've thought about him—it's actually the twelfth, but who's counting other than me, so let's round down to ten so it's less depressing. I don't know if he's alive. Or if Fort Caroline immediately detained him and tortured him for information about where I am, no matter how many times he said he's the one who killed Danny Rosewood's son, not me.

Maybe they'd use him as an example and execute him.

Amy has just gotten Henri-Two down and turned in for the night. Next to me, the Kid lets out a big yawn. I'm not strict with his bedtime because I know he usually passes out when he needs to. Right after dinner, which we finished a couple of minutes ago.

Across from me, Taylor pokes the fire with a stick. She's been quiet all day. Probably missing Jamar.

"You want us to go back?" I ask. We haven't gotten that far away from Faraway yet, so it would be okay if she did. But she looks up at me and shakes her head.

Cara looks over at her. "We could try to find a car. See if there's one in a garage nearby that the owner isn't using anymore."

Great euphemism, Cara.

"Oh, can we do that anyway?" Rocky Horror asks, rubbing at his feet. "I got way too used to being carted around by the Nomads."

"I'm fine," Taylor says. "Except yes about the car."

"Yes, tomorrow we'll get off the highway and find a car."

Cara opens her mouth but stops. She looks over my shoulder, her eyes squinting. Then they go wide. "Who's there?" Her voice is low and anxious.

I spin around and peer into the dark. There's a noise, but it's so quiet I can't tell if it's my imagination. But then I see movement.

I grab the rifle, holding it up to whoever or whatever is there in the darkness. My mind immediately goes to alligators.

And then, for just a second, I hope it's Jamie.

"Wait! Don't shoot, it's just me!"

But that's not Jamie's voice.

Taylor is at my side. "Jamar?"

"Yeah." He comes a few steps closer. I lower the gun as Taylor runs over to him. She stops short and it almost becomes a replay of (what I assume was) their first kiss. But they both seem to be too nervous to do that again, so instead she knocks the wind out of him with a hug.

"Jesus, don't sneak up on us like that," Rocky Horror says.

"What's going on?" Amy asks, sounding groggy.

"Jamar followed us from Faraway," I say. Amy grunts and goes back to sleep.

"What about your sister?" Taylor asks.

Jamar winces. "I left her a note. When she gets back with Jamie, he'll have someone to leave with him."

Rocky Horror gives me an anxious look that I pass along to Cara. Niki is going to be pissed. And she's definitely following him. *If* they come back. But I have to stop thinking like that.

When they come back.

Thirteen times.

Rounded down to ten.

Jamar sits by the fire, very close to Taylor, and eats while we ask him why he left. Obviously he did it for Taylor, but I'm curious to know if he rationalized it to explain to Niki.

"You know she's going to be pissed, right?" I ask him.

Jamar nods. "For a while. But when she catches up, she'll realize why I did it." He holds out his hand to Taylor, who takes it eagerly. "We don't have our grandma anymore. It's just me and Niki, and we never really found a place we belonged after Grandma died, no matter where we went to. Then we met you." He looks at Taylor when he says this. "I know Niki feels the same, but she's just worried about me and not about herself. This is right for us. And she'll realize that, too."

I love his optimism. I want the optimism of a thirteen-year-old in love for the first time.

Fourteen rounded down to ten.

"Hey, guys," Taylor says. She points at a shopping center to our right. It's the next morning and we've gotten off the road to look for a neighborhood with a car we can borrow. I saw the shop signs from a ways down the road, though judging by the names listed, I'd assumed we wouldn't find food there. But Taylor isn't pointing at a food store. "Mind if we stop in here for a sec?"

It's a Books-A-Million.

"I've been meaning to look for an atlas," Cara says. "Ours is still in Jamie's pack." Then she gives me a nervous glance, realizing she just said the J-word.

"Yeah, we should probably stop and get one."

We head over to the store. Like most, the front glass has been smashed in. But where hardware, clothing, and grocery stores all look like they experienced a full-on siege, the bookstore looks like one lonely individual threw a brick through the front doors and walked in.

In fact, when we pass through the second set of doors, there's a brick on the floor.

The Kid runs off in the direction of the toys and children's books. Rocky Horror looks at Cara and me for backup, but I shake my head. "We're getting the road atlas."

"I'll go with you, RH," Amy says, carrying Henri-Two over the glass, then following the Kid.

Rocky Horror cups his hands over his mouth and shouts, "Oi! Kid! Don't touch any wild animals."

Taylor and Jamar go off on their own as Cara and I search for the travel section. Most of the shelves are still full of books. I wonder why. Maybe if there's a big reader nearby, they use it like a library, taking only what they want, then returning them when they're done.

There's a spiral-bound Rand McNally road atlas. Cara grabs it and we head back to the front of the store to get more light. While she skims the pages, I find a pack of expensive calligraphy pens by the counter. I rip open the box and hand a couple of pens to her, then head back to check on Rocky Horror and Amy.

"You have two stuffed animals already." Rocky Horror is pointing at Bobo and the stuffed Pokémon. "Why don't you pick out a couple of books?"

"I don't know how to read," the Kid says like it should be the most obvious thing in the world.

Rocky Horror sticks a thumb in my direction. "Neither does Andrew, and he's doing great."

"Which is why you should pick some books," I say, taking the Kid's hand and steering him away from the toys. Then I shoot a threatening glance back at Rocky Horror. "Maybe Rocky Horror will be nice and read them to us."

"Guys, come here!" Taylor shouts.

"One sec!" I point the Kid to a section of picture books and tell him to pick out three with cool pictures. "Where are you?" I shout.

"Back here."

I follow Taylor's voice and turn the corner to see her and Jamar standing in the romance section. How appropriate. But they don't look like they've been very romantic back here. Aside from Jamar holding Taylor's hand.

She points at a shelf. "Look."

I scan the books and come to a stop on two full shelves of paperbacks that make my heart break.

Daphne De Silva's name is bigger than the titles.

Rocky Horror, Amy, and Cara join us.

"Holy shit." Rocky Horror takes one of the paperbacks down and looks at the cover. "I knew she was a writer, but I didn't realize she was *prolific*."

"Oh yeah," Amy says. "She was very popular. After a couple bottles of wine one night a few years back, she told me she also wrote horror under a pen name but wouldn't tell me what it was."

I grab another book; this one's titled *A Second Chance at Forever*. The cover is illustrated and split diagonally down the middle by a crooked line. It shows two straight white couples, one younger, one older. I flip to the back and see a quote from a bestselling author about how "delightful" the book is. Below it are a couple of paragraphs about the people on the cover. It's the same couple years later—high school sweethearts who are pulled apart after a tragic car accident during their senior year. Then a chance meeting fifteen years later draws them back together and they try to pick up where they left off, hoping to get a second chance at happily ever after.

I flip it open, and inside is a page that lists all the other books available from Daphne De Silva. There are over fifty-four novels listed, seven novellas, and two listed separately under the "Detective Farrah Wallace Series."

Cara snorts and shows me another illustrated cover of a male rock star in a ripped shirt and jeans and a woman who looks like she's walking the red carpet of a movie premiere. The title makes me laugh, too.

Starry-Eyed and Rock-Hard.

Taylor takes off her backpack and starts grabbing one of each book from the shelf.

"You planning to carry all of them?" I ask.

She looks determined. "I want to read her work. And, yes, I want to read all of them."

Cara and I share a look. But it's Rocky Horror who speaks, taking a copy of *Pen and Paper Hearts* down from the shelf. "I'll carry a couple for you."

"Me too," I say.

By the time we're finished, we have twenty paperbacks of Daphne De Silva's life's work divvied up among our bags.

That night, since it's cold, we set up camp outside so we can have a fire. When the Kid is asleep, Taylor reaches into her bag and pulls out the books she got from the bookstore.

"What should I read for us?" she asks. She reads out each book title and the back blurb one by one. It's unanimous. We want *Love at First Swipe*: the story of Lucy, a woman who swears off dating after a string of horrific boyfriends and finds a no-strings hookup on an app. But what's supposed to be no-strings turns into something more when fate keeps putting the two together in hilariously awkward situations. It sounds like a Hallmark movie, and my heart aches remembering how much Jamie loved those.

Taylor starts reading it, and within minutes all of us are laughing, trying to stay quiet. When Lucy and charming, successful business-man Dan finally meet up for no-strings-attached sex, Rocky Horror gasps.

"Daphne, girl! You're a freak!" He says it as though she's still with us, and we all laugh.

Taylor shakes her head. "I am not comfortable reading this."

Rocky Horror holds out his hands. "Well, shit, I am. Hand over the smut."

He picks up where Taylor left off, and yes . . . even with Rocky Horror's carefully placed euphemisms and censoring, it is pretty steamy. Again, I find myself aching for Jamie. Wishing he were here with us, experiencing this moment. Though maybe all the Daphne De Silva smut would be too much for us.

After their steamy sex scene, Rocky Horror dog-ears the page and closes the book, but Taylor holds her hand out for it. She asks Cara for one of the markers she isn't using to mark the road atlas. Cara hands over a purple one and Taylor opens the cover and writes something in it.

"What are you writing?" I ask.

"I'll show you later." She even covers the page when Jamar tries to look.

We turn in for the night, but I'm still thinking about Jamie. And us together. Tears sting my eyes as I look up at the sky, so scared that I'll never see him again. Or that something bad will happen. Or that I will see him again, but he might not be the same person.

I have to trust that we'll have our own Second Chance at Forever. Pretend we're in a Hallmark movie, or a Daphne De Silva romance novel, and it's only a matter of time before we're together again.

Thirty-one, rounded down to ten.

The next day it's rainy and cold, but we're back on the road, still skirting the highway and checking houses for food, so while Amy, Taylor, and Jamar look after the Kid and Henri-Two, we head to a neighborhood with pretty big McMansions.

The third one gives us a real win.

When we break in, I smell the rot before I see the body on the couch. There's a blanket on top of them, but the flesh is pulled tight on the skull. Cara plucks the edge of the blanket and draws it up, over the head.

There are canned goods in the pantry and in the garage is a newish Volvo—probably one of the last couple of thousand cars sold before the flu. We pull the emergency cord on the garage door opener and lift the door up. The car is locked, but a quick search of the first floor turns up the keys. It's been sitting, unused, for probably over a year, but Cara still turns the key in the ignition.

The car engine tries to turn over but doesn't catch. She tries it again. This time, the engine comes to life. We all cheer.

"How much gas is in the tank?" I ask, peeking over her shoulder.

"Holy shit. Almost half-full!"

Rocky Horror throws his bag in the front seat and pulls open the glove box. "A lovely way to look at it. Let's all thank . . . Mr. Doyle"— he spins an expired insurance card around for us to read the name Christopher Doyle on it—"for his excellent planning and gas conservation." We thank Christopher Doyle and head back to Amy and the kids.

When we're all squeezed into the Volvo, we get back on the highway. Cara and Rocky Horror switch off driving while Taylor continues reading from *Love at First Swipe*. The book is filled with innuendos—some Taylor doesn't even realize as she's reading them aloud, but Amy will snort or Cara and Rocky Horror glance back at me with wide eyes—and when she gets to a sex scene she dog-ears the page and says, "You can read that part later, Rocky Horror."

When a dirty joke comes up that Taylor gets—or an inappropriate word—she either skips to the next sentence or comes up with some other word that has Cara, Rocky Horror, and me cackling.

We stop for the night in North Carolina. We should reach Bethesda tomorrow, and I can tell Amy is in high spirits. She might have been unsure about leaving the Keys, but she seems excited knowing how close we are to Henri now.

286

It's Rocky Horror's turn to read. We're getting to the end of the book, so he spares Taylor and Jamar embarrassment and skips over the final sex scene—telling us he'll read that to himself tomorrow morning at breakfast—and we listen, rapt, as Lucy and Dan confess their love to one another in a coffee shop after not realizing they've moved across the country to the same city.

The best part is, Dan ordered Lucy's coffee order—a nonfat, no-water, double dirty chai—instead of his usual black coffee. So they both go to reach for it when the barista calls out the order. And they see the universe has brought them together again.

The next morning, after Rocky Horror has read the sex scene to himself while boiling water for the day, Taylor takes the book from him and writes in it. Then she hands it to me.

I smile and pass it to Cara, who hands it to Rocky Horror.

"I like that," he says, then hands it back to her. Taylor places it on the ground, in the middle of the road. And we all stand in silence for a moment before packing up and getting back in the car. There's less than a quarter tank of gas left, so who knows how far it will get us, but it'll be close enough. We're almost there.

As I pull the Volvo door shut, I look back down at the book on the road, remembering how Dan and Lucy were thrown together over and over, the universe conspiring to get them back into each other's lives.

I just hope the universe does the same thing for me and Jamie one day.

Infinity rounded down to ten.

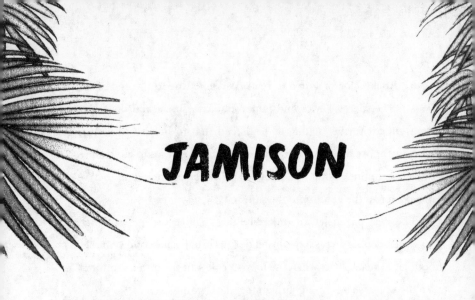

JAMISON

WE START SEEING THE WANTED POSTERS AROUND Columbia, South Carolina. Scattered on the ground or stapled to trees and utility poles, tucked under the windshield wipers of abandoned cars like take-out menus. There are even two white billboards with the same text as the posters painted in dark red or black—some of the words misspelled.

There are probably more in Georgia. Maybe even a few going up I-95.

We end up camping in Orangeburg, South Carolina, for two days, and the longer we stay put, the more anxious I get. Denton has become the main source of intel for Cal. He's spent most of the past few days describing the layout of Fort Caroline, drawing crude maps, and explaining the ins and outs of the community.

I listen as often as I can, trying to distract myself from wondering if Andrew is okay back in Faraway and also trying to figure out what exactly Cal's plan is. So far it's been nothing concrete. At least for me. They've been taking people aside, giving them all tasks. The guy from the back of the RV came to me after he got his. He's supposed to find out where Fort Caroline is doing army training and see if he can join up. From there he'll start asking around to figure out who's most dissatisfied with Fort Caroline.

This whole mission could take months. I'm getting even more nervous because I have no idea how the hell they plan to keep me alive for that long. Or what Niki and the other people of color are going to do. We only saw white people in Fort Caroline while we were there, so best-case scenario is they say Niki and the others can't stay. I'd feel better knowing Niki isn't in danger.

Finally I get tired of worrying and waiting around for Cal to tell me what his plan for me is—because it was *his* plan; he was the one who came to me with this, and he's the one in charge. I go over to the RV and open the door, climbing up into it. He's sitting at the dining table with three others.

"I want to know what the plan is," I say. "I'm sick of waiting."

Cal nods. "Of course. We were going to come get you tonight, but since you're here, this is what we've planned so far."

He points to some maps and papers on the table. The map is ripped out of a book on the table called *Georgia Atlas and Gazetteer*, then taped together and marked up with boundaries and some color-coded routes.

"Our plan is to just go through the front door." Cal points to a red-outlined road. "Your friend Denton says there's a toll plaza that they turned into a security checkpoint. We'll tell them we're looking to join up with them and say we have you as a show of good faith."

My stomach tightens with anxiety. "So I'm your bait." It's not that I thought I'd be given a prosthetic nose and wig and told to pretend

I'm someone else, but it's still a terrifying notion. Bait doesn't usually survive.

"Were you expecting something else? We're open to suggestions." He looks at me but, honestly, I don't. I doubt most Fort Caroliners would really recognize me, but Danny Rosewood won't have forgotten my face.

"What if they just kill me right there?"

"They won't," Kevin says. "And if they try to, we'll stop them."

"Denton says morale is at an all-time low," Cal says. "At least it was when he left a couple months back, and places like this, they don't usually get much better. They need little moments of hope and joy— maybe an ice cream day or a rock star shows up and agrees to sing a couple hymns in church on Sundays for some extra food. If their leader's been looking for you so hard, he's gonna want to use you as an example. One of the morale-boosting moments of joy. 'We got the bad guy! Sure, he's a kid, but we got him!' And they're going to want to keep that rolling for as long as they can, so it's in their best interest to give you a lengthy trial. Something for all the old ladies to gossip about."

"Cal's going to use you to get close to Rosewood. Put a bug in his ear about all the above and make sure he's on the same page."

"What if he isn't?" I ask.

Cal frowns. "Look, you know there's an element of danger here, yeah?"

"Yeah, but dying wouldn't be ideal for me."

"It's not ideal for any of us," Cal says. "But we're risking our lives, too. Look, if you don't want to be involved, you can leave. We don't need you as bait; they'll let us in regardless. But you can't have any other role in this, because if they find out who you are, we all go back to square one in terms of gaining their trust."

Of course I can leave, but then I wouldn't know what happens in Fort Caroline. And I especially want to know what happens to Danny Rosewood.

I want to stop him from ever hurting someone else again.

"What about Niki and the other people of color who are with us? Has Denton told you about the lack of diversity in Fort Caroline?"

"He has, but according to him, they've never turned anyone away, and they don't kill anyone because of the color of their skin. It's more aggressively making those folks feel unwelcome."

That doesn't make me feel better.

"Unwelcome how?"

He looks at me like I'm being dense, and he's right—I do know exactly how they'd do that. It was similar in the mainly white, conservative town near my mom's cabin.

"Just tell me you have a plan to keep them safe."

"Niki is coming into town with us. She says she wants to, and I know she can take care of herself. I've seen her do it. I've also seen Carlos, Helena, and William take care of themselves, and I know they can handle it." He points to a wooded area on the map by the highway. "But if it makes you feel better, anyone who feels they're actively being targeted—regardless of the color of their skin—there's going to be a group here camping and waiting for us. Denton says no one takes the road next to it, so it's the safest place. And they're our backup if things get bad."

I stare at the atlas. It's not a foolproof plan by any means. But I do want to check with Niki one last time before we get too close. She still has time to turn around and go home if she wants.

"Okay," I say. "I'm in. But if it looks like they're about to kill me before Rosewood is killed, I'm doing what I can to take him out."

Cal laughs. "Trust me, he'll be taken out before anyone even thinks of killing you."

"I don't mean taken out of power; I mean killed." I watch the men's faces, trying to decipher their looks, making sure they understand it's important that Rosewood dies. If I die doing this, I can't let him come after anyone else.

But they all just nod.

"Understood," says Cal. "We're just finishing up, anything else you want to add?"

"No. Thanks."

"Get some sleep, everyone," he says, rolling up the maps and stacking the papers. We all leave the RV, and I go over to my sleeping bag, where Niki is waiting for me.

"They talked to you already?" I ask.

She nods. "I also spoke with Denton. I know how the people in Fort Caroline are, and I know what to expect. To be fair, I'm a Black woman who grew up in Arkansas. I know how to stay out of trouble. Even if other people are looking to put me in it."

I nod. "I know you do. And I know this is your decision—"

She interrupts me. "Yes. And I like you, Jamie, but I'm not doing this for you. I don't think Cal is either. I'm doing this for Jamar. Because when the last settlement tried to throw him in jail for keeping my grandma alive, and I took his place, I swore I'd do anything to protect him. And that means doing this. Making sure these people don't find their way to Faraway."

"In case no one told you recently, you're a great sister."

She chuckles, shaking her head. "Tell me that again when there's a prize for it." I laugh and she grows serious. "And, Jamison, tell me that again when we make it through this."

I nod. She gets into her sleeping bag, and my eyes survey the camp for Denton, finding him sitting by a fire. He's not talking to anyone, just watching the flames.

Then, as if he can feel my eyes on him, he looks up. I lie down quickly, pulling up my sleeping bag and closing my eyes.

The next day, we don't get going until a little after noon. I'm back in the truck bed again and the cold wind whips around the winter coat I stitched together from the pieces Andrew and I found. Niki is next to me, nervously chewing at her chapped lips. I pull a knit cap down over my ears and bury my face against my knees.

At least it's not raining.

My stomach is a sea of nerves. It hits me in waves, getting stronger and stronger the longer I sit in silence, like a tide coming in. I try to breathe deeply and purposefully. With the wind, it's easier to let out the shuddering, nervous breaths without anyone hearing.

We stop five miles before the toll plaza, and Cal goes around and double-checks that everyone is prepared and still ready and willing to do this. He holds his gaze on me especially, and I nod.

"All right." He grabs a strand of rope, like the kind we used on the boat back in the Keys. "Hop out, Liam's swapping places with you. You'll be in the cab with us the rest of the way."

I jump out of the truck, and Liam moves behind me as Cal tells me to hold out my hands. He starts tying a knot.

"One thing I didn't tell you about the plan," he says.

My stomach tightens along with the knot around my wrist. This feels like a trap. I have no idea what Cal could want that Fort Caroline would give, but it could all be a ruse, a way to get some kind of reward for turning me in.

"What's that?" I ask.

Cal sighs. "We gotta make it look real. You understand what I'm saying?"

My eyes drop to the rope around my wrists, then up to Cal. He cracks his knuckles and then I understand. I've only been in a fight once, in fourth grade, and it wasn't even a real fight. It was one punch that I threw and an elbow to my face, and that was it before the recess aide ran over with her whistle. After that, I got a stern talking-to from my mom about fighting. And of course all the horror stories about people who thought they'd be fine throwing one punch and then that one punch hit just right and killed the person.

"It'll be quick. Liam'll hold you steady."

Liam grabs my arms tightly and I close my eyes so I can't anticipate the hit. It comes less than a second later, right in the center of my face. I feel my nose crack and blood flows instantly.

I cry out and my knees buckle, but Liam holds me steady.

"Hey!" Niki shouts from the back of the truck.

"One more," Cal says.

Christ. I brace myself and the second hit comes, this one right into the side of my mouth. My lip splits and I bite my tongue as my jaw snaps shut. I spit out the blood and open my eyes. Cal is looking at my face as though he's studying a painting in the Philly Museum of Art. I blink away tears as he nods.

"I think we're good to go."

"Wonderful." I spit out more blood and glance back to see Niki still standing in the truck bed, looking concerned. I give her a quick nod as Liam helps me into the truck cab before climbing into the bed.

Now my head is pounding, and my stomach is still roiling with anxiety. I try to wipe my bloody nose on the rope, but it keeps dripping anyway.

"Tilt your head back," the woman next to me says. I do it, but I feel the blood running down the back of my throat and it makes me gag. I try plugging the nostrils with my fingers and wince.

"I think my nose is broken," I say.

"It'll be fine," Cal says.

"Right."

We arrive at the toll plaza just after sundown. Cal slows the truck and the RV behind us follows suit.

"Denton said there'd be people here," Kevin says from the passenger seat.

"Maybe there's a shift change?" Cal says.

I lean over to look out the windshield. There's no one at the toll booth. When Denton drove Andrew and me through last July, there were people with rifles stationed here.

"Something feels off," Kevin says. "Let's get Denton. The last thing we need is to drive into this place unannounced and get shot up."

Cal puts the car in park and unbuckles his seat belt. "Yeah."

Everyone gets out, and Cal even helps me out as well. He gets to the RV as Denton comes down the steps, but I hear Niki's voice from the truck behind me.

"Look." She's pointing in the direction of Fort Caroline.

I turn and see several pillars of black smoke floating up from over the leafless trees.

Denton looks just as confused as everyone else. Cal turns back to him, then me. He unties my hands.

"Looks like we're late to the party."

Driving through Fort Caroline now feels so different. Eerier somehow. Buildings are burned and there are bullet holes in windows and the sides of disabled trucks. As we head farther into the town, the truck's headlights drift over bloodstained asphalt. It's clear that something big happened here and a lot of people died.

But I don't see any bodies.

Cal stops the truck. Ahead of us, across the entire road, is a blockade of burnt cars. We get out again and walk toward the wreckage. The town is silent, but smoke still hangs in the air.

"Denton," Cal calls out. He points to the wrecked cars in front of us. "Was this a barricade in case you guys were invaded or attacked?"

Denton shakes his head. "There were shelters set up, and units to protect each shelter. This wasn't part of their plan."

"Shelters where?" Kevin asks. He sets the maps on the hood of the truck.

As he speaks, Denton points out locations and cross streets. "The old library, sheriff's department, the food depot . . ." He continues to point out several more, but something rustles in the park behind us.

I spin, bringing my gun up.

"What is it?" Niki asks. She raises her gun, too. It's dusk, and the smoke in the air and the setting sun make it hard to see. The tree limbs are leafless, but the branches still cast shadows in the low light, and the brown grass and weeds are waist high.

"I heard something," I say.

There's another rustle and Niki flinches. "I heard it that time, too."

"Cal!" I yell.

But it's too late—a group of people leap from the grass, and even in the darkness I can see the guns pointed at us.

"Don't move!" a woman shouts.

"Weapons down, hands up!" says another voice, this one from the other side of the truck behind us. I turn to see more people emerging from the shadows.

The blockade was a trap. And now we're surrounded.

ANDREW

"I HAVE TO GO."

I look down at the Kid as he pulls on my hand.

"Right now?" I ask. "We're going to find a place to stop for the night. Can you hold it for five more minutes?" He can pee behind the first house we check before we settle in for the night. But the Kid shakes his head quickly. "All right. Hey, guys, Kid's gotta pee."

The others ahead of us stop and the Kid takes off his little backpack and runs into the trees beside the road.

"Don't go far!" Rocky Horror shouts.

But he doesn't have to, because the Kid knows how far to go. Especially with the sun setting. The western sky is bright pink and purple where the light breaks through the clouds.

Taylor rolls her eyes at me, which is strange but kind of nice to see. It means she's getting back to a more sisterly relationship with him instead of the overly adult guardian demeanor she's had since Frank and the others died.

We were supposed to be in Bethesda by now, but we've been

delayed by a torrential downpour for the past day and a half. We also ran out of gas, so we're back to walking. Cara and Rocky Horror are talking about which direction we should go at an intersection up ahead, so I take the moment to drink some water.

But then something chills me to the bone.

A tinkly version of the Mexican hat dance drifts through the leafless trees.

Taylor's and Cara's eyes go wide.

"Shit."

"What is it?" Rocky Horror asks, clearly seeing our concern.

"We heard that same thing back when we were camping with the Nomads." I pull at the jacket I'm wearing—the one Jamie stitched together from the shredded rats' nest in Dick's Sporting Goods.

"What is it?" he asks.

"No clue. We left before we found out, and I think we should do the same now. Let's get back on the highway," I say. "Maybe go an exit or two farther just in case."

"Yeah, that shit sounds ominous." Rocky Horror puts the road atlas away as I call out for the Kid to finish up.

The Mexican hat dance ends, then starts over again.

Then again.

Still the Kid doesn't emerge from the trees.

"Kid!" Rocky Horror shouts.

He doesn't answer.

No way he would walk *toward* that sound. Right?

I look at the others to see if they're thinking the same thing, and they don't seem to feel as optimistic as I do. Taylor shouts for him again, her voice anxious. But I run to the trees, the others calling after me.

"Kid!" I yell. But not too loudly. Because if we can hear the Mexican hat dance, it means the person playing it can also hear us if we get too loud. I look around the trees, trying to see if the Kid is just having a bad tummy day—I mean, it happens to the best of us on the road, so we've got to have a nice way of putting it for the Kid.

But he's not here.

I call out again, keeping my voice low as I step farther into the woods.

A twig snaps behind me, and I turn in the dimming daylight to see Taylor, followed by Jamar. They whisper-shout his name, too. But now I think he's more drawn to the sound of the ice cream truck music. Because what kid wouldn't be? It's been over a year and a half since he saw an ice cream truck in real life, so why wouldn't he walk toward one?

A million horrific possibilities pop into my head. The loudest being the most terrifying. It could be some psychotic child killer who survived the bug and decided to use an ice cream truck to lure kids with no parents out of their hiding places. A postapocalyptic Pied Piper.

The image is horrifying, and it's enough to get me running *toward* the music, the Kid's backpack swinging in my hands. Fuck being quiet.

"Kid!" I scream.

Maybe the others figured out what I was thinking because I can hear them behind me. All of them, running, yelling for him.

The music gets louder, and through the trees I see headlights. And a fire. The chug of a diesel engine below the tinkly music.

The truck is on. Of course, it would have to be if it's playing music through the speakers.

Which means it can drive away before we catch up to it.

"Kid!" I shout, getting closer to the lights. The music is louder now.

There's a clearing up ahead. I burst through the tree line. No weapons, nothing in my hand except for the Kid's backpack. My left arm throbs with pain and I clutch it to my chest.

The truck really *is* an ice cream truck. It's painted pink and seafoam green, the words *SEÑOR HELADO* written in yellow above the window cut into the side. The lights inside the truck are on. There are two folding chairs set up by a fire.

But nothing else.

No one else.

Behind me, Jamar is the first to emerge from the woods and slides to a stop next to me. He sees the truck and slowly shakes his head. "I'm surviving the apocalypse and I'm absolutely worried about ice cream truck serial killers."

"You forgot all the others," I say. "Point for Niki."

"Yeah, you can be the one to tell her when we get out of here."

Rocky Horror bursts through the tree line, the rifle in his hand. The others follow him, taking in the scene. He turns to Jamar, Taylor, and Cara, telling them to go back into the woods and stay out of sight. "If something happens, run. Get out of here."

Cara nods and leads Jamar and Taylor into the trees as Rocky

Horror turns his attention to me. I run around to the rear of the ice cream truck—the Mexican hat dance drowns out something Rocky Horror calls after me.

The back of the ice cream truck is open. I round the corner, expecting some horror show to greet me.

Instead there's a short, thin man with light brown skin. He's shouting out vocalizations to the music as he vigorously whisks something in a large steel bowl. He glances over at me and startles. His whisking hand goes wild, and something thick and syrupy goes flying up to the ceiling.

He puts his hand to his heart and shouts something, but I can't really hear him over the music. Rocky Horror joins me, pointing the rifle, and the man's hands fly into the air.

"Don't shoot!" That I understand.

But the man is alone in his truck. There's no Kid in sight.

"Let me turn off the music!" he shouts, pointing toward the front of the truck. Rocky Horror motions with the end of the rifle for him to go ahead, and the man cautiously walks to the front. The music snaps off and he returns, his hands still high above his head.

The man is in his forties, maybe. He has a salt-and-pepper beard, but the gray hasn't spread yet to the thick waves of black hair slicked back on top of his head.

"Please," he says, speaking with a Spanish accent. "Don't shoot me. My brother, he is alone out there. I play the music for him."

"Andrew?" I turn to see the Kid standing by the trees. He's holding the hand of a boy with Down syndrome. Rocky Horror immediately lowers the gun.

The man in the truck jumps down between us, his voice rising to sound happy and excited, but I can still hear some anxiety in there. He says something in Spanish that I can't recognize but then repeats it in English—I assume for our benefit. "Hector, come meet our new friends." He puts his hand out to Rocky Horror, using the other to gently push the rifle down a bit more. "I'm Ramiro. My brother is Hector."

"Rocky Horror."

Ramiro quirks his head and smiles wide. "Beautiful name. Nice to meet you." He turns to me. "I assume, then, that you are Andrew?"

I say yes and shake his hand.

The others emerge from the woods and introduce themselves. Ramiro says hello to everyone, the atmosphere slowly growing less tense.

"Hector!" he calls out to his brother. "Why don't you come say hello if you want, and let our friends warm themselves by the fire while I finish the ice cream."

Ice cream? I mean, I know it's an ice cream truck but, one, it's probably not even forty degrees out, and two through one million, it's the fucking end of the world. How is he making ice cream?

But before I can ask, Hector comes over, reaches out, and hugs me. "Hi, Andrew, I'm Hector," he says.

"Nice to meet you, Hector."

He turns to Rocky Horror and introduces himself and hugs him, too. Rocky Horror tells Hector his name and watches him go say hello to, and hug, the others. And I realize Amy isn't there. Cara tells me she waited by the road with Henri-Two—probably worried we'd all be murdered and wanting to spare her one-year-old that fate—and says she'll go get her. Rocky Horror turns and follows Ramiro into the truck. Knowing the Kid is safe with Hector and the others, I follow him.

"Do you like ice cream?" Ramiro asks, back to whisking.

"How do you *have* ice cream?" Rocky Horror asks.

Ramiro motions around him. "It's an ice cream truck." Then he winks at Rocky Horror and laughs. "I would not call it *real* ice cream had the whole world not shit the bed. I love that phrase, *shit the bed*. But ice cream, yes. Sadly, until I can find a cow small enough to fit in this truck, we are stuck with—" He moves the metal bowl and opens the steel door to the chest freezer, taking out several bags followed by cans and a plastic bottle. "Powdered milk, condensed milk, evaporated milk, and on those depressing days when we no longer have shelf-stable milk, raspados." He shakes the bottle of cherry syrup, then drops it all back into the nonworking freezer.

"Unfortunately"—he shrugs as he returns to whisking the fake ice cream—"Hector is not a fan of raspados, but I make him ice cream as long as I can find the ingredients to do so. If I do it well enough, he hardly can tell the difference."

"That's a very nice thing for you to do." If I didn't know Rocky Horror to be a cynical bitch like I am, I'd think there was a bit of joy in his eyes. But, yeah, even I can see the kindness in Ramiro's actions.

Ramiro turns to look at us again, then out the open window of the ice cream truck. "Well, there isn't much else left to do these days. Why not spend the time we have doing kindnesses for those we love?"

Again, my heart breaks for Jamie. The kindness that's missing from him. Was it my fault? Was I not doing enough to remind him that there can be good in the world? Maybe I should have stayed with him. Gone with him to Fort Caroline and tried to stop him before he got there.

"Rami." We turn to see Hector at the ice cream truck window. He motions for Ramiro to come over. He bends down while Hector whispers in his ear.

Ramiro smiles wide at us and shrugs. "I don't see why not. Hector would like to share. Do you all want to stick around for some ice cream?"

"We don't want to impose," Rocky Horror says as Hector turns back and starts talking with the Kid, Taylor, and Jamar.

"I think the imposition would be telling Hector no. And you don't want to disappoint him, do you?" Ramiro puts a hand to his chest as though scandalized by the thought. He gives Rocky Horror a playful nudge. "I'm playing with you, sweetie. He'll be sad, but he'll get over it."

Sweetie? Is . . . Ramiro flirting?

Rocky Horror lets out a loud laugh and nods. "Well, we'd be happy to stay and maybe also share our food with you?"

He turns to me, the inflection at the end of his sentence making it clear that he knows we don't have enough food, but also if we're getting free end-of-the-world ice cream, it's a fair trade, right? I nod.

"No need!" Ramiro dumps the mixed ice cream into a soft-serve machine bolted to the wall of the truck and turns it on. He hands Rocky Horror the dirty bowl, then opens the other side of the freezer and takes out a few cans of food. "You're our guests this evening. We rarely get visitors in our truck, and between you and me"—he means Rocky Horror and him, because I have quickly become the invisible third wheel in this ice cream truck of love—"I've missed hosting dinner parties."

Oh, definitely queer. Welcome to the group, Ramiro.

Hector spends most of the night talking to the Kid and Jamar about Pokémon. He knows the names of every single Pokémon and has a notebook he's drawn most of them in. I try to take part in the conversation at one point—if only to give Rocky Horror and Ramiro a moment to flirt in peace—but it quickly goes over my head, so I ask Cara to help me change the bandages on my arm.

Soon after dinner—and dessert—the Kid and Hector both fall asleep. Henri-Two is still awake—probably wired from her first taste of ice cream. The look on her face almost made this whole trip worth it. The rest of our group enjoys the remaining ice cream by the fire.

It's cold and very sweet, but it's been so long since I've had real ice cream, I can't even tell it was made with imitation vanilla extract and powdered milk.

"It's because of all the sugar," Ramiro says after I tell him this. He shakes his head, looking over to Hector in his sleeping bag by the fire. "I should have reminded him to brush his teeth when I saw him getting sleepy."

Henri-Two finally crashes, and Amy turns in for the night with her.

I'm finishing the stale ice-cream cone—my second, and honestly just as amazing as the first—when I decide to come clean about the last time we ran into Ramiro and Hector. How we heard their music through the small town in South Carolina and we thought he was probably an ax murderer.

"I'm sorry!" he says, wiping the tears away as he laughs. "It's for Hector. When I'm in the truck, sometimes he wanders, and I play the music so he doesn't get lost. Oh, speaking of."

He jumps up and goes to the truck—which has been running since before we arrived. The soft-serve machine was running off the battery, but he keeps the freezers switched off and uses them as storage. The truck is diesel, and Ramiro showed us the pump and hoses secured to the top of the truck that he uses to pump the tanks at gas stations.

Apparently, Ramiro and Hector have been driving from Cabo San Lucas all around the country. Ramiro owned the ice cream truck and always said he'd take Hector to America for a vacation, but life kept getting in the way. Then Ramiro and Hector were the only ones in their family left after the bug. So they decided not to stay in Cabo, and went on their road trip instead.

Ramiro cuts the engine and lights and rejoins us.

We throw more wood on the fire and talk. All of us sharing stories about our lives one by one, except for Taylor, who fakes a yawn and excuses herself. She wraps her body in her sleeping bag and lies by the fire with her back to us.

Taylor has always avoided talking about her family in the before times. I honestly can't blame her. It's hard talking about life before.

"How old is Hector?" Rocky Horror asks.

"Thirty-two."

He nods. "I had an older brother with Down syndrome. He died before the flu. Maybe twenty years ago?"

I turn to Rocky Horror, fascinated. I never knew this about him.

He's never talked about his family from before; I always assumed it was because there weren't any happy stories to tell about them. But the look on his face says this story is a happy one.

Ramiro scoots his folding chair over to Rocky Horror and takes one of his tattooed hands. He says something quietly in Spanish that I don't understand, but it sounds comforting. Then he adds, "I'm so sorry for your loss."

"It's okay, I've had enough time to grieve him. But more time to remember him."

Ramiro nods aggressively. "I love that outlook. What was his name? What was he like?"

"Vinnie—well, *Vincent*. I called him Vinnie. And he was the only one in my family, I believe, who truly loved me. I told him one day, I asked him to use my new name. He asked why, and I told him it was because I never felt like the person our parents had named me. I said I was a boy." Rocky Horror's eyes flit over to Ramiro, then down to Ramiro's hand holding his before rising to meet mine.

I'm as surprised as he seems to be. It's almost like he didn't expect to say that out loud just now. Rocky Horror never hid who he was when we were in the Keys, but on the road—even with the Nomads— he was reluctant to trust too easily. This must have been an accident, but he's never slipped before. I wonder what that means. But after a brief pause, he continues.

"He was the only one who never had a problem. He messed up maybe three times his whole life, and it was just because he was excited about something. Meanwhile my parents deadnamed me for years. I never understood why Vinnie got it so easily, but they couldn't."

I can see Ramiro squeeze Rocky Horror's hand tighter. "Because Vinnie loved you."

Cara and I share a glance and smile at each other. Something passes between us—a telepathic message that says these two should have some time together alone—so I wait a few moments before I take a page from Taylor's book and fake a yawn.

"I should probably get some sleep."

Cara stands. "Me too."

Ramiro turns his attention back to Rocky Horror. "I'm going to stay up for a bit—I'm kind of a night owl. Would you mind if I left you all here? I'll make my own fire over there."

He points to the truck a little farther away.

"Can I join you?" Rocky Horror asks.

"I would love it if you did."

We say good night to them, Cara and I trying our hardest not to let on that we're whispering behind their backs about how cute they are together.

"Why Señor Helado?" Rocky Horror asks as they gather some wood to make a smaller fire separate from us. "You'd get the alliteration if you went with Señor Softie."

"Sir!" Ramiro says. "No one has *ever* referred to me as soft."

"Holy shit!" I whisper to Cara. She immediately falls into a fit of giggles that she has to smother in her sleeping bag. I try to hide my own laughter as well. Several times throughout the night, I wake up to throw more wood on the fire. Each time, I can hear Rocky Horror and Ramiro talking quietly by the truck.

* * *

309

The next morning, Hector and the Kid are up before the sun. I hear Ramiro whisper something to Hector. Even with no real Spanish vocabulary, I recognize the sound of an older sibling scolding a younger one.

I get up with them and the three of us go to where Hector says there's a stream. I fill up the water bottles and they help carry them back to the camp, where the others are beginning to stir, including Rocky Horror, who wipes his face, clearly exhausted.

"You two were up late," I whisper as I set down a pot on the side of the fire and fill it with water.

"Hmm" is all he says. "Gotta pee." With that he gets out of his sleeping bag and heads into the woods.

Hector pulls at Ramiro's arm and points to his lips. Ramiro bends down and gives his brother a kiss, saying good morning. Then he turns his attention back to us. "I have something I have been saving for a special day, and I think meeting new friends makes this the perfect occasion."

He turns and heads back to the truck.

"Oh, please let it be a bottle of prosecco," Amy prays. Sadly, Ramiro returns with a giant can in his hands.

Freeze-dried bacon and eggs. The can says there are nine servings in it.

"Holy shit!" Amy yells. "It's better than prosecco."

Ramiro tsks. "Hardly. Oh, I'd kill for a mimosa."

We boil the water and wait for it to rehydrate the eggs. I'm halfway through my own bowl before I realize I need to savor this. It's salty and hot and delicious. And honestly, when I'm finished, I feel amazing. Completely rejuvenated.

While the rest of the drinking water boils, Rocky Horror crouches next to me. "Can I talk to you?"

Here it is. The "can we ask them to join us" talk. And it's going to be a quick talk because, yes, absolutely.

But that's not what Rocky Horror asks. In fact, he doesn't ask me anything at all.

He says, "I'm going to go with Ramiro and Hector."

My stomach drops and I stare at him.

"I already know what you're thinking and, trust me, I thought it, too, for the last several hours. But there's something here. I was never the kind of person who believes in fate or God moving us around like chess pieces, but this all seems to fit too well. *We* fit too well. Like maybe with fewer people in the world, there are more chances for divine intervention."

That phrase Cal said to Jamie comes to mind. Universal convergence. If that's true, I hope there's some good intervention coming up for Jamie and me.

"And we can both feel it," Rocky Horror continues. "We spent the night talking. The whole night." He leans against a tree, bracing himself on his knees, smiling. "I honestly haven't done that since . . . maybe college. After?"

"Okay, but why don't you ask if they want to come with us?"

His face clouds. "For one, they have their own plan, and I don't want to be the person who changes that. He and Hector went from Cabo to the Grand Canyon to Vegas. Along the northern border and down south again and up the coast."

"Where are they going next?" I ask.

"He says he wants to show Hector everywhere he can drive to. They have general locations in mind all the way up the coast, then through Canada and back down to Mexico and maybe beyond. Basically, they're going to travel until they can't find any more diesel or the truck breaks down."

"Are you sure they'll let you go with them?" I ask.

"Ramiro asked me last night. I already said yes. I don't think I've ever said yes to something so fast in my life." He blushes as he says it.

I'm happy for Rocky Horror. But I also know how much I'm going to miss him.

"Who's going to help me when I have an existential crisis?"

Rocky Horror pulls me into a hug. "It's cute you think I'd care about your crises." There's the Rocky Horror I know and love. And am going to miss so damn much.

We say goodbye later that morning. Rocky Horror already has an arm around Ramiro's back, holding him at his side. He takes it away long enough to hand me Jamie's rifle.

"You sure?" I ask.

"We'll be okay," Rocky Horror says.

"Hector," the Kid says, "you can have Albie." He holds out the stuffed Pokémon—which Hector has explained is a Bellibolt.

"Thank you," Hector says. He and the Kid hug, and he kisses the Kid's cheek. Then he goes down the line and kisses each of our cheeks, saying bye along the way.

Rocky Horror gives us the food out of his pack—as well as a few more cans from Ramiro and Hector, since they have more than enough in the truck.

Then he crouches next to the Kid. "You're in charge now, 'kay?" Rocky Horror points to me with his middle finger. "Try not to let this one fall off a cliff or anything."

The Kid nods and gives him a hug. And if I'm not mistaken, it looks like Rocky Horror might be sad to see the Kid go.

When he hugs Cara goodbye, I hear her whisper, "Adios, Mary Poppins." Rocky Horror snorts and moves on to me.

"What's the plan after you all get to Bethesda?"

I shrug. "Guess we have to talk about it."

"Something you're not great at."

"I'm trying."

He opens his arms and I step into his hug. "Try harder. I know you can do it."

With that, we say goodbye and head back to the road. If we find another car, we can be in Bethesda by the end of the day. For the first time in a long time, I'm full of food and hope. But it's not enough because Jamie isn't here.

Our little fellowship is getting smaller and smaller. And each time, the hole left by Jamie's absence feels bigger.

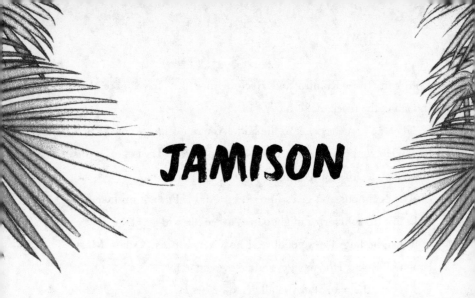

JAMISON

"ON YOUR KNEES!"

My nose whistles with clotted blood, and the handgun shakes in my sweaty hands as my heart races. Niki and I drop slowly, setting our guns down on the ground in front of us. Everyone else does as they say. As some of the Fort Caroliners hold us at gunpoint, a few others run to pick up our weapons.

I glance back at Cal and Denton to see if they have a plan or want to give some kind of signal. But they both have their eyes trained on the people pointing weapons at us.

"Check them," the first woman who spoke says. She walks around us as someone to her right comes forward and starts patting us down. He moves on to Cal.

"Traveling with any bags?" he asks.

"We checked them with TSA," Cal says. The guy gives him a shove and a fake "ha-ha."

Then Denton speaks. "Lacy?"

The woman—a white woman in her forties with her hair tied back into a ponytail—turns to him. "Holy shit, Denton?" She walks over to him and holds out a hand, helping him up. She pulls him into a hug. "We thought Rosewood had you killed. Nadine?"

"She's alive. She's with . . ." He turns to everyone else around him, still on their knees. "We're good; we're not here to hurt you."

Lacy nods and motions for us all to stand. "Give them their weapons back."

Her men do as she says while Denton launches into his explanation—how Nadine got him out when she heard that Rosewood and a few others were planning on framing him. Then he asks what's going on.

"Things got worse after you left," she says. "People were starving. Kids dying. We'd finally had enough."

"Rosewood?" Denton asks.

She shakes her head. "He's somewhere in there." She nods toward the line of cars. "We cornered him and his people about a week ago, set up a perimeter and have been waiting them out. We know they're low on food. It's just a matter of time now, so we have teams stationed at every intersection."

"Where is he?" Cal asks.

"We don't know," Lacy says. "We could do a house-to-house, but it would take too long, and he and his men might have set their own traps by now. We figure we can wait them out longer than they can wait us out. Eventually they'll run out of supplies and his little army is going to turn against him."

"Where are your blockades?" Cal asks.

Lacy goes over to the truck and takes a red marker out of her pocket. I watch as she marks off the roads around us on our map. It's a rectangle that looks to surround fifteen or sixteen blocks. Smack-dab in the middle is the sheriff's station. When we first came to Fort Caroline, that's where we had to register our guns and request ammo.

It was one of the places Denton had mentioned Rosewood might be holing up. And if there was always a plan to protect it, maybe that's where he's hiding out right now.

"How much longer do you think they can survive in there?" Denton asks.

"A week?" says Lacy. "Maybe two, but that's it. Even if they don't starve, they'll be out of water soon."

"How do you even know they're still in there?" Cal asks.

As if on cue, gunshots pop from the blockade behind us. Someone from Lacy's group drops, and bullets hit the ground around us.

"Take cover!" Lacy shouts. We run to the other side of the truck and RV, ducking down. Niki is to my right, and I see Denton crouch around the back of the RV and lock eyes with me. Our group returns fire.

But then there are more shots from the overgrown baseball field to our right. Lacy yells to Denton and Cal that we need to seek cover, and four people from her group start shooting in the direction of the baseball field. We grab our packs and weapons, and Denton latches on to my shoulder, pulling me to my feet. I reach for Niki, but she falls behind.

I shrug off Denton's hand and run back to her. We stay low and he watches us, waiting until we're next to him before following Lacy and the others.

Once we're behind another blockade—this one made of concrete barriers and wood—we stay down while Lacy and her team talk to Cal and a few others about how to push back. The shots keep coming. Denton and Niki are listening intently. Lacy talks about retreating to another group for reinforcements, but when she points at the map in front of her, it's in the opposite direction of the sheriff's department.

A group of four provide more cover as one of Rosewood's people leaps over the blockade from the direction we came. When we have to move again, Denton glances back to make sure I'm following. A bullet whizzes past my ear and I duck. Someone to my right falls, hot blood spattering the side of my face.

There's another blockade ahead to our right.

"Look out!" someone on our side shouts. But it's too late.

The person in front of me stumbles backward—all their weight drops on me, and I fall to the road. And more people are shooting. Everything is chaos. This isn't how this was supposed to go; it was supposed to be more gradual, less violent. We didn't realize Rosewood and whoever sided with him would be so desperate. Because that's what this is. They've been trapped and have only days left before they begin to starve.

The person on top of me is gasping like they can't breathe. I recognize him. It's the young guy from the back of the RV. The one who said he wouldn't mind a little firefighting. But the fear in his eyes as blood spills from his mouth and the holes in his chest says the opposite. His hands grab mine; they're already cold and clammy.

I remember how the bullet felt in my own side when Fort Caroline shot me, and I squeeze his hand tight. He won't live, but I don't want him to be alone when he dies.

"Jamie!" Denton is there, trying to pull me up. But I don't want to let go of the guy's hand yet. He's still alive, but not for long. Denton keeps trying to get me to move as gunshots echo around us. Niki is there now, too, and she helps Denton, pulling the young man's hand away from mine. Someone else from our side is shooting back the way we came, but bullets tear through the front of their jacket, narrowly missing Niki. She screams as the person drops to the ground, dead. I push Niki ahead, and Denton shoots blindly behind us.

This is just going to continue every day until Rosewood and the other leaders are dead. Which means every day, more people are going to die. But if Rosewood dies tonight, it's over. And if I'm right about where he is, I can end this; not wait a week or more for them to starve or die of dehydration. Or for them to get even more desperate and kill more of us. Like Niki, who shouldn't be here but just wants to protect her brother.

Or me. Who shouldn't be here either. But this is for Andrew, to protect him so he can protect the others. I have no clue how many people have died already for Danny Rosewood, but no one else is dying tonight. Especially not for me.

When we reach another roadblock to our right, neither Niki nor Denton notices as I fall back and let everyone pass me. I stop, waiting for them to look for me; when no one does, I turn away from them and run for the barrier. None of them seem to notice, as there are no shouts after me. I climb up onto the cars that make up the roadblock, black soot coming away from the cracked and burnt paint.

In under a minute, I'm over the blockade and on the other side.

Alone.

The sheriff's department is only a few blocks away. I can check it out on my own, see how well guarded it is. Maybe Rosewood is there, out in the open. And if he is, maybe his men will let me get close enough to take him out.

I turn down a road, sticking to shadows. I'm moving in the opposite direction from the gunshots, so things are getting quieter.

There's movement in the street ahead of me, so I duck into an alley and wait. Voices drift through the night, getting closer and closer. I back down the alley, away from the street, hoping the shadows between the building are enough to hide me.

A young man is speaking. "—probably distracted by the assault on Stillton. I say we make a run for it while we can."

Another voice—younger, more boyish—answers. "What if they just shoot us?"

"They won't, bud," answers the first. "We'll just go out with hands up and—" Their voices get farther and farther away. Still, I don't risk going out just yet.

Halfway down the alley, there's a right turn, and I glance down it at the white cinder-block sheriff's department. Smoke drifts slowly beneath an orange light at the front corner of the building. There's gotta be a generator. And if they've chosen to power a generator using the limited resources they have, it must be because the leaders are there.

That's where he is, I know it. Like some dictator hiding out in his bunker while the opposing troops close in.

And judging by the two men I just heard, they seem ready to give up. Maybe if they know their leaders are falling, they'll be more willing to lay down their guns.

I sprint down the alley toward the station. The road is clear, but I look both ways to be sure, then take my chance and cross the street to the empty sheriff's station parking lot.

I run around the back, into the shadows. There's the low hum of a generator farther along the building's back wall. I turn back to see the alleyway is still dark. No one is following. I continue around to the other side and hear voices from the front of the building. Yelling. But I don't know what they're saying.

There's a truck on this side with tarp-covered boxes in the back of the bed.

More gunshots, six or seven overlapping pops. But they're much closer than any others I've heard.

Someone rounds the corner, limping. He's a short, thin white man with a gray mustache and bald head. Blood drips down his face from a cut across his forehead. There's more blood on his chest and a thick, dripping trail behind him.

He doesn't see me in the shadows. Neither does the man with the gun behind him. My heart stops and everything goes silent except for the pounding in my ears.

Danny Rosewood lifts the pistol in his hand and fires one final time into the other man's back. The bald guy drops to the ground, tries to crawl, then stills.

My fingers tighten around the gun in my own hand.

There he is.

Rosewood limps over to the man. There are red splotches of blood on his white suit. One near his shoulder. And another on the right side of his abdomen. Almost exactly where the scar on my side is.

He throws his own gun—a six-shooter, of course—aside and reaches down for the other guy's gun. Another six-shooter. Probably standard-issue for the selectmen of Fort Caroline. Something that looks old-school, dignified, and Wild West-y. It makes sense given the wanted posters. Rosewood picks up the gun and goes to open the chamber but stops when he sees me.

I've stepped out of the shadows, my legs moving on their own. My arm must, too, because I don't remember raising my gun, but there it is. Pointed right at his chest.

He seems nervous for a moment and puts up his other hand like he's about to surrender.

"It's all right, son," he says. "No need to go shooting anyone now. I was just defending myself is all."

That's like a slap in the face. The casual way he says it. The way he calls me "son," as though I'm just some random person he's never seen before. I study his face, and it takes longer than it should for me to realize he doesn't even fucking recognize me.

"You . . ." I start, but can't say anything else.

He nods and puts on all the southern charm he can muster with a pained face. "I'm just going to go ahead and get in this truck. Sound okay to you? You can come with if you need. I think we oughta get out of Dodge, like, now. We got a tow truck set up—if you drive that in the opposite direction and pull down the barricade, I can drive right on through. I'll wait for you to hop in, and we'll get out before they even realize what happened."

You liar. You'd tell that to anyone and leave them to die in the tow truck. But that's not what pisses me off.

"You don't know who I am?"

He studies my face and nods. "Sure, I do, son. It's just remembering names has never been my strong suit. Why don't we talk about it in the truck, and you can refresh my memory."

"You chased me to Florida," I say, stepping toward him and keeping my gun trained on him. "You've been looking for me for over five months. You sent people down to the Keys for me and destroyed the home we were trying to make."

Home.

Saying it aloud makes it all sound possible. The Keys *would* have been a home if Fort Caroline hadn't been looking for us. If Rosewood had never sent his son after us, and I was never shot. If I never killed Harvey Rosewood to protect Andrew. If I was never terrified that they would show up and kill us, I could have let myself trust the people in the Keys. Andrew and I could have been safe and happy there, even with the storm. We could have helped rebuild, and I would have been able to let the others in—Daphne, Rocky Horror, Liz, Kelly, the kids, all of them. But I couldn't, because of him. This sad, forgetful old man.

He's still looking at me as if he has no idea what I'm talking about.

"I shot Harvey," I say. And saying it aloud feels like the moment I realized what I did all over again. His face, the blood. My stomach turns and threatens to throw up whatever's in it, just like that day.

And then Danny Rosewood's face changes. Because *now* he knows exactly who I am.

"Shit," he says. It's the first time I've ever heard him curse. "It is you." His face becomes a mask of rage. "You killed my boy!"

"He tried to kill me first."

"He should have!" Rosewood snarls. "I thought him surviving the flu meant he'd change. Like he was chosen to be a leader finally. To grow a pair and stop fuckin' around with his life!"

That one sentence changes everything I ever thought about Harvey Rosewood. The way he looked at me and Andrew. How he tried to kill us and the horrible things he said. Now, hearing this anger from his father, Harvey's voice in my head sounds almost like a parrot. The words are there, but not the understanding.

For the first time, I feel bad for Harvey Rosewood.

Rosewood motions around us. "You're the reason things around here went all to shit! You weren't in the Keys, we wasted all this time and supplies going to get you, and now look. You happy with yourself, boy?"

He raises the gun.

But mine is already up.

I pull the trigger.

Nothing happens. The safety is still on. Because the safety is always on. Because I hate guns and I don't want to hurt people, not even Danny Rosewood, not in this moment or ever. The whole time I was coming here, I was trying to psych myself up to do this, right now.

Shoot him.

Despite everything, I still can't. But more than that, I don't want to.

Another gunshot rings out in the quiet night. So close and so loud that it makes my ears ring.

I don't even feel the bullet hit me, but I flinch anyway and drop my own gun. I close my eyes, waiting for the pain. For the blood and cold that come as the life starts draining from my body.

But there's no pain.

I open my eyes, and Danny Rosewood drops to his knees, clutching the center of his chest, trying to stop the river of blood spilling between his fingers.

For a moment I feel like I must be imagining this. That I died and this is some last-minute hallucination before I lose consciousness forever. But then I turn and see Grover Denton coming up beside me. Niki follows him, her gun at the ready, her chipped pastel nail polish bright against the black steel.

Denton steps up to Rosewood and kicks the guns away from him. Rosewood looks up and grumbles his name, blood spilling from his lips, before he falls over.

Niki reaches out for me. Asking if I'm okay. I nod, but I don't know if I am. Physically, I'm fine, but I also feel numb. It's like I don't know if I'm scared or happy or frightened. Empty is all I feel. I join Denton at Danny Rosewood's side. Rosewood looks like, if he could, he'd strangle us both so hard our necks would snap.

"My boy . . . ," he gurgles, staring up at me, "shoulda killed you when he had the chance."

"He tried," I say. "Maybe that will make you proud of him. To know that the last thing he did before he died was try to shoot me."

"Shoulda been you."

I nod. "For a while I wished it was. And for an even longer while, I thought he deserved to die, but maybe he didn't. I'm sorry he's dead, but I'm not sorry I'm alive."

Rosewood coughs up another clot of blood. "Well, I am. I hope you never have . . . a moment's peace. Ever."

He probably thinks this is supposed to make me feel worse, but it doesn't. If anything, I feel bad for him. It also makes me feel bad for Harvey Rosewood. This spiteful, angry man was his father, and maybe all that hatred in Harvey Rosewood's heart came from him. I'd like to think maybe there is another universe—one where the superflu never happened and maybe Danny Rosewood didn't pass his own hate on to his son. Or if he did, maybe Harvey was able to end the cycle.

I'd like to think in that universe, Andrew and I still found each other.

"I hope . . . ," Rosewood continues, "you suffer."

"Okay," I say. I put my hand on Rosewood's. It's sticky with blood, and he's already getting cold. I remember that feeling, thinking I was going to die. How scared I was. Even through the mask of rage Rosewood wears, I know he must be scared, too. It makes me pity him and every terrible decision he made. All the selfish hate he's filled with.

I know I don't want that same hate in me. The hate I had for Danny Rosewood drove a wedge between Andrew and me and ruined everything we built together. It made me someone I didn't want to be.

And I don't ever want to be that person again.

"I forgive you anyway," I say to him.

"He doesn't deserve forgiveness," Denton says.

I shake my head. "I'm not forgiving him for everything. Just for me."

Rosewood coughs again and I see his eyes change. First more anger, then frustration, then sadness maybe, then suddenly fear or a different kind of anger. Finally, he lets out a shuddering breath. And he's dead.

Danny Rosewood's blood has soaked through the knees of my jeans, and my hands are sticky with it. I don't feel the relief I thought I'd feel from his death; more than anything, I just feel sad. Like I wasted so much time worrying for nothing, because he barely remembered me. At the end of the day, yes, I'm sure he was devastated that his son was dead. But it seemed like he would have reacted similarly if his son had died in an accident.

The Danny Rosewoods of the world only care for Danny Rosewood.

Denton fishes in Rosewood's pockets but comes out with nothing.

"What are you looking for?" I ask.

"The keys."

"The road is blocked," Niki reminds him.

He nods. "Then we take the truck Cal drove in here."

"What about the others?" Niki asks.

He shrugs. "I'm not worried about them. You came for Rosewood, right?"

I don't know the answer to that anymore. Originally, yes. I did. But now I don't know.

Denton takes my silence as confirmation and continues, "Whatever happens here will happen whether we're here or not. Your part is done. As far as I'm concerned, so is mine."

"So we just go back to Faraway?" Niki asks.

Andrew won't be there. He and Amy will have moved on to Henri's.

"You're all safe now, right?" he asks. It feels like a non sequitur, and I don't understand what he means. Then it all clicks. We *are* safe. At least as safe as we can be given the end of the world. Gunshots still ring out in Fort Caroline, and tomorrow morning when the sun rises, someone will be there to pick up the pieces. But they won't be thinking of me or Andrew or Cara.

"Yeah," I say. "We're safe."

"Then, yes, let's go back to Faraway. Cal and the others can help clean up here if they want."

"We came here to stop them," Niki says. "To stop people like him from growing into power and making this world shitty for everyone who isn't him."

"No," Denton says. "I came to make sure Jamie didn't get himself killed." He turns his attention to me. "In Florida, when we found you and Andrew, I tried to tell the others to keep moving, but they wouldn't. We saw Andrew first, and they went for him, then they went for you. I heard you tell Andrew you loved him, and I knew we'd fucked up. I'm sorry, Jamie, truly. I never meant for either of you to get hurt. I knew we couldn't take you back with us, so when you ran off into the woods, I started figuring out how to get Rosewood to stop looking for you. I had to appeal to his bullshit whims and tell him he was wasting supplies and that people would turn against him if he kept it up. I wish I could have done more, but I couldn't. Now I feel like I did. You're alive, Rosewood is dead. So let me get you to safety again so you can go home to Andrew. Please, just let me do that."

I stare at him, trying to figure out how much of this is true and how much is just him trying to look like a better person. But I can see in his eyes, the way he's pleading with me—it's real.

I wipe my bloody hands on my pants and stand. Niki and I follow Denton over the barricade.

When we reach the truck, Niki looks back in the distance, where the gunshots have stopped. The town is completely silent. It's only a matter of time before someone finds Rosewood's body.

"Come on," I say. "It's done here."

"What if it isn't? What if there are still people here who are that willing to kill others?"

"*We* aren't those people." I reach out and take her hand, the one she doesn't hold a gun in. The new polish on her nails chipped because she's been nervously picking at them since we left Faraway. "This isn't us giving up or running away. We have our own people to worry about. We have to make sure Jamar, the Kid, Taylor . . ." Andrew. "That they don't become those people."

We have to make sure they don't become like us. Seeking revenge through violence. All we can do is protect and love them, and hope we can survive this world with love instead of hate.

"You're a great sister," I say, keeping my promise to remind her when we were done in Fort Caroline. "Let's go home."

Denton climbs into the driver's seat of the truck. Niki hugs me tight, sobbing quietly against me, and whispers, "Okay. Let's go home."

Before we're even buckled in, Denton pulls a U-turn, going back the way we entered Fort Caroline.

We drive in silence, the falling settlement fading into the distance.

***

Denton drives through the night. The truck had a full tank of gas, and he gets us to Faraway a little past one in the morning. He directs us to the showers, where I can wash up. It's pitch-black and the water is freezing cold, but it seems to wake me from whatever stupor I've been in, and I realize it's really over.

I thought I wanted Danny Rosewood to die, but none of that even mattered. I risked everything because I was angry that people like that still existed and still hurt others even after we've already lost so much.

I sob under the freezing-cold water. How could I make a mistake like this?

Denton is waiting for us by the lodge with Nadine, Hannah, and a third person. It's Kelly. She runs to me, pulling me into a hug. It's nice to have someone from the Keys on my side again. I never gave her the chance to get close when we were there, but she's here now, and she's hugging me, and I cry again.

"Where's Jamar?" Niki asks.

"So what's your plan?"

In the sunrise, I look over at Denton and shrug. "Andrew and the others went to Bethesda. Niki and I will follow them and see if we can catch up."

Denton laughs. "Yeah, Niki seemed pretty pissed."

I smile. She absolutely was, but it was nice to see. Like the old Niki we met on the road. Not the terrified Niki looking for revenge like I was. She's worried about Jamar, but she knows Andrew and the others will protect him.

"You can take the truck if you want," Denton says.

I snort and give him a shrug. "Niki and I don't know how to drive." But even if we did, I don't think I'm ready to catch up to them just yet. Andrew was right, I was on a revenge mission, and if he knew that before I even did, it means he knows how close I came to losing who I was. He might not trust me again, at least not off the bat. Maybe some extra time will make it easier.

But my chest aches at the idea of not seeing him soon.

That afternoon, Niki and I say goodbye to Faraway and head northeast to Bethesda.

ANDREW

ONCE WE'RE CLOSE TO BETHESDA, I PUT Amy and Cara on high alert. Taylor carries Henri-Two and Jamar holds the Kid's hand. We stopped in Virginia to find more guns for Cara and Amy. At first they didn't want them, but I reminded them about the escaped zoo animals in DC. And how far out they'd been hunting.

Cara points her handgun at the side of the road. The sun is low in the sky and casts the clouds in beautiful cotton-candy pinks and orange.

"I think we're okay," I say. "It doesn't look like whatever is out here is as human-hungry as the lions in DC."

There's a flu victim lying face up on the sidewalk to our left. Their flesh is tight against their skeleton, but there are no bite marks, no gunshots.

"Maybe leopards don't like human jerky," Cara says.

My stomach rolls. "That's the most disgusting thing I've ever heard you say."

"Maybe no talking," says Amy. "Just in case."

Cara nods.

Amy is leading us now. She took over as soon as she started to recognize the area. It's changed since Jamie and I were here. For one, it's winter, so the leaves have fallen from the trees and most of the grass has gone brown. Dull-green vines grow up the sides of houses and from under car hoods.

Every day since we left Bethesda last June, this area has become more like a jungle. Maybe that's what the zookeeper who let out the animals hoped for all along.

Amy takes us around a corner, and I see it right away. Henri's house. It's still boarded up and the grass is overgrown. But the brick-and-metal fence around it remains. The lock is still on the front gate.

Cara reaches for the padlock, turning it over in her hands. "Should we just shout for her?"

Amy opens her mouth to answer, but the front door swings open.

And there she is. She looks so much thinner. Smaller. Older. It's only been a few months, but any longer and I might not have recognized her right away. Her white hair is braided and curled into a bun. She squints at us—the shotgun points down at the ground—then recognition lights up her face and her mouth drops open. She puts the gun to the side of the door and marches into the winter afternoon.

"Amy?" Her voice is hoarse, as if she has a cold.

Her eyes flick to Cara, then back to me. They crinkle as she smiles and takes out a key to unlock the gate. Her hands are shaking with excitement, and I immediately lose the ability to talk. Her smile drops a bit when she looks back up from the lock. Amy is sobbing, her hands on the gate. "Mom."

"Oh, honey." Henri swings open the gate and wraps her arms around Amy, and I lose all composure I have left as Amy hugs her mother tightly.

"Shh, it's okay," she whispers, lovingly rubbing the back of Amy's neck. This moment makes everything worth it. I was worried it wouldn't, but here we are. Amy and her mother are back together. Jamie and I traveled so far and lost so much, but we still managed to make this happen, and it's all worth it. I wish he were here to see it.

Cara turns away, but I can see her wipe tears from her own eyes. Taylor is grinning, and Jamar has wrapped an arm around her, but the Kid's eyes are locked on me. He watches me wipe at my cheeks, and I nod that everything is okay.

Then Henri holds Amy out at arm's length, looking at her. "You look great, pumpkin."

Amy wipes at her eyes. "Please, I look like death warm—" Her voice trails off and I follow her gaze to the front door of the house.

"Amy?"

Another woman stands there, in her forties—she looks just like Amy. And beside her is a girl around Taylor's age who is a young version of the women in front of me. The girl runs toward us.

"Auntie Amy!"

"Ellie!" Amy loses it again and pulls the girl into a hug. The other woman runs out and joins her, crying. Henri watches them with tears in her eyes. Then she looks at me and laughs, opening her arms wide for me. I hug her, burying my face in her warm sweater.

"Thank you," she whispers. "Both of my daughters are home with me."

Both of her daughters. This must be the one who was in Colorado. She was alive after all.

"Your granddaughters, too," Amy says, turning and looking to Taylor.

Taylor holds out Henri-Two to Amy, who takes her. "Mom, Kristy, Ellie, this is Henri-Two. Er, *Henrietta*!" She catches herself, laughing and shaking her head. Then she gives me a glare. "Can't believe you made that nickname stick."

I shrug. "It fits."

Henri-Prime takes Henri-Two in her arms. "I think it's perfect. Just like her."

Amy introduces us to her sister, Kristy, and niece, Ellie. Henri-Prime holds Henri-Two out for Kristy to take and falls into a fit of coughs. Something passes over Kristy's and Ellie's faces, as if they're worried. But Henri-Prime waves as Amy goes to her.

"It's fine, just a cough from the cigarettes."

"You're not still smoking, are you, Ma?" Amy scolds.

Henri-Prime gives her daughter a haughty look. "Not unless tobacco has become a cash crop in the apocalypse." Amy rolls her eyes as Henri waves to the yard around her. "It's just the cold, so let's get inside where it's warm. Or at least it was . . ." She points to the open door. "Now we're heating the neighborhood."

Kristy locks the gate behind us as Henri leads us inside. I introduce Henri to Cara, Taylor, Jamar, and the Kid, then we sit quietly, letting Amy catch up with her family. Ellie plays with Henri-Two, making her squeal with laughter.

But Henri's eyes are on me. Then they drift over to Cara and the others before coming back to me. She wraps a blanket around her shoulders and looks like she wants to ask me a question. Like where Jamie is, maybe.

She coughs again. Kristy gets up to get her a glass of water and comes out of the kitchen with a pitcher full, offering some to the rest of us. Eventually Taylor and Jamar sit with Ellie and keep Henri-Two busy.

When Kristy asks Amy to help her with dinner, Cara offers to help as well. Ellie asks her aunt if she can bring Henri-Two outside and after Amy says yes, Taylor and Jamar follow them.

Leaving just me, Henri, and the Kid.

"The Kid, huh?" Henri asks, looking at him. "I like your name."

"Thank you," he says. Maybe at this point he doesn't even remember his own name. I've been calling him the Kid so long, he just goes with it.

Henri chuckles and falls into another fit of coughs.

"Are you okay?" I ask. "Really?"

She nods. "Yes." But her voice is so hoarse, and she's so skinny. "You brought my daughter all the way up here. Which I assume means you went all the way down to her. So, yes, I am more than okay. Really."

"That's not—"

"I know what you mean, Andrew. And I'm still telling you that today, for the first day in a very, *very* long time, I am wonderful." Still, she coughs again. Like a lie detector test narcing on her.

"Are you sick?" asks the Kid.

"I think so," she tells him. "But don't worry, it's not the flu. You can't catch what I have, sweetie."

"What is it?" I ask. She stares at me for a moment, almost like she's scolding me for asking. Then she shakes her head.

"I guess it could be a cold? Pneumonia? Could be . . ." She trails off and shrugs. "Could be I'm just getting old. Even just surviving can take it out of you eventually." Before I can ask anything else, she brings up the only topic that she probably knows will get me to stop asking questions. "Where's Jamison?"

The Kid also turns to me. He asked me the same question and I gave him a half-assed lie about him taking a trip to make sure we were safe. I guess the Kid deserves the truth, too. He's been with us this whole way; he deserves to know where Jamie went.

So I start with the day we left here. I tell her about going to Reagan Airport and finding out the rumors of the EU convoy were just rumors. Then our trip down to Florida, including the run-in with Fort Caroline, Jamie getting shot, and his revenge mission once he found out they were still looking for him.

"That doesn't seem very like him," Henri says once I'm done. I look at the Kid to gauge his reaction, but his face is blank.

"It doesn't," I say.

"The two of you have been through a lot," she says. "So I understand how that can change a person."

"But it's not that he suddenly wants to become a mechanic or likes mushrooms. It's a fundamental shift from who he was."

She nods slowly and takes a moment to clear her throat. "And that change isn't something you can ever accept."

Of course it isn't. He's going to kill someone—actively choosing to do it, not because he's trying to save me or himself. He *thinks* he's protecting us, but that's not true. We could easily hide; the two of us could go back to his cabin. It was his plan all along, so I can't understand why he couldn't just do that. Why he had to go looking for Rosewood.

But then it all clicks into place.

This whole time, he's been keeping everyone we've grown close to at a distance. Even after we left, he said he wanted to take Amy to Henri, then go to the cabin, just the two of us. We could have done that, left Faraway together, but he chose to go after Fort Caroline.

I look down at the Kid, who is still latched on to my hand, and my chest aches with a weird combo of love, frustration, and sadness. Jamie finally let himself love everyone else in our group. He went to kill Rosewood because he doesn't want any of us to get hurt. He doesn't want what happened in the Keys to happen again.

Maybe that was driven partly by revenge, but a large part also has to be because he was scared. And not just for himself.

For all of us.

My heart aches again for him—with fear and worry but also so much love. I wish I could have reassured him, found a way to convince him to change his mind.

"Maybe?" I finally say to Henri. Maybe one day I can forgive him. Knowing he finally opened his eyes to our found family and just wanted to protect them. Us. "I think I can. Maybe with more time."

Henri smiles. "Well, that's the good news about the apocalypse. Nothing but time."

Still, her eyes are sad. Like she knows that's not true.

Not for her.

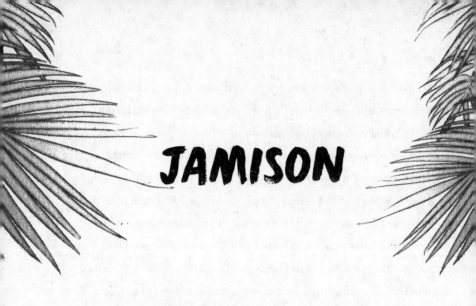

JAMISON

A COUPLE OF DAYS AFTER LEAVING FARAWAY, Niki and I have to stop for the afternoon. It's raining nonstop and our shoes are soaked through. We light a fire in the fireplace of an empty house and raid what's left of their pantry—there's not much, but it's enough to feed us for the night. The following day is clear, so we set out early, looking for a place in town that might have food.

We check a few houses first and come up with five cans—black beans, corn, pears, and vegetarian refried beans—and a tin of sardines. Still not much.

"Maybe the others came through and cleaned out most of it," Niki says.

I nod. "Andrew would absolutely leave the sardines."

We check a few more places—gas stations, churches, a dentist office kitchenette—but find nothing substantial.

I go into a discount grocery store while Niki watches the front and double-checks the map. I find a few more cans, but wherever we stop for the night, we'll have to go looking for more food before we leave in the morning.

"Jamie!" Niki's voice sounds full of fear, so I sprint through the messy aisles out the broken door. She has her rifle pointed toward the parking lot. I reach back for my gun but stop.

There's a dog sitting halfway between a light pole and us. Just sitting, their mouth open in a pant and eyes squinting. They're a big dog, but skinny. Large satellite-dish ears are splayed out on either side of their head and their white, brown, and black-speckled fur is thick and matted.

"It's okay," I say, putting my hand on her rifle and pushing it slowly down. "I don't think they're going to hurt us."

"Have you *met* the postapocalyptic dogs? The ones who survived are feral again."

"Does this one look feral to you?"

"Yes!"

Almost as if to prove a point, the dog yawns and returns to panting. I take a step forward.

"Hey, uh . . ." I check, just to be polite. "Guy. You hungry?"

"We don't really have food for *us*," Niki mumbles.

"We have enough." I take another step forward and hold out my hand. The dog stands and takes a few strides over to me, keeping his head down. He smells my hand, gives a light lick, then presses his face into it. I scratch behind his ears, and he starts kicking his hind leg.

Teeny fleas jump off onto my hands. My flesh crawls and I step back, shaking them off. The dog sits down hard and continues scratching behind his ears with his hind leg.

"He's covered in fleas," I say. Probably ticks, too. Poor guy. "Wait here."

I go back into the store as Niki calls out after me. There's a pet aisle, but I doubt they have flea and tick treatment in a discount store. They do have a brush and a small, bristled metal comb specifically for combing out fleas.

I grab both, then a bottle above them catches my eye. Flea and tick shampoo. What do you know. I check the back to make sure it's going to get rid of the fleas, not just make him smell like lavender. But the bottle says it's unscented and kills fleas and ticks on contact. Perfect.

"Jamie, hurry up!"

"Coming!"

I head back to the front but stop myself, turning back and grabbing a hard plastic chew toy that says it's supposed to be good for dogs' teeth and a soft plush hedgehog. I give it a squeeze, and instead of a squeak it makes a huff sound.

Outside, Niki yelps and glass crunches at the front of the store. The dog stands in the doorway, his head quirked to the side and one ear up.

"You heard that, huh?" I ask him. I squeeze it again and his thick, fluffy tail sways back and forth. "You gotta follow us if you want it."

I probably should get a leash and collar, but it's not like he's *my* dog. And he's been surviving on his own well enough, it seems, so I decide to just let him come with us as long as he wants and leave when he wants.

He jumps up for the hedgehog toy and I pull it out of his reach. He sits down and lets out a little whine.

"Don't torture him," Niki says. She seems to be coming around now that he hasn't decided to attack us.

"Okay, go get it?" I toss the hedgehog into the parking lot, and he bolts after it, scooping it up, giving it a shake and making it huff before trotting back and placing it at our feet. I pick it up and throw it for him, only this time when he launches after it, Niki and I follow. When the dog realizes we're coming with him, he runs ahead a bit, then turns back and circles around us, chomping down on the hedgehog.

Huff. Huff. Huff.

We both laugh as he circles us with his new toy. I don't think either of us has laughed or even smiled in weeks. It feels odd. And it reminds me of when I first met Andrew, how he tried to make me laugh, but it didn't feel appropriate after everything that had happened. The thought only makes me smile more, and this time it's a little easier.

Niki points us in the direction of a housing development near a river. While she settles into a house, I head to the river with our bottles and a bucket I found in the house's linen closet. The dog follows me, probably not realizing what I'm grabbing the bucket for. I fill up our bottles and the bucket and head back to the house, where Niki has already set a fire in the fireplace.

She joins me on the back deck because we've already decided the dog isn't coming inside until he's cleaned off. And given how cold the water I splashed on my leg is, he's probably going to decide against sticking with us anyway.

"I put an empty pot by the fire," Niki says, closing the sliding glass door behind her.

"I'll refill the bottles when we're finished cleaning him," I say.

"Then we can boil it to drink."

I try to wrestle the hedgehog away from him, but he latches on tightly, shaking his head.

"What should we call him?" Niki asks.

"I don't . . . know. Drop it!"

He drops it.

"I don't think 'Drop It' is a very good name," she says, snorting.

I tell him to sit, and he does but then promptly stands back up when I set the hedgehog on the railing. "Where are we again?"

I take off my shoes and socks and roll up the bottoms of my jeans. It's probably about forty degrees out, but I'd rather be cold for a bit than cold *and* wet. I take off my jacket and shirt and gently take the dog by the scruff of his neck. He doesn't pull away, just keeps his eyes on the hedgehog.

Meanwhile, Niki has the road atlas in her hands and is skimming pages, trying to find where we are.

"Newton, North Carolina," she finally says.

"Oh, Newton is a cute name."

"Newt. I like it."

I turn the dog's head so he's looking at me. "What about you? You like the name Newt?" He pants, his tongue sticking out of his mouth, which is probably as much confirmation as we're going to get. "Newt it is. Now that we have a name for you, I have to say sorry for what I'm about to do, Newt."

I let go of him and pour a bit of water from the bucket over his hindquarters. He lets out a whine and immediately starts trembling.

"I know, buddy," I whisper. "But it will make you feel better, I promise." I cup a little of the cold water in my hands and pour it over his head, then start shampooing.

Newt trembles, shakes, pants, and whines the whole time, but he stays put. And after I have a nice lather worked up around his ears, he seems to enjoy it a little. At least until I rinse him off with the rest of the water. When I'm done, I tell Niki to back up as he does a big shake and water goes flying everywhere. I can see flecks of dead fleas in the suds on the wooden deck, so the shampoo seems to have done its job.

"I'll go get more water," Niki says. "You go inside and warm up."

I thank her and grab the hedgehog, and Newt follows me inside. I throw it close to the fire, where Newt runs after it. There are still towels in the linen closet, so I grab a stack, dry myself off, then go back to find Newt working hard at ripping the noisemaker from the hedgehog.

"You're going to be very disappointed when that isn't making sounds anymore," I tell him. He ignores me and keeps gnawing at the stuffy while I rub him with a towel. Once he's a little drier, I set about combing out the mats and dead fleas—and a few ticks, which I throw into the fire.

When Niki returns, we boil the water and open a few cans of food. We give Newt the tin of sardines, which he laps up in seconds, then stares at both of us, trying to get us to share our food with him.

After it's clear we won't, he decides to punish us by jumping onto the couch across the room and curling up, burying his nose under his tail and watching us resentfully.

"What are you and Andrew going to do when we get to Bethesda?"

343

Niki asks me after dinner. The fire is crackling, and outside, rain patters the windows again.

"I don't know."

I'm not even sure if Andrew will be happy to see me when I get there. It doesn't matter that I didn't kill Rosewood. I left Andrew with the idea that I would, and Rosewood's still dead and Fort Caroline has fallen, and even though I didn't cause either of those things, he might still see me differently.

I kind of see myself differently. Maybe it was just temporary insanity, but I couldn't go on trying to survive in this world knowing someone might show up at any moment looking for revenge. I kept imagining them tracking Amy and Henri-Two to Bethesda. Or finding Taylor and the others at Faraway. Finding the Kid. I could never live with that constant fear.

But even with all that behind us, I don't know where that leaves Andrew and me.

And I'm scared to find out.

"Faraway seemed nice," she says. "Maybe we can all go back. I'm sure they'd love to have us."

I nod. "Yeah. It was nice. We'll do that."

Andrew wanted a community in the Keys. If he wants to stay in Faraway, that would be good for everyone. But if he doesn't want to see me, I think I'll just keep going. Back up to my cabin. I know how lonely I was up there before Andrew came, but I don't think I could stand to live in the same place with him if he hated me. It was bad enough when we were fighting in the Keys.

Plus, the settlement that robbed us is still up there, and they did say they were just trying to scare us into joining. Maybe that's what I'll do if Andrew and I are over. He can go back to Faraway with the others. I'll go back home.

Then everyone will be happy.

"Jamie."

Niki whispers my name two more times before my eyes snap open. I turn to my right and she's smiling, holding a finger to her mouth. It's early morning and the fire has burned down to crackling embers. The rain also seems to have stopped.

Niki points down between our sleeping bags.

Newt has splayed himself out on his back between us, one paw sticking straight up and the other bent at the wrist. I smother a laugh as Niki does the same.

"I think we might be stuck with him," she says.

"I think you're right."

I reach out and rub his belly as he stretches out a little more.

"Newt! Leave it!" I yell. It's a fun game he has us playing. I have no idea how many things he's eaten that he shouldn't have throughout his postapocalyptic journey to us, but I'm trying to keep it to a minimum now. He spends most of his time sniffing things on the side of the road, licking things he probably shouldn't—my chest aches at the thought of how Andrew would make a joke here—and often we catch him chewing something, but "drop it!" is not a command he is willing to listen to when it comes to food. And "leave it" doesn't seem to be working either.

"What is it this time?" Niki asks.

"I don't know." I jog ahead and push him away from whatever it is he's sniffing. But it isn't food; it's a thick, waterlogged paperback book.

On the front cover, bigger than the title, is the name Daphne De Silva.

My heart feels like it fills my chest to almost bursting, and I reach down for it. I turn the book over, examining every inch. On the back page is a black-and-white picture of Daphne that makes me laugh. She looks like she did in life—like she had the juiciest gossip and just couldn't wait to share it with you. I can even hear her warm laugh.

"Oh my . . ." Niki says, coming up behind me.

The pages are all stuck together, so I carefully hold the book before flipping to the front cover again. But something catches my eye. Purple stains on one of the front pages. I open the book to see someone's handwriting.

Daphne De Silva, still with us on our journey.
Started: Rocky Mount, NC 12/27
Finished: Cushman, NC 12/28

Still with us on our journey. Still! It has to be Andrew and the others. It's not Andrew's or Cara's handwriting. It must be Taylor's. Because of course she'd think of something like this.

I hug the book to my chest, tears welling in my eyes, then look back at the writing.

December 28.

Shit, that was a week ago.

"We passed through Rocky Mount," Niki says.

That was days ago, but they got here in only a day. "They must be driving."

We won't be able to catch up to them, but we know where they're going, and we'll get there eventually. And now we have Daphne on our side, too.

I squeeze as much moisture as I can from the book and put it in my pack. I'll leave it out to dry whenever I can. I just hope it doesn't get moldy. But for now, I feel rejuvenated. Even my sore feet aren't enough to slow me down.

Newt is looking up at me, his tail brushing the wet leaves and weeds on the road.

"All right," I tell him. "You did good." I take the hedgehog out of the pack and throw it ahead for him.

We'll see everyone soon. And though the thought of seeing Andrew again still scares me, finding this book makes me feel like I can handle it. And maybe, just maybe, he'll be as happy to see me as I will be to see him.

ANDREW

WE'RE GOING TO LEAVE HENRI'S SOON. HENRI, Amy, and her sister have all decided to stay, regardless of whatever happens in Fort Caroline. Henri even gave a laugh and said she'd like to see them try to come here.

Amy said she'd cover for us, tell them we went to Connecticut. I even gave them my home address so she could pass it on to them.

The night before we're planning to leave, Cara asks to talk with me outside.

"I'm going to stay here. Maybe not with Kristy and Amy, but close. Unless they don't mind me staying. But we're just three or four days' walk from my hometown. I haven't been since . . . August, the year of the flu. I'm not ready to go back yet, but I think I might be one day soon."

"Do you want us to wait? We can go with you." Maybe this is me trying to find an excuse not to go to Jamie's cabin. I made the decision so firmly, but now it kind of scares me. Especially without Cara coming. We're losing members of our fellowship left and right, and what if it's just me soon? Alone.

"I don't want you to go with me. I want—I *have* to go alone." A fat tear spills over the edge of her eyelid. I put my good hand out to her, and she snatches it, holding tight. I try to put my injured hand gently over hers. The nerves shoot pain up to my shoulder and I try to hide the wince. She takes a deep, shaky breath before she speaks. And when she does, it's like she's practiced this for months.

"No one in my family got sick. My dad was a pediatric nurse, my mom was an oral surgeon, and when things got really bad, they both helped at the hospital as often as they could, but they still never got sick. All their patients died but they never did. When the hospital had to close and they came home, they didn't get any of us sick. My grandmother was still living with us, my sister, my aunt Tracey. I knew they were trying to help people, but I was so scared they would catch it from someone."

Cara pauses and I let her take whatever time she needs, because if I say anything she might retreat into silence, and I think she *needs* to get this out.

"Still, they were healthy. So were we. One morning in November, I heard from my neighbor that one of the grocery stores was getting a food shipment. This was after the internet stopped working and we were only hearing rumors from the other people left in our town. I left early, alone, because the last time we went things got a little crazy. Anyway, I managed to get a couple bags' worth of canned food, and as I was walking back, I started smelling the smoke."

She pauses for a long time.

"They set my house on fire. They burned them all alive because someone heard a rumor that they were asymptomatic carriers. My mom and dad had been in the hospital, trying to help, but people who'd lost their own loved ones were grieving. They started talking about how my family was fine and they said we were spreading the virus. That people like us who didn't have symptoms just kept giving it to everyone else. Do you think that's true?"

"No. That's not what happened."

She nods as though she might not believe me but wants to. "I know people were scared. All of us were, but they . . ." Her voice breaks, and she pulls her hands away from mine, pressing them to her eyes. "I want to . . . I hope that . . ."

She doesn't seem to know what she wants to say next, like this is the part she didn't practice. Then finally she gives a quick, short exhale.

"I *want* to go home. And I *want* to try and . . . forgive them. Even if they're dead and there's no one left, I want to be able to forgive them. I want to remember why they were so scared, and I want to be able to forgive them. Do you think that's weird?"

I shake my head. "I think it's brave." Cara—who isn't a hugger—wraps her arms around me, tight.

"Sure we can't convince you to stay?" Amy asks as Henri-Two scrambles in her arms, reaching out for my hand.

"You have your hands full with this one," I say. "You don't need a bunch of orphans in your way, too."

"Andrew." Her voice is warning me that what I said is ridiculous and completely not true.

"I know, I'm ninety percent joking." I don't know what's wrong with Henri-Prime, but judging by what she's told me so far, she doesn't think she has much time left. I'd rather she spend as much of it with her daughters and granddaughters as she can.

Taylor, Jamar, the Kid, and I will try to find our way back up to Jamie's cabin. It's a terrifying thought, waiting up there and hoping he'll show. And the longer we wait, the more likely it will be that he's dead. But I'm trying this new thing where I let myself hope for the best-case scenario—that he realized what a dummy he was and turned back around.

Of course, I was hoping he'd make it here by now, but it's been four days. Four days of us eating Henri and Kristy's food stores.

We can't stay here any longer. We have no clue if Jamie and Niki would even come here or go straight to the cabin. Or something even worse. We could wait and wait and . . . I can't think like that, though. I have to hope they'll come to the cabin eventually.

I hug Amy goodbye and pretend to eat the side of Henri-Two's face, which sets off a round of giggles just like it always does. Then move on to Kristy and Ellie before stopping in front of Henri.

"You could just move next door." She hikes a thumb over her shoulder to the rancher next to her. "Help bring the property values back up."

"That's gentrification, Henri, and you're better than that."

Her laughter turns to coughs again, and I wait until she's settled before hugging her.

"Take care of yourself," she says. "And them, too."

"I will."

She gives me a long kiss on the cheek and cups my face in her warm, thin hands. "Thank you for bringing my girls back to me."

I can't even get a "you're welcome" out because my throat is tight, so I just nod. They all walk us to the street, and as Henri unlocks the gate, I take the time to remind Cara where she can find us.

"Whenever you're ready."

She nods.

"Who's that?" I look to see the Kid pointing down the street.

My heart leaps and I follow his finger to the horizon.

But it's not a person and my shoulders slump. Three large brown beasts and a little baby beast trot behind a parked car and into a yard.

"Bison," says Henri. "More Smithsonian animals, but I'm hoping they become a big old herd." Then she lowers her voice so only the adults can hear. "Lots of meat on those suckers."

"He'll be here soon," Cara whispers to me. She sounds so sure. "And I'll send him after you."

We finish our goodbyes, the Kid takes my good hand, and we head off in the direction of the bison—giving them a nice, wide berth. I don't need any more zoo animal encounters, thank you very much.

Do you know how many "burgs" there are in Pennsylvania? I mean, obviously there's Pittsburgh and Harrisburg—though one has an *h* and the other doesn't. But there's also Dillsburg, Mechanicsburg, Elysburg, and Bloomsburg. All of which we pass by in the two-week trip from Virginia to central-ish Pennsylvania. Like, did the person putting in I-81 have to name these places and just think "something-burg!"?

But now I'm at the part where things get a little hazy.

I was hoping that I'd recognize some landmarks along the way, a car or a highway that looked familiar. Unfortunately, everything looks different than it did the last time we came through. Maybe it's the seasonal difference, but I assume by the time spring rolls around, this place will look even more different from the last time I saw it. Than it does now, even. That's the reality these days—with every season that passes without humans to maintain things, once-familiar places will look newer and stranger.

"Maybe we should find a place to stop," I say.

The sun is still in the sky, so it's probably midafternoon. But I don't want to be stuck out in the open at night.

Taylor stops and looks at me. "How much farther is it?"

"Uh, I'm not really sure. I'd have to look at the map to estimate." Man, I wish Cara were here.

"I'll get it." Taylor starts to take off her backpack, but I hold out my hand.

"Why don't we stop for the day and check out the map when we find shelter?"

"Because if we're five miles away from the cabin, why wouldn't we just walk the five miles and stay there?"

"I think it's farther than that," I say, trying to bluff. "And, honestly, the last time I was around here and wasn't careful, I stepped in a bear trap. So it's safer for us to find a place to stick it out for the night and get a fresh start tomorrow."

Taylor shakes her head as though she's disappointed in me. I almost ask her what that look is for, but I know the answer and I don't need her to say it aloud.

She knows I have no idea where Jamie's cabin is.

It's kind of why I found it to begin with. At the time, I'd just had my first bad interaction with other survivors. So I got off the highway and started wandering aimlessly down side roads and less busy highways.

But then, passing through the town where I eventually found the cabin, I heard people. They were on ATVs or dirt bikes—I only heard the revving of their engines.

So I got off the road and went into the woods.

And that's when I stepped in a bear trap.

I should tell the kids the story, but I can do that when we *find* the cabin.

If we find the cabin.

We'll find the cabin. Right?

We come to a quiet small-town street that either looks familiar or it's my own hopeful mind playing games with me. It's easier to *not* be optimistic because then shit like this doesn't happen. My mind doesn't say "Hey! This might be the place!" But lately I really have been trying to be more optimistic.

I think it's because of the others. How they agreed to stay with me even though we were going to a strange place where they had no idea what was waiting for them. They became the optimists because they trusted me.

Yeah, maybe I should have been a little more honest that I needed to do some exploring to find Jamie's cabin again. But it's nice that they trusted me! We're here, we have time. It will be fine.

See? Optimistic.

It's not too cold, so we should be okay in any building, even one without a fireplace.

"How 'bout there?" Jamar points to a two-story house painted pink with purple shutters. The supports and handrails on the wrap-around porch are also purple, but the spindles in the railing have been painted pink. There's a crooked sign swinging in the breeze. It's hanging from one hook, the chain on the other side scraping the top of the purple railing.

The sign reads: "Marnie's Kitchen Café."

"Why not?" I say, happy with anything that gives me a little more time to check the road atlas and see if there's a town or a street or *anything* that sounds familiar.

We go up onto the porch and try the front door, but it's locked.

"Try around back?" Taylor says.

I hold out my hand to the Kid, who takes it and lets me lead him around the side of the porch, where there's another door. But that one's locked, too.

"What kind of lunatic locks doors during the apocalypse?" I ask.

"Maybe this is someone's house," the Kid answers.

"I think it used to be a house," I say. "But then someone named Marnie turned it into a restaurant."

"It's a restaurant?" The Kid sounds impressed, and I realize he probably thinks Marnie is still around and turned it into a restaurant postapocalypse.

"I mean before the bug, Kid. It's not anymore. Not a great time to start a business, with the collapse of civilization and all."

"Yeah," the Kid says, as if he understands the fall of capitalism. We climb down from the porch and continue toward the back of the house.

"Hey, can you try this window?" I ask, pointing to a window about six feet off the ground.

"I can't reach!" The Kid uses Bobo—who is looking in deep need of professional cleaning—to point up at it.

"Yeah, dude, I was gonna lift you."

He raises his arms, letting me pick him up. First with my good arm only. I'm trying not to put too much weight onto my injured arm until I need to. He senses this and manages to climb onto my right shoulder, letting me hold his legs steady.

"Try and push it up if you can." Ahead of us, Jamar is rounding the corner as Taylor hangs back and watches us with a smirk. I know the Kid's not going to be able to open the window, but I just like giving him things to do sometimes. Makes him feel like he's an integral part of the team.

But the window does open.

"Holy shit!" I say.

"Holy shit!" repeats the Kid, surprised himself.

"Don't say *shit*. Can you push it open any farther?"

He puts his little fingers in the opening and grunts. It moves about half an inch, then stops.

"Put your hand under the window and I'll push you up, just keep your arms straight, okay?"

"Okay!"

He does as I say, and I push up on my tippy-toes, using my shoulder as leverage. The window slides up with a loud groan. It's just big enough for him to slip through. But I pull him back down and put his feet firmly on the ground as Jamar comes back around the corner.

"Okay, I need a break," I say. My left arm is starting to throb.

"Back door is locked, too," Jamar says.

I point up at the window. "Kid opened the window for us."

"Good job!" He puts out his hand and the Kid high-fives it.

I crouch down to him. "If I boost you up there, think you can go in and unlock the front door for us?"

He nods and puts his hands in the air again.

"I can do it," Taylor says.

"The Kid's got it." I kinda want him to be able to celebrate the win here. She seems to get that—and that she can be the backup if he can't figure out the door or there's a bolt that's out of his reach—so she shrugs and nods.

I lift him up using only my good arm and supporting his feet with my injured arm, and he climbs into the window. Rising to my tippy-toes, I hold on to his feet as he slips inside.

"You good if I let go?"

"Yeah!" the Kid calls back. I let go of one foot, then the other. There's a loud bump that makes me worried that I just dropped him on his head—I have no clue how far the drop is on the other side. But then the Kid's smiling face pops up in the window and he waves. Taylor laughs and tells him to go to the front door, and he disappears into the darkness.

We head back up to the porch, rounding the corner to the front of the restaurant—

And there's a man there. He's a stout white guy, a little older than me, with a brown-and-red beard. He wears a bright yellow beanie and a green puffer coat.

And he has a rifle pointed at us.

"Who are you?" he asks. "What are you doing here?"

My hands go up, not to the rifle on my shoulder. "Just looking for shelter. I used to live in a cabin around here, but we're stopping for the night. We're not here to hurt anyone."

"What cabin? I know everyone in the area, and I never seen any of you before."

"We came from a settlement down in Florida. We got hit by a hurricane and the settlement was destroyed, so I brought everyone up to the cabin."

"Where's the cabin?"

Oh shit. This isn't going to sound great for us.

"I . . . kind of forget."

"Andrew!" Taylor says my name like she's my mother scolding me.

Then the lock on the front door of the restaurant pops and the door opens.

The man turns.

"No!" I yell. My legs move on their own, pushing past the guy. The rifle falls off my shoulder onto the ground and I wrap my arms around the Kid. Taylor screams.

The man falls on his ass and when I turn to look, he points his gun in my face and pulls the trigger.

CLICK.

I open my eyes to see the look on the guy's face. Like *he's* the one surprised that he doesn't have ammo. Did he forget?

He looks at the end of the gun for a second before his eyes drift down to Jamie's rifle.

The rifle that *is* loaded.

I turn to grab it, but he swings the end of his rifle around, smacking me in the side of the face. The pain is sharp and makes the world flip and go blurry. I fall back, bracing myself with my hands, and pain shoots up from my chewed-up left arm. Taylor calls out my name and I hear the Kid crying.

Warm blood drips down the side of my face onto the porch. I put my hand up, and it comes away covered in red. I can taste iron. My tongue moves to the side of my mouth to feel a chunk of flesh where I bit my cheek.

Next to me the Kid is crying, his arm across my chest. Blood drips from my chin onto Bobo's nose. The guy in the yellow beanie shouts at the others to stay back, but he's the one backing away from us, Jamie's rifle in his hands.

"Just go," I say, though it comes out a little messy because my face is starting to swell.

"No," he says. "All of you down here, now."

"We don't have anything useful for you," Taylor says. "Just take the gun and go. We're not going to follow you."

"There's three groups in the area!" he shouts. "You don't come from any of those groups because we all know each other, so you're coming with me until we sort all this out."

"What's there to sort, man?" I ask. "We said we're coming through looking for shelter. We're not going to hurt you. The Kid is seven, those two are thirteen—" I thumb back in Jamar and Taylor's direction. "We're all just kids."

He looks at us like he's not sure he believes me. Then he shakes his head. When he speaks, he sounds a little less frantic.

"I'm sorry. But I need you all to come with me, okay? Please?"

"Are you going to shoot us if we don't?" I ask.

"I can't let you go."

"So, because you can't let us go, your only option is to shoot a bunch of unarmed kids?"

"Please." He sounds panicked and he moves his whole body when he says it, like he's begging us without getting on his knees. "Just come with me and the others can figure it out."

"Okay," Taylor says. I turn back to look at her. She gives me a slight nod that says either *I have a plan* or *what other option do we have?*

I stand, feeling a little dizzy, and Taylor comes over to catch me.

"Bring my rifle," the man says. Taylor grabs it and slings it over her shoulder.

I reach down for the Kid and pick him up, my bad arm again throbbing with pain. I glance down at it to see one of the healing scars has ripped open a bit and blood trickles down my hand. The Kid cries into my neck—on the side of my face that isn't bleeding—and we take the steps down the porch as the guy backs away.

When we come to a stop in front of him, he points to the road with the rifle.

"That way, go on. I'll tell you where."

We turn and go back to the road, where he tells us to turn right. He follows behind us, keeping Jamie's rifle pointed at our backs.

I can't help but return to my pessimism. Wondering if this would have happened if I'd known how to get to the cabin without Jamie.

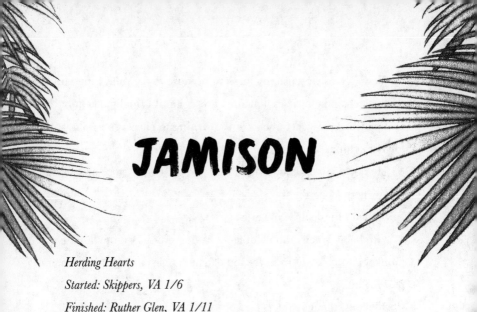

JAMISON

Herding Hearts
Started: Skippers, VA 1/6
Finished: Ruther Glen, VA 1/11

WE HAVEN'T FOUND ANY NEW DAPHNE DE Silva books since Ruther Glen four days ago, but maybe they ran out of them. Or maybe they're just not finished with whichever one they're reading now. Walking down the streets of Bethesda toward Henri's house fills me with more anxiety than I've ever felt. More than the hours leading up to tests in school. More than when I started to realize my feelings for Andrew. More than choosing to go back to Fort Caroline.

Because I don't know what's waiting for me when I get there. I know *who*, but I'm not sure how I'll be received. I don't know if Andrew will even be happy to see me, and I don't know what the others think of me either.

I'm also worried about the Kid. Taylor and Jamar are probably old enough to understand why I left, but there's no way the Kid could understand the complexities of my decision. Or even my reversal of that decision.

Newt seems to sense my anxiety because every time I give him the hedgehog, he nuzzles it against my leg until I finally take it back and he trots a few feet ahead of us, turning to check that we're still following him.

He doesn't even know where we're going, but he stops and sniffs everywhere along the way.

"What's his deal?" Niki asks.

"Probably smells the wildlife." On our way in we saw a pair of monkeys watching us from the top of a light pole in a shopping center parking lot.

No lions, though. Yet.

Hopefully Newt will warn us if he smells them coming—and knows to run from them.

We turn the corner of Henri's street and I stop. My feet completely unwilling to let me continue any farther. Niki makes it a few more paces before she turns back. Newt has stopped as well.

"We came all this way," she says. "You can't just stop here."

Of course I know she's right. But I can feel my hands trembling, and some of the anxiety has been replaced with excitement. I really do want to see everyone again. Whatever their reactions might be.

When the front door opens, Cara runs out with keys to unlock the gate. My heart leaps into my throat. Someone else appears in the doorway, but I can't see who they are because of the tears stinging my eyes. Cara yanks open the door and wraps her arms around both Niki and me.

"I was worried." I can't even speak. She holds me at arm's length and her voice lowers. "What happened?"

When the tears clear, I look up to see Amy and another woman watching us. Amy smiles, but the woman gives me a cautious look.

"Where's Andrew?" I ask.

After dinner, Cara, Amy, Niki, and I sit quietly by the fire out back. Henri, Henri-Two, Ellie, and Kristy have all gone to bed.

Newt is fast asleep at my feet, his head on my right shoe.

Henri's house is just as crowded as I thought it would be—it's only slightly bigger than the cabin Andrew and the others are heading for right now, so that's bound to get even more crowded.

"What do you think, Jamie?"

I look up from the fire to see Niki, Cara, and Amy staring at me. Niki was talking, but I wasn't listening at all.

"Sorry, what?"

She looks frustrated but repeats herself. "Stay tomorrow, and depending on weather we can leave the day after. Lead me up to the cabin where I can wring my brother's neck. With love."

"They might have gone back to Faraway." I don't believe that, though.

Cara probably knows I don't and frowns at me. "Andrew said he was going to the cabin."

That still gets me. I have no idea why he would go back to the cabin instead of waiting for me here. Maybe because he knew that if I didn't come here, I might have still been out there. But if I didn't come back to the cabin, it meant I was dead. If he had just waited a little longer, though, we could have gone up together. Unless he wasn't ready to see me yet.

"What if he took everyone else to Faraway before he went back to the cabin?"

"The Kid *left* Faraway to chase after them," Cara reminds me. "And Taylor chose to leave Jamar, which is how he ended up following us."

Niki shakes her head, still angry at Jamar, but I feel like she also might respect his decision. As long as it doesn't get either of them killed.

"Okay," I say. "We'll rest here tomorrow, then head for the cabin the next day."

But the following night, it starts snowing.

ANDREW

WE WALK ABOUT FOUR MILES BEFORE THE guy tells us to turn up a driveway of cracked asphalt. A half mile later, the thick woods surrounding the road open onto structured rows of leafless trees as far as the eye can see. The driveway turns to dirt and stone, but we continue walking.

My face throbs with pain, but my nose and the scratch below my eye have stopped bleeding. The Kid holds my good hand while I keep the bad one pulled close to my chest. The pain seems to be coming from everywhere in my body.

I turn to Taylor and whisper, "I need a fucking vacation."

The look she returns says, *Seriously? You're joking about that now?* I shrug because what can I say, it's true.

There are what look like seven housing structures on the property, which I'm now starting to assume is a farm of some kind given the cute little farmhouse that shall be known as structure number one. There's also a big, weathered wood barn that's a dead giveaway. But the other structures look like modular homes joined together by wood beams as an afterthought. Each has a steel chimney emitting white smoke. A few faces look out the windows at us.

Someone emerges from the farmhouse, coming to a stop at the top of the porch steps. They watch us for a bit before they turn around and duck back into the farmhouse, then come out again. This time they walk down the steps and approach us.

It's an older Southeast Asian man with short white hair and a clean-cut white beard.

"What the hell happened, Jeff?" the man asks.

"They were breaking into the restaurant downtown."

The man looks confused, then shakes his head. "Marnie's? What the hell would they have taken? We took everything of use over a year ago." He points at my injuries, then looks back at Jeff the Jerkoff. "And I'm assuming this is your fault?"

"They're not from around here," Jeff says.

"Guess the accent gave it away, huh?" I ask.

The older guy laughs, then walks up to Jeff and holds out his hand. "Give me the gun." Jeff hands it over and he pulls the bolt. I watch as his eyes go wide. "Where'd you get the round?"

"That's mine," I say. "The ammo, but the whole rifle, too."

Taylor steps forward and holds out Jeff's empty rifle. "This one is his."

The man takes it, thanking her, then throws it to Jeff. "Go back to your bunk, wait there."

"But—"

"Now!"

Without another word, Jeff hunches over and heads to one of the modular homes. The man looks at me in the dying afternoon light and winces.

"Sorry about him," he says. "He's jumpy, that's why he doesn't usually have ammo."

"Didn't stop him from pulling the trigger on an empty chamber," I say.

He groans and then motions for us to follow him. "Come on, let's get you cleaned up." As he starts walking toward the house, another man comes out to the porch. It's not until we're about ten feet away that I recognize him.

"You've got to be kidding me," I say.

On the porch, Howard Didn't-Get-a-Last-Name-Because-the-Last-Time-I-Saw-Him-He-Was-Robbing-Us is giving me a look that says I seem familiar, but he can't quite place me. How many people *did* you rob, Howard?

"Everyone, take out your food and give it to this asshole," I say.

"Asshole," the Kid repeats.

"That's right, Kid."

Hearing my voice must connect the dots for him because his eyebrows jump. "You and another guy were in the cabin about ten miles that way."

He points southwest. Ten miles! I'm only ten miles away?

Shit. Ten miles and now I'm probably going to have to pay a tax or some shit for trying to break into Marnie's. Howard's eyes drift over the others, but then come back to me when he realizes Jamie isn't here.

The other man speaks. "Jeff says they were trying to get into Marnie's downtown."

"Why?" Howard looks at me when he says it.

"Trying to find a place to shelter for the night before we go back to the cabin."

He mulls this over for a second, then turns back to the other guy. "Robbie, get them set up in one of the bunkhouses." Then he adds quickly, "Not Jeff's!"

"Yeah, no shit," Robbie mumbles.

He points at me. "You. I'll walk you to medical and we'll get you cleaned up."

The others look at me with concern, but from all the context clues they've been throwing around, it sounds as though Jeff is the only one we have to worry about. But the Kid is still holding on to my hand. I bend down and look him in the eye.

"Go with Taylor and Jamar, okay? I'll be right behind you after I fix my mug." I wave my hand around my face, then gently run my fingers down his face like I'm pulling off a mask, making him smile. He nods and takes Taylor's hand, and Robbie leads them off.

I watch them go—just in case the context clues were intended to throw me off—and Howard joins me at the bottom of the porch steps.

"Howard," he says. I see his hand out, but I don't take it.

"I remember. Andrew."

"I'm trying to be cordial."

"I think my face got enough cordiality from Jeff."

"*Cordiality* isn't a word."

"Yes, it is. Who taught you grammar?"

He frowns. "Is it?"

"Yes, and you can consider my teaching you that a down payment on whatever taxes I have to pay to stay in the cabin."

Howard seems embarrassed. Which, good, I'm glad. It was him and a group of others from this camp who showed up at Jamie's cabin demanding our food as taxes for living on this land he suddenly claimed in Postapocalyptic Eminent Domain. "Look, all that shit about taxes was just . . ." He flicks his head to his left. "Walk with me, that cut on your face needs to be cleaned."

I look back to see the others being led into a blue modular home, then I follow Howard.

"Sorry," he says. "We knew you were out there—we saw the other guy—"

"Jamie."

"Yes. We saw him out getting supplies in town one day and they followed him. Left you alone for a while, hoping you'd go out searching for other survivors and find us, but when spring rolled around and you didn't—"

"You decided to rob us."

"We were trying to scare you into joining us."

"Ah, yes, because intimidation is so inviting."

He shrugs. "Yeah, that was my fault. My wife told me it was a bad idea, but I think I was underestimating you. We'd had a couple of bad run-ins with other groups in the area, so we thought it best to scare you into joining us and make it seem like we were your best option."

"Stealing our food and trying to starve us to death makes you our best option?"

"We left enough food to last you a week, and we went back to the cabin three days later to check on you and invite you back here to live. But youse were already gone, so we figured you had joined up with one of the other groups."

I watch his face, trying to figure out how much of this is true. "Jeff said there's three groups in the area?"

"Including us, yeah. There's a farm about fifteen miles south with around ten people living on it. And the next closest is a group of twenty in a motel six miles west."

"A Motel 6 or a motel *that is* six miles west? Again, who taught you grammar?"

"The second one," he says, sounding as if he's trying not to laugh.

"How many people are here?"

"Forty-two." We reach a small corrugated-metal building painted white with a red cross on the door. Howard pulls it open for me. "Watch your step."

The room is dark, but I can see there's a large step up that would be easy to trip on. I step inside and Howard flips on a light switch.

The building is one room with four recessed lights in the corners that barely light it up when they flicker on.

"Solar panel on the roof is good for maybe forty minutes of light. They're LED, so they get brighter the longer they're on."

In the center of the room is a padded exam table that's only missing the disposable butcher paper that made me feel like deli meat at my pediatrician's office in the before times. There's a rolling stool pushed into a corner, cabinets above a sink, and a large, locked closet on the wall to my right.

"Have a seat." Howard motions to the table and goes over to the sink. He squeezes soap out of a dispenser into his hands and uses his foot to hit a pedal below the basin. After a few pumps, water pours from the spigot and he scrubs his hands. Then reaches into the upper cabinet. I see boxes lining the shelves, and he takes one down. It's a box of assorted bandages. He opens the other cabinet and takes out a towel.

He places them on the table next to me, then goes to the closet, which he unlocks using a ring of keys dangling from his belt loop. He removes a bottle of alcohol, a tube of ointment, and a glass jar filled with long Q-tips.

Once he has everything, he dampens the towel with some alcohol and holds it close enough to my face that I can smell it. "This is going to burn."

"I've felt worse."

His eyes drop down to my hand. "What happened?" He puts the towel against the cut on my cheek and the burn is immediate. I suck air through my clenched teeth as he dabs at it, the yellow towel coming away brownish red.

"Alligator attack."

"I'm sure you can make up a better lie than that."

"Oh, I absolutely can. But sadly nothing beats the truth."

He looks at me like he's not sure he understands the joke. "An alligator."

"It's a long story involving the breakdown of the food chain, but let's stick with grammar before moving on to biology."

Behind him, the door swings open. A Black woman with her hair in short locs enters. Howard peeks back, then returns his attention to me.

"Andrew, my wife, Raven."

"We've met before, when your husband was robbing us," I say with faux-cheer.

She looks at me cautiously, letting the door close behind her. "I remember." Her hand drifts down to her belly, which is much bigger than I recall. I guess the Howard-Raven family is expecting a new addition.

"It's fine, darling," Howard says. "Jeff just ran into them before we could."

Raven huffs. "Dipshit." Then her face clears up and she moves to stand so she can look at her husband while talking to him. "They have a kid with them. Do we have enough water treated for him?"

"We should. Ask Cookie to boil some extra before dinner."

"We can get our own water," I say.

"It's fine," Howard says. "We use our water for cooking, irrigation, and washing up, mainly. It got to be too much, trying to treat the water for drinking."

I stare at him, then Raven. "So . . . you all just don't drink water?"

Howard smirks. "Well, Raven does. For about seven months now. And if anyone wants to, they boil it off for themselves. But you see all the trees on your way in?"

"Yes?"

"Apple trees. Back in the day, before there was large-scale water treatment, people used to drink beer, wine, and cider more than water. Fermented drinks were healthier for them."

I stare at them, wide-eyed. "Yeah, and they also used to do blood-letting as a treatment for insanity. So, you're all just drunk all the time?"

Howard chuckles. "It's low alcohol. Our apples are less sweet than what you're used to, and we don't add sugar. But just to be safe, pregnant women and kids get water."

"Or milk," Raven adds.

"If there's extra from what Cookie needs it for."

I clench my jaw, trying to figure out a polite way to say this—which, honestly, they robbed Jamie and me, so do they even deserve politeness? But on the other hand, they are helping me right now. "So, you have a cow—I'm assuming—"

"Your assumption is wrong. We have goats. But only four, which doesn't go as far as you'd think."

"Okay, you have *goats* and cider and apparently a whole-ass farm. Why did you rob us? And don't say it was to scare us into joining you, because I'm not buying that. You could have knocked on the door and said 'We got goats! Come see!' and my ass would have been here in seconds. Goats are fucking adorable."

Raven swats Howard's arm as he opens the tube of antibiotic ointment. "See?"

"At the time, we didn't have everything we do now. We weren't producing our own crops—even that was hard this year."

"The bugs?" I ask.

Howard looks at me as if he's surprised, then seems to realize it must be a universal issue. "Right, breakdown of the food chain. Thankfully we still can make cider from the apples the bugs have gotten. Just adds a little protein."

"Ew."

Howard continues, "But we weren't completely set up then. We needed more people and supplies. We've been through some tough times, and there's a big learning curve to becoming a self-sustaining community. We're still learning, honestly. But we're doing it." He lightly places the bandage across my cheek. "We do it by learning from each other and trying our best. Sometimes an extra hand or two comes in . . ." He pauses.

"Oh, please don't say handy," I say.

He and Raven both laugh; it's absolutely what he was going to say. But he decides on, "It's useful. So now we'll do this the way we should have from the start. We would love to have you all join us."

I stare at them, thinking it over.

Then Raven adds, "We got goats!"

I point at her, staring daggers at Howard. "See? How hard was that?" They laugh, but I'm still not sure. Living with groups hasn't been what I expected. I prefer when it was just Jamie and me making our own decisions. Or even Niki and the others. I wouldn't say Jamie was *right*, but I'd say now I better understand where he was coming from—and I wish he were here so I could tell him.

If we all lived at the cabin, it would be cramped, but we could make choices for ourselves. We could reach out to this group if we needed help, help them when they need it. Separate, but still part of their community.

"I have to talk to the others," I say. "They can decide what they want to do, but I think I'm going to pass. That cabin is home for Jamie and me. We're willing to help you out and be friendly, but I'd rather live there."

Howard seems disappointed but nods anyway. "Okay. And all that about the taxes, just forget it."

"Yeah, I was gonna do that anyway, but thanks."

Raven pats Howard's shoulder. "I'm going to go check on the water for the kid." Then she looks at me. "What's his name?"

"He won't tell us, but he answers to Kid."

Howard's eyes light up and Raven shakes her head. "No."

"I told you it was an option!" he shouts at her as she leaves the room. She shouts "no" back. "I suggested that for the baby's name." He starts cleaning up and I hop down from the table.

"I agree with her. You can't have two Kids walking around. Especially with the goats!"

"I never thought about it like that." He shows me out of the room, and we start walking back toward the other buildings.

"Any chance someone can walk me to the cabin? I can't really find it from here, and the last time I went wandering through these woods I stepped in a bear trap."

He stares at me as if trying to figure out if I'm joking, and no, I'm not joking, Howard. Then he finally says, "You have terrible luck."

"Tell me about it."

The next day, the others stay at the farm—Howard and his crew call it Bittersharp Farm based on the type of apples they grow—while he and I walk through the woods to the cabin. As we walk, I tell him about our journey from here, why we left and why we came back. It's a shortened version of events, because we only have three hours to cover the past eight months.

Howard seems impressed, but I'm probably doing a bad job of telling the story. It's all the excitement, none of the bad shit. Of that, there's plenty.

I see the shed first. Greenish-brown ivy grows up the back of it, wood peeking around the leaves. The blue tarp over the woodpile has started to shred and come apart. The grass in the backyard is about waist-high and brown.

We stop at the edge of the tree line. This is where I first saw Howard while Jamie and I were sitting on the back deck one afternoon.

Now my view of the back deck is blocked.

A large tree has fallen on the cabin. It looks like it landed on the room that I used to sleep in, crushing the roof and continuing over to the bathroom and maybe even part of the kitchen. The top of the dead tree lies across the backyard.

Given everything that happened to us, this seems fitting.

"Well, shit," I say. Am I numb? Is this what being numb to the fortunes of the world is?

Howard steps around the fallen tree and I follow him. We go to the front of the cabin—taking a long way around the roots that have pulled up from the ground.

From the front of the house, it almost looks as if the tree missed it. At least Jamie's room is intact. Howard walks up the porch stairs, but I stop at the bottom of them. The steps are covered with leaves. I use my hand to push some of them aside, and there she is. A garden gnome sitting on a toadstool with a fat little sheep in her lap. The Mother's Day gift Jamie bought one year.

"Hey, Holly," I say, picking her up. "Long time no see!"

I put her in my backpack as Howard opens the front door. I see right back to the cracked window over the kitchen sink. One of the wall cabinets has fallen down, and it looks like the drywall is moldy and wet from where the tree landed.

The house smells like a mix of mildew and decaying organic matter. Something scratches across the floor to our left, and Howard points a flashlight. A fat raccoon runs down the hall toward the fallen tree.

"I always wanted a pet trash panda," I say.

"You're not seriously considering staying here."

I shrug. "Maybe I can cut up that tree and rebuild the wall. Jamie and I only need the one bedroom."

Howard shakes his head. "Look, I know we pissed you off, but it sounds to me like you were gonna leave anyway. Just stay with us. We'll keep you safe; you can have whatever freedom you and Jamie need when he gets here. We'll keep Jeff forty feet away from you at all times."

I laugh. "I get it. Stop feeling guilty, you fed us last night, we had a warm place to sleep"—thanks in large part to the modded-out modular homes with the woodburning stoves—"but you really don't owe us anything else. The others can stay, I'm sure they want to, but this is where Jamie is coming when he finds his way back. I know it."

And I know he's still alive. I can feel it in my gut. It's not me being optimistic—I just know he is. All the bad things that happen to us, they happen because we can survive it. Together or apart, the worst never happens, and I'm starting to believe it never will.

"We'll help you," Howard says. "Come stay with us, then every weekend a few of us will come out, help with cleaning this place up."

I stare at him. "Seriously?"

"Yes. We can split the wood from that tree. We'll figure out a way to turn it into supports for the new walls. Get rid of the raccoons—"

"I mean, maybe they can stay in the shed."

"We make amends. We rebuild, you all can stay here but know you have neighbors who are there to look out for you."

This is not what I expected. If anything, I thought Jamie and I would have to hide here the rest of our lives, being careful not to let it seem like anyone is here. But, honestly, how long would that have lasted?

"You're really serious about this," I say. "Not just trying to pull me along so I can help on your farm, and every weekend it's 'Oh, we can't, something came up, next weekend for sure.'"

"You have my word. Sure, there are bound to be times when it seems like a bad idea to leave the farm—blizzards, for instance. But as long as weather allows, yes. You help us, we help you." He holds out his hand to me. I stare at it, then look around at the walls. There are tiny spots of mold and mildew. Moss grows on the tree trunk where the bathroom should be. The floors have warped and discolored with constant water intrusion.

Fixing the house might be an impossible task. But having others there to figure it out might be helpful.

I take Howard's hand and shake on it. "Okay. Deal."

"Great, let's head back, then. If we're going to be camping here every weekend, I'd rather do it with more supplies than we have now."

"One second." I walk around him into the dining room. Some of the pictures scattered across the wall have fallen—probably when the tree hit the house. I bend down and pick one up. The glass is cracked, but the frame is intact.

In the picture are Jamie and his mom. Jamie is almost a foot taller than she is, and she's trying to kiss his cheek but he's laughing and pulling away. She's wearing green scrubs and he's in a black suit and blue shirt with a navy tie. There's a flower pinned on his lapel. I assume he was going to some high school dance, so it was probably only taken a couple of years ago, but he looks *so* young. Completely different from the boy I know now.

I put the frame in my bag with Holly. And one picture, still on the wall, catches my eye. It's Jamie as a little kid on the beach with his mom. He's missing baby teeth and there's a glob of sunscreen on his shoulder. His smile makes me feel light and buzzy and fills my body with warmth. It's a kid who has no idea what's ahead for him. I tell myself it's okay. Someday I'll see him again. And maybe he'll even smile like that again.

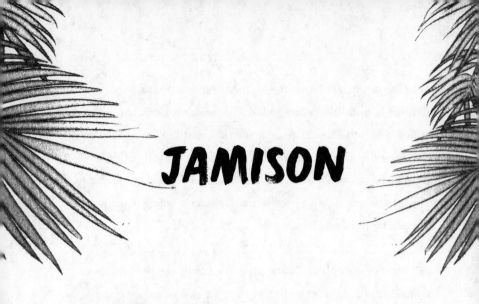

JAMISON

HENRI MADE IT UNTIL APRIL. BUT IN the end, it was her choice. Her breathing had gotten worse, and she said moving around exhausted her and it felt like there was a weight on her chest.

The storm the night after we arrived kept us snowed in for weeks. We stayed inside, bundled in blankets, while fat snowflakes drifted slowly from the sky. Kristy told us stories about their family—most of them about Amy and the trouble she would get into. Like when Amy was eight and she tied a rope to the handlebars of her bike. Then she waited by the bus stop on the corner, and when the number 29 bus stopped to pick people up, she looped it around the bus's bumper. She didn't realize how fast the bus would go, nor how fast *she* would continue to go when the bus stopped. She collided with the back of the bus, falling off and scraping her knees. When she stood up to brush herself off and get back on, the bus pulled away—still not realizing the bike was attached. It dragged the bike down the street, hitting parked cars and doing who knows how much damage before the bike got caught under a pickup and the rope snapped. Amy left her bike there and ran home, telling Henri she got hit by a bus.

Kristy was in tears laughing as she told us about it. The doctors rushed Amy into scans to make sure she wasn't internally bleeding. It was Henri who finally realized Amy's story started changing slowly but surely with every doctor who asked a new question.

We told them about our time in the Keys and all the good memories we had. Skipping over all the bad memories on the road. Then, when the snow let up and the sun went down, we set a fire in the fire-pit and made dinner while Henri and Ellie sat warm by the fire. That day was one of the best I'd had in a long time.

We went out a few times—Kristy, Niki, Cara, and me—looking for supplies. But the cold snap stayed over Maryland for weeks. Some days more snow would come, but nothing like the original blizzard. Still, going out for supplies was hard enough. No matter how anxious Niki was to find her brother, she wasn't planning to freeze to death to do it.

Any time she seemed to panic, Cara would remind her that Jamar was with Andrew, and he'd never let anything happen to him.

Henri and her family never asked us to leave. It seemed like every time we started talking about going, Henri sensed it. She'd say something about how glad she was that we were there. She'd tell me how much it meant that I did so much for her.

Every time, it felt like she was asking us to stay.

Or maybe it was me, making excuses so I didn't have to leave. Because I'm scared of what I might find at the cabin. It's been four months, and Andrew could have shown up here at any moment. Henri has been dead for three days, and I'm still here.

Still saying just a couple more days.

My eyes keep drifting over to the little mound where we buried Henri in the backyard. Just five feet from the garden.

I swat another bug as it lands on my neck, but my hand comes away clean, so whatever it was, I missed. I return to weeding Henri's garden with Ellie while she sings. I hear Cara emerge from the house behind us.

"Ellie, your mom needs your help in the kitchen."

Ellie jumps up and heads back to the house as Cara crouches down next to me and pulls out something green. I watch her add it to my pile of weeds.

"That was a tomato," I say.

"Oops." She gives up on weeding and just sits on the edge of the raised bed. "How long are you planning to stay?"

I shrug and my eyes drift over to the mound again.

"You aren't required to, you know." Her voice is soft, low. Did the others send her out here to have this little intervention?

"Are they getting annoyed that we overstayed our welcome?"

"No. Amy asked me how long you were staying, but more than anything, I think she's concerned about you. She's heard more 'Oh-This-One-Time-Andrew' stories than *I* even know. I think she's worried you feel obligated to stay. Henri didn't expect you to hang around here to look after everyone."

Of course Cara would know my own reasons for staying better than I ever could myself.

"It's not just them."

"I know you want to see Andrew again, so why are you still here? Kristy and Ellie will be fine—they walked across more than half the

382

country to get here. Amy carried her daughter up here with us; the two of them will be fine. *I'll* be fine. And since the weather has gotten better, I think Niki is less willing to make excuses to stay, but I know she won't leave without you."

I'm not sure how to explain it to her, but it's like I'm lost and don't know what to do. I thought going to Fort Caroline would change things because I was taking action. Instead of waiting for them to find us, I went to them. But we don't have to worry about them anymore. And Andrew got Amy home and Henri got to spend her last days with what was left of her family.

I want that.

We survived the superflu, and there are still thousands or millions of ways we could die now that there's no infrastructure of society to maintain us. But I don't want to worry about that anymore. I want to spend the time I have, however long that might be, with the people I love.

I've stayed here because I know there are people I love here. I stop weeding, and the pit in my stomach that's been slowly expanding like a sinkhole finally reaches its full width and threatens to swallow everything.

"Because if I get to the cabin, and he's not there—"

"He is. He's there and he's been waiting for you."

"What if he's not waiting for *me*?"

"He is. And if you don't move your ass, he's going to be pissed."

I laugh and pull another weed. "And if he's already pissed?"

"You just have to go, Jamie. If you want me to go with you, I will—"

"No, no. Stay here, I understand." Although I do want her to come with us. Because I'm going to miss her. And I'm only now realizing how much. "I'm going to give you the address. I get it, what you have to do. But if you go to Easton and . . . I dunno, if it ends up not feeling like home again—you always have a home with us."

She reaches out and wraps her arms around my neck. I hug her tightly and try not to cry. She lets me go and sits back down on the edge of the raised bed, but I see her wipe away a silent tear quickly before she asks, "So answer my question: How long are you planning on staying?"

"We'll leave tomorrow."

Cara nods. "I'll let Kristy and Amy know."

The next day, the four women are at the front gate to see us off. Newt is already out of the gate, sniffing around and peeing on things one last time. I think Ellie is sadder to see him go than she is me or Niki. They each give us a hug goodbye. Cara kisses me on the cheek.

"Remember what I said. You always have a home with us."

She nods. And I really do think I'll see her again. Maybe not for a few years, but I know it's not the last time we'll see each other. So instead of goodbye, I tell her, "I'll see you around."

Cara's mapped out the route for us, but it's familiar. It's the same route Andrew and I took into Bethesda—only I asked her to make sure to avoid the roads with tunnels.

There's something about starting this journey home in the spring that feels almost right. Life returning. As if Henri planned it this way, to have me stay until the grass began to turn green and the buds on the trees started to sprout. For the cold winter months to be a distant memory instead of a constant, stony presence.

It fills me with hope. Something I haven't had in a while.

"You ready?" Niki asks.

I nod and whistle for Newt, who trots over to us. We wave back at the others and start our journey home.

ANDREW

"HAVE YOU SEEN THE KID?" I SHOUT out to Taylor. I throw the last bag into the wagon as if I can't see his little sneaker under the blanket in there. Or hear his tittering laugh when the bag lands on him.

Taylor smiles, knowing full well where he is but playing along. "I don't know! Maybe he's over by the root cellar again."

"What a little shit!" I yell out, walking around to the ATV and grabbing the helmet. "I can't believe he's not here to say goodbye."

The Kid pops up from beneath my bag and yells, "I'm not a little shit!"

I grab him under the arms and hoist him out of the wagon. "Don't say *shit*." I put him back on the ground, but he promptly stands on my foot and wraps his arms around my leg. Lucky for him, there's no rain in the forecast, so that leg isn't hurting. Oddly enough, that same superpower isn't working with my left hand—which has healed nicely over the last few months, but still doesn't work like it should. The nerve pain is less, only an odd zap every once in a while instead of a constant throb of agony. But the index and middle fingers still aren't mobile and probably never will be.

Luke, one of the actual smart people at Bittersharp, made me a glove that has metal wire splints in the fingers. He cut off the pinkie and ring glove-fingers—and sewed up where the thumb should be—but left the other two with the splints sewn in. I can bend and reposition them so they hold things. Like ATV handles, for instance.

I walk over to the others with the Kid hanging on tightly, then he hops off and goes over to them. Howie, Raven—their daughter, Lydia, who is a little over a month old, is fast asleep in her father's arms—Taylor, and Jamar are all there.

"You all don't have to be here," I say. "I'm probably coming right back tomorrow anyway."

"And we're probably coming out to see you all the time," Taylor says. "What's your point?"

"I don't like an audience when I leave. Remind Jamie to tell you about that when he gets here."

And then everyone gives me that look that says, *We absolutely will when that absolutely happens.* But I know it will. Sure, it's almost May, but I know he'll get here when he gets here. Maybe he's the one who stepped in a bear trap this time and has to wait until he's healed. They all probably think I'm delusional, but I don't think I'm at that point yet.

I'm optimistic, not delusional.

Because of all these people, I'm the one who's truly an optimist.

"All right!" I say. "Better get going. If you hear an ATV in the middle of the night, it's because I heard a noise and got scared, so don't shoot me."

I head back to the ATV. There's a dirt path to the cabin now. Worn down—and cut down—after almost four months of weekend work back and forth.

"Andrew, wait!" Raven calls out. I turn, expecting to see her coming to give me yet another hug, but it's the Kid who's running after me.

I crouch down and he wraps his arms around my neck. I look up to the sky, trying to force the tears burning my eyes back into the ducts where they belong.

"Kid, this is embarrassing. You're making us look so uncool."

"I miss you," he says.

Jesus, does he have money on getting me to cry?

"I'm not even gone yet; how can you miss me?" My throat tightens a bit because I'm going to miss him, too. "Be good for Raven and Howie, okay?"

He nods and I finally lose my composure when he says "Okay," his voice watery. I hug him again, rubbing his back.

"All right, that's enough." I let him go and stand. "Now get out of the way before I run you over." He nods and starts walking back to the others. I turn back to the ATV, but something tugs at my heart again. The way I said it. I know it was just a joke, but what if the Kid doesn't? I keep going into a full-360-degree circle and call back out to him. "Kid!"

He turns and I close the distance between us and crouch down to hug him again. "I love you, Kid."

Then he whispers, "Albie."

"Huh?"

He steps back and rubs snot from his nose. "My name is Albie."

Well, shit. My mouth hangs open, then I smile and nod. "Albie the Kid. Pretty fuckin' badass."

He gives me a devilish grin and whispers, "Badass."

I shake my finger. "Don't say *badass*." I stare at him. He's only a short ride through the woods, but not seeing him every day is going to be hard. I wish he hadn't gotten so comfortable here with Raven and Howie; maybe he'd want to come live at the cabin. I had a few moments where I imagined them all living with us—Niki, Jamar, Taylor, Cara, and the Kid—cramped and arguing in the cabin. Still happy, though, and safe. But it's better for him here with everyone. "I'll miss you, too, Albie."

He runs off, this time heading for Raven, who runs her fingers through his hair as he wraps his arms around her leg. Without looking back again—because I know I can't keep doing it—I pull on the helmet and hop on the ATV.

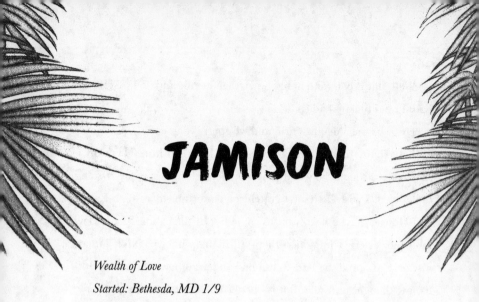

JAMISON

Wealth of Love
Started: Bethesda, MD 1/9
Finished: Bel Air, MD 1/13

Perfect Mess
Started: Bel Air, MD 1/14
Finished: Jacobus, PA 1/16

A Second Chance at Forever
Started: Jacobus, PA 1/16
Finished: Port Trevorton, PA 1/22

ANDREW AND THE OTHERS HAVE STUCK TO the exact route Cara mapped out for them. The Daphne De Silva books are like breadcrumbs, leading us home. Each one I pick up fills me with more love and hope and excitement.

And we always seem to find a book when we need it most. On our first day out after a two-day rainstorm. When we get low on food. When we're tired and our feet ache and it seems like we can't go on.

Each time, there she is, in the middle of the road. With a note from Taylor, reminding us Daphne is still with us.

And it really feels like she is.

Four more days.

Four more days till I see Andrew again.

ANDREW

ABOUT FORTY MINUTES AFTER LEAVING BITTERSHARP, I come to a stop behind the cabin. The new cabin. This one comes complete with one less bedroom than it started with, a root cellar, a slightly bigger kitchen without a refrigerator, and a luxurious outhouse!

I traded the solar panels on the roof to Bittersharp so they could use them. And in exchange I got some nice additional raised beds to plant in, which are slowly sprouting up.

After rebuilding the walls and roof of the cabin, they helped dig the well, since the components that supplied running water to the house were no longer getting electricity.

Now it's all done. Different from before, but still good. A little like my left arm, I guess. But it's still Jamie's home. *Our* home, whenever he gets here. Honestly, I don't know when that will turn to denial— sometimes I do try to convince myself I'm just in denial that the love of my life is dead and the sooner I get over that, the sooner I can heal.

But I know it's not true.

I can feel it in my gut almost as much as I can feel the rain coming in my leg and the random shock of nerve pain in my scarred arm. Those two traumatized extremities constantly at odds with the comforting buzz in my chest that tells me he's coming. He'll be here soon.

Grabbing one of my bags from the wagon attached to the ATV, I head around the front again. I set the bag on the stone walkway and take out the gnome from inside.

"Welcome home, Holly." I place her on the ground next to the stairs before going back into the bag. I put the little neon turtle—*FLORIDA* painted across his shell like a threat—next to her. Then I take a few steps back and look at it all. When I saw it for the first time, I thought it was empty.

But now it looks like someone's lived here since we left it.

It's warm and inviting.

Home.

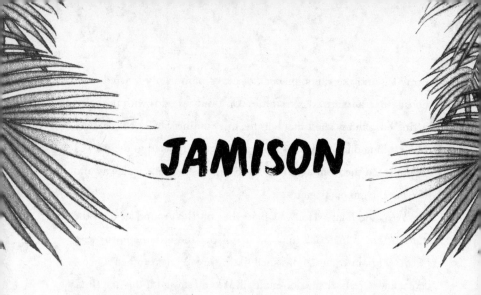

JAMISON

BEFORE THE SUPERFLU, SEEING THE CABIN WAS a relief. It meant the three-ish hour drive from Philly—depending on traffic—was over and we could get out and stretch. Seeing it now just brings fresh anxiety.

"Go ahead," Niki says, probably sensing the worry of what—or who—I'll find in the cabin. "I'll give you five minutes. Newt, stay."

Beside her, Newt sits and waits patiently until she hands him a few Cheerios from her jacket pocket, which he munches loudly. His obedience training has gone well the past few weeks, especially after we learned stale Cheerios are considered a high-value treat in Newt's mind.

I take a deep breath and walk up the driveway to the cabin.

The door is locked when I reach for it, which is odd because I left it unlocked when I followed after Andrew. My body starts to buzz at the thought. Someone else is in there, and either it's Andrew, or I'm so desperate for it to be him my body refuses to believe any other possibility. Because this isn't the buzz of fear or anxiety anymore, it's excitement and anticipation.

Instead of knocking, I grab the spare key that's still hidden in the compartment under Holly the Gnome's toadstool, and my heart flutters again at the neon turtle next to it.

After I unlock the door, just for a second, I worry I've broken into the wrong cabin. But then I see the gun pointing at me.

And the boy holding it.

"See?" he asks, his voice full of frustration. "How do *you* like it?"

I laugh, and my chest feels like either it's about to burst or I'm about to crumble into dust. Something otherworldly and uncontainable. Hearing him make a joke so easily—after not seeing me for such a long time—it means maybe things could be okay with us.

He sets the rifle down and we close the gap between us in half a second. His arms around me, mine around him. Holding tight, as though we're trying to fuse ourselves together. It's familiar and lovely.

"I've been planning that bit for months," he says. "Just so you know."

"Was it worth it?" I ask.

"No. But every other part of this is." He leans away but keeps his arms wrapped around me. His smile drops down into a look of uncertainty. He wants to ask about Fort Caroline.

I shake my head. "It's a long story, but I didn't . . . he's dead and I don't think Fort Caroline is going to be the way it was, but I had nothing to do with it, in the end. You were right. I'm sorry. You were always right, about the Keys and about the revenge mission, and I never should have left you. I should have been open to creating a new family with everyone, but I couldn't."

"You were scared." He kisses me, holding my face in his hands. "It's okay. You're allowed to be scared."

"I know, but I shouldn't have let that get in the way."

"It's okay." He kisses me again. "You're here."

My eyes return to the walls. From where I stand, the kitchen looks bigger. The walls aren't painted and instead have dark, minimalist gray wallpaper plastered over them.

"What did you do to my house?"

"Shhh." He kisses me. "Don't worry about that now."

I laugh against his lips and pick him up, so he wraps his legs around my middle.

"I'm sorry," I say.

"Don't worry about that now either." A short bark from behind us makes him startle in my arms and he pulls away from me. Newt stands in the doorway, his tail waving slowly behind him.

"Oh yeah," I say. "This is Newt."

Andrew gasps and drops down off me. "I love him!" Newt, sensing Andrew's energy, bounds into the cabin and slams his backside into him, immediately demanding pets.

Then Niki appears in the doorway. "I gave you enough time. Andrew, where the hell is my brother? Hi. Nice to see you again."

"Oh, hey, Niki." His cheeks turn red as he looks over to me like I'm going to help him out. "He's . . . nearby. There's a farm through the woods they're all staying at. Really nice place, I think you're going to love it."

Her jaw goes tight. "How far?"

"Ten miles?"

She slumps. "More walking."

"There's an ATV?" Andrew tries. I have no idea where he got an ATV from. Maybe he's made an alliance with this farm and doesn't have to pay Howard's land tax. Then he looks over at me. "But I do think we should walk. We have some stuff I've got to bring you up to speed on. Newt, wanna go for walkies?"

But Newt turns away from him and hops up onto the couch in the living room.

Andrew shakes his head. "I thought we had something, Newt."

"We do have to talk," I say. Most of it is going to be me apologizing for not letting anyone in, and for not listening to him about going to Fort Caroline. But I want to tell him what happened there, and of course I have to tell him about Henri. My tone seems to be making Andrew anxious, so I try something else to help him understand. "But I do want to see the Kid, Jamar, and Taylor. I missed them a lot."

Andrew seems to relax, and he puts his hands to my cheeks, smiling again. And that's how I know he understands what I'm telling him. That he was right. These people are our family.

"They missed you, too."

"Save all this for the walk," Niki says, without hiding her annoyance.

After coaxing Newt off the couch, Andrew leads us around back to the new pathway. Niki starts marching down the dirt road and Andrew takes my hand, linking my fingers with his. Then he kisses me on the cheek.

"Welcome home."

"It's good to be back."

The next night is our first night in the house alone together—a little over a year since we left it. I make us dinner and after we eat, we sit on the back deck watching the fireflies by the low light of a kerosene lantern. Newt snores under the table, lying against Andrew's leg. I take the faded green raffle ticket out of my pocket and put it on the table in front of him.

He grins and takes it, putting it into his own pocket. "Okay. Which movie?"

"Not a movie," I say. I go inside and grab the last book Niki and I found on our journey to the cabin. *A Second Chance at Forever*.

I hand it to him, but he shakes his head. "No, this is her masterpiece—seriously, it's amazing. I won't paraphrase a word of it." He turns up the lantern a bit and adjusts his chair. Beneath him, Newt grumbles, then gets up and lies down by the stairs.

Andrew motions for me to sit down and he props his legs up on mine while tilting the book into the lantern light. He begins to read.

EPILOGUE

APOLLO'S HOOVES CLOP SLOWLY ALONG THE DIRT road, while somewhere in the woods I hear the snap of twigs as Luna sniffs and hunts. I know she'll bark before she goes running off, so I let her explore. She always seems to get more antsy around this part of the journey.

It takes five more minutes before I reach the clearing of Andrew and Jamie's house—which has gotten much wider since the first time I was here about nine years ago.

I let out a sharp whistle. "Luna! Here!"

The black-and-white mutt comes bounding out of the trees, giving Apollo a wide berth because she knows he can get pissy when she follows too close at his legs.

The back door of the cabin opens, and Luna's butt begins to shake like a counterbalance to her swishing tail. She lets out little whines of excitement, waiting for her command word.

"LUNA!"

And there it is. She bolts across the yard, then clambers up the steps to the deck and jumps onto Andrew, trying to lick his face. I climb down from Apollo, leading him over to the well, where I tie him up and bring up the bucket of water for him to drink.

When I get back to the deck, Luna has gone belly-up and stares at me, tongue lolling to the side of her open mouth as Andrew gives her belly scritches.

"One day, she's just going to stay here," I say. "Leave me forever for a life in the woods."

"That's because I love her so much and everyone at Bittersharp just enjoys the good job she does."

I scrunch up my face. "Um, would we really say she does a good job?"

"Albie, don't be mean to her. The *jobs* are good, she's just awful at them, and that's why I love her so!"

He's right. She really is a terrible goat herder, hunting companion, security dog, etc. The only thing she's good at is being dopey and adorable. Luckily, that means she gets to be *my* dog. Besides, the other dogs are good enough at their jobs to make up for her.

The back door opens again and Luna's up in a second. She jumps onto Jamie, who quickly scoops her into his arms so she can lick his face.

"You shouldn't let her do that," I say. "Who knows how much deer shit she's eaten on the walk here."

Jamie groans but doesn't try too hard to pull away from her before finally setting her down.

I take off the backpack and set it on the wooden table.

Andrew turns back to Jamie. "Babe, grab the bread and cheese. I'll get some water."

"Hold on," I say, pulling out the jug of cider. "This is one of Nat's new brews. She wants your opinion."

Andrew wrinkles his nose. "Hopefully this one doesn't taste like fermented onions like the last batch."

Jamie shrugs as he goes back into the house and shouts back, "I liked it!"

Andrew shakes his head, giving me a sad look. "Fucking lunatic."

Jamie returns with a wood platter of bread and soft cheese and three glasses, setting them on the table. We sit down and Jamie pours out the cider.

"Sláinte," Andrew says, and we toast. The cider is tart and makes my cheeks clench. I flinch as Andrew lets out a "whoo!" "Tell her I like the sweeter stuff."

Jamie shrugs again. "I like it?"

"You like everything," Andrew says. "I'm going to find something you don't like one day."

"It's your own fault for forcing hen of the woods on me," he says.

"Did you not like mushrooms?" I ask.

"He hated them!" Andrew says.

"To be fair, what I hated was canned, rubbery mushrooms. And everything tastes better with butter."

"Oh, right!" I lean over and dig back into the pack. I take out a wax-paper-wrapped slab of butter, a pound of flour, and a small tin. I slide the tin over to Andrew, who sighs.

"Thank you!"

"Gemma added eucalyptus oil," I say as he opens the tin. He uses his right hand to take some of the balm out and rubs it on his left hand

401

where his thumb is missing and the index and middle fingers have started to lock up.

"How is everyone doing?" Jamie asks as I rip off a piece of bread.

"Good. Raven's due in a month."

Andrew nods. "I have it in my calendar. Plus, I have a bet with Howie that it's another girl."

I laugh. "He says he thinks it's a boy."

Andrew snorts. "He thinks that every time. Howie's a great girl dad. I don't know why he's trying so hard for a boy. You'd think *four* girls is enough of a sign from the universe."

Jamie puts his glass of cider to his lips. "Has anyone heard from Jamar and Taylor?"

I shake my head. "Niki is talking about going to find them."

"And Cara is telling her to stay put, right?" Andrew asks. Jamie reaches over and squeezes his arm gently.

"She's trying." I shrug. I can't really blame Jamar and Taylor. They said they wanted to show their son, Eli, what the rest of the world looked like, but I'd bet that they just wanted some time away from Bittersharp. Maybe a way to show Eli where Jamar and Taylor met, where they traveled. The life they lived before he was in the world. And maybe that's good for Eli, even if he is only five. I vividly remember things after the bug. But everything before is muddled.

Sometimes I remember my parents' faces, but I don't remember their names. If I try really hard, I can remember some scary parts from before everything fell.

But I do have one good memory of my parents. It was a holiday in the summer that we don't even celebrate anymore. I had to have been maybe three or four. We sat on a blanket by a lake and the sun was setting. I remember it being exciting because usually I was in bed by the time the sky looked like that. I was tired, though, and wanted to go home. But then the sky exploded with lights, and it was scary, but none of the adults around me seemed to be scared. So I just watched. Dad kept asking me if I thought it was neat and I nodded, but that was a lie. I thought it was magic. Papa pulled me over into his lap while Dad said, "Ohh! Oh, it looks like the willow tree in our backyard! Wow, look, it's a green one!" I remember a firework that looked like the willow tree in our backyard, but I don't remember the willow tree.

"Well, keep an eye on her for us," Andrew says. "If she says she's leaving, tell her to come see me first. I'll try to talk her out of it, or I'll go with her."

Jamie lets out a sound like he's going to scold Andrew but stops himself.

"It's fine," Andrew tells him. "Between me and Cara, I think we can keep her calm. Things aren't as scary out there as they used to be."

I nod, remembering our own time on the road—and Andrew's stories about him and Jamie traveling before they met us in the Keys. Everyone left after the flu knows we have to rely on each other if we want to survive.

Andrew continues, "Niki knows they'll come back. Even if it takes a few years."

Jamie reaches over and squeezes Andrew's arm again. A show of agreement.

"Anyway," Andrew says, attempting to wave away the bad vibes. "What about you? Masie didn't want to join you today?"

Jamie laughs. "Yes, you made her feel very welcome last time."

Andrew looks offended. "I was *very* welcoming. It's not my fault she doesn't understand my sense of humor yet." He looks at me. "She does know I like her, right?"

"I told her you do, but she definitely thought you hated her."

"Great, now I have to be on my best behavior." He frowns as if it's the worst thing we could ask of him.

"Well, don't do that," Jamie says, putting cheese on a piece of bread. "You'll scare her off for good." He hands the bread to Andrew, who takes it and bites into it.

We talk until the sun falls below the trees, then they walk me over to Apollo. Jamie gives him a soft pet and feeds him the end of the leftover bread.

"See you guys next week, right?" I ask.

Jamie looks to Andrew. "What's next week?"

"Howie and the Hornblowers concert."

I snort. "That is not their name."

Andrew shrugs. "It should be. 'The Bittersharp Band' needs to workshop their shit before they take the show on the road."

"Raven's going to have to let him fulfill his dream of a nationwide tour after his fifth daughter is born and he has a mental breakdown."

Jamie and Andrew laugh.

"Say goodbye, Luna."

She gets pets from Andrew while Jamie hugs me goodbye. Then they swap. Andrew wraps his arm around me.

"Love ya, Kid."

"Love you, too."

I climb up onto Apollo, then whistle for Luna to follow. She runs ahead on the path. I look back to see Andrew and Jamie standing at the clearing, waving goodbye. Their arms around each other.

ACKNOWLEDGMENTS

Acknowledgments are a funny thing because, for the most part, I assume people outside of publishing don't read them because they'll think, *Well, I'm not in it so why bother?* In my acknowledgments I always thank the reader, and it usually goes a little something like this: "And to you, the reader, if you bought this book, received it as a gift, checked it out from the library, or even borrowed it from a friend, thank you. You helped keep all the people above [in publishing] employed."

But this time I want to start by thanking every reader, bookseller, and librarian reading this. Not for buying the book—which, yay, thank you if you did!—but for reading *All That's Left in the World* and loving it so much that you recommended it to other readers and asked for a sequel. I had planned more than one book out when I wrote *All That's Left in the World*, but after living through a pandemic, I never wanted to revisit Andrew and Jamie's world. Only after receiving many comments, emails, and pleadings at book events did I rediscover the joy in writing about Andrew and Jamie in the postapocalypse. *All That's Left in the World* was my debut, and without the word-of-mouth buzz surrounding it from readers like you, *The Only Light Left Burning* wouldn't exist. Even if you only read *All That's Left in the World* after *The Only Light Left Burning* came out, you have contributed to my success as an author. This is my dream job. Something I've been working toward since I was a kid. And hearing that my stories are connecting with people, and in such an emotional way, makes me proud every day.

I will say, this is the end of Andrew and Jamie's story. They deserve peace and happiness, don't you agree? That doesn't mean this world will never be revisited in the future. But for now, I hope you are pleased with how their story ends. I hope you forgive me for all the trauma I put them through and all the stress I put you under as a reader. But thank you for coming along on this journey with them—and me.

Now about the publishing: thank you to my editors—Kristin Rens at Balzer + Bray, and Katherine Agar, Noah Grey, and Naomi Greenwood at Hachette. This book was entirely rewritten twice, and it only exists and makes sense now because of the work you all put into helping me get it there.

I also have to thank my former editor, Tig Wallace, who moved on to another position at Hachette before I even started work on this, but still listened to a pitch of what the sequel would look like. And his parting gift was this title, which fit perfectly!

Thanks also to the following behind-the-scenes folks who were integral to getting this book into your hand. First, at HarperCollins: Chris Kwon in design, production editors Caitlin Lonning and Alexandra Rakaczki, editorial assistant Christian Vega, Melissa

Cicchitelli in production, Michael D'Angelo in marketing, Lauren Levite in publicity, Kerry Moynagh and team in sales, Patty Rosati and team in school and library marketing, and Maria Nguyen, who illustrated the beautiful North American cover.

At Hachette: thanks to Joana Reis for Hachette's in-house design, and Joe Stansbury, who managed to create such a beautiful cover that complements the first book. Thank you to desk editor Laura Pritchard; Alexandra Haywood, who handles marketing; Joey Esdelle in production; my wonderful publicists, Lucy Clayton, who taught me many valuable things while babysitting me on my book tour in the UK, and Anna Cole, who spent an entire day walking me around London and still went back to the office afterward. And special thanks to Siobhan Tierney, the sales director for Hachette Ireland, who makes sure all the booksellers in Ireland are my biggest fans.

Writing is solitary, but publishing is a team effort—as you can see by all the names above. Still, even before the writing starts, the people who represent me do a ton of work. So immense thank-you to my agent, Michael Bourret: you're much smarter than me, which makes you the best business partner I could ask for. You also somehow always know which of my ideas are the good ones. Thanks also to the entire team at Dystel, Goderich & Bourret, including assistant Michaela Whatnall, rights director Lauren Abramo, and rights associate Gracie Freeman Lifschutz. And thank you to Anna Carmichael at Abner Stein, who represents me in the UK.

It being my third year as a published author, I'm so honored to get to thank the other authors who have welcomed me into their world as a colleague and a friend: Jennifer Dugan, Naz Kutub, Susan

Lee, Brian D. Kennedy, Anna Gracia, Jason June, Josh Silver, David Fenne, Zachary Sergi, Steven Salvatore, Adam Sass, Julian Winters, and honestly so many more I know I am forgetting, but I will make it up to you by continuing to buy your books!

Thank you very much to all my friends and family who deal with me while I'm moody or distant when drafting a book. I promise I'm never mad at any of you, just my characters.

And to Michael Miska: fiction requires conflict, but real life is so much better when partners are in agreement and understanding. I'm so thankful to always be on the same page with you in our adventures; even the scary parts are less scary because you're there. I love you, and I'm excited to see where the next stage in our journey leads.